CIRCLE OF THE MOON

A Soulwood Novel

Faith Hunter

D0101204

ACE
New York

ACE
Published by Berkley
An imprint of Penguin Random House LLC
1745 Broadway, New York, NY 10019

Copyright © 2019 by Faith Hunter
Excerpt from *Flame in the Dark* copyright © 2017 by Faith Hunter
Penguin Random House supports copyright. Copyright fuels creativity, encourages
diverse voices, promotes free speech, and creates a vibrant culture. Thank you for buying
an authorized edition of this book and for complying with copyright laws by not
reproducing, scanning, or distributing any part of it in any form without permission.
You are supporting writers and allowing Penguin Random House to continue to
publish books for every reader.

ACE is a registered trademark and the A colophon is a trademark of
Penguin Random House LLC.

ISBN: 9780399587948

First Edition: February 2019

Printed in the United States of America
1 3 5 7 9 10 8 6 4 2

Cover art by Cliff Nielsen
Cover design by Katie Anderson

Praise For Faith Hunter's Soulwood Novels

"Rich, imaginative, and descriptive, Hunter's latest novel in her Soulwood series shines . . . The intriguing, inventive plot coupled with the bone-chilling tension make this story an unforgettable read." —RT Book Reviews

"I love Nell and her PsyLED team and would happily read about their adventures for years." —Vampire Book Club

"Faith Hunter does a masterful job . . . and has created a wonderful new heroine in Nell, who continues to grow into her powers." —The Reading Café

"Faith Hunter delivers. Just like Nell's plants that bloom when and where they shouldn't—it'll grow on you." —Kings River Life Magazine

"An exciting paranormal adventure." —*Library Journal*

Praise For Faith Hunter's Jane Yellowrock Novels

"Jane is a fully realized, complicated woman; her power, humanity, and vulnerability make her a compelling heroine." —*Publishers Weekly*

"Hunter has an amazing talent." —SF Site

"Readers eager for the next book in Patricia Briggs's Mercy Thompson series may want to give Faith Hunter a try." —*Library Journal*

"Hunter's very professionally executed, tasty blend of dark fantasy, mystery, and romance should please fans of all three genres." —*Booklist*

"Seriously. Best urban fantasy I've read in years, possibly ever." —C. E. Murphy, author of *Stone's Throe*

To my Renaissance Man,
who keeps our castle safe and full of laughter.

Acknowledgments

David B. Coe/D. B. Jackson, author of the The Islevale Cycle series for info on Tennessee.

Mark Dudley for info on Tennessee building codes and housing.

James R. Tuck, author of the Deacon Chalk series and more, for tattoo advice.

Teri Lee, Timeline and Continuity Editor Extraordinaire.

Mud Mymudes for all things planty and doggy, for beta reading and PR.

Let's Talk Promotions at ltpromos.com, for getting me where I am today.

Lee Williams Watts for being the best travel companion and PA a girl can have.

Beast Claws! Best Street Team Evah.

Mike Pruette at celticleatherworks.com for all the fabo merch.

Mike Prater for printer and computer help.

Lucienne Diver of The Knight Agency, as always, for applying your agile and splendid mind to my writing and my career, and being a font of wisdom.

Cliff Nielsen for the glorious cover art.

And to my Copy Editor, Sheila Moody. Any CE who can see what is not there is priceless.

As always, a huge thank-you to Jessica Wade of Penguin Random House. Without you there would be no book at all!

ONE

The night sky was a wash of cerulean blue over the trees and the roofline, with a trace of scarlet and plum on the western horizon. A silver wedge of moon would rise soon, no longer full, an important consideration when eating a picnic with a were-creature. Other than the stars, our only light came from an oil lantern propped on a flat-topped rock, casting shadows over the blanket and used paper plates and the half-empty bottle of Sister Erasmus' muscadine wine, and even that would get snuffed as soon as the meteor shower began.

I was safe on Soulwood land, even in the full dark, and had no need to worry about my surroundings. I was primarily concentrating on the danged wereleopard lounging in human form on the picnic blanket beside me, looking amused, and maybe just a bit smug. *Dang cat.* "Take. Off. Your. Shirt," I demanded again.

"Why, Nell, sugar, if you were so desirin' of seeing me in my naked glory, all you had to do was ask."

I blushed, which didn't show, not with my new coloration, but I knew Occam could smell my reaction and hear my suddenly galloping heart. But we had been over this conversational ground on two separate evenings. Two official dates. This was our third and I wasn't taking no for an answer. I inhaled a steadying breath and leaned in until my face was an inch from his, wiping out the horizon. He had no choice but to focus on me. Quietly, almost a whisper, I said, "This ain't my first rodeo, cat-man. I been fighting recalcitrant males for mosta my life. You died. You're still scarred and mostly hairless and moving slow. *Now.* Take off the shirt. Lemme see the scars so I'll know what to do to help heal them."

"My face is bad enou—"

"No arguments. You been putting this off for days. Lemme see so I can help you."

Occam eased away from me, his body dropping back from the elbow that held his weight, his western-booted ankles uncrossing and recrossing as he sat up. His face lost the laughter and teasing and took on a wary expression. His Texan accent grew stronger. "You brought me back from the dead, sugar. You did the best you could. There ain't no point in this. I'll heal eventually from shifting."

"Yeah? You ain't getting better fast enough, not even when you shift here on Soulwood under the full moon." I shoved my head forward the way the werecats did when they were irritated. Bumped his nose. "You ashamed a your'n body, Occam, *sugar*?" I asked in my strongest church accent, using it as a weapon to get my way. But it didn't work.

"No." He bumped me back. "You ashamed of yours? I'll take off my shirt if you take off yours."

Shock and excitement and fear and laughter shot through me like lightning. I settled on laughter, a sputtering, staccato sound that echoed back from the house and the massive trees that ringed the acreage and flowed down the hill toward the lights of Knoxville in the far distance. I said, "I ain't ashamed a nothin', kitty cat."

Occam laughed at that, a purring sound that rumbled through his chest and the earth beneath us. It was well after the three days of the full moon—part of the reason I'd picked tonight for our picnic—at a time when were-creatures could shift if they wanted to, but weren't forced under control of their creatures. Occam's cat was reckless at all times, however, and he reached for the hem of his T-shirt with his damaged left hand, the scars on the two ruined fingers bright white in the darkness.

Our cells dinged with incoming texts at almost the same moment. *Of course.* "Dagnabbit," I cursed. Occam's laughter deepened, a catty purr. His good hand found my neck in the dark, his palm heated and smooth, his fingers long and bony and firm. Determined. He pulled me to him. His lips found mine and his body rolled me over, his elbows holding him above me. Not prisoning me. Not aware that I wanted him to lay his weight over me and throw caution and worry to the wind and—

He kissed me. Hard and hot. That very improper kiss he had promised me long months ago. His scruffy, scarred face scrubbed against mine. I kissed him back. Dragged him closer. He shoved his body higher, over mine, his jean-clad legs tangling in my long skirt. The scent of his sweat was manly and healthy . . . not like John's scent at all. My body simultaneously loosened, boneless, and clenched.

"Ohhh," I murmured into his mouth as his tongue claimed mine. Twisted and thrust. Occam's need and desire pressed against my abdomen. My heart thundered and warmth rushed all through me, a strange and wonderful electric heat that settled low in my belly. *Desire. This is what desire feels like.*

The cells dinged again, reminding us. Occam cursed and I made a sound that was close to a moan as I eased away. I dropped my head back to the blanket I had spread on the too-long summer grass for our picnic. I breathed out a laugh, the sound only a little frustrated. That was what I told myself. Only a little. Stars were visible around the edges of Occam's head, his thin hair looking brittle even in the pale light.

"Look!" I said, pointing. A shooting star raced overhead and blinked out. "First one. Make a wish!"

"I'm pert' near certain that my wish has already been ruined by that text, Nell, sugar," he said. "You go ahead. Maybe you'll have better luck."

I said my quick wish and turned my head to him, knowing he could see better in the dark than I could. I wasn't human, but my kind of paranormal didn't have any superpowers like better night vision. My wish was carnal and sinful and full of hope. And also ruined by the text.

Occam rolled off me and we reached for our cells, answering them to see identical texts from PsyLED. *Get to HQ ASAP. Trouble,* it read. The text was from JoJo, second in command of Unit Eighteen.

"No court in the land would convict me if I killed her," Occam growled.

I laughed again, remembering the feel of his weight over me, pressing into me. Remembering the shot of excitement that flashed through me like lightning before settling deep inside. Excitement. Not fear. *Desire.* The physical need I'd read about and—

The cells dinged again, this time from JoJo's personal cell. It read, *If your cells were any closer they'd be making cell-babies. I hate to say stop, because I really hope you two are getting busy, loud and long and satisfying, but I need you at HQ. Both of you. Days off canceled.*

Occam pulled me to my feet, still cat-strong, though not so flexible as before the fire. That part of his were-taint abilities hadn't been affected by the instinctive and peculiar healing I had managed the night he was burned and had died, and my up-line boss nearly so—the night I'd hauled them back from the claws of death. Occam might look a mess yet, he might move slower than before, but he *was* getting better, bit by bit, every time he shifted into his spotted leopard. That was a natural part of the were-taint gift. I helped where I could, when he shifted on my land, drawing on the power of Soul-wood, feeding him the way I did the land when it was injured. If I could see his scarring, see what he needed, maybe I could help more or better. But Occam was stubborn about me seeing the scars on his body. Which was why my secret wish on the shooting star had not yet been fulfilled. *Dang cat.*

"Gear up," he said. "I'll drive."

"And that means I'll have no form of transportation back here in the morning."

"'At sounds about right."

I hid a smile in the darkness and let him lead me to my own front porch. And wondered if *sounding about right* meant he intended to pick up where we left off.

We walked into HQ together, Occam at my six, protecting me or heading me like a cat after prey. I didn't know. Didn't rightly care. I'd learned at Spook School that the most experienced fighter/shooter always came last. If an enemy was waiting and attacked the first person in line, then the man at six was able to take the bad guy out. If the most experienced is at point and is ambushed, then the bad guy will likely get the second person in line too. Perfect logic.

Second in command of PsyLED Unit Eighteen, Special Agent Josephine Anna Jones—JoJo—met us at the top of the stairs. She was supposed to be writing the final summation report on a possible sighting of a devil dog in the hills east of Knoxville, but from her expression, this call-out was more than that. She said, "Where's Mud?"

It was a strange question. "She's spending the night with Esther and Jedidiah."

"Jedidiah Whisnut, right? She safe with him?"

Safe was important. The men of God's Cloud of Glory Church, a polygamous cult from which I had escaped, weren't known to protect women. My sister Mud was twelve. That was close enough to make her prey to some of them. "She's good."

"Better be. You two are making a run. Rick sent a text and needs . . . hell, I don't know. Backup? Help in some non-lethal situation? Kent's gathering Rick's four-day bag, backup weapon, extra key fob, and extra cell. I'll text you the coordinates."

T. Laine was visible at the end of the hallway, loaded down with gear.

JoJo, scarlet skirts swaying, whirled and rushed back along the hallway, part of the full moon and leopard tattoo on her neck catching the overhead lights, her turban glistening. There were gold and silver threads woven through the fabric. JoJo did not dress by PsyLED dress codes, and so far no one had told her she had to comply.

"Rick's in trouble?" Occam asked as we weaponed up.

JoJo shouted back, "He didn't send a nine-nine-nine, so I'm assuming he's ruined his clothes and gear. Went for a swim. Something. But he texted from an old, outdated cell number, and now I can't get through to it. So wear your vests. Just in case."

Code-999 was for officer down, urgent help needed. No 999 meant things weren't dire. Request for his gobag and gear? Yeah, that sounded like he fell in the river.

"Specifics?" Occam asked, seeming irritated that he was having to ask for details.

JoJo read from her screen, shouting down the hallway. " 'Need pickup. Weapon. Gobag. Cell. Car fob. ASAP. Send Occam and Nell.' "

T. Laine said, "Rick's bag, packed with backup weapon,

extra official cell, charger, car fob, shoes, and a change of clothing, as ordered." She tossed Rick's gobag at Occam and he caught the bag with catty reflexes, though still not as fast as once before. "Move it, CC."

CC stood for Crispy Critter, which was the term emergency crews and law enforcement used for burned bodies in a very hot fire. It was not a nice thing to say. It was also the exact thing Occam needed to hear—a reminder that his team knew he was disfigured, ugly, as far as social standards went, but still considered capable. Still part of the team. "Jo and I've got comms," the resident witch added. "I was heading out, but I'll stay over until we know what's happened. I'll update you on the way."

Occam and I left the gear we didn't need and headed back down the stairs to his sporty car, putting on comms systems as we went, our own one-day gobags over our shoulders. Occam used only one earbud, because the ear cartilage on the damaged side of his face hadn't regrown. Yet.

"You copy?" Lainie asked over the earbuds.

"Receiving loud and clear," Occam said as he started his car.

"Receiving," I said. "I just plugged in the coordinates and Rick is on the bank of the Tennessee River in the middle of the night?"

"Nothing about the request or the destination makes sense," T. Laine said. "And the request for backup came in over a nonsecured number, that old flip phone he keeps in a gobag in the glovebox of his car."

"No other details?" Occam asked. "Grindys?"

"Not a one. No info on the grindys. I'm still trying to get back through. No luck."

Grindylows were cute, neon green, kitten-sized were-creature killers. They appeared when a were-creature was in danger of transmitting the were-taint and killed the offending were-creature with extreme prejudice, no recourse, no appeal.

As the newest official special agent in PsyLED Unit Eighteen, and the one who had spent six months as part of a forest, on the injured and disabled list, I seldom was allowed to leave the office, my job these days being predominantly database searches and intel correlation. Excitement skittered along my nerve endings like ants in an electric current.

* * *

We made good time, most of the streets and pikes being fairly deserted at this hour, but finding a lone man outside of Knoxville proper, on the banks of a river that twisted and turned like the track of a snake, was difficult. Rick's GPS coordinates were on a tongue of land between the confluence of the French Broad and the Holston rivers, where they merged to become the Tennessee River. We drove slowly along Riverside Drive, poorly lit, totally deserted, watching for Rick. Not knowing what we'd find. I normally would love a drive along tree-lined country roads, under a night sky, watching the stars and a metor shower, but I didn't like this one. The things we were told to bring along suggested that Rick had a problem, and anytime a wereleopard had a problem it was dangerous.

"Dial his old cell number," Occam said.

Rick had acquired a new cell number while I was a tree. Something about a problem in New Orleans, involving Jane Yellowrock, one of his exes. No one seemed to know what had happened between them, but Rick had kept the old number and the old cell. A way for Jane to reach him if she ever wanted. Rick's love life was as broken and emotionally maimed as his psyche.

A lot had happened while I was out of commission. I had been back at work only three weeks and I was still getting accustomed to the changes. Rick answered, sounding out of breath and wary at the same time. "I see your lights. Pull over to the right," he said. Satellite maps showed that the right side of the road was pasture or field, and beyond that was the Tennessee River. Occam braked onto the grassy verge.

A hundred feet ahead, Rick appeared in the darkness, a thin orange blanket printed with black puppy paws wrapped around his middle. His silver and black hair caught the light, too long, flying in the breeze, his face scruffy, signs of a recent shift.

His chest was bare, the headlights giving me a glimpse of the ruined, scarred tattoos across one shoulder and scars from wounds that should have killed him. A lot of scars, especially for a were-creature.

Long after the blood-magic tattoos had been applied, Rick

had been infected by the were-taint, bitten by one black
wereleopard, then chewed on and tortured by werewolves, and
then spelled by Paka, a second black wereleopard. All that in
a matter of months, which had affected the magic of the were-
taint, leaving him unable to shift until the last seven or eight
moon cycles.

Rick had been a were-creature only a few years, and in that
time had been dragged through hell and back. Lately he had
been looking what I called antsy—twitchy and agitated. Tonight that was multiplied times ten. Magic rolled off him,
making the air itself seem to spark as he moved, balanced and
cat-like, toward the car.

Beside me, Occam hissed in a slow breath, picking up the
sizzling energy that Rick was throwing off. He gripped the
steering wheel hard enough to make the leather covering
squeak softly.

"Rick doesn't look entirely in control," I said quietly. "Why
isn't Pea or Bean here?"

"No humans nearby," Occam said.

I realized why I had been sent with Occam, not one of the
other agents. I was more tree than human and was immune to
the were-taint that would turn others into a were-creature. If
Rick attacked me, I could heal as soon as I got my fingers into
dirt. I also had some small control over Rick because of his
tie to my land. Occam and I were most likely to survive if
Rick attacked. I had been expected to understand all that and
I hadn't. Until now, when I put it all together.

Right, I thought.

"Besides, I got this."

"Hmmm," I said, trying to decide if he really did. Occam
lived in more harmony with his cat than Rick with his, possibly because Occam had spent twenty years in a cage getting
to know his spotted leopard. Rick's cat had been chained into
the human body even at the full moon and was now half-feral,
prickly, and intent on winning dominance games and fights.
The two men got along okay, but the cats, not so much. They
were alphas, and the status of who was more dominant between them—the mature spotted leopard or the more powerful but immature black leopard—was always in flux. They
hunted together but were solitary cats. It was complicated.

Rick's puppy blanket glowed in the headlights as he got closer and so did his eyes, the green magic of his cat still close to the surface. Beside me, Occam shifted in the seat and a low vibration began in his chest. A growl, quickly cut off. I glanced sideways at Occam, who said, "His cat is close." His voice was laconic and heavy with Texas twang, trying to hide his reaction.

"Uh-huh."

Occam grinned unrepentantly, his scarred face dragging up on one side. "I got this," he repeated. He blew out a breath and, in my peripheral vision, I saw his hands slacken on the wheel.

I shook my head, returned my full attention to Rick, and got my first good look at the infamous scarred tats on his chest and shoulder. In the harsh light, I couldn't tell what the mangled artwork had been, but the colorful inks and scars covered his left collarbone, ran down his pectoral, and wrapped around his entire upper arm. All that was left in the puckered scar tissue were the amber discs, like eyes, and they were reflecting gold, bright in the lights of the sports car. There was a circlet tattooed on the right biceps, less scarred and more recognizable. Possibly barbed wire. That one drew my attention and held it.

I was wrong about it being barbed wire. The tat was really a depiction of twisted vines with curved, retractable big-cat claws and raptor talons and a few drops of bright red blood interspersed throughout.

"Huh," Occam said. "The tats on the right look better than they used to. This is the first time I've seen them since you healed us. You do that?"

It was interesting—or perhaps disturbing—that the right-side tats were of vines and claws. The right tat reminded me of the vampire tree (now more like a grove of vampire trees, though they were all one root system) that was growing at the edge of my land and in the church compound. Fear spurted through me as thoughts and memories and worries collided. "I don't know," I murmured.

It too was complicated. To mix his were-magic up a little more, I'd claimed Rick a few times for Soulwood, for healing. Rick's cat was now bound to my land and trees.

He was close enough for me to see he carried a crumpled gobag in one hand and a folded flip phone in the other. Rivulets of sweat traced down his flesh. His black and silver beard had grown out an inch and he was nothing but skin over corded muscle and bone. I realized that the golden orbs of his tats weren't reflecting the headlights, but glowed from within. They looked heated and painful.

Rick stopped in front of the car, wrapped waist to thighs in the paw-print blanket, his feet shoulder-width apart, his stance aggressive, his entire body tense and glistening in the muggy heat, his eyes glowing cat-green in the dark.

"Nell, sugar, you okay?"

"I'm fine," I lied, as worries knotted themselves all through me.

"Uh-huh," he said, hearing the lie. "Stay in the car," Occam said softly.

"Right."

Occam reached behind the seat, retrieved Rick's office gobag, and left the car, closing the door softly. He approached Rick in the glare of the headlights, his body bladed, cautious, stepping slowly, his feet lifting and setting down, cat-like, or dancer-like. Rick hunched down, as if drawing paws beneath him. He snarled. Rick's teeth were part cat, as if he was caught in the shift or the power of the full moon. But he should have been in command tonight, with the full moon past.

Occam tilted his head and snarled back in warning. He dropped the full gobag between them and his fingers curled as if he was growing claws. This was about to go all catty with blood and claws and fangs and I didn't know who would win in an all-out dominance fight, or if one of them would die. I didn't want to draw on Soulwood for fear of tying them even more strongly to my land, but I was pretty sure that if I didn't, there was gonna be blood and a lot of it.

I cracked open the car door and leaned out, putting a fingertip to the dirt. I closed my eyes and reached out to my land. It was close enough, and in midsummer the trees and plants and grasses and veggies were in full leaf and full bloom. The land was powerful and playful. It slammed into me, like an oversized young dog at a dead run. I fell back hard, against the metal of the car. My breath shot out. The might of Soulwood filled me and wrapped around me, warm as a wool blanket in front of the stove at my house. I laughed softly. "Hey there." I soothed the land for a few breaths, and then reached for the cats in the dark, sharing the joy and peace that was my land. The magic of Soulwood.

Even with my eyes closed, I felt the cat-men calm and swivel to the car where I sat. I felt them step away from the coming fight. Felt their aggression vanish. I opened my eyes and sat upright, to see Rick walking away, into the night, his full gobag with its change of clothing in one hand, the second small gobag and his antiquated cell in the other. The car lights picked out scarring on his back at his kidney and over his shoulder. Claws had raked him deeply enough to leave puckered flesh, an old injury.

Occam walked toward the car. He was caught in the headlights, the left side of his face and skull fully illuminated, the scars showing a shocking white in his tanned face, his mouth and eye drawing up on the side. His ear a shriveled mass. The scars were a patchwork and a veining of pure white that spread down his neck, likely onto his torso, along the outer part of his arm, and down to his maimed hand. Two fingers had been burned away in the fire that had killed him and hadn't grown back properly. They curled inward, the tendons permanently contracted like curled vines, not much more than scars over bone. He blinked against the glare.

The automatic car lights went out, leaving us all in the dark.

Occam opened the door and slipped inside. Closed it. Silently, we stared into the night, waiting for Rick to dress. He said, "His cat was loose. About to shift."

"I noticed," I said.

"You pulled on Soulwood."

I frowned, uncertain.

Occam touched my forearm with an unscarred finger. "It's okay. I felt a sense of peace. I smelled the firs and the poplars. I felt the soil and the grass and knew it was a safe place to bed down. I felt . . . Soulwood. I felt you, Nell, sugar. I knew *you*."

I looked down at my hands, fingers laced across my lap in the dark. And studied his right hand, the contact between us the pad of a single, warm finger just above my wrist. I said, "I shared the land with you both. I wondered if you could tell."

"Can't say as I always know when you draw on Soulwood, but this time I could feel it. It felt good. Peaceful. As if the moon wasn't in charge of what and who I am. As if you gave me a different kind of power over my cat, that I don't normally have." He withdrew his hand and I missed the warmth.

Rick, dressed in dark jeans and a white T-shirt, reappeared, moving smoothly in the night. Occam opened the car door and the overhead light came on and the wild poured in. Evergreens and heat and mosquitoes. I hated summer in Knoxville. Rick said, "Thanks for coming. I have something to show you. Ingram, you too. Got your field boots?" It was as if the previous scene had never happened, and since Occam seemed fine with it, I guessed I was too.

Rather than reply, I unzipped my one-day gobag and kicked off my sneakers, hauling on the boots. While I changed shoes, Rick ate a protein bar. It smelled nasty and I bet it tasted nasty too. I'd tried making protein bars for the cats, but the whey protein powder was awful, the egg-based protein was dreadful, and the powdered fishmeal protein was yucky and hard to work with. Come fall I could make venison jerky and wild turkey jerky from kills the wereleopards brought me. I could also smoke trout from mountain streams. I had ordered some dried skipjack tuna shavings to increase the protein content. Until I got the shavings and hunting season was right for butchering meat, the cats were stuck with the icky commercially prepared stuff.

Stepping out of the car, I twisted my silky skirt up between my legs and tucked it in at my waist, making a kind of baggy drawers. Not having cat eyes, I flicked on my flashlight and slid my gobag over one shoulder as Rick led us into the dark, off to the right, away from the road and toward the Tennessee River. We crossed a field planted with a healthy crop of soybeans, the knee-high plants swishing as we moved, grasshoppers flying up, most moving slow, nearly dead from the poison I felt/smelled/tasted as we walked toward the water.

When the moon rose, it might be bright enough to see something, but for now, my flash was a thin beam on the plants of the field. I sent my awareness into the land as best I was able without touching skin to earth. The land wasn't dead. It was full of nutrients and organic matter from the last flood, the soil rich. Despite the current moderate drought, the soy was healthy, putting out lots of bean pods, not that I would eat anything from this land. The pesticides that were killing the grasshoppers and other critters that attacked soy had been absorbed by the roots and leaves and into the bean pods. I closed my eyes as I walked, feeling for the life in the ground. Even amid the poisons, I could feel the magic in the land, tendrils twining around and deep. Black magic.

Occam gripped my shoulder, jerking me back. "I forgot you can't see in the dark," he said. The cats had stopped. I hadn't. I'd almost stepped across a witch circle. I had been so involved with my thoughts, walking with my eyes closed, the magics flowing up through my boots, I hadn't even noticed the soy had ended. That was stupid.

"Thanks," I said, not sure how I felt about Occam watching over me so closely. And then he released my shoulder and walked away, following Rick, the two of them walking widdershins outside the circle, sniffing the air for scents humans might miss.

"Anything?" Occam asked.

"Something sour, like sickness. Dead cat." The boss shrugged.

The twenty-foot-wide circle, drawn with what looked like powdered white chalk, studded with crow and buzzard feathers, was a witch circle unlike any I had seen in Spook School. Instead of a pentagram inside a circle, which created a pentacle, this one had angles like the spokes of a wheel. In each of the spokes, there were shapes that might have been runes drawn in the dirt. The spokes connected to a smaller central circle, maybe three feet across, and in the center of that was a dead black cat, blood all around, soaked into the ground. It was hanging upside down from a makeshift wooden tripod, its throat slit. The cat had been sacrificed.

Bloodlust rose up in me, demanding, insistent, needing. *Feed the land.* Soulwood, so recently invoked, wanted the blood.

"I was driving," Rick said.

I yanked back on the need, holding it down, trying to smother it.

"I felt something . . . happening inside me," he continued,

halting, his voice growing raspy, "like a moon-calling, but . . . different. I pulled over, secured my weapon, shifted, and I woke up there"—he pointed—"lying near the circle, but outside it. And—" He stopped, shook his head, and looked around, his eyes puzzled and perhaps a little bit sleepy. He looked bewildered, as if he had woken up in the middle of sleep-walking.

Occam paced to Rick. He didn't touch Rick but stood close, looking slightly to the side, cat-like.

Rick said, "That's a black-magic circle. On the bank of a river, a dead black cat in the center."

"Yeah, Hoss, we see that," Occam said, his tone kind. "Anything else you need to tell us?"

"I . . . I don't know." He stared at the dead cat. "My cat grabbed the gobag holding the blanket and my old cell. I ended up here. But I don't know how I kept from being drawn into the circle."

Rick must have felt the death of the housecat in the circle and tracked it by . . . I had no idea.

He shook himself, more dog-like than cat-like, his silvered hair flying with the motion. Sounding more like the senior special agent I knew, he said, "Black magic isn't illegal in the human world, except for the cruelty-to-animals part. We need to report this. This could indicate a psychopath, a serial killer, trying out her skills."

"Statistically speaking," I said, remembering my studies from PsyLED Spook School, "black-magic users don't usually become serial killers." Rick turned his attention to me and I gave a tiny shrug. "It's a new course for continuing ed. The Statistics of Magic. It isn't the death or the torture that witches want, it's the power that the deaths bring."

"That makes a weird kind of sense," Rick said. "I can barely smell death on the cat. No release of bowels or urine on the air." To Occam, he said, "It hasn't been dead long. Maybe three hours?"

Occam lifted a thumb, an ambiguous agreement. "Maybe less. After sunset."

A good six feet from the edge of the circle, I continued widdershins around it, stumbling in the dark, taking photos with my camera, the flash too bright, shocking in the night, but revealing the runes in the ground, in the spokes of the wheel. Keeping busy kept the bloodlust at bay, but I shouldn't have—wouldn't have—drawn on Soulwood had I known about the cat.

Occam said something that was lost on the night air.

"River is that way." Rick pointed. "Twenty paces. North is there." He pointed in a different direction. "Moonrise will be in that general area." He pointed.

I made notes on my cell, aligning with the north point on the witch circle. I tackled the pink elephant in the room. "Did the spell call you here? You specifically?"

Rick shook his head. "I don't see how. To summon a human or a were-creature, the witch needs something personal from them—blood, hair with roots, fingernails with a bit of flesh on them. There's nothing of mine here."

"T. Laine—Kent," I amended, "should be here, not me. My witch-magic knowledge is nothing compared to hers."

"I texted Kent while I was dressing," Rick said. "ETA ten. Meanwhile, will you read the land? Are you up to it?"

"Except for the dead cat, yeah." Death and blood called to my magic. The team knew about me being easily caught up in the earth, but not about my bloodlust. If I got caught up in the land, hopefully someone would knock me out and stop me before I killed someone. Risking a brain injury was better than risking me killing someone.

"Manageable?" Occam asked, reading my worried expression, or maybe my worried scent.

"I think so." But I'd discovered that most magical things were manageable with Occam around. Two dissimilar species of predator were seldom compatible, but, strangely, being guarded by Occam's cat soothed my own predatory instincts. Maybe because we suffered bloodlust for two very different reasons. I hadn't yet told Occam that his cat was so important to me. I didn't like being dependent on others for something so basic as self-control.

I unfolded my faded pink blanket, settling it on the ground, at the north point of the circle but outside. I sat, my knees decorously covered. I'd learned not to place both palms flat on the ground and thrust myself into the earth, but rather to put one index fingertip on it first and take a peek down. It was my version of testing the waters with a toe.

Rick was behind me, Occam to my left in case he had to cut me free of the earth. It had happened. I touched the ground with the tip of one, then both index fingers. Something wriggled beneath the ground. I jerked my hands to my chest, hugging myself.

"Nell?" Occam asked. "What?" He was kneeling near me, Rick beside him, all our faces on a level. Occam's white scars and Rick's strangely silvered hair caught the flashlight's beam, creating voids of shadow and inky night where their eyes were. It was creepy, but I figured I better not say that. I frowned. Gingerly I put my right index fingertip on the earth. And frowned harder.

"What?" Rick demanded.

"Maggots. Lots of maggots." For me that meant vampires. Vampires had been here in such numbers that I felt them stronger than the black magic.

"Why?" he asked, understanding what I meant.

"I don't know. I'm going deeper." I closed my eyes.

I heard the sound of a knife being drawn from a Kydex sheath, a snap/slide/plastic/steel sound. Without opening my eyes, I knew that Occam had drawn his blade. Just in case. Sometimes the ground got a little too excited when I was around and the earth had been known to send up vines and roots and tendrils to stick into me, to tie me to it, to pull me down. "So far so good," I muttered.

I dropped slowly through the layers, past the sensation of maggots on the surface, where I encountered the black magic that permeated an inch below. It felt icky, slimy, like burnt motor oil and something I might scrape out of my compost pile. Underneath the magics, I slipped through soil poisoned with pesticides where modern farming had been continuous for decades. Below that was disturbed soil with evidence of earlier farming methods: an iron tip from an old tiller; bits and pieces of metal and old diesel fuel in one spot that felt as if some machine had broken and been repaired on-site; a refuse pit with rusted tin cans and broken bottles.

Below that were bones, the memory of blood and death. A

battle had been fought here once, in the distant past. My bloodlust wandered through the bones, the evidence of blood spilled, and violence. The memory of blood and terror and—

"Nell! Nell, wake up! Come back to the surface." Occam. Upset. Excited. Worried.

I felt his ravaged hand on my shoulder, hot and shaking me, more claw than fingers. I eased my mind back from the battle and took a breath. Blinked. Occam was cutting me free of the ground. My fingers were buried in a tangle of rootlets and leaves and vines. Occam cursed when one extruded a thorn and bit his wrist.

From somewhere in the dark, Rick snarled. "Why is the circle attacking Ingram?"

A woman's voice said, "It's not the circle, boss. That magic has been expended. This is Nell's magic."

Occam sliced me free of the last rootlet/vine and picked me up, stepping away fast, holding me like a child. It was nice. I was suddenly cold and he was cat-heated. I rested against his hard chest, his arms holding me easily.

Rick yanked and ripped my blanket free of the vines. Cursing. Mad. His Frenchy black eyes glowing cat-green. I didn't know if he was still reacting to the magic or to an attack on a member of his team. Both probably.

"Don't mess up my blanket," I said. "I need it."

"I'm not messing up your blanket, Ingram," he growled.

"We were afraid of you going all woody and branching out," the woman said.

I swiveled my head to her. "Hey, Lainie."

"Hey, Tree Girl. You got all leafy again."

"I did?" I lifted my hands in the light of her shielded flash. My nails were greenish brown and leafed out, the skin of my fingers nut brown. I put a cold palm against Occam's unscarred cheek, which was scruffy. His eyes were glowing gold. "You cut me free again." Occam growled softly. I smiled up at him. "Thank you. You can put me down now."

Occam's arms tightened on me.

"Or not." I rested my head against his chest, watching the action in the field. Kent was doing some kind of arcane measurements with a stick and the psy-meter 2.0 and recording numbers on a pad in the light of her flash.

"Levels one and four are redlining, which is not typical for a witch circle or a witch."

"What is it typical for?" Occam asked.

"Nothing I remember from the databases. But with the cat and the strangeness of the circle, I can agree with your evaluation. It's *black magic*," T. Laine said, the words sounding as if they tasted bad. "It's a strange spell. I'll know more after I finish analyzing it." Lainie was the unit's witch and her analysis would be arcane as well as mundane.

Rick—properly referred to as LaFleur on the job—said, "When you get back, open a file on this, Kent. Run it through the local law enforcement databases and see if there's anything similar."

T. Laine asked, her voice carefully emotionless, "What do you want me to say about how you ended up here?"

I shifted in Occam's arms at that question. The query may have sounded simple, but it was loaded with intricate potentialities. If Rick had been summoned by the spell, it made him a liability to the unit. If we left mention of him out and it was later discovered that he was a liability, then we'd be in trouble for not including it. Internal Affairs would be all over us.

Rick turned his head so he was looking back over the circle; I couldn't see his eyes. "Say exactly what happened. I was attracted to the working after it was over. Make the file PsyLED Unit Eighteen eyes only for now. I'll call the up-line bosses and report." Which was walking a very fine line between the prospective problems. I was impressed despite myself.

"I'm taking Nell home," Occam said. "She's growing more leaves. She needs to be back on Soulwood."

I held up my hands and studied my fingers. "Mighty leafy." Then I laid my head on Occam's chest and fell asleep, hardly noticing when I was placed in his car, and waking only when he picked me back up. I sighed and stretched and yawned and pushed away from his body to look up at his disfigured face. But he was still Occam. And he had become a safe haven for me.

That thought coiled through me, foreign, alien. Except for Soulwood, I'd never had a safe haven before.

TWO

"I can walk, you know. I ain't broke and I ain't a young'un."

"True," Occam said. But he didn't put me down, just rubbed his jaw on the top of my head like a cat, scent-marking me, carried me up the steps to my door, and leaned down so I could open the lock. Then he carried me through the dark to the tiny bath and placed me on the toilet seat, which was all kinds of uncomfortable even with both of us fully clothed. "You're cold. Get a shower. Get warm. Put on your winter pajamas. Get in bed. I'll add wood to the stove and let the cats in."

"That sounds nice, you bossy cat, but the stove's cold so there ain't no hot water. I don't burn wood in summer. I take cold showers and use the AC window unit upstairs and the fans downstairs to keep the place cool. I cook on the brazier outside or use the microwave."

Occam hesitated in the doorway, watching me with golden eyes. He hadn't been around long enough to know how people living off the grid survived the heat of summer.

"Get on outta here. I can take care of myself." I couldn't see him well in the dark, but I knew he wasn't happy at the thought of leaving me. I could feel his disquiet through my connection to Soulwood and that disturbed me. I shook my head at my land, more than at Occam. "I'm good. Go on," I said more gently. "I can tell you need to shift and run and hunt, and I'll feel better knowing you're here, close by. Just don't take a doe. All the does on the land have fawns. There's a small bachelor herd to the north, and one is too big for his britches. Take him. He's young enough to be tender but old enough to make trouble. And I think we got a family of coyotes skirting the property. If you find them, be careful. They're shifty and tricky and they might get the drop on a big-cat."

Occam shook his head at the impossibility of a canine species getting the drop on him. Without a word he slid into the muggy darkness. I heard the back door open and felt more than saw the mousers race in from the back porch. I heard the lock click and knew he was gone to shift and hunt and watch over me. I sighed and let go of the tension that was holding my shoulders tight.

While Jezzie, Torquil, and Cello wound around my ankles, *mrowing* for kibble and voicing their displeasure that the big-cat was gone, I made it to my feet and stripped off the clothes I'd worn to date Occam. Rinsed, shivering, under the tepid shower water. The house was muggy and sticky hot from the day's heat, even with the single window unit struggling to cool it down, but my body was cold as an oak in winter. I padded to my bedroom and dressed in pajamas, then called Mud, my baby sister, who was coming to live with me soon, to see if she was all right for the night. Somewhere in there, I poured out kibble and ate a leftover sandwich from the picnic. Finally I crawled into bed with the electric blanket on a two-hour timer and cats settling in on top of me.

I woke when a pan clanged in my kitchen. The cats were gone and the smell of bacon and coffee was bright on the air, though judging by the angle of the sun, it was well after noon and long past breakfast. My sleep schedule had been odd since I'd come back to the fauna side of the flora and fauna biology spectrum, and working PsyLED hours was not helping me to sleep at night like normal people. I snickered softly. Normal people. I was definitely not normal people.

I rolled off my sweat-damp mattress, knowing that at some point in the last year, I had become a spoiled city girl. I'd never survive another summer without doing something about an air conditioner. My bedroom was hot and sticky and so was I. Sleeping, I had thrown off the blanket and it was heaped on the floor at the foot of the bed. I managed to stand on wobbly legs and stripped the sheets. Caught sight of myself in the mirror. I was browner than before. Leaves were growing out of my fingers and my hairline. They were bright and deep summer green, shaped vaguely like the love child of grape leaves and oak leaves. Vines were tangled in my redder-than-once-before hair. My eyes were the green of corn husks, flecked with the darker green of . . . of zucchini maybe. I was going vegetarian. I laughed.

I knew vaguely who was in my house and if I'd tuned in more closely I could have named them. Most of Unit Eighteen had invaded the living room and kitchen and I couldn't remember if this was a planned visit or not. Either way I had company and couldn't go traipsing around in my altogethers. I wrapped a robe around me and trudged to the shower, dropping off the sheets on the back porch, which served as a laundry room, cat romp-room, hammock sleep space, and catchall. Without greeting or even looking at my uninvited guests, I got ready for my day. Showered; clipped my leaves; gooped the ends of my hair; jerked on loose pants, white T-shirt. The weapons harness and weapon went into my repacked gobag, just in case. Slippers on my feet. Because I was not dressing for work on my day off in my own house. Decent, I went to face my home invaders. Though I guess I had to call them visitors since they had cooked breakfast.

"File is 'LaFleur/Circle,'" JoJo said, referring to the report on our screens, one I hadn't read yet. "We have a black-magic/ blood-magic spell with a dead cat, and the possible presence of vampires at the site either before, during, or after the spell was cast. Rick was called to or attracted to the site, in cat form, though by the time he arrived the spell was ended. Due to the timeline, we haven't established causality. T. Laine? You're up."

"From the beginning . . . ," T. Laine said slowly, as if trying to sift out conclusions. She was sitting in my rocker, her tablet balanced on her thigh, with one knee thrown up over the arm of the chair, the other foot bare to the floor, pushing her forward and back. She was dressed in pants that ended at midcalf and a tank top to combat the heat. She had kicked off her shoes at the door and looked perfectly comfortable in my home. ". . . Rick loses conscious volition, yet somehow drives toward a site where a black domestic cat has been sacrificed in a black-magic ceremony. He shifts to cat, grabs an old gobag containing a blanket and a flip phone, which is perfect for being carried in cat fangs. Goes overland to the witch circle. He doesn't enter the circle. He shifts to human. Texts for help. Wraps himself in the blanket. Waits for backup.

"Occam was not called to the witch circle, though he *was* farther away and *busy*." T. Laine slid a sly glance my way and then back to her tablet.

I was too much of a tree for my blush to show, thankfully.

She went on with her summary. "Rick *is* a black cat. Rick has magical cat tats, though not black cats. JoJo has a big-cat tattoo and she isn't called. And Occam, who is a cat, but not a black cat, wasn't called to the same spell. I'm not sure what part is coincidence, but I'm thinking causality is in there somewhere. Either way, coincidence is a rare bird."

I wasn't certain what birds had to do with cat spells, but I agreed with the coincidence factor. I nibbled on a piece of cold toast, letting the conversation flow through me like a stream, searching for eddies and pools where logjams and detritus of thought had gone overlooked.

Breakfast had been really good, even though it was only microwaved scrambled eggs, toast, and jelly. The washed dishes were piled on the kitchen counter, except for the last of the toast and jelly on a platter in the middle of the coffee table. The work-related tablets and laptops were scattered around, as were glasses of iced cola or tea. Everyone had brought their own drink. I was sipping on my own cold mint tea to try and keep cool. It wasn't helping much. My single-unit air conditioner had never been intended to chill down a house this big, in daylight, warmed by this many people. John, my deceased husband, may have planned to get more window units, had the children he wanted ever appeared. Living alone, I hadn't needed them, but Tandy, Occam, T. Laine, and JoJo did.

Rick, our senior agent, was in an interagency conference all day at Knoxville FBI headquarters, with the assistant director of PsyLED—Soul—and with the regional heads of the FBI, CIA, ICE, ATF, the Tennessee and North Carolina National Guards, the state bureaus of investigation from Tennessee and North and South Carolina, MEPS (the U.S. Military

Entrance Processing Command located in Knoxville), top Highway Patrol chiefs, and Homeland Security. It was a big meeting of the biggest LEO brass from three states, working on creating protocols for potential security and terrorist threats of all kinds, human and paranormal, homegrown and foreign.

Our new up-line man, the special agent in charge of the eastern seaboard, Ayatas FireWind, was at the Pentagon for high-level meetings about vampires. FireWind spent a lot of time on planes, jetting around, dealing with politically delicate paranormal criminal cases, often with the vampires, who seemed to be in an uproar since Leo Pellissier, the former Master of the City of New Orleans and most of the southern United States, was no longer in charge of his Mithrans. We were on our own today. FireWind had run other units and even other regions, but they had been primarily human units. Unit Eighteen was the first largely para unit, and though I hadn't met him yet, I had gotten the feeling that things hadn't gone nicely the first few times FireWind was in the office. There was some smoldering discontent in the unit, and clearly they didn't want to discuss Rick around HQ, where the boss might walk in unexpectedly.

Since electronic equipment allowed us to run the office remotely, and since Occam had hunted as he protected my land all day, the office meeting was here and we were unobserved. It was kinda nice.

T. Laine's lips puckered and her eyes went distant, still thinking. She said, "Rick seemed . . . odd this morning. Even for a moon-called beast, he seemed distracted, agitated, preoccupied, and even more distant than usual."

"It's not new," the unit empath said. "He's been unvaryingly unpleasant inside his own skin for weeks, the way he is on the three days of the full moon. I'm glad he's not here. He's throwing off confusing emotions that make my skin itch, and he's pacing like a cat in a cage. No offense, Occam."

"None taken, Tandy," Occam said. "You're a lightning rod who reads minds. I'm a cat. We all have issues."

Tandy gave a breathy laugh. He had been struck by lightning three times, which had ignited his empath gifts and left him with permanent Lichtenberg lines on his skin. Issues.

True, I thought. Occam had surely done his share of pacing during twenty years in a cage, in cat form. T. Laine was a witch without a coven. JoJo was the Diamond Drill, the highest level of hacker known. I was turning into a plant.

Right now, Occam was stretched out on the sofa, his jeans and T-shirt damp with the heat. He was stroking Cello's head, the once-feral cat purring and stretching under the big-cat's hand. "That's why I called our meeting here. We needed a break from HQ and a chance to voice our thoughts."

"How far from the circle was Rick when he was called?" I asked. "If he was really called, that is, and it wasn't coincidence." We were all dancing around that possibility, that Rick was in danger personally and was also a liability to the unit. "Which side of the river?"

Occam twisted and leaned over the coffee table, punched a key on his laptop, and whirled it around to show us the screen, before dropping back to his lazy position. On the laptop, a small map of Knoxville and the surrounding area appeared, marked with a circle and a dot. The center of the circle was near the river. The dot was tagged as Rick's car. "I checked that. He was on the same side of the river, and within five miles of the circle as the crow flies."

"What was he doing?" Jo asked.

"Driving home from dinner and drinks with a hungry feeb," Occam said, referring to an FBI agent who was low on the food chain. "He pulled over, secured his weapon, and shifted. His cat grabbed an old, mostly empty gobag that contained an old flip phone and a blanket, and went overland."

I remembered Rick saying that part and added, "Pulling over, securing his weapon, and then his cat taking the gobag took critical-thinking skills and problem-solving ability."

"Right," Occam said. "He felt something was coming and got ready for it. He was driving, and though he doesn't remember it, he drove himself two miles closer to the circle, shifted in the car, ruining his clothes, and went on overland. We still haven't found his new cell, his car key fob, or his right shoe, but his weapon was under the seat, which, while not locked in the gun safe in his trunk, was put away, not in plain sight on the car seat. His memory is spotty until he woke up at the circle site, still in cat form, bag and flip phone beside him."

"That preparation suggests he was in his right mind," T. Laine said, in agreement with me, "though not remembering the drive suggests something else."

"At the scene he thought the cat had been dead about three hours," I said. "When you discount our drive time, that leaves about two hours and twenty minutes from the time the spell was at its zenith to the time Rick was sane enough to call for help. It takes him something like twenty minutes each time he shifts shape. So that takes away another forty minutes, leaving an hour twenty or so. How long did it take him to get to the spell site?" I asked. "Did he smell vampires when he got there?"

"He didn't know, and he doesn't remember anything about vamps," JoJo said, her mismatched earrings swinging silvery in the light of her laptop screen as she tapped keys. "But he was alone each time he shifted. Good questions, probie."

I ducked my head in pleasure. "In that case I have another one," I said. "If the purpose was to call Rick, then the spell succeeded. Why wasn't the witch waiting for him? Why do the spell and leave? By not being there, that suggests coincidence, not causality."

T. Laine brightened and said, "Yeah. My gut feeling is that this blood-magic caster didn't know Rick would come." She pointed a finger at me approvingly. "Our blood-magic witch initiated the spell in the inner circle, slit the cat's throat, closed the inner circle to let the spell run its course, and then stepped outside the outer circle and reclosed it too." She took a long draw of her iced drink through the straw, trying to combat the heat of my house. The tiny window-unit air conditioner was straining. Come full dark, when the temps outside dropped lower than the temps inside, I'd open the windows and doors and let the winds sweep out the heat, but for now it was just miserable. "It's a freaky working," the unit's witch continued. "I still don't know what it's supposed to do, but I think the spell was a fast one. She killed the cat and once it was dead, the spell ended and she left."

"And the maggoty feeling Nell got?" JoJo asked the witch.

"I'm spitballing here, but I think the vamps showed up and left before Rick arrived. And no, I have no idea if vamps were there for the working, or were summoned, or if that's an accident too."

JoJo adjusted the elastic waist of her sweat-damp skirt, plucking at the thin cotton fabric printed with big aqua blooms, smaller bright pink flowers, and small green leaves. "Dear God, I'm hot. Nell, this place reminds me of my great-grandmother's place in Georgia." Jo took off her turban, which was a one-piece thing like a toboggan, tossed it to the kitchen table like a Frisbee, and gusted a hearty sigh. "Great-Gramma had AC but never used it. Said her bones were cold all the time. Her place was a sauna too."

I almost said that I was sorry, but it wasn't my idea for the unit to invade my home, so . . . no apology. It was nearly August. It was hot.

"Yeah, I know," JoJo said, reading my face the way Tandy could read emotions. "I have to deal."

"According to the calendar," Tandy said, hiding a grin, "last night was a waning half-moon, days after full. It wasn't a moon working, which would take place on the full moon. It didn't look like an earth magic working or a water working. It wasn't any recognizable or standard magical working. Which adds to the possibility that this was an accidental summoning. A deliberate summoning of a were-creature would most likely be on the *full* moon."

"What *do* we know about the circle?" JoJo asked T. Laine. "Anything expected and ordinary? Anything we can use as a jumping-off point?"

"The circle was downright strange," T. Laine said. "Nothing traditional about it except the starting point aligned to magnetic north. Most circles that big need multiple witches to invoke. This was a one-woman circle. Most are geared to the element the witch is called by. I'm a moon witch, so I'd only attempt a big circle on the full moon, using moonstones as focals. An air witch would use feathers and fallen leaves and even carved wood amulets from wind-downed trees. This circle had focals from all the elements and some of the focals were totally unfamiliar to me. There was a branch freshly broken from a black walnut tree, the leaves wilted, and is the only thing that might point to an earth witch. There was a lump of unformed clay, probably from the nearby riverbed, which might point to a water witch. A golf ball and golf tee, both new looking. I got nothing for them. There were two glass vials full of black liquid that stinks like old blood. A rotten scrap of gauze or cheesecloth stained with what might be blood. There was a small steel paring knife. A cheapie."

"I've sent everything off for analysis," JoJo said, "but it'll all go on the back burner since there's no crime involved with the circles and I have no favors I'm willing to call in yet. It could take weeks."

"No witch would combine all the things she did and then add steel to it," T. Laine said. "Steel is disruptive to magic. And no witch leaves behind focals. When the working is done, they end the circle and take all the goodies away."

"Steel. Black walnut," I said, trying to make sense out of it. "That wood is somewhat toxic. Is it possible that she was going to go back later to gather the focals and make sure the working was really completed, but we got there first?" I asked.

"That's as good an idea as any," T. Laine said, sounding grumpy. "Too bad I didn't think to put up a freaking camera or two."

"Occam, what can you tell about the gauze?" JoJo asked. "Is it blood?"

"Yes," Occam said, "but what species I can't tell. It's years old."

"So why did she leave all her focals behind? This stuff has to be hard to gather. Was the witch a novice," Jo asked, "untrained and trying to make it up out of nothing?"

"Maybe she didn't know she was calling a black leopard and Rick scared her off?" I suggested.

"Hmmm. I don't think so. The circle was powerful. All the power had been emptied out, used up, but the traces of the working were there, so strong they practically sizzled. For all I know, more powerful focals may have been taken when the witch left. But the strangest part of the circle is the runes." T. Laine propped her tablet on its stand so we could see the rendering on the screen. The unit's witch had re-created the circle but made it of dotted lines, so there was no way to accidently invoke it. "Every single rune was merkstave—reversed—and none of them are traditionally used together. There were twelves spokes on the circle and four runes, each used three times. There were merkstave versions of Uruz, Fehu, Thurisaz, and Wunjo, all of them calling for awful things to happen to the person being spelled. For instance, Fehu reversed means greed and slavery and bondage and failure." T. Laine looked around at us, making sure she had our attention. "It was a curse circle. It was powerful. And Rick happened to be nearby. If the working had been intended for him, he'd never have called us because he'd have been dead. This is why I think Rick's attraction to the circle was an accident of proximity."

Occam asked, "What happens when the local witch coven finds the caster?"

"She'll be put in a null room for a long time. This circle was very, *very* bad business," T. Laine said.

"Rick's hair looked whiter this morning. Did this spell age him even more?" JoJo asked. Rick's hair had been turning white for the last few months, and no one really knew why.

"I don't know," T. Laine said. She scrubbed her head with both fists as if trying to knock something loose from inside her brain. "I don't know about the witch or her focals. I don't know much of anything. Rick's been aging, but he's only been emotionally weird off and on for the last few months. I can't tell what's causing the aging, or if the problems with his magics have resulted in the white hair *and* made him more likely to be called."

"Did you scan Rick for latent magic, something left over from the spell and not part of his own magics?" Jo asked.

"First thing. His magics look the same in a . . . let's call it an *inspection* working, one that lets me see overlays of magical energies. Nothing is clinging to him. Whatever the circle was, the *curse* working had dissipated before he got there."

"Occam," Jo asked, "did you feel anything from the circle when you were there or anything like a calling last night? A need to go catty?"

"Not a thing. It was a peaceful night." His eyes traveled slowly to me, and when they met mine, he gave me a Mona Lisa smile, his expression reminding me what we had been doing when the call came in. "Very . . . peaceful."

"Stop it, Occam," Tandy said, clearly embarrassed. "Please."

"Yeah. It's hot enough in here already without you two starting up whatever you were doing last night when I texted you," JoJo said.

"Ummm. Details later, bestie," T. Laine said to me.

Blood fought to heat my cheeks. The women in the church never talked about the night before on the day after. It just wasn't done. I didn't know how to respond and so simply lowered my eyes, mortified.

"So Rick was the only werecat called," Jo went on, either oblivious to my embarrassment or ignoring it.

I pushed away my discomfort and said, "We know that Paka bound him magically and that she used were-magic in her binding. I sorta bound him in some way to heal him. Twice. It's possible"—almost certain, but I didn't want to say that—"that I tied him to Soulwood. And maybe, through his own cat and the tattoos, and the were-magic Paka used, he's more susceptible to spells that deal with cats?"

"I like," T. Laine said, her eyes going unfocused and distant.

"And why don't we just ask him?" I added.

Both T. Laine and JoJo hooted with laughter. Jo said, "The boss doesn't talk about his tats. Like not *ever*."

Occam was still giving me that faint smile and I couldn't meet his eyes. My awkwardness about the previous night, added to my prevarication about tying the werecats to the land, was amusing to him. He could feel the pull on his magics; he knew I had tied him and Rick both to the land when I healed them. When I brought him back from the dead.

"Back to your comment about him being susceptible to cat spells. Twisty, but possible," Jo said, taking a slice of toast. "And in my opinion, tied to your land is better than being dead."

T. Laine said, "My personal worry is that his unfinished tats and blood magic, mixed with our old friend Paka's spells, may have created a magical opening into Rick's soul, an opening that's still there."

Occam sat up, swinging his feet to the wood floor, sliding Cello to his lap. "You're telling me Rick's psyche might be open? That any witch worth her salt, or maybe any fanghead strong enough, can reach in and take him over?"

"Yes," JoJo said.

"No," T. Laine said at the same time. "Not exactly." She swung her leg off the chair arm, to the floor, and sat up in the rocker, her motion mimicking Occam's and making her dark

bob swing. "Okay, it's like this. And though none of this is a
secret, it stays in this room until further notice. Verbal discussion only."

We all nodded.

"You know how Rick has music he plays during the full
moon. He got it to help keep him sane back when he couldn't
shift into his cat. And you know how it eases all the shifters
who've tried it."

The music was a big part of the full moon protocol in HQ.
Occam nodded slowly, his fingers sliding down the cat body.
The cat started purring.

"When Rick was turned, things happened fast. He was bitten by a black leopard and the taint got into his system, starting the change. Immediately he was kidnapped by werewolves
and they chewed on his tattoos. Think about it. There was
werewolf taint in his flesh while he was going through the
change into a black wereleopard. That had to cause problems
on a first moon-calling, and we all know he couldn't shift into
his cat for two or three years." She leaned in. "Rick was still
with Jane Yellowrock at that time and Jane is the one who got
the music for him. Jane is friends with Molly Everhart True-
blood, of the Everhart witches, but Molly is not an air witch.
I'm guessing that Molly found an air witch somewhere and got
her to make the music spells that disrupted the magic in Rick's
unfinished black-magic tats."

The magical music also kept the were-taint from consum-
ing his sanity, helping to interrupt the attraction of the moon
keeping him from going crazy. The music also had a side effect on all were-creatures, keeping them calmer, more stable,
and better able to resist the change, which was why we still
played the music in the office on the full moon. Something
about that tugged at my brain, but before I could take it apart
and inspect it, T. Laine went on.

"You have more control over your cat than Rick does, but
even you are more peaceful when the music is playing, right?"

Occam nodded, his eyes narrow as he thought back over
the past year of his life. "Yeah," he breathed. "I am."

T. Laine said, "What I figured out a few months back,
while you were putting down roots," she added to me, "is that
the music also has the ability to plug the hole in Rick's magic.

Plug isn't a good word, but it'll do. When the music is playing, it keeps out other workings and dark magics. It also has a cumulative effect, making him more resistant to outside influence. I thought the plug had made Rick totally safe, unresponsive to other workings. I was wrong, and I have to figure out how this curse got through his defenses."

"So how did Paka get in?" I asked, finishing off my toast and licking the jelly off my fingers. Occam's eyes darted to my mouth as a finger popped out, too interested. I stopped. Wiped my fingers on a cloth napkin instead.

"If Paka had come along six months later than she did, her magic might not have gotten in so deep," T. Laine said. "He might have resisted her. Unfortunately she showed up in the first few months he was a werecat."

"You told Rick all this?" Occam said, more a statement than a question.

"Long time ago, yes. Rick and Soul. I assume the new guy knows it too."

"I read what I could in the report about the werewolf attack and Rick's rescue, but big parts were redacted," I said. "The parts that tell who actually rescued him have been removed. If I didn't work at PsyLED, I'd have no idea that Jane Yellowrock and Leo Pellissier's people helped to get him free."

"Security clearances are so entertainin'," Occam drawled.

"The most important part wasn't in there at all," I said, "which was: did any of the wolves escape? Are there any still floating around who might hire a witch to target Rick? Or is there any other were-creature in Rick's past who might hire a witch to target him? Anyone considered the possibility that Paka hired a witch, who is trying to get Rick to turn someone, so the grindy'll kill him?"

"Ohhh," T. Laine said. "Never thought about that one." She and JoJo exchanged glances I couldn't interpret before bending over their tablets. Tandy and Occam were equally involved in file searches, fingers tapping.

Brainstorming was fun.

Sounding as if she was speaking while the primary part of her brain was otherwise engaged, Jo said, "Brute, the unit's white werewolf, disappeared before you joined us and is currenly staying with Jane Yellowrock. So not him."

My head swiveled to her. I'd heard about the werewolf, but never seen him. I had thought for a while that the unit was pulling my leg about having a werewolf as part of the team. "Rick hates werewolves."

"Yeah. We know. He didn't stay long once we landed in Knoxville, and it was weird having him around." JoJo yanked on her earrings. "Brute has his own dedicated grindy and is unable to shift to human, so he isn't after Rick. We have records that other werewolves appeared in the mountains and bit humans but so far as we know, they were all tracked down and dealt with. There's no indication that any of the werewolves who bit Rick or participated in his kidnapping or torture are still alive."

"A lot is redacted about his rescue and, unless Rick tells us, we may never know specifics," Tandy said. "However, two werewolves were in jail at the time of the raid that rescued Rick."

Occam said, "I got names and socials for those. Sending them to you. I don't see where they are. Not in the system. Not confirmed kills by grindylows."

"You guys have the weres covered. I'll compile a list of witches who have interacted with Rick in the past," T. Laine said.

"What about Jane Yellowrock?" JoJo asked.

"Jane is direct and impatient," Tandy said, thoughtfully. "If she wanted Rick dead, he'd have been dead a long time ago. A headless corpse. She isn't the kind for machinations."

Occam said, "If it makes you feel better, Rick doesn't talk to me about his past either. He's pretty closemouthed about it all, even to the only other werecat around. I'll have to drag anything new out of him, which might involve a major catfight and not a little blood for very little info."

And that was the crux of the matter. Rick was close-mouthed about everything. His family, his relationships with women prior to being bitten, his undercover life, which went on for far too many years. Rick protected people he felt deserved protecting, even against law enforcement agencies. Maybe even against us. If the witch circle had really targeted him, then his entire life would have to be inspected to track down the potential bad. Everything. Every detail of every case. No more secrets. Rick would *hate* that. And all of us were too chicken to address the issue.

"Tandy? What's Rick feeling about the witch circle?" JoJo asked.

"Worried," the unit empath said. The Lichtenberg lines that were part of the legacy of three lightning strikes went darker red against his pale skin. "Depressed. Angry. Tied up in knots. And now that you mention the possibility of his life being turned upside down, it makes sense." Rick was in a lot of emotional pain lately. It was clear as day on his face. Tandy was having trouble working through Rick's emotions. "I tried to speak to him. But he . . ."

"He what? He looked at you mean?" JoJo asked.

"No," Tandy admitted. "He snarled and showed me his teeth. And he hissed."

"That right there was relevant information," I said, pointing with the jelly spoon. Tandy was supposed to be our unit's therapist. Instead he was scared of his boss. "Rick must be deeply troubled that he'd introduced one security breach to the unit with Paka and now might find his personal and professional life rummaged through like a yard sale."

The empath sighed and took a black-headed cat from Occam's shoulder, holding and stroking it. Torquil, named for the helmet-like black head, had once been wild; now she purred. The werecats had tamed all my mousers. I still didn't know how I felt about that.

For the first time, it occurred to me that in a lot of ways, they might have tamed me too. I scowled. "Just 'cause you don't like one a Rick's reactions don't mean you get to keep it secret," I said, sounding a little too churchy. I reined in my accent and finished my thought. "Secrets are dangerous."

"I know," Tandy said, seeming to take comfort from the cat. "But if I write up a report about Rick being difficult, and maybe a security risk, then what? Rick *is* a security risk, but no more than the rest of us. Soul went rogue and killed salamanders during the fight that injured our cats, and she might even have killed the ones in captivity at HQ. I lost it a few months back when I was exposed to abnormal energies and forced emotional changes on the humans around me. JoJo did a little drilling again." He looked at his girlfriend.

Her eyebrows were reaching high at being outed for illegal activity. Not that we didn't all know anyway. But no one talked about any of this.

"In the interests of protecting the public," Tandy amended.

"Uh-huh," JoJo said, in a tone that carried a threat if he continued. But he did.

"T. Laine needs a coven and doesn't have one yet because she keeps pissing off the locals." Tandy's face was turning red, the Lichtenberg lines going darker. "Occam spent months in Africa being healed and he still isn't a hundred percent. Paka still signifies a compromise to the security of PsyLED and she vanished into the wilds of Africa, making her impossible to track. If she shows up here again we'll have a fight on our hands, which could put our badges and careers on the table. And we have an unpredictable grindylow keeping inconsistent watch on our werecats."

I didn't say anything to that, though I could have. My land and magic had claimed Paka. She was no threat. If she came to the United States again, I'd feed her to the land and she would be gone, every hair, every skin cell.

As if he heard my thoughts, Tandy turned his reddish eyes to me. "And how many secrets are you willing to share if we start making reports, Nell? Are you willing to share just how powerful Soulwood really is?"

That was a low blow and hinted at a desire to argue with me. I narrowed my eyes at him but didn't take the bait he dangled. If Tandy and I were ever gonna argue, it would be at a time and place of my choosing, not his. I'd learned that from the mamas.

I said to JoJo, "Anyone considered the possibility that Paka is doing this to Rick from afar?"

"That one's mine," Occam muttered. Louder he said, "I've got contacts in Africa trying to keep tabs on her. They got a hint of her whereabouts last month, in the middle of a tribal war. Nothing since, but my feeling is that she's too busy trying to stay alive to deal with Rick. There's nothing to suggest her involvement."

So the entire unit except for me had assignments looking into Rick's history. I scowled harder and thought more outside the box. "Or maybe the witch really is trying to call Rick so

Rick will turn her. Maybe she has some terminal disease and thinks she needs were-taint to live."

JoJo looked up from her tablet, eyes narrowed and appraising. She said, "You're spitballing pretty good, probie."

"I got more. We've all noticed that the grindys are not concerned with Rick's unusual shifting or moods. They ain't— they haven't been in HQ since the witch circle. Maybe the spell is affecting the grindys too."

"I think I hate you," T. Laine said, slapping the coffee table.

I grinned happily, figuring that meant no one had thought about some of that.

"This is a lot to incorporate and keep straight in our individual reports," JoJo said, "but we keep all info about Rick and Paka and the grindys off PsyLED's informational systems for now. This is an in-office inquiry, not an investigation. I'll update Soul when she gets free from the meetings, voice only. No way am I creating a report that's a career-killing move for my boss." She looked around the room, making sure we all agreed, her fingers tugging on her earrings, a personal tic that looked painful but had become endearing. She continued. "Inside this unit, we need to know everything. I expect everyone to keep apprised of all ongoing developments, and this is a good time to make use of the internal network." That was a system of files available only within the unit itself. I hadn't used it much, but it was handy in times like this, or when we needed to schedule meals together or send a group e-mail that wasn't case related. "We keep Clementine off," she added. Clementine was the unit's voice-to-text system and when she was on, she recorded and transcribed everything. "We partition off anything that relates to Rick being a possible security threat until Soul says otherwise."

We all agreed and JoJo turned gleeful eyes to me. "And since you brought up the grindylow, you get to research every single appearance of grindy-related deaths since they first appeared in the United States, and compare and contrast with the very rare times when the grindys didn't execute judgment. It might give us insight into why they're ignoring Rick's problems." Her tone said it served me right for spitballing so well.

"I can add that to my search," I said. Research was my

forte, and I had been updating records of recent grindylow kills since I had come back to work. Tracking para activity was a big part of PsyLED's mandate, and this simply took my investigation deeper.

Occam said softly, "Nell, you should talk to Rick. He might open up to you."

Because of the tie to Soulwood. "Secrets," I sighed, my tone saying that I thought they were dangerous and stupid. But. Tandy's accusation had been on point. I hadn't written a report about my land. Or my bloodlust. Or killing people and feeding them to Soulwood. And I never would, that being murder and all. "Fine. I'll talk to Rick." I knew I'd been maneuvered into the talking-trap when everyone relaxed. But at least that little chore could wait until morning. Or later. Much later.

I studied my guests. Where once there had been ties between a few of us, but no real cohesiveness, now there were bonds forming. We were becoming a team, the five of us. But not Rick. He might be the impetus that was driving the unity I could feel around the coffee table, but he was still outside of it. It might be up to me to bring Rick into this sense of accord. And my social skills were not the best.

I flapped my hands at the unit and said, "You'uns go play at the office. This is the last of my days off and I need my hands in the dirt."

They left, all of them departing through the front door.

I changed into overalls and work boots and rubbed some of my homemade bug-be-gone on my exposed skin and went out the back to work in the garden. Occam was there, his back to the house, looking over my split wood supply. It was under a blue tarp to keep it dry. John had been planning to build a shed for the wood, but he died before he could knock one together. The tarp worked fine for me. Occam stood there, framed by the blue of the tarp, one knee bent, that leg out to the side, his feet hidden in the grass. He was taller than me, rangy and lean, but broad across the shoulders. The faded jeans were tight across his backside and I flushed, shook my head, and dragged my eyes away from the vision as I squashed my imagination of what that backside would look like without the jeans. It was a bizarre thought and not one I had ever had about a man. I hooked my thumbs into the bib of my overalls and walked up next to him, knowing he would hear and smell me as I approached. Espccially as I was covered in bug gunk.

"What time of year do you start looking for firewood?" he asked.

"Been looking around already. There's a couple of guys I can call. And I toss deadfall into my truck when I find it. Split it when I get it home."

"You split your own wood?"

I didn't hear censure in his tone. In the church it wasn't considered womanly for the weaker sex to handle an ax. John had said he figured that was to keep a woman from knowing how to use a weapon and I'd agreed, but I'd kept that thought to myself. John might have saved me from become a concubine in God's Cloud of Glory polygamist cult—not a church, not really—but he still had strong feelings about a woman's place in the home and in society. "John taught me. The same week he found out he had cancer and it was . . . pretty much everywhere already. He was gone a few months later, but in between, he worked on my shooting, taught me how to clean all his weapons, hunt, field dress a deer. Showed me how to butcher and clean doves and pheasants and even small hogs. Taught me maintenance on the well pump and the windmill. He made sure I was self-sufficient so that if I married again it would be my choice and not because I was starving to death and needed a roof over my head."

"He loved you." Occam said the words softly.

"Yeah. He did."

"Did you love him?" he asked, even softer.

"Much as I was able. I respected him. I was and am eternally grateful to him and to Leah for marrying me. For saving me from the Colonel." The Colonel, Ernest Jackson, the leader of the church, had wanted me for a junior wife or concubine. Even though I'd led his enemies to him and I was pretty dang sure Yummy the vampire had killed him, the thought of him still had power. I shivered in the heat. "I'm grateful to John for leaving me the land and enough money to survive. And sometimes, a man's kindness, a woman's loneliness, and that kind

of gratitude are enough to make it seem like love." Occam
didn't respond, and we were both staring at the small pile of
wood as if it was the most important thing in the world.

Occam said, still softly, "The churchmen who came courting you. They wanted your land."

"Yep. In their eyes, I was useful, and as a woman, I would
surely be stupid enough to fall into their arms and give away
all John left me. But if I'd not had the land, none a them
woulda come calling. It wasn't me they wanted, it was my
land, except the Colonel, and he was a filthy pedophile and a
sexual predator both."

"I like hunting on your land. But I'll never try to take it."

My face softened from a stiffness I hadn't noticed. "That's
good to know, Occam. That buck. He made you work to catch
him."

Occam nodded, a smile lighting his eyes. I could see it
from the corner of my eye, along with the fused fingers of his
left hand. They looked a bit more fleshed out. Shifting on
Soulwood was good for Occam's healing, and he hadn't done
that much while I was a tree, and not enough since I'd been
mostly human again. "He gave me a chase. He was big and a
little mean. It was a good fight. He was tasty too."

"Come fall, when I have the wood-burning stove going
again, and you kill a big one, bring me what's left after you eat
the innards. I'll make some venison jerky." I tilted my head to
Occam and whispered, "I got my own recipe of herbs. You'll
like it."

"I am quite certain that I'll like anything you cook, Nell,
sugar. Anything at all."

But the cat in him was thinking only of meat. My smile
went wider. "Turnips? Collard greens? Pickled and fermented
cabbage?"

"Now you're jist being mean."

I laughed.

"Let's say I'll be willing to try anything you cook. Always."

"Deal. Now you got to git. I need to put my hands in the
earth."

"Okay, Nell, sugar." But he didn't move. His head swiveled to me. "Nell, sugar, would you consider it okay if I kissed
you?"

My heart did a somersault and my lips seemed to grow tender at the thought. "A properly improper kiss?"

"That's the only kind I can think of at the moment. My mouth on yours. My arms around you and yours around me."

"I'd like that," I managed. But I didn't turn to him. I was frozen, staring at the stupid blue tarp. He eased my hand from my bib. Turned me around and stepped close to me, holding me, as if he knew I'd fall if I tried to move my own feet. He placed my arm around his waist, on his sweat-damp shirt where it was tucked into his jeans. My other went around on his other side all by itself. His arms came around me. And his lips met mine.

I thought about the kiss—all of those kisses, because they had gone on a long time before Occam pulled away, and brushed my face with his hands, and walked to his car—as I worked in the garden. Late heirloom tomatoes were ripe; herbs were ready to be picked. Fall seeds needed to be planted, the garden needed to be weeded, and I needed to sweat. I had discovered that working the land was good for the land and for me. The farm had seemingly figured out that if I was a tree, there would be no one to work the soil and it liked me around. Now, as I worked, the leaves on my neck and hands broke off and the vines fell free, a calming sacrifice to the land, not bloody and violent as other kinds. Getting my hands into Soulwood was beneficial to all of us.

I ripped weeds out like a machine—grab upper roots and stem, grip, angle hand down, yank out the roots, toss away. Over and over again. But. As I tore out weeds I found a root that didn't belong in the garden. "Dagnabbit," I cursed. I fell onto the worked soil, backside first, work boot soles flat, knees high. Resting my forearms on my knees I dropped my head and caught up on my breathing. When I was satisfied that I was calm and breathing normally, I put my fingers into the aerated earth and dug until I touched the tree root again. "You can't be here," I told it. "This is *my garden*. I get nourishment from this garden. You take too much and don't give back enough. Now you'un get back to your'n spot and stay there." Nothing happened. I pushed with my magics. The rootlet jerked away, back in the general direction of the vampire tree grove that had taken up residence—with my permission—on the church side of our properties. The tree was both many trees and one tree, all sharing one root system, but with many trunks. It—they?—seemed to have the ability to grow roots faster and farther than kudzu did. The vampire tree—I settled on singular—was getting restless and it liked the energies of my land, maybe a little too much.

I dragged my hands from the soil and yelled, "You stay outta my garden, offa my house, and away from my critters. You hear me?" I had no idea how much English the vampire tree understood, but it understood enough, and it was learning more. The fact that the tree was probably sentient was a secret I hadn't shared with Unit Eighteen. "Pot, meet kettle," I muttered to myself.

The roots didn't reappear; new shoots didn't surface.

I'd accidently forced the original oak tree to evolve and mutate when I used the tree's life to heal myself after I'd been gut shot. Afterward, not knowing I had caused a mutation, I'd abandoned the tree to its own devices. It had developed a sort of sentience and a taste for blood, trapping and killing small animals and birds in the vines it grew, eating their bodies. Hence the name vampire tree. And it had learned how to grow thorns and send out rootlings over pretty far distances.

I went back to work extracting the last of the weeds and mulching the freshly worked soil, my sweat dripping onto the earth.

Soulwood perked up and nudged the ground beneath my feet. I had more company coming. The road up the mountain was getting a lot of wheel time today.

I hung my hoe, three spades, one weeding fork, and two shovels on nails on the back porch and toed off my work boots. I dropped off the basket of tomatoes, cukes, squash, peppers, and onions at the sink and put the three flavors of mint, rosemary, and sage in a bucket with water. I was stinky and sweaty and had just enough time to shower, dress, and grab my weapons before this next batch got here, whoever it was. I ducked under the cool shower and dressed fast, in jeans, T-shirt, and weapon harness, then twisted an elastic around my hair, as the curls had massed around my head and shoulders in a red halo from the heat and humidity. I was still unaccustomed to the change in my formerly straight brown hair.

I seated my PsyLED service weapon in its Kydex holster and picked up one of John's old shotguns as the large van turned into my drive. There was a logo on the side of the van, but the sun was glaring off the van windows and into the house, so I couldn't make it out. However, the vehicle wasn't a church truck, so I unwound a bit, watching as the van eased down the drive and parked next to my Chevy C10. I walked out onto the front porch, ready to do battle if necessary. It wouldn't be the first time nor the last time the churchmen of God's Cloud of Glory Church tried to take me back for punishment. Women didn't leave the church without repercussions.

A familiar frame climbed out of the truck and I broke open the shotgun as Brother Thaddeus Rankin of Rankin Replacements and Repairs emerged into the heat. "Hello, the house," he shouted into the glare. It was a country greeting, a visitor calling out to the house during the day, when a farmer and family would be out in the fields, working, informing them they had visitors.

"Welcome and hospitality," I called back. "It's cool on the porch. You want some tea?"

"That would be mighty welcome, Sister Nell," he said, climbing the steps into the shade of the porch. He stopped dead at the sight of the shotgun. "You been having more trouble from that church of yours, Sister Nell?"

"Not my church," I said, repeating the denial as I always did. "Cult. And no. Not recently. But I didn't recognize the van."

"Ah. New. The old truck died and Deus suggested that we go for advertising on the sides." He looked proud. "My boy's gonna be great when he takes over the business."

"Set a spell. I'll get that tea."

Thad took a seat and I reentered the too-hot house. I put the shotgun and my weapon harness on the kitchen table. Not something I'd have done if Mud was here, but it was expedient. I poured sun tea from the fridge, added ice cubes to the glasses, and dropped sprigs of fresh lemon mint into a small bowl. I put everything on a tray and added a small jar of simple syrup, spoons, and cloth napkins. Back on the porch, I put the tray on a small table and said, "The tea isn't sweet. But there's sugar syrup."

"Sister Nell, in this heat, the cold is what I'm after." He took a glass and held it to his dark-skinned face. "Ahhh. That's nice." He sipped the tea. "And delicious, just like it is, though I have family who would skin me if they heard me say unsweetened tea was good."

"Me too." Ignoring the swing, I took another chair, sat, and sipped my tea. I twisted two mint leaves and dropped them in. Tasted. Better, I decided. The cold was refreshing.

After the socially appropriate time to enjoy the tea, Thad opened our conversation with, "This heat is a killer."

I nodded. "It is a hot one." In the South, weather was an acceptable topic of discussion in every social situation, appropriate for business, politics, friendship, finances, therapy, courting, and religion. I didn't know which direction he was going, but opening with the weather meant that I was ready with an appropriate social rejoinder.

"I got your message about improvements for the house. I'll have you an estimate by the end of the week," he said. "I've got the measurements on file and can pull permits at any time."

I nodded. I planned to petition the courts to have my sister come live with me, and for that, my house needed things most people took for granted, like updated electricity, a bathroom upstairs, all sorts of things. I had thought Brother Thad might be here to bring me an estimate, but it seemed I was wrong.

He continued. "It's going to be even hotter by the end of the week. How you holding up with just the window unit and the fans?"

It hit me what he was asking and my eyes flooded with tears at his kindness. "Oh. Brother Thad. Are you here to check on a widder-woman?"

"Of course, Sister Nell. How you holding up?" It was what the men in his church did. They made sure the people in their congregation were safe. I had only been to his church a few times, but . . . it seemed I might now be listed among the people the men of his church took care of.

"I'm . . . I'm good." I dipped my head and stared into the tea as I blinked my tears away. Being taken care of wasn't something I had much experience with. In the confines of God's Glory, a man took care of a woman's needs as part of a sexual contract, favor for favor at best. This was something different. This was kindness. "The heat's manageable."

"And next week?" he asked. "Heat index is going to rise considerably."

"Next week I may close off the upstairs and my room, put the window unit in the front window"—I thumbed at the window to my side—"and sleep on the sofa. Or in the hammock on the back porch."

Sweat sliding down his cheeks and neck and into his collar, Brother Thad nodded. Sipped. "That's good. That's good. You need me, you call me."

"I will. Thank you, Brother Thad."

"You get ready to . . ." His words trailed away and he started again. "You ever decide to install more solar panels and upgrade the current system, I'll give you a fair bid."

"I know that, Brother Thad," I said, not sure why he had phrased it that way. Rankin's was the only company I had ever used.

"Mighty pretty here. Peaceful." He was staring out over the property, deep into my old-growth trees, which had not been so large when he first began to come visit me. I wondered what he was thinking about my land, but if he had been about to speak of it he changed his mind and stood. "You have a nice day, Sister Nell."

"And you, Brother Thad." I watched him walk to his van. Felt his vehicle roll down the mountain and off of Soulwood.

THREE

Esther and her husband dropped Mud off at the house at four p.m. and drove off in their truck before I could even get to the door. Esther hadn't talked to me since I admitted to my family that I was part tree and that I thought she might be too. She hadn't admitted a thing to anyone about whether she grew leaves or not, but refusing to talk to me suggested Esther was hiding something, running away from a difficult truth. It hurt. I figured it always would. But too much water and blood and time had flowed under the bridge for my family to fully trust me. And Esther, if she was a plant-person like me, had too much church conditioning to adjust to being nonhuman.

I opened the door to see Mud trudging up the steps, her dress soaked with sweat and streaked with dirt, her fingernails crusted with black rings, and her bunned-up hair half-fallen down one side. In both hands were damp paper bags with green leaves growing out of the tops. "Let me guess," I said. "You spent the day in the greenhouse."

"It was wonderful! They got fourteen kinds of basil growing. Fourteen! And they got thirty kinds of sage. Did you'un know there's over two hundred kinds of sage?" She reached the porch and started into the house.

"Boots," I said.

"Oh. Right. Here." She thrust the paper bags of cuttings at me and dropped to her backside to tug off her boots. Her fingers hit mine and her excitement and contentment and pleasure zinged across the brief connection. The emotions I felt from her touch were all braided together in a jubilant delight that called to me of joy and fecundity and life. "But," she grunted as she yanked at a boot, "I need to get the cuttings in water. Is it okay if I pot-plant 'em when they root?"

"Sure. What do you have?" I closed the door on the heat and Mud followed me to the kitchen.

"Basils and sages and stuff, plants to look pretty and to eat too. Raspberry Delight and Blue Steel Russian and Pineapple and Scarlet and Grape. Grape sage gets big, so it has to go in the garden."

"We can try to overwinter them on the front porch, but they may not survive." I placed the bags in the kitchen sink near the herbs and veggies I had brought in earlier, and opened the paper. The rich scent of sage leaves spilled out and filled the room. The spicy scent of Thai and lemon basils added to the mélange of fragrances. I separated the plants and lifted down narrow-necked vases and cups with broken handles and other good rooting dishes. I hadn't cleaned my own veggies beyond hosing them off outside, or dealt with the cuttings I had brought in, so I piled everything together, turned on the water, and went to work.

"We could cover 'em with plastic on cold days and nights," Mud said, "or . . ." She stopped. Her color went high, her face bright red, and not with sunburn.

My hands stilled all by themselves and my body hung loose as if I was about to face a fight. "Or what?"

"Or we could build a greenhouse," she whispered. It was the tone of a faithful supplicant in a cathedral, one full of reverence, hope, and not a little awe.

I went back to separating the plants and snipping off the bases of the stems, removing leaves to create a good spot for roots to start, and putting all the leftover green matter in the compost bucket. Carefully, to keep from getting Mud's hopes up, I said, "I've considered a greenhouse. But this is a hard time to build one for lots of reasons. You're starting school, we have a court date to be set, we have to consider child care, I have cases at work, we're learning how to live together. A proper greenhouse is expensive."

"Them's all problems we can deal with," she said earnestly. "If we had a greenhouse, I could practice my growing skills and we could have plants ready for the ground in spring. We could have fresh lettuces all winter. And tomatoes starting early. Please, please, please!" Hope and groveling laced all through her words and tone.

I never wanted my sister to grovel or beg me for anything. Women were used to begging in the church. Asking was okay. Begging was for victims. "I'm thinking about it. But it's costly, Mud."

"Not if Sam and Daddy build it."

We both went still and silent. When I could move again, I put three basils into vases. Five sages, then three more basils. I separated my mints and put them into a separate shallow bowl. Softly, I said, "Daddy and Sam still want us in the church."

"Nope. You grow leaves," Mud said with satisfaction, "and I might."

I studied my sister as my fingers continued to separate plants, working by muscle memory. Mud was dirty and tired and full of both angst and animation, what churchwomen might refer to as "being fraught."

"You think they want to help us but not bring us back into the church because I grow leaves."

"I think they want to keep an eye on us because they have future generations to look at and their young'uns might grow leaves too. I'm thinking they want to have a safe place for their plant-people to live if necessary. I'm thinking we'uns—sorry—*we* need to make hay while the sun shines. I'm thinking we need to get a greenhouse outta their worry."

"That's very Machiavellian of you, sister mine."

"That sounds like a dirty word, but if'n I get a greenhouse outta that, then I'm okay with it."

I chuckled and placed the last cutting into a canning jar. I washed my veggies and set them aside. Washed my hands. I looked at the water pouring from the sink and sighed. If we got a greenhouse, I would need a separate cistern since my well was wind powered and a slow draw. A separate system was costly. I shut off the water. "I'm okay with family—but only family—providing labor for a greenhouse. But I have to be able to pay for the supplies, materials, equipment, and any nonfamily labor."

"Deal," Mud said instantly, digging in a dirty pocket. "Sam

came up with a . . . not a bid, but a materials and costs list." A grin that might have riven the Red Sea split her face.

I took the folded piece of paper. There were three columns listing prices and materials, based on the size and type of greenhouse. The totals made my heart pound. "I'll think about it," I managed. What I was thinking? Even the smallest greenhouse was *sooo much money*!

Nell said, "I gotta shower. Then I gotta tell you'un about the vampire tree. It's been retreating for months and last night it let the bulldozer go. And it ain't ate—hasn't eaten?—an animal in weeks!"

Mud was determined to get a greenhouse. Family discussions were hard, despite the fact that there were only two of us. Mud had the ability of most churchwomen to finagle, manipulate, and guilt me into too much. I'd been raised the same way myself, but years living with John and Leah, my husband's senior wife, and years more on my own, had dulled my abilities to wheedle to get my way. It wasn't an ability that I particularly wanted to encourage in either of us. It was a cult woman's way—a victim's way—of negotiating in a household where multiple wives had no control over the purse strings.

I'd been working to get Mud to understand the difference between negotiation and wheedling and was making progress. For that reason—or that's what I told myself—I let Mud talk to me about the possibility of a greenhouse. "Not one a them little ones neither, but a *proper greenhouse*," she insisted, tapping the kitchen table with her fingertip on each of the last four syllables.

"Oh?" I asked, knowing exactly what she meant. Mud wanted a church-style greenhouse—a twenty-by-forty-foot structure, dug down into the soil, with French drains, cement-block foundation, galvanized steel supports, raised beds, a working water supply, a planting station, shades to block extreme heat and sun, easy-to-open vents, and eight-millimeter twin-wall polycarbonate cover material. A *proper* greenhouse had been my dream for years, and so I let her talk, showing me illustrations on her new computer tablet, having fun with a device that had scared her silly the first time she held it, only a week or so past.

"There's lots of reasons to build a proper one. Logical reasons," she concluded.

"I'm listening."

"We can save money by growing our own food." Finger tapping with each point, she continued. "We can trade veggies for half a pig in the fall like Mama does." Tap. "We can sell veggies at Old Lady Stevens' and Sister Erasmus' market"—tap—"and at the town farmers' market on Wednesdays." Tap. "And we can show the lawyer and the judge how we can eat cheap and fresh. That'll make 'em feel good about you getting custody of me."

"Now you're pulling out the big guns," I said, secretly amused, and pleased that there had been no whining. Yet. "We'd have to go into debt," I said.

That shut Mud up. Debt was against everything the church taught.

"I'd have to get a loan," I said, "and the supplies you're suggesting would run me a good ten thousand dollars, Mud. For ten thousand, we can buy from the church and still eat organic, still put up veggies and fruit. Ten thousand is a lot of money, and we'd still need to buy seeds and plants and roots. *And* we still need to address upgrades for the house like air-conditioning and a real hot water heater and a redesigned bathroom and laundry room and maybe even central heat. And add to that the cost of child care until you reach the age of sixteen."

"I don't need no child care."

"You can't be here alone at night if I'm out at work. It's expensive. We need all that to make this place a proper home for you, according to what the court is likely to require. That's a much bigger part of the custody problem than not having a greenhouse."

"I reckon that's a lot."

"It is. And it's what it'll take to bring us into the twenty-first century." I studied my sister and said, "I have the list of upgrades to the house suggested by the lawyer. Brother Thad will have me an estimate soon."

Mud took a breath as if diving into deep water. "You make

more'n fifty thousand dollars a year," she said, looking at her hands tightening into fists on the kitchen table. "And your living costs last year were around fifteen thousand. You being a tree for six months meant your income was less—due to you bein' on disability and everything. But your cost of living while you were a tree was negalable so you came out ahead."

Oho. "Negligible," I corrected, wondering how Mud had figured out all this. JoJo had hacked into my accounts and paid my few bills while I was out on "disability," but Jo would never give out my private information. My family thought I had been undercover, not on disability. The story had been a total fabrication to appease the Nicholsons until a solution could be found for calling me back from being a tree. Only Mud had known, and she must have gone through my bills, my bank statements, my mail, all my financial papers. "Somebody's been sneaking around, searching through my financial records."

Mud blushed at the accusation, though she looked more defiant than ashamed.

"And talking to an adult who surely gave you the logic and reason for this argument."

"I ain't told nobody. I sneaked through your'n private papers while you was *supposedly* undercover."

My sister had just called me a lying sneak. Interesting. I leaned over the counter, bracing my elbows on the top.

"Then I got Sam to take me to the library and your friend there helped me research what happens to the money when a government employee goes on disability. When I knew most everything I could find, I added up all the money on the calculator on your computer, so I know everything. I *should* be ashamed." Her face went mulish and she plowed on. "But I ain't. Not really. I want a greenhouse."

"And now we have the change in tone that says you're trying to get your way as opposed to us working together, making good decisions for our family."

Mud looked up at me with a fierce delight in her eyes. I had a sudden fear that I was about to be bested at this discussion.

"If I'm supposed to make good decisions, then I needed all the information to make them. Knowing family income is part of that decision-making." Mud's glee spread. "That there?

That's what's called being hoisted on your own petard." When I didn't reply she went on. "*Petard* sounds nasty, but it ain't. What you'un did? Saying you'un was wantin' me to be a modern woman all the while keeping me in the dark? That there is what a churchman would do."

The insult landed on me like a roundhouse blow. "Not exactly," I said, putting my feet flat on the floor and drawing through the wood to the land for calm and steadiness. "What I'm wanting is for you to grow up into an honorable woman, not a sneak. Churchwomen sneak around because that is the only way they can ever find out things. You and me? We aren't churchwomen anymore and I don't expect you to act like one."

"That ain't fair."

"It's totally fair."

Mud's lips firmed and she scowled. "But how'm I supposed to find out stuff if I don't sneak?"

"You could have asked," I said calmly. "I happen to think you're old enough to know financial things, so I'd have told you the truth. But you didn't give me a chance. If you're going to live here, we both have to be honest and respect my privacy and my rules."

Mud's entire face puckered up in irritation and confusion and maybe a little culture shock, deliberating. She raised a hand and smoothed her hair as if noticing that it was bunned up. Absently, she removed the pins and finger-combed it down. "I'm sorry. I want to be an honorable woman. A city woman, but an honorable city woman. What do I do now to fix things?"

I sat down at the kitchen table, thinking over the chain of logic and arguments that led us to this point. "Apology accepted. As to your request, your argument was succinctly reasoned and effectively debated. Sam help you with that?"

"Only the sal'nt parts. But the delivery was all mine. So . . . Did my sneaking around keep us from getting a greenhouse?"

"*Salient*. But you used it properly. There's a lot of ifs and buts. *If* the custody hearing goes our way, and *if* we can afford the cost of the house upgrades, and *if* Sam and Daddy want to provide greenhouse labor, and *if* I can afford the greenhouse materials too, then yes."

Mud threw back her head and shouted, "Whoop!" and proceeded to dance around with a total lack of decorum. I was elated to see my sister being so happy.

"We'll still have to get a loan," I said, over her whoops.

Mud stopped. Scowled at me.

"We'll need a full plan, which also has to include legal and court fees for the custody papers. Bids for bathroom, laundry, AC and heat, and more solar panels. If we're going to do this, we're going to do it right. Pavers, raised soil beds on both sides, and a path next to the walls. A separate cistern so I can make an aerated compost tea to feed the plants, add fertilizer, and deliver it without mess."

"You been thinking about this too," Mud accused.

"Forever. What's a plant-girl without a greenhouse?"

Mud spluttered in laughter.

"I didn't have the money until I started working for PsyLED. I barely have ten thousand dollars in the savings account, and even if I did, I don't want to drain every single dime, because we'll need a good ten thousand for me to get custody if Daddy contests it." Mud started to argue that Daddy had said he wouldn't contest it and I held up a hand to stop her. "Just in case. I'm not touching that money. And getting a loan takes time."

"Or Daddy could—" Mud stopped.

"Or Daddy could loan us the money? Mud, was Daddy part of the discussion for this greenhouse?"

"Yes." Her scowl went deeper. She crossed her arms over her chest and stared at the table, avoiding my eyes. "I reckon this is more a my sneaking. I'm sorry. Again."

"Did you tell Daddy about my finances?"

Mud's eyes jerked to me, hazel gray and shocked. "I'd never tell that. That's family business. Our family, you and me."

Something warm spread through me at the words. "Okay. Good. In that case, as soon as I have estimates and know the court costs, I'll talk to the bank. And we can have our first serious family talk about finances."

"Second. 'Cause this'un was pretty serious."

That decided, we started putting a meal together while chatting about the lawyer we had seen the previous week, in the first steps to custody. Discussed the upgrades to the house.

Chatted about the public school Mud would be attending starting in August. She had been tested to see where she fit in
scholastically. Mud was twelve years old, but a fierce desire to
read everything and anything had placed her at tenth grade
level in English and biology, and eighth grade in math. She
was at sixth grade in computer, chemistry, and history.

She would start school in eighth grade with remedial classes
and be adjusted as needed, attending Cedar Bluff Middle
School. The school's emblem was a large green tree, and the
motto was Go, Giants. The emblem was like the hand of God,
or maybe Fate, pointing us in the right direction. We also
talked about getting a scholastic tutor for the subjects she was
behind on, and a computer tutor for immersion in the how-to
of the future. And a new wardrobe.

We were in the middle of a late lunch when I felt an unfamiliar
vehicle coming up the road. Mud looked up. "What?"

"Someone's coming." And no one from PsyLED had texted
me to say they were on the way up.

Mud rushed to the windows and looked out. Checked the
weapons that I kept near the front windows, under a chair. I
placed John's old single-shot, bolt-action shotgun across the
chair arms and took up the double-barrel break-action shotgun. Both barrels held three-inch shells. I might dislocate my
shoulder, but if I hit them, the trespassers' blood would feed
my land.

Mud appeared at my side and lifted John's lever-action car-
bine .30-30 Winchester. "Keep your hand off the trigger," I
said.

"We shoulda given me more lessons," Mud said.

"We'll remedy that soon. I promise."

A truck appeared between the trees on the one-lane road
that led to my house, passed out of sight as it turned into the
drive, and reappeared as it slowed to a stop. I hadn't noticed
the heat in the house until now, and I started sweating, feeling
it trickle down my back. The overhead fans turned, pushing
cold air around from the window-unit air conditioner. Not
enough coolness in the heat of a late July day.

A man got out of the truck, early twenties, lanky, medium height. Carrying a wilted bunch of flowers. I recognized the face but couldn't place the name.

"Dagnabbit," Mud said, sounding frustrated.

"Who is it?"

"That's Larry, second son of Brother Aden. Him and his first wife, Colleen, done signified an intent to court me."

"Daddy told him no," I said. I'd heard about the interest of the Aden family back when one of the Adens had wanted to court me. "The church voted to disallow marriage of underage girls. They agreed to follow Tennessee law on marriage age."

"Don't look like Larry is of a mind to listen to Daddy or the law neither," Mud said.

Larry started up the steps. He was an average-looking man with an obstinate jaw and broad shoulders. He looked capable if not kind, determined if not affable.

"Has he been coming around?" I asked. "When you're at Mama's or Esther's or Sam's?"

"He was at Sam's when we was talking about the greenhouse—" She stopped, realizing that talking about anything in the presence of churchmen was dangerous.

I looked Larry over. If he was armed, it was in an ankle or spine holster, hidden under his church-made jeans or his church-made, starched, ironed, cotton plaid shirt. "We'll see what he has to say. But he'll be talking to the business end of the shotguns." I opened the door. Stepped out, shotgun at the ready. Mud moved out beside me. Larry stopped, his eyes going wide.

He swallowed, the sound rubbery, and he wilted like the flowers he carried. "I . . ." He swallowed again. "I come to call on Miss Mindy."

"Mindy's daddy told you no."

His chin went up. "I've been led to understand that you'un had taken custody of her, so I don't rightly think it matters what her daddy done said."

I hadn't been expecting that one. But he had a point. "No. Not now, not later, not ever."

"I'd like to hear it from Miss Mindy herself."

"Mindy's a minor."

"Not by church law."

"No," Mindy said. "I ain't interested in marrying into the Aden clan. I ain't interested in marrying at all."

"Every woman wants to marry, little miss. Your witch sister been spreading her lies to you? Sounds like you'un's needing some protecting from her and her devil talk and her devil ways. I aim to make you'un respectable and keep you'un safe from the world and its dangers." He held out his bouquet and took the final step to the porch. "I brung you'un flowers."

"I said no," Mud said, her voice as cold and hard as mine.

"Okay. Let me make it plain." I slid into church-speak. "Get offa my land or we'uns'll fill you so full a holes the undertaker will have to hold your corpse together with duct tape and baling wire." *No. I'd feed him to my land.* There would be nothing left but his gun, if he was carrying. Even his clothes and shoes would be gone, absorbed by Soulwood.

Beneath me, the land came awake. And hungry.

Bloodlust slammed through me. And for maybe the first time in my life, I laughed at a man who was threatening me and mine. "You can get off my land, church boy. You can stay away from my sister. Or you can die. Not many choices between life and death." I stepped toward him, the barrel aimed center mass. "I said, get offa my land."

Something in my face made Larry Aden pale and his eyes dilate. He backed slow down the steps and headed to his truck. Somewhere along the way he dropped the flowers.

I felt his fury as he strode across the land; felt the land's response as Larry took his last step and got in the cab, started the engine, and backed away fast, throwing gravel. All along his trail between steps and truck, vines erupted from the ground. Vines with dark, thick green leaves and scarlet petioles, vines with thorns and self-will. Parts of the vampire tree.

As Larry whipped his truck around and roared down the road, I fired into the ground, directly at the vines. Furious and angry and scared all at once. I yelled, "I told you to get off my yard. Don't make me fight you, you danged tree!"

"Nellie?" Mud asked, her tone doubtful.

I pointed at the gravel parking space. "Two birds, one stone, as it were." Then I saw my fingers and the fresh leaves uncoiling from the tips. "Dagnabbit!"

Mud giggled, a tiny, tentative *snurf* of sound, took my elbow, and led me back inside. "I'll make us some herbal tea. Somethin' with chamomile and lavender."

"I do not need to be calmed down," I said, holding my cell. "And it's too hot for tea."

"Uh-huh." She took my gun and pushed me onto the couch. Secured the weapons just like I'd taught her.

"Leave my gun on the chair near the door," I instructed into the silence.

"Okay. Who you calling?" she asked.

"Sam. Then Daddy. Then my boss."

"I understand family. Why your'n boss?"

"Because I just fired a gun in a situation that might be construed as an attack on an unarmed man. Because who's gonna believe I fired at a tree that likes to kill things?"

"I reckon that's a good point."

I dialed Sam. "Hey, Nellie," he said.

"Did you know Larry Aden was coming over here to court Mud?"

"What? No! Absolutely unacceptable. We told him no, in no uncertain terms."

"Seems he's decided that since Mud will be living with me, without a man present, that means our opinions and plans have no value. And that means he gets to ignore you. So you pass the word, brother mine. The next churchman or church boy who comes onto my land without my advance permission gets shot. Period. Are we clear?"

"We're clear. I'm sorry, Nellie. This shouldn'ta happened to you."

"You're right. It shouldn't have happened to any of the women or girls of the church, ever." I hung up. I had broken out in a sweat during the conversation, and not just because the house was eighty-four degrees inside, but because I was so mad. And getting madder. I dialed Daddy. Gave my free hand to Mud to clip my leaves while I talked.

"How's my girl?" Daddy answered, his voice not as hearty as it once had been. We were three weeks past his surgery to repair a persistent bleeder and clean out a lot of scar tissue from when Daddy had been gut shot. The original surgery, while keeping him alive, hadn't been quite enough, and the doctor had made it clear after this second one that he might need a third one. Daddy had been shot protecting his family. Remembering that, the worst of my anger simmered away. More of the anger bubbling through me cooled when I remembered that Daddy knew Occam was a wereleopard and hadn't objected to us working together and maybe-sorta courting. He could have made my life very difficult, but he hadn't.

"I'm good. Mindy is good. But we have a problem." I described Larry's visit and he listened with patience. Made a few angry "Mmmms," and few more sounds that sounded like growls.

I took a steadying grip on the kitchen table, wood from Soulwood trees, wood that knew me. "I told Sam I'd shoot any churchman or boy who comes calling. I mean it. You spread the word."

"Nellie—"

"Don't 'Nellie' me." My voice dropped. "You pass along the word. I got beefs with the church about a mile long. I'll shoot anyone who comes here without a specific invite. Shoot 'em dead. Got it?"

"I understand," Daddy said softly.

"You make sure the churchmen know my rules. They come to my house? They die." I punched end.

Mud put a big glass of iced herbal on the table. I had seen the new jar next to my mint tea. Plopping down on a chair at the kitchen table, I picked up the glass and rolled it across my forehead. Mud took the glass and placed it in my other hand so she could clip the leaves on the free one.

I sighed, a long unhappy sigh full of pathos. Or maybe self-pity, if I was honest.

Mud released my neatly trimmed fingers and I sipped the tea. The florals were amazing together, which was handy since I really wanted to change the subject. "Is this your blend? It's wonderful."

Mud flushed with pleasure. "Organic. I'm thinking about going into business making organic soothing, calming teas. Most teas need sugar. I'm gonna make sure mine don't and can be enjoyed hot or cold."

"Business?"

"When I turn eighteen. I'll already have my blends and recipes and flowers growing."

It hit me what she had done and I chuckled. "And you plan to move them to the new greenhouse."

"Yep. So I got a question. I overheard Sam talking today. What happened to Brother Ephraim?"

If I'd had leaves at the moment I think they might have quivered at the question. "Um . . ."

"'Um' ain't no answer. You know something, don'tcha."

I sighed and decided on honesty, if not total and complete. Mud deserved as much of the truth as I could give. I put the glass on the table and took a cat up in my arms for the comfort. It was Cello, the quietest of the mousers and the least loving, except to the werecats who came calling from time to time. Right now, Cello let me hold her and I put my head to hers. She started purring, which was soothing. "It isn't my story to tell, not all of it. But what I *can* tell you is that Ephraim came here to try and force me back to the church. He attacked me. Then he attacked an officer of the law. This was before you and I got to know each other. And it's the darker part of our magic."

"You kill him?" she asked, casually, as if murder was fine and dandy.

"Not exactly." This was the part of the story that wasn't mine to tell. I went on with what I could tell. "He was injured and dying. So I fed him to the earth. To Soulwood."

"He tasted bad, didn't he?"

I spurted a laugh that was as much relief as amusement. "I reckon he did. The land didn't take him at first. He caused a few problems before I found a way to . . . absorb him. I reckon that's a good enough word." I pushed away the glass, and condensation made trails across the wood. "I killed him," I said, softer. "That's murder. Manslaughter at the very least."

"I heard Sam say one time that some men need killing. I reckon the man who punished Mama fits that description."

In church parlance *punished* meant raped. I hadn't known that Mud knew that story. I tilted my head, less in agreement than to indicate that I'd heard the same argument.

"Your'n friends at PsyLED know about it?"

"Rick LaFleur guesses." Paka knew everything. If she came back that might be a hold she would have over me. But Soulwood had a hold over her, so maybe they would cancel out each other out. Maybe.

"I think it's best that we keep it between us, then, don't you?" she asked.

I nodded. "You okay knowing all this grown-up stuff?"

"I'll keep our secrets. And I'm good, long as you ain't totally shutting out the possibility of a greenhouse. But, since we'un's chatting, I need some clothes for school. I need two pairs of khaki pants to start the year on account of it being so hot. And some sneakers. I got a list. I been looking on my tablet and I like the prices at Kohl's and Walmart."

I smiled and drank some of her tea. "We can shop. You really want to go into business making teas?"

"Yep. Soulwood teas. Only the very best local ingredients, hand grown, hand harvested, organic. That's what it has to say on the tins. But you gotta make up to Daddy so he'll build us that greenhouse. You hung up on him. He's gonna be mad."

"Well. Okay, then. He'll be mad." I picked up the phone and dialed Rick LaFleur, my up-line boss at PsyLED Unit Eighteen. He didn't answer, so I left a message telling about Larry and the shotgun blasts.

Mud and I spent the hottest part of midafternoon outside, deciding where to put the possible greenhouse, how to situate it so it got the best sun in fall and winter. But it was too hot to stay out for long. I had to work come evening, and so I called it a day in late afternoon, took another cool shower, and grabbed an hour's nap.

It was evening. I hadn't slept enough to make it through my usual twelve-hour shift without nodding off. I had dropped Mud off at Daddy's and went in to apologize for my anger and rudeness. Not that I took the threat to kill churchmen off the table. Any who came on my property were still at risk of death. I just phrased it with a smile, as if I was discussing tea and scones instead of self-defense by shotgun. Daddy accepted the apology and brought up the greenhouse. It was a nice visit, all in all, mainly because I wasn't being judgmental or causing problems. This time. There was a time and place for that later, in what would be an ongoing, lifelong battle, I was sure. I left Mud in deep conversation with Mama Grace about how to make her special cheese biscuits.

As I walked to the door, Daddy looked up at me and then at my youngest true sib, in a sort of a promise. "You got child care worked out?" he asked.

I was nowhere near a solution, but I nodded. "Getting there."

"She'll be safe here tonight. I'll keep an eye on her. And on Larry Aden." Daddy might not make the best decisions all the time, and getting him to walk into the twenty-first century wasn't easy, but Mud was safer with the Nicholson clan than with me tonight. Until she grew leaves and the churchmen burned her at the stake.

FOUR

I dropped my four-day gobag off in the locker room and took a few seconds to trim back stress-growth leaves at my hairline. Talking to Daddy hadn't been horrible, but it hadn't been easy, either. I'd been a tree for about six months after the last big case and that experience had left me leafy and viny and rooty. I didn't so much indulge in personal hygiene as landscape myself. Half of the team was equally injured and had been in rehab of one kind or another. Unit Eighteen had been working a skeleton crew for months—paperwork, protocol, and research. Now that Occam was back from healing, and I wasn't so rooty, we were a full crew. It felt good to be back to work.

When I was presentable, I went to my cubicle, stuck a finger into the soil and herbs at the window, and locked my one-day gobag and weapon in the drawer. The weapon wasn't needed in HQ. The herbs were too dry, which severely limited the salad flavors I had planned on for supper. I fished an empty bottle from the recycles bin, filled it with tap water, and emptied it slowly over the herbs. "There you go, my pretties. Sorry about the chlorine. I promise not to clip you for a day or two to let you recover, and I'll bring better water tomorrow." Kissing the air over them, I picked up my laptop and two tablets and carried them to the conference room, where Tandy was bent over the unit's main system, the one where orders and comms originated. I took my place at the conference table and logged in to the PsyLED system. "Hey," I said.

"Evening, Nell. I brought salad fixings for supper," our resident empath said. He wasn't prescient, but because of his empathy gift, he sometimes seemed to be expecting things ahead of time, like what I wanted for supper. He'd explained that it was a part of knowing us so deeply, not a form of psychic mind control or prophecy.

"I can do salad," I said, proud that I sounded like a modern city girl. I'd never be hip or cool or chic, but at least I fit in now, sharing a more common accent and language syntax. "I'm sending you my report on the black-magic circle from last night."

Tandy nodded, the sharp overhead lights picking out the Lichtenberg lines that traced across his skin like scarlet lightning.

I read over the summation reports for the last few days and the latest on Rick's black-cat-in-a-circle case. There wasn't much. The focals—the bloody gauze, the knife, the golf ball and tee—from the circle had been sent to the lab, signed for, and placed into a queue for eventual testing. No date for actual analysis had been sent to us. T. Laine still wasn't sure what the circles were for, but causality needed to be proved or disproved in law enforcement, and she was working on the "Rick being called by a black-magic spell" aspect to see if it was happenstance or deliberate.

Someone had asked Rick if he played golf and he'd said, "Not for years." The tee and ball looked brand-new. No tie there.

Lainie had gone through the runes in the black-magic circle, trying to provide us with an interpretation. Tandy had chatted with the owners and managers of the businesses on Riverside Drive, the street near the circle. Two employers had recently fired several people, and one young woman had been fired for smoking marijuana and crack on the job. The woman was in her twenties, short and slight, and the manager had provided Tandy with her ID and address.

Tandy and T. Laine had run the ID. It was real, but the address on it turned out to be an empty lot behind the wastewater treatment plant off of Neyland Drive. They had tracked down her parents, who lived in Nashville, but they hadn't seen their daughter since they kicked her out for stealing and pawning her grandmother's silver. There had been no indication of witch genes in the lineage. No one had been able to find the woman and there was no way to determine if she had cast the circle.

The local witch coven had been asked to take a look at photos of the circle and they had no idea who had cast it. They also had no idea what it did except something bad. They had refused to go to the circle in person and had broken off contact. Which they had done before when bad magical things were taking place in Knoxville.

We were no closer to knowing if the witch circle had been a deliberate call to Rick or if he accidently answered it because of proximity and the black cat used as sacrifice. We had nothing except bloody gauze we couldn't track to the blood source, a bunch of weird focals, and . . . Nothing. Except that someone was casting nasty curses with unknown magic. This alone had everyone worried, especially the werecats.

Tandy was in charge for the night and also handling comms, should we get a case. As long as no one took a day off or went on vacation we had enough people to staff the office twenty-four/seven. On nights when that wasn't possible, calls were autorouted to Rick or JoJo and they called us in. Computers were grand things when they worked. Satisfied that I was caught up on everything, I went to work on my assignment, tracking grindylows and their kills and why grindys were indifferent about Rick. PsyLED's mandate was to investigate paranormal crimes, keep paranormal records, track paranormal trends, and I had traced and amassed a lot of records in my time at Unit Eighteen.

On my first break, well after midnight, the waning moon was visible and the sky was black against the city lights as seen though the windows. I trimmed back dead leaves—on the herbs in the windowsill boxes, not on me—and enjoyed the novelty of air-conditioning. Novelty because I was still mentally stymied about going on the grid or adding to my solar array and solar batteries just for comfort. It was hard to turn away from a lifelong independence. I weighed it all as I worked on the plants.

"Nell," Tandy called over the in-house speaker system. "Come to the conference room, please." I put down my small watering can and went back to join him. "It's probably nothing," he said as I stepped in the doorway, "but Knoxville PD called in something and are asking for an agent to liaise."

"You want me to go on a call? Alone?"

He didn't look up at the obvious excitement, apprehension, and delight mixed together in my voice. "Sending coordinates and address to your cell. Meet Officer Holt at the scene. Convenience store robbery a little after midnight, on the heels of an earlier title loan shop robbery as the employees were closing. The businesses are within a mile of each other and the perpetrator in both cases was described as male, five-nine, black hair, pale skin, and 'acting strangely.' He stole cash and a gun and ammo from the pawn shop and food items and cash from the convenience store. Neither business' security footage shows the unsub's face, but both describe bloody clothing. The descriptions were similar enough for KPD to put them together. They want the place read for vampire."

Unsub was cop-speak for unknown subject. "Species profiling because of blood and pale skin? Maybe he's a butcher."

Tandy didn't look up, but the amusement was clear on his face in the glare of his tablets. "You get to decide what species. If human, you can give the investigation back over to the local PD."

So, no crime workup, just a reading. Scut work. I gave a long-suffering breath and gathered my gear—my weapon and Kevlar/antimagic vest, the psy-meter 2.0, and a comms set.

I didn't push my old red truck, didn't run lights and siren. The C10 wasn't designed for the strain of pursuit or emergency driving, and since the delivery of my official vehicle had been delayed while I was a tree, I had to protect my only mode of transportation.

I reached the address to find a Pilot Gas and Convenience store just off Cumberland Avenue. Before I stopped, I drove around and found the title loan shop, an odd business for what was a midscale retail area. There was no crime scene tape, no indication of a crime committed, which was odd. I motored back to the gas and convenience store. The Pilot was newish, open twenty-four hours a day, with bright lights and a lot of traffic. It wasn't the kind of place I'd expect a robbery during heavy business hours. After two a.m. maybe, but not before that. Again here, there was only a single strip of bright yellow crime scene tape around one entrance and one cash register, but no plethora of detectives.

I parked beside the KPD unit and pulled up the security

footage of the Pilot robbery itself, which Tandy had sent as I drove. I watched on my tablet as the skinny unsub in jeans and a dark hooded jacket walked through the entrance and pointed his pocket at the cashier closest to the door. The pocket could have concealed a hand holding a weapon, but looked like the tip of a finger. It was hard to say. The cashier removed a handful of bills from the drawer and handed them to the subject, who reached out and accepted the bills, his hand narrow, thin, and shaking, as white as any vamp's. He left the Pilot at a steady, slogging pace. Not running, not panicked, but not acting odd in any way I could see. No cameras caught his face, and he seemed to disappear into the shadows across University Commons Way toward the Walmart.

Something seemed odd and I watched the video again, realizing the male unsub could be a gangly female. The slender hand. The way he, or she, ran wasn't suggestive of gender.

I read the rest of the report. The kid—estimated to be about seventeen by the cashier—had asked for four hundred dollars. Not everything in the register. Just four hundred dollars. That was weird. I looked up felonies and discovered that in Tennessee, a robbery involving less than five hundred dollars, and committed without a weapon, (fingers didn't count) was a misdemeanor. That explained the lack of police presence here, just the one police car, Unit 102.

I accessed the surveillance cameras from the earlier title loan shop robbery. Same slim form, same white skin, same hand in pocket. A finger. He had stolen a gun and ammo as well as money. Here, the lanky thief stole less than a hundred dollars and the .32 Smith & Wesson. He—I chose male for convenience—had calculated the value of the gun and ammo, adding them to the cash. Stealing a gun carried heavier penalties. I was guessing he didn't know that. But, if both robberies had been connitted by the same person, he or she had been in possession of a gun on the second robbery, and hadn't used it. So why steal the gun?

I clipped my badge where it could be seen, adjusted my vest and weapon, and stacked my tablet on top of the psymeter. The robberies hadn't been violent, but the robber wasn't in custody. He'd taken off on foot, was smart enough to dodge security cameras, and was armed. Better safe than sorry. I checked my comms unit and went inside, spotting the cop right away, leaning over the counter, chatting with the Pilot employee. I said, "Officer Holt?"

The cop turned and looked me over, a frown on his face. He muttered, "You gotta be kidding me," just loud enough to make sure I heard. Holt didn't like female special agents, especially ones who looked too young to have come up through the ranks and paid their dues, as he had. And based on the hint of fear in his eyes, he especially didn't like paras, and I didn't look quite human right now.

His attitude got all over me like deer ticks on a dog. "Not kidding at all, Officer Holt." I looked him up and down just like he looked at me, my eyes alighting on his thinning hairline and his paunch, which he sucked in to make himself look in better shape. "You were hoping for a nice big former Green Beret with scars and wartime experience? You call PsyLED about a nonviolent, very questionable vamp robbery after midnight, and you get me. Special Agent Ingram. You got a problem with that, you can call your headquarters and see if they'll let you run and hide from the big bad para." I tapped my chest.

Holt flushed.

"Did you get all that, Special Agent Dyson?"

"Every word," Tandy said into my ear. "Making friends, there, Ingram."

"I got your report," I said to Holt. "How about you stand outside and ask people to wait out there for five minutes while I read the premises." I turned my back on him and set the psymeter on the counter near the Slim Jims and Ho Hos. I heard the door open and close and I caught sight of Holt walking it off outside. I hadn't done a very good job improving interagency relations. LaFleur would probably have a few things to say about that.

To the clerk I said, "Okay if I tape our interview?"

"Sure." The cashier nodded. He was in his midthirties, with patchy facial hair and an old odor of alcohol and weed about him. Idly I wondered where he'd hid his stash when he'd had to call the police. His name tag read HANK.

"Okay, Hank. Speak into the tablet. Tell me your full legal name, the date, and the current time. Then tell me what happened." I set the tablet to record and as he talked I calibrated and did QC on the psy-meter 2.0. His story was pretty much what I had seen in the security cameras. "Can you describe the alleged thief?"

"Kid. I'm saying male. I mean, chicks don't rob stores, ya dig?" I nodded, encouraging him to talk. "Probably between seventeen and twenty. White skin, black greasy hair to his shoulders, skin was dirty, medium height. Skinny." He added, "He was shaking like a junkie, but the thing that made me think vampire was the white skin and the blood on his clothes. And he talked funny, so I was thinking fangs."

I was betting that this kid loved horror movies and read vamp porn. "But you never saw fangs?"

"No, ma'am. Just the blood on his clothes and the white skin. But I thought bloodsucker and the cop agreed."

"Uh-huh. Right. Okay, with your permission, I'm going to read you, then take a reading everywhere the perpetrator stood." I calibrated the four levels to zero and then scanned Hank, who was excited to be part of a PsyLED investigation and who read fully human. But his countertop read moderately low on psysitope one, slightly lower on two and four, and a rise on three, giving a nod to every para in the book. The Pilot store had a lot of traffic and the residue had accumulated. I frowned. Such an accretion of psysitopes didn't make sense. I pulled up a map and compared the location to the Glass Clan Home and to the address of the leader of the local witch coven. The store was close enough to these social gathering places to be used for gas and late-night purchases, hence the readings. "What made you think the subject was male?"

"I only got a good look at the chin," he admitted, "but it had a few hairs on it like a kid trying to grow his first beard. If it wasn't a dude, then she was the ugliest chick I ever saw in my life."

"Hmmm." Mentally, I ran through the possibilities. Vamps were white skinned, and both robberies had been after dark, but vamps had mesmerism abilities and would blood-kiss-and-steal to get money, not rob. Juvenile Welsh devil dogs were skinny and apt to be unkempt, and it was possible that one had slipped by in the recent roundup of the horrid, foul shape-changers. Maybe a witch wearing a glamour to look like a male? Could be; a glamour would mess up my readings. Male witch? Not likely. Male witches succumbed to childhood cancers with a regularity that was scary. Because of the childhood mortality rate, male witches, sometimes called sorcerers, were once rarer than hen's teeth. With modern medicine, more males had begun to survive to adulthood, but the percentages were still low. If the pale unsub was a sorcerer, he might be sick. Even dying. There was a single report in the PsyLED databases that a sick sorcerer had thrown off strange psysitope readings. For now, I was betting on human junkie. I touched the counter and felt no maggots, but that meant nothing since the robber hadn't touched the counter.

Reading the rest of the store took a full three minutes, and I saved my readings on my tablet before thanking the cashier and leaving the store. I went up to Holt and said, "It's all yours." I didn't wait for his reply and got into my truck. I drove away, across the street toward the Walmart where the robber had seemed to be heading when he raced away on foot.

I drove around the Walmart, past big rigs parked in the shadows, a few RVs and travel trailers. Spotting the security guard, who was riding around in an orange vehicle with a flashing orange light on top, I followed and flashed my blue lights to get his attention. Unlike Holt, former KPD sergeant Wellborn was genial and chatty. We sat, driver-side door to driverside door, and gossiped over the window edges for a while about the robbery and the homeless and drug problem in Knoxville.

He pointed to the back of the Walmart and said, "We try to keep them from bothering the shoppers and joggers. When there's two of us working and when the numbers get too bad, we help the local boys flush them out of the greenery along the greenway back there."

I assumed that *local boys* meant KPD and not armed yahoos looking for excitement.

"But they don't need much more than a bush to sleep under in summer, and with Third Creek back there and nearby places to beg, they have everything they need to survive for six to nine months a year. Come winter, things'll change up a bit, but for now, it's homeless heaven."

I pulled up the video of the suspect. "You ever see this guy?"

Together we watched both sets of footage and Wellborn shook his head. "No. Dark jacket, jeans, sneakers, maybe an old pair of Jordans. Moves like a female. I have to say, robbery by the homeless isn't as common as most folk think. They make more and better money begging, without the fear of ending up in jail."

Making a note to check the statistics, I considered the darkness behind Walmart. The security lights didn't reach beyond the parking area, and though the moon was still up, it wasn't providing much illumination. I really didn't want to go back there, but . . . "I need to inspect it, to see if I can spot the perpetrator."

"If you want to take a look, drive around and come in the back way, on the far side of the creek. Shine your lights at the creek and the back of the store. You'll see some. See a campfire or two. Maybe a tent. If you want to wait till I'm off shift I'd go with you, but I'm the only one on tonight and can't go now."

"Thanks. I'm good. I'll call for backup if I see anything that means I need to get out of the truck." I shook his hand across the space between our vehicles and followed directions to the far side of the creek. I motored in behind a storage building or warehouse—there wasn't a sign on the back road to tell me what it was—braked, and measured with the psy-meter out the window. The readings read background normal, and I moved on down the road. On my GPS it was called Unnamed Road, which seemed an appropriate and sad place for the human homeless. I made three stops, working from inside the truck cab, and found only tents, tarps, trash dumps, an abandoned campfire, and glimpses of people escaping into the brush, until I got past the Walmart. The psy-meter 2.0 went off, spiking and holding at level one and level four, the readings matching the circle that had called Rick. My heart rate rocketed. There was something witchy on the bank of Third Creek.

I called Tandy. "Got something, but not what I expected."

"Describe."

"Checking psysitope levels on an open field in the direction the subject had been walking after the robbery. High readings on one and four, holding at redlining, no downward movement. I don't know what it is, but I'm requesting backup. Is T. Laine on call?"

"Roger that. Putting in a call for KPD and Kent. Do not—repeat, do *not*—leave your vehicle."

"Roger that," I said. "I'll write up reports while I wait in the Walmart parking lot with Wellborn, formerly of KPD and armed."

In my report, under "Comments," I speculated that the store thief was human, but couldn't rule out a witch using a glamour or carrying a charm that might affect the psymeter.

Lainie made it to the parking lot in under an hour and a small KPD night-shift team met us in the parking area behind the warehouse-type building on Unnamed Road. Lainie and I went over the psy-meter numbers I had collected, and made an informed guess at the location of whatever or whoever awaited us in the brush near the creek. It hadn't moved. I mentioned the robberies and the remote possibility that the two were related, based on my theory of a witch under glamour.

The KPD team listened in. There were six of us, the cops looking psyched at going into the wild and kind of freaked too, probably at the combination of an armed, magic-using suspect in the area, though I explained that the readings were wrong for a witch lying in the grass or for a vamp. There were no apparent heroes and no obvious para haters in the cop group, so that was good. Better was the fact that we could all share a single communications channel. After the crazy things that had happened with strange magic in the last year, KPD, KFD, and the Knox County Sheriff's Department had dedicated a single frequency to ops involving paranormal investigations or creatures. Most cops call it the para freq, and laughed.

Together we moved into the brush, every officer except T. Laine with service weapon drawn, tactical flashlight glaring, and wearing a vest. Over a shoulder, I carried a gobag with my pink blanket, tablet, and the psy-meter 2.0. T. Laine was armed with bright yellow number two pencils that R&D at PsyLED central in Virginia had imbued with a *null force*

working to stop magic and magical attack. The null sticks
were impossible for a human to activate, and painful for a
witch to handle, making it nearly impossible for T. Laine, our
moon witch, to carry a gun too, so she wore night-vision gear,
both low-light and infrared oculars, and took a track beside
me and a little ahead so my flash didn't interfere with her
headgear.

The null sticks were General brand pencils, with the word
semi-hex on the side, surely a joke on the part of the witch who
had spelled them. T. Laine carried one by the eraser and was
ready to toss it at will.

As we moved through the tall grasses and brush, the only
sounds were the trickle of water in the creek ahead and the
swish of the summer grasses on our clothes. We'd have to do
a thorough tick search when we got back to HQ. Maybe Lainie
had a tick-search spell. That would be handy. Stupid thoughts
to indulge in when there was something magical on the creek
shore ahead.

"Halt," T. Laine said softly into her mic. She turned to her
right in small angled degrees. "Two o'clock from my location,
twenty paces ahead. No live bodies in infrared, no DBs on
low-light, but . . . something. The null sticks just flashed hot."

"They shouldn't flash hot unless there's an active working,"
I said. "Let me read the earth." Which meant, let me put my
fingers to the ground.

T. Laine tapped her mic and explained to the others, as she
swished through the grass around me, "Ingram will be vulner-
able, unable to seek cover in case of attack."

"Copy," several voices said.

Surprisingly, Lainie was setting a circle around the two of
us, which I didn't expect or understand. She tapped off her mic
and added softly to me, "There's mundane cover and there's
magical cover. I can handle the latter if not the former, hence
the circle around both of us."

I holstered my weapon and withdrew the pink blanket and
the psy-meter from my gobag. I partially opened the blanket
and sat on it, making a nest in the tall grass for my backside
and legs, which I folded under me. I opened the psy-meter,
which had gone to sleep, and pointed it at the direction Lainie
indicated. Levels one and four redlined instantly. It wasn't a

person. It was a thing, and whatever it was, it was big. And its magic was still active.

Gingerly, I placed a left fingertip on the ground and pressed through the tightly interwoven roots to the soil. I jerked away so fast that I nearly rolled off the blanket. "It's very active," I whispered into the mic. "And there's something dead there." I pointed. "Something cold, been dead a few hours."

"Human?"

"No. Too small. Maybe a pound or two?" I suggested.

"Cat?" T. Laine asked, thinking about Rick's black-magic circle.

"No. Smaller. Maybe half that size. Maybe a kitten?"

"Okay. Pack up," she said to me. I shoved my gear in my bag, strapped it around me, and took my weapon in a one-hand grip, my tactical flash in my free hand, held out to my side. If someone had us in their sights, I wanted any targeting mark to be out to my side, not midline on me. As I stood, Lainie dropped her circle and said, into the mic, "Let's move in."

The cops said, "Copy that," in unison, and we all moved forward, spreading out.

Just ahead, the grass fell away, as if cut too close so that it had died in the summer heat. A small flat area appeared on the bank of the creek. In its center was a witch circle, about twelve feet in diameter, with spokes that ran out from the center. In the center of the circle were three dead white rats.

Laine tapped off her mic and murmured to me, "Not a black cat."

"But an active witch circle," I said, "close by two robberies likely perpetrated by a para." And the circle was very similar to the last one we had found, which neither of us said aloud.

Lainie tapped her mic back on. "Maintain positions. I want to check something." She tapped it again, going to PsyLED freqs. To Tandy she said, "Dyson, call LaFleur. Get his twenty and condition. Tell him what we found." What she meant was, find out if he was human shaped. "Report back to me."

"Roger that," Tandy said. "I've been monitoring. If he doesn't answer, I'll get Occam there ASAP."

We were currently assuming the same potential scenario, that Rick might have been called by this witch working too, and could show up in black leopard form. Rick hadn't been a werecat for long and control over his beast was sometimes precarious. The grindys assigned to Knoxville were juveniles and didn't always show up at the right time. None of us wanted to have to shoot our boss to keep him from biting a human. We would, of course, but it would bother us.

Moments later, Tandy said into the PsyLED-only frequency, "LaFleur responded. He is en route to your twenty. ETA twelve minutes. He recommends that you pull back. Suggests that you thank KPD for their assistance and send the officers on scene back to their units." That meant Rick was human shaped. His order was not entirely unexpected. Humans near an active working might accidently set in motion a magical working that had been initiated but placed on hold and not yet fully launched, injuring themselves or others. In a slightly different tone Tandy said, "Alerting PsyLED agents on scene: Pea is with LaFleur."

Lainie shot me a look through the dark, not one I could decipher. Pea hadn't been around much in the last few weeks. The grindy hadn't appeared at the other circle. Why did she show up—I looked around at the nearby humans. *Right*.

T. Laine slid her dark eyes to me and said into the shared para freq, "Copy that, Dyson. Officers, this is an active witch working. Repeat, an active magical working of unknown intent. We've been advised by Knoxville PsyLED HQ to evacuate humans from the premises." To get them going, she shooed me back toward the cars and the cops began to follow, tactical flashes swinging slowly back and forth. "PsyLED appreciates your assistance," she said, to get them moving faster, "but we need to evacuate this area."

"Copy that, but I thought we were looking for a robbery suspect," one of the cops said.

"We were. That is now officially on the back burner. Officer safety is paramount to PsyLED, and we've stumbled on what is a dangerous paranormal scene."

Stumbled on? Or were led to? By a witch under glamour? Or something else?

"What about the homeless?" the cop pointed across the creek to the camping area.

"Most likely took off when you guys showed up. And running water will keep them safe," T. Laine said.

* * *

T. Laine and I were sitting in her official vehicle, the engine running and the AC pumped up high, when LaFleur coasted up. We all got out, the neon green grindylow sitting on Rick's shoulder holding a cat treat in her front paws and nibbling on it, like a squirrel might. Rick wasn't wearing a vest or headset, but his badge was clipped to his jeans and his shoulder rig was prominently displayed against his white T-shirt. Usually Rick was cool and collected at paranormal scenes. This time he looked fidgety, as if he was holding anxiety down by force of will.

"Update," he said.

T. Laine brought him up to speed on the night's events and finished by saying, "Did you feel anything? Any attraction to shift and come here? Do you feel anything now that you are here?"

"No," Rick said, one hand smoothing the grindy's tail along his shoulder and down one arm. "Nothing." He tilted his head like a cat and sniffed. "I don't smell anyone. Don't sense moon-calling magic at all. Is it active right now?"

I opened the psy-meter 2.0 and reread the earth. "The levels are dropping, pretty close to midhigh," I said. "And I agree. No witch other than Lainie or human in the immediate vicinity, including the large group of homeless camping on the other side of the creek."

T. Laine pointed across the creek toward the Walmart. "I can make out a few tents. More upstream. A few campfires. No people on infrared."

Rick grunted, unconvinced.

"Let me inspect the circle. Alone," T. Laine said. "I want you two behind the engine blocks. There's enough iron in them to frazzle any working that might get by me."

Get by me meant any working that exploded and killed her. "You will *not* die," I ordered.

"Roger that," she said.

"Don't get too close," Rick said, giving permission even as he backed away. "Use a personal indicator light so we can follow you."

"Okay. I'm going to cast a *scan* working and a *seeing*

working. Wish me luck." T. Laine moved back into the weeds, wearing the night-gear headset and a comms set, no weapon drawn, a tiny green light on her shoulder. She was holding a small moonstone amulet carved into a bear. We followed her progress as she moved slowly through the weeds. I started to follow.

His voice strained, his body taut, Rick said, "Get back here, Ingram. If she triggers it and explodes there's no point in you getting hurt too."

I wanted to say something like, *Wow. Show some concern, why don't you?* But the female agents I worked with had told me that I tended to overreact to male authority even when it was appropriate, like a male boss giving a perfectly reasonable order. So I swallowed the insubordinate words before they left my mouth, scuttled behind the iron engine block, and crouched close to him. Our positions put two engines between the working and us.

"What did you get when you read the earth?" Rick asked.

"The magic was hot, like getting a shock from a live wire. The feeling of death was fresh and strong, but small."

"No feeling of maggots?"

I frowned. I had forgotten the sensation of maggots I had picked up at the other circle. "No. What does that mean?"

Rick shook his head, barely visible as his silver locks caught the meager light. He didn't reply. Silently we followed T. Laine's slow, methodical progress in a straight line to the location of the magical working. She started walking widdershins to the circle, then stopped and backed away, and started back sunwise, which was unusual. It could mean a lot of different things, depending on what she was sensing in her magical scans.

A good fifteen minutes later, T. Laine moved back toward us. When she was close enough for us to hear without comms, she said, "Same markings and style of circle as the last one. Same runes. It's the same magic signature, but the animals are three white rats, not a cat. Smaller animal mass and radius of the circle means a less powerful spell. And the rats were carried here, not summoned here."

"Different pattern," Rick said, thoughtful. To me, he said, "Tap on your comms and ask Tandy to compile a listing of all the pet stores in the area that sell white rats. Tomorrow someone will need to drop by and ask about recent sales and request surveillance footage."

"For now?" T. Laine asked him. She stopped about halfway between the working and the vehicles.

Rick said, "Can you safely disrupt whatever working is in progress? I'd like us to get up close and personal ASAP."

"Can do. Back in a bit."

T. Laine moved back through the wild grasses, stopped, and began to mumble, nothing in English, but with lots of *s*'s and *l*'s and something that sounded like she was dying of consumption. Maybe some form of Gaelic. She raised an arm and made a tossing motion. Nothing happened, and her shoulders went slack. Louder, she called to us, "It's down and safe."

I noted that Rick was less stiff, his posture less rigid. LaFleur had been prepared for the working to explode. Or he had been ready to fight off a calling.

Before we could take a step, T. Laine had her personal light on high beam and was searching the ground. We moved in close but kept our feet far outside of the circle, which had been cut into the ground with a spade or narrow shovel.

The circle was smaller than the last one, but at twelve feet across, it was still a big circle for one witch to make and handle. There were runes drawn into the earth but no focal items except two more golf balls and one tee, what looked like a used facial tissue with a trace of lipstick on it, and a shoelace from a man's dress shoe. Rick bagged the tissue, golf implements, and shoestring, hoping for a DNA match with the witch or with the intended victim of the circle. They bagged the rats for a necropsy at PsyCSI. We worked with a sense of reprieve. Rick hadn't been called.

Rick and T. Laine took measurements and photos and made drawings and I went back to my original task, taking readings of the foliage around Third Creek and back behind the Walmart. I got zilch. The robber wasn't here anymore if he or she had actually come this way. Eventually I left T. Laine and Rick at the circle and headed back to HQ to finish writing my reports. Something about all this seemed off. But I was a probie. What did I know?

FIVE

I stretched and went to find a cup of Rick's dark French roast Community coffee. The stretch in HQ, before five a.m., doing paperwork and database scans, was hard on me. Trees slept in the night and the urge to lie down and snore was strong, but as probie it most often fell on me, and would until September when the budget said we'd be getting a new probationary officer (unless there was a new hiring freeze), or when I got custody of Mud, whichever happened first. My schedule would change then. For now, I was night shift and I needed the caffeine pick-me-up with three packets of sugar and a dollop of real cream. I made a second cup for Tandy and considered which fixins to add. I had learned that his coffee preferences tended to change based on who he worked with, so I situated the painted metal travel mugs and creamer and sugar packets on a small tray. I placed his coffee at his side and fell into my chair. "Dark. Creamer and packets of sugar and sweetner to the side if you decide to come to the light side."

Tandy smiled, his skin white, the scarlet Lichtenberg lines vibrant in the light of the screens. "*Star Wars*? Impressive, Ingram."

I smiled and sipped. "Does my being so sleepy cause you to feel sleepy?"

"Yes, Nell. It does. It's easier when there are several people in the building, as the effect of any single person's emotions is mixed and blunted. But with everyone off shift but us, your . . ." He paused. "The force of sleepiness is strong in this one."

Tandy pushed away from the keyboard and took a sip, opened a tiny plastic tub of cream, and poured it into his mug. Sipped again. All of our mugs had been painted by an anonymous artist, Tandy's with clouds and lightning, which was kinda mean, though he seemed to find it amusing. Mine was painted with green leaves. Tandy asked, "Do you hate paper trails as much as I think you do?"

"I'd rather have a bad cold than have to do an NCIC search and now I have two of them."

"Summation?"

"Grindylows are scary. The list of were-creature kills is spectacular and a little terrifying for the U.S. grindys.

"Also, blood-sacrifice witch circles are a pain in the neck. I've been paper-tracking through police records for reports of sacrifice on the bank of any river or creek and trying to tie it to waning moon cycles. So far I have nothing. You got any idea how *not*-user-friendly NCIC is for magic-related records?"

The National Crime Information Center—NCIC—might be the lifeline of law enforcement, but it was downright painful for *us* to use. The agency was an electronic clearinghouse of crime data available to virtually every criminal justice agency nationwide, twenty-four/seven. It had helped LEOs identify terrorists, track down and apprehend fugitives, locate missing persons, and convict serial killers. It had been estimated that there were currently thirteen million active records available, and searchable according to specific keywords. But not magic keywords.

And it was boring.

"I'm aware," Tandy said. His understanding smile was sweet as he continued, "JoJo loves it, which I'll never understand."

"Are you and JoJo getting married?" I asked.

Tandy's cup bobbled in his hands and some of the creamy coffee splashed out onto the table. "What?"

I frowned at him and maybe at my own unexpected and blunt question. "Well. Ummm. You don't think that it's a secret you two are practically living together, do you?"

"No. But, married?" The last word squeaked.

I frowned at him. "I'm less and less inclined to find importance in the institution of marriage, but for most people it tends to be the next logical step in a sexual relationship."

"Nee-e-ell." Tandy dragged out my name and I thought he might have blushed, but I couldn't be sure. He stood and mopped up his spill with a roll of paper towels kept on the

windowsill, silent as he worked. I waited, not sure what I had said wrong. "This is a most inappropriate line of discourse," he said after a too-long silence, and he sounded uncomfortable and snippety, which I found odd.

"Really?" I asked, trying to figure out what was going on. "It's all anyone in the church ever thinks about: who's proposing concubinage or marriage to who—whom?—and when."

Tandy tossed the towel in the garbage and sat back down. "Okay. I guess I understand that." He met my gaze across the table and dragged his cup closer, fiddling with a spoon and sweetener packets. "Meeting her parents would be the next logical step, and JoJo hasn't asked me to do that."

"Why not?" I stirred my coffee, watching from the corner of my eye as he dipped the spoon and stirred his coffee—without adding anything more to it. He blushed harder, the red a certainty now, but he hadn't walked away, so I went on. "Tandy, why hasn't she asked you to meet her parents?"

"I'm this white guy with crazy red hair and bizarre red lines on my skin. I'm fine for a roll in the hay but not for taking home to meet her parents."

"I know for a fact that JoJo would never say something like that."

Tandy smiled slightly, but didn't retract his statement.

"You asked her to meet your parents?"

"My father is . . . not around. And my mother is an unsubtle racist and a bigot. She kicked me out of the house when I was struck by lightning and developed the lines and my gift." He paused and sipped his coffee again, his expression pained. "She touched me when she threw me out. Her hatred and fear were palpable, so terrible that I—" He stopped. "I haven't been back and have no intention of ever going back."

I had nothing helpful to say to that. Sifting through my limited, recently acquired, socially appropriate lines of comfort, I said simply, "Families can suck all the red offa life's lollipop."

Tandy burst out laughing, his muscles unclenching. "Yes, they can. Why do *you* think JoJo hasn't asked me to meet her family? Has she said anything to you?"

"Not a word. But the reasons can be all over the place. You should ask her instead of assuming it's the color of your skin."

"And when I read her emotions when I ask that? And I know exactly what she's feeling about it? That's a terrible invasion of privacy, Nell."

I hadn't thought about it that way. "So send her an e-mail. You won't be there when she reads it. She can think about it for a while before trying to answer."

"Isn't that taking the easy way out?"

"No. If you tell her in the first paragraph that you're doing it this way to give her emotional privacy, then it becomes sweet." I thought about words normal people might use and added, "Mushy sweet."

Tandy laughed again, and I remembered the anxiety-ridden man he had been the first time I met him. He had changed a lot. We all had.

"I'll take it under consideration," he said. He changed the subject. "You need to examine the soil on the roof. It's been a while and with so little rain and the winds last week, it might have blown away."

"I'll do that," I said, but I tucked the reminder away for later. I could tell the soil was still up there. I could feel it. Rick and Occam had carted ten five-gallon buckets of dirt from my land and deposited it onto the flat roof, as soon as I was human enough to think of returning to my job. They wanted me to have a safe place to rest should I need Soulwood to rejuvenate. Or heal. Or a place to plant green things. Or anything. I wasn't planning to use it, but it was nice to know it was there and even nicer to know that my coworkers—my friends—cared enough to do that for me.

He looked up and I heard the door to the stairwell open. T. Laine trudged up the hallway. Tandy asked me, "So what did you find in the dreaded NCIC database?"

"Local sheriff's deputy reports about witch circles that were not routed to us, going back over three months."

T. Laine dumped her gobag and laptop on the conference room table. "Yeah. That means I'm not getting any sleep tonight," she groused.

"Should I have waited till morning to send them to you?" I asked.

Tandy tilted his head as if trying to read our emotional reactions.

"No. You did right. Update me."

"I've found ten witch circles reported to the sheriff's department that were *not* routed to us, plus the two we already know about. Three had dead black cats, two had white rats, one with a raccoon, four with no sacrifices on-site, all of them located on the bank of a creek or river."

"Needless to say," T. Laine said, "there might have been more circles that weren't discovered or reported. And near running water is not an ideal location because of the possible disruptive action on workings—unless we have a water witch involved."

"Was Rick in town on the other black cat ceremonies?" Tandy asked.

"No," I said.

"I'm doing a prelim comparison on the photos of all the circles," our witch said, her words slow and her tone thoughtful. "So far, they all bear the same magical signature." She punched buttons on her keybord and photos of the circles I had gathered appeared overhead. "The runes are confusing. The focals are mismatched. Nothing about any of the workings or circles makes sense under the accepted rules of magic. Most importantly, according to the lunar calendar, none of the circles appear to have been worked at the full moon, which I would expect to be the case for any working calculated to hit a were-creature. Rick being called, showing increased signs of aging, but not being killed when he shows up at the circles, still only makes sense as coincidence. In which case the curse is for someone else and that someone is in danger."

"But none of us believe in coincidence." Tandy pushed back away from the table and turned up the lights. "Let's finish our workups. Send out the reports. In-house only. We'll backtrack the local reports and see who sent them out."

"Already done," I said.

Reading my reports, T. Laine said, "And it isn't just one officer. Multiple reports, five officers, and that doesn't make sense."

"It does if they send them all to one up-line officer who is supposed to liaise with us," I said. "Tracking that requires more access than I have. Or an internal search."

"Ah. That sucks donkey—" T. Laine stopped. "Oops. Sorry."

An internal search meant someone in KPD looking through the records for us. Or a certain hacker going in for a look. Tandy and I stared across the table at one another, neither of us willing to take that step. Knowing I was being wimpy by passing the buck up the chain of command, I said, "I think we should send it to Rick and let him handle that info through proper or improper channels, as he sees fit."

"Proper channels means we'll never know who was suppressing reports to us, because KPD will never share that."

"Copy that," I said. I started typing my summation report to Rick. "The sacrifices appear to be evolving, accelerating and decelerating in terms of the focals used and the animals sacrificed." I stopped typing and looked out the window into the night. "She's good at killing things." I put my fingers back on the keyboard and took up where I left off. "The runes in the circles suggest preparation and planning toward a greater black-magic spell. Future human sacrifice cannot be ruled out as an ultimate intent." That part hadn't occurred to me until I typed it out, and a chill went through me.

T. Laine said, "I just pulled up Rick's schedule. He was hundreds of miles away on some of the older black cat circles. Either he felt a calling from way off and didn't tell us or the summoning spell has a limited footprint. I'm going with a limited footprint. But we need to talk to him."

Haltingly, Tandy said, "But—well—I have to tell you both, privately." We both turned to the empath. "I've noticed an increase in anxiety, irritation, and temper from Rick on the waning moon for the last two or three moon cycles."

"That's not good," T. Laine said. "Is it getting worse?"

"No." Tandy looked puzzled at that. "And it goes away. Coincidence again?"

"Or he's lonely and that's the time of the cycle where he feels it most?" I suggested.

"Were-creatures are sensitive to lots of things," Tandy said, "and I may be the only empath to ever work closely with werecats, so I don't know what's normal."

"Occam acting jumpy?" T. Laine asked.

"Not at all. Rick is . . . different." The empath stood, went to the coffeepot, and refilled his mug. Black this time.

I held a hand over my own cup. Tandy started pacing and sipping his coffee, his body movements beginning to take on a human version of Rick's lithe motions. I realized he was drinking coffee the way Rick drank his and I was fascinated at the transformation. T. Laine sat up in her chair, watching the change, her eyebrows up in surprise.

"You felt maggots at one site," he said. "I think we need to know if Mithrans had been called there. Maybe before Rick got there?"

"Could be. And if so, then the fact that we got to tonight's circle so fast could mean the vamps arrived but were able to stop approaching the circle before we saw them." I stopped and drew out the site of that circle on a legal pad, including nearby roads and parking areas. "Yes, there could have been vamps present. I never read with the psy-meter here"—I pointed to a warehouse—"here"—I pointed back to Walmart—"or here"—I pointed to the roads near the creek where a vamp might have parked. "I haven't been to all the circles, so I don't know if there were vamps there or not. Why?"

"What if there's a para hate group with a single witch attached, calling on the undead, trying to capture or kill a vamp, and Rick just got caught up in one of the spells with a black cat," Tandy said.

"It's been tried before," I said, recalling a few cases I had studied at school. Under a different file, I added to the list of possibilities as we worked through them, and said, "Someone in the CIA leaked info on paranormals to the Human Speakers of Truth. The Speakers are all dead or in jail, but we never discovered who in the Central Intelligence Agency leaked the info."

"Brainstorming, here. Maybe targeting vamps with the objective of delivering true-death?" he asked, his syntax remarkably Rick-like. "Or blood theft? Or using the vamp in the circle, sacrificing the undead as part of the casting."

"Or since Rick was called, maybe all the para species in the area are being targeted, one at a time."

"Maybe with an emphasis on law enforcement paras? Which means a spotted cat might be sacrificed next and call to Occam," I said, a strange feeling settling in my chest. I was good at research, but I didn't like where this was going.

"And since the KPD hasn't notified us, we have to consider that a faction of the department is involved. This could get messy."

"I'll add the possibilities to my reports," I said. "Oh. And with the proximity to the witch circle, we have to consider the possibility that the thief at Pilot Gas was a witch hiding under a very good glamour."

"I have to hit the sack," T. Laine said, groaning. "Morning comes early, so I'll use the mattress room. Later." She left the room.

Tandy nodded and the body mechanics of his boss fell away. Tandy returned to the coffee tray and added cream to his mug. *Interesting.* Tandy was very, very interesting.

Rick came into the office before daybreak. He was walking more slowly than usual and dropped by his office before joining us in the conference room, where he filled his own mug. It was painted with a black leopard on the shiny finish, with the letters *SAC*—special agent in charge. As he poured coffee he said, "I read your report on the lack of interagency communication between a certain sheriff's office detective working up possible paranormal crime, and Unit Eighteen. Good summation, Ingram. I sent it up-line, but Soul and FireWind were called to Maine, working a crime scene involving the Master of the City of New York. I doubt either of them will address the issues anytime soon, as it might require a face-to-face with KPD and the sheriff's office."

Tandy was watching Rick's careful movements. "Are you hurt?"

"No."

Even I could tell Rick was lying, but Tandy didn't call him on it, saying instead, "Do you think *we* can wait until they get back to address the issue of the local LEOs not alerting us to the presence of a black-magic user in the area?"

"No. I don't. I'd like Ingram to call her friend at the FBI and prime the pump."

"I don't have a friend at the FBI."

"Sure you do. In your report you described her as a 'Coffee addict going on a four-hour withdrawal. Dark-skinned, African-American female FBI agent, jacket and pants, hair cropped close. History of familial witches.' She called you her telepathic new best friend. Ring any bells?"

"Oh. Special Agent Margot Racer." Margot had a strong truth-sensing ability, which I had left out of my report, though I had told Rick privately. It seemed important that my boss know when he was talking to a walking, talking lie detector. Like Tandy. "But she isn't my friend."

"Racer called—how many times was it, Dyson, while Ingram was out on disability?" Rick paced along in front of the window, sipping, just as Tandy had done during the long night.

"Five times," Tandy said. "The last time was a month ago."

I squinted up at Rick, a silhouette against the graying skyline. Margot Racer calling me was strange. Unless . . . unless she had more than a strong truth-sense. I had wondered if she was a budding, true empath. But what if she was a budding precog instead? Or something even more arcane. "Why did she call?"

"Your disability was a secret only from your family. Racer called to see if you were getting better. Why not call her back. See what she knows."

I frowned, thinking. I wasn't sure how to do that—call up someone and question them.

"Ingram?"

"I can do that." But even I could hear the uncertainty in my tone.

Rick smiled, not unkindly. "Give her a call and go for coffee. Offer to share what's happening in return for any info she might dig up on the local LEO who isn't passing along information. It's called quid pro quo, Ingram. You don't have to do a spa day or become BFFs or anything."

"Okay. I can do that," I repeated, but more certainly this time.

Rick took his seat and rubbed his head. Tandy looked from Rick's hand, massaging his temples, to me. Rick was in pain. "Are you okay?" I asked the boss.

"Headache." Rick dropped his hand and said, "Kent's having no luck tracking the witch via arcane means. We somehow got *lucky* last night and found a second black-magic circle. I don't believe in luck. Is it possible that we were lured to the most recent circle? I want you to contact your friend with the Mithrans in addition to talking to Racer. See what they know."

He wanted *me* to call the vampires. I had expected him to contact Ming of Glass.

I studied Rick. There were dark circles under his eyes, his skin was sagging, and the fine wrinkles that used to be laugh lines had become deeper, downward frown lines. "How long have you been having headaches?" I asked. "Now that we know there have been circles for a while, do we need to posit that the circles are giving you headaches?" *And making you act fidgety,* I thought.

Rick's tone was sharp. "I don't know." He shrugged slightly and amended, "A couple of months."

I considered the timelines of the witch circles. "The same time as the circles. Okay. Take some Tylenol. I'll make the calls, then I'm heading home. While I'm gone, the team needs to ask our boss some pointed questions about witch circles." I glared at them and left the men sitting in the conference room, Tandy watching Rick, Rick looking ornery. At my desk I made calls. Yummy was on the security team of the new Master of the City of Knoxville. I got a voice mail, but as it was after sunrise, I didn't expect to hear back until after dusk. The voice mail left on the service of FBI Special Agent Margot Racer was more tentative. "Hi. Um. This is Nell Ingram. I thought we might have coffee tomorrow. If you want. If you have time. If you're in town. And not working a case. And, um. Yeah. Okay. 'Bye." I gave my number and hung up. "And that didn't sound like a twelve-year-old desperately trying to make a new friend, at all."

Being a PsyLED special agent sounded all exciting, but most of the job was combing through boring databases, talking to people, and brainstorming, trying to make sense of disparate and mismatching puzzle pieces. And working long, tiring hours through the night and into the morning. I grabbed my gear and clattered down the stairs into the dawn, looking for Occam's car in his parking spot, just in case he was getting to work early. Empty. I had hoped to see him, even if only just briefly. And wasn't that like that twelve-year-old being lovesick. Sometimes it was as if I'd never grown up at all. I was halfway to my truck when I heard a scrape behind me.

And the world exploded into brilliant white sparks on a black sky.

I woke blind, cramped, my arm under me, twisted and dead-feeling. My head was throbbing and white sparks were going off behind my eyes. Bumping. Moving. I rammed into the thing behind me. More sparks. I dry-heaved, and the smell of vomit let me know it wasn't the first time. Something wet and cold trickled from my scalp along my face. I had a head injury. Concussion. Arms and ankles bound. Hands numb and tingling painfully. Not gagged. In a trunk of a car. The car bumped over something. I heard voices and I managed to kick the side of the trunk and shout, but the car cruised on.

At Spook School I'd taken a course on how to escape from various places including the trunk of a car, but the course instructors hadn't included having bound and useless arms and legs. The main thing they shared was to get away before the kidnappers reached their destination, their own home ground. I tried to position to kick out the taillight but just managed to bang my booted ankle bones on the sidewall. I gagged again and groaned. My only hope was that Tandy had seen my abduction on the parking lot cameras.

The car slowed. I heard a rooster crow. I knew that rooster. It had once belonged to Daddy and Mama and I had sorta managed to free him.

I was on the grounds of God's Cloud of Glory Church. Fear and fury slammed through me in equal measure. My head exploded with pain in reaction. The blinding stars behind my eyes grew and fell like snow. I retched again.

The car stopped. The engine died. Everything happened fast.

The trunk opened. Daylight seared my eyes and skull. I tried to scream.

Larry Aden snarled at me. Reached in, grabbed my hair in one hand, and stretched around me to grab my bound hands. He yanked me up from the trunk.

I bit him. I caught his wrist in my jaws, biting down with

all my might. I tasted blood. He shook me like a dog shakes prey. I bit harder. Ripping skin. Sucking his blood into my mouth. Bloodlust rose in me like desire, like addiction, a need so strong I whimpered and shuddered. I *wanted* him. Wanted his death. Wanted his body and blood for the land. I spat his blood to the ground. He was *mine*.

I could take him, *right now.*

Kill him. Feed him to the earth.

Devour him body and soul. *Neeeeed* slithered through me.

Instead, I whipped my body, bucking. My scalp tore. His flesh ripped. He cursed and dropped me.

I called on Soulwood.

The vampire tree's root system answered faster.

Vines erupted through the ground and wrapped around Larry's booted ankles. Slithered up his legs. Constricting. Thorns rammed into him. Pierced through his clothing, into his legs and thighs, securing him in place. He screamed.

Need quivered through me.

Thick dark leaves unfurled beneath me. The vines lifted me and, rustling, carried me several feet away before the tender shoots whipped up over me. Creating a mattress below me and a cage of thorns over me, a bower and a prison. Protecting me, ensnaring me.

Near me, Larry screamed and thrashed. His voice was abruptly cut off. He gurgled. Joy shot through me. My enemy was now my prey. *Mine.* I reached for his body and blood.

Voices sounded. Shouting. I came back to myself, just a fraction. Just enough. I gripped my bloodlust in tight reins. I owned it. My bloodlust did not own me.

Soulwood reached for me through the ground. I could feel its agitation, its desperation. More of my blood dripped on the ground from my scalp. My land responded, frantic. The leaves were keeping me from touching the ground. "I need to touch the ground. Let me down," I whispered to the vampire tree. "Let me down, *now!*"

The leaves parted and my face landed on the dirt and gravel of a parking area. Scraping. But there was enough soil. "I'm okay," I whispered to my land. "Calm. Calm."

Both the tree and Soulwood slowed, reassured, appeased, though still worried, still ready to attack. It was strange to

have both Soulwood and the tree respond to me, separate but
working together. I had a single blazing image of a knight on
a pale green horse, carrying a tall pole that bore a flag. On it
was a living tree. Something to think about when I wasn't in
so much trouble.

"What happened?" Sam's voice interrupted.

"I thought you'un said that tree was done rooting up everywhere and killing," another voice said. I shifted my eyes that
way and spotted Ben Aden through the leaves, the man who
had wanted to marry me not so long ago. He was standing in
a group of men, young and old, maybe eight or ten of them.

"We're not dead," I managed to say. "The tree didn't kill
anyone. Sam, it's me. Nell. Under one of the . . . mounds of
leaves."

"Nell, what the Sam Hill?"

I chuckled at Sam's choice of cursing. "Larry attacked me
in the parking lot of PsyLED." I tried to turn over using only
my heels and backside and shoulders, but my arms were a raging sea of needles and stabbing pain. I had to give up. "I'm tied
up. He hit me over the head. Put me in the trunk. Brought me
to the church."

"She deserves to be punished," Larry gurgled, hoarse.
"She's living in sin, working with a man, alone, in an office all
night. A Jezebel! And that devil tree attacked us!"

"Nell?" Sam asked, wary. "I'm not sure what to do."

The tree. It killed things. It was big enough and mean enough
to kill people if it wanted. And it was sentient. It had tried to
talk to me, if my vision was an indication. A knight on a horse
carrying a Soulwood banner. *Oh. No. The Green Knight? His
weapon a staff made from fire-hardened wood? Was the Arthu-
rian tale a reality? Maybe.* I swallowed down the bile that rose
up my throat and said, "Call the police. You got no choice, Sam.
Larry attacked an officer of the law. It'll be on the security
camera at PsyLED. Photo evidence. You cut me free and I'll—"

Sirens cut the dawn air. Cars tearing into the church grounds.
Skidding to a stop. Doors opening. Occam shouting, "Arms
up! Get on your knees!" A growl entering his voice. "Get on
your knees!"

Rick shouted, his voice overlapping, "PsyLED! On your
knees! On your knees!"

"Do it!" T. Laine shouted. "Put down your weapons!"

The churchmen started quoting their constitutional rights to the cops. Loudly. I shouted, trying to be heard over the clamor. "I'm here! I'm okay!"

Rick shouted, "Don't do it, farm boy. On your knees!"

Sam said, "Nell?" Fear and violence in his words. Churchmen, two wereleopards, a witch, and too many guns.

I sobbed once, hard. My relief was potent, overpowering the last of the bloodlust, as much because I had been saved as because I hadn't killed Larry. To the tree, I whispered, "You'un gots to let me go now. I'm safe."

"I said, on your knees!" Occam growled.

"Nell!" Rick shouted again, his voice catty. He was about to shift.

T. Laine shouted something that sounded like, *"Cactus est somnum."*

Sam said, softly, "No . . ."

I felt bodies hit the ground, solid thumps. A unidirectional sleep spell had hit the churchmen.

The leaves beneath me quavered and the rock-pocked soil juddered and shook. The vines protecting me rolled back. I rotated my hips to sit upright.

Occam knelt beside me. His eyes were glowing the gold of his cat. "Nell?"

"I'm tied up. My arms are numb. Cut me free."

"Jeez. Your fingers are blue."

I felt/heard something grinding, a peculiar rubbery sound, and then the bonds around my wrists snapped free and pain shot up my arms and down to my fingers. The awful pain in my shoulders eased, to be replaced with a different kind of pain as my numb arms dangled helplessly. Occam sliced through the silver duct tape holding my ankles together on top of my socks and work boots. He sheathed the blade and carried me to his fancy car, opened the passenger door, and placed me inside. I closed my eyes, sick with vertigo. *Concussion.* From somewhere a cool cloth wiped my face clean of blood and vomit. I had a quick thought of a cat tongue and managed a smile I didn't explain.

Occam took my hands and, gently, began to peel off the tape. A strong smell of solvent made my eyes water as he worked the tape off my wrists. The cleaning burned, but I didn't say anything as he peeled. It had to be done and, unlike on TV and movies, taking duct tape off wasn't an easy thing. The smell faded and he began to massage my fingers and wrists, working the circulation back into them.

"Nell?"

I got my eyes to open without throwing up.

Rick LaFleur was kneeling beside Occam near the open door, concern on his face. "How bad are you? I don't smell much blood."

I knew better than to lie. "I'm hurt. Concussion. Hands without circulation too long. But not anything that needs the hospital." Hospital meant the paranormal ER of the University of Tennessee Medical Center. They couldn't help me. They didn't know what I was. They wanted to study me. "No hospital," I repeated and closed my eyes, sick to my stomach. Occam continued to massage my hands and lower arms. "Ow, ow, ow, ow."

"Feeling's coming back," Occam said, his voice rough with his cat. "It'll get worse before it gets better."

"It hurts like fire ants and hot peppers, but don't stop."

"The guy who took you?" Rick asked. "Is he here?"

"The one still trapped with thorns is him. Larry Aden." I got my eyes open again and indicated the prison over him.

An expression crossed Rick's face too fast to be certain, but he looked . . . fiercely delighted. "Well, well. The one who tried to take our Mud?" He had gotten my message the day Larry came by and I fired into the ground. Rick didn't wait for me to answer. He kicked at the man's foot.

"Make the tree let him go, Nell, sugar," Occam murmured. "We got more witnesses coming." His long-fingered hand rested on my arm, skin to skin. I was cold, icy with shock, and wanted to curl up against his heat, but this wasn't the time.

"Let him go," I whispered to the rootlets that confined Larry. When nothing happened I added, "We'll take him for punishment."

The tree shook, all its leaves quivering. The vines whipped away from Larry, who was still asleep, leaving the thorns embedded. They'd have to be extracted by a doctor. They might be poisonous. I almost felt sorry for Larry. But not quite.

Rick cuffed Larry and picked him up. Werecat strength. He carried him away from the vines. I didn't tell Rick the vines could follow. That might be considered creepy. More sirens sounded in the distance. Rick began to zip-tie all the men, even Sam, and T. Laine joined in, using stronger ties for the men's ankles. I caught Occam's gaze with my own and said, "Not Sam."

Something flashed in his eyes and was gone, something predatory and possessive. "They were all present at the discovery of a kidnapped federal agent." He leaned to me, closer, so I could hear the cat-growl of his words. "Be sure about this, Nell, sugar."

"I'm sure. Sam was trying to help."

Occam looked around and said to Rick, "Nell says some of them were trying to help."

"That isn't exactly what it looks like," Rick said to me. There was no give in his tone, no . . . mercy. An alpha male protecting his kits, his leap of leopards.

"Nell, sugar, it does look like they all were part of it." Occam frowned and lifted a hand as if to touch my hair, which was brighter red and leafy. "We called out the sheriff's department, so we can't go messing with evidence. This might get personal. Intrusive. And though I want more than anything to haul you straight back to Soulwood to safety and protection, I can't." I didn't answer and he went back to scrubbing my hands. "Nell? Talk to me, sugar. Did you hear what I said?"

Prickles of nerves coming back alive bit me worse than the vampire tree's thorns, but I didn't jerk away. "I heard. I know. Ow, ow, ow."

"Sorry, Nell, sugar. About the pain and the loss of privacy this might mean."

"This stinks. Dagnabbit."

He maneuvered in front of me, protecting me from sight, and tucked my hair back from my face. "Yeah. It does. It will." He flipped open his pocketknife and cut away all the leaves growing in my hairline, tossing them to the ground. He was a cat, grooming me, shielding me from unwanted attention, because he hadn't been able to protect me.

SIX

The sheriff came with his deputies—five units and six uniformed county men and women—and three city units followed, all with lights and sirens, taking up the meager parking with the three PsyLED vehicles and officers. Any problem on church grounds was likely to create an excess of law enforcement, a development since the first time the compound was raided and children in danger had been taken into protective custody. The gunfight that came months later and resulted in loss of life and serious injury had only made things worse. And then there was the case of the kidnapped vampires, the abduction of their children, and the presence of devil dogs. The church was desperate to avoid entanglement with the law, but it seemed to happen with increasing regularity.

That didn't stop the churchmen and churchwomen from gathering and standing silent, watching, including Daddy and the mamas. Mama was holding back Mud, keeping her away from me, but our eyes met and I gave a tiny nod, telling her I was okay. Except for family, the churchmen were staring at me, eyes accusing, muttering angry imprecations at the cops, all just loud enough to barely be heard, comments about witchcraft that had attacked their churchmen in clear violation of their civil right to worship as they chose. Their right to be protected from evil. Things about due process. Legal wrangling. Typical churchmen stuff.

The cops ignored them, which seemed to make some of the church folk madder, and to make things worse, the men on the ground began to rouse, complaining of headaches and demanding to know why they were tied up. Three of the Jackson coterie, my family's enemies, showed up holding hunting rifles, and my heart began to race. Mama stepped back toward safety. Mud resisted. The deputies drew weapons and pointed them at the crowd. "Put the weapons down. Put the weapons down now!" the deputies shouted.

"Occam?"

"I'm seeing, Nell, sugar."

Things looked as if they were about to escalate, and I glanced down at my chest. No shoulder rig. No weapon. Not that I'd be able to fire a weapon if things went south. I tried to make a fist, as if gripping my service weapon. My fingers didn't close. I needed to find my service weapon. The crowd began to move in.

"You'un boys! Put them weapons down!" The words echoed across the church grounds. I knew that voice. It was Brother Aden, Larry's daddy. "We are a people of peace. We will not attack law enforcement doing their duty. Put 'em down." When no one moved, he roared, "Put 'em down or be sanctioned." The three churchmen lowered their weapons and stepped back, disappearing into the crowd, which I figured was better than nothing. The cops didn't chase them. Suddenly I could breathe again.

Brother Aden moved to his son, cuffed and bleeding, and the cops let him through. It looked like the brother's heart was breaking as he stood over the still-comatose Larry. He shook his head, his lips firm and tight, turned his back on his son, and took a place beside the Nicholsons, shoulder to shoulder with Daddy and the mamas. Ben Aden joined them. Mud looked up at them both in surprise.

Now that the lines between church and law enforcement had softened, Mama and Mud shoved through the cops and came to me, Mama gathering me up in her arms. She pushed Occam away. "Thank you'un. I got her. It's okay, baby girl. I'm here," she whispered.

"Thanks, Mama," I whispered back as Mud wriggled into the car and curled around my back.

"You'll need to work on Nell's circulation, Mrs. Nicholson," Occam said, standing. He took in the church folk, who had been watching him rub my hands and arms. Angry churchmen seeing a stranger touch one of *their* womenfolk. I wanted to shoot the God's Cloud crowd just for that presumption and possessiveness, but luckily my hands were not functioning and the world was still tipping and whirling. Mama started rubbing my hands, her fingers tanned and strong on my much-browner ones, her head bowed so I could only see the crown of her head. Beyond her, a small grouping of the crowd stepped slowly toward Occam.

Occam rested one hand on his holstered weapon. It was a reminder, a potent one, that he was a cop, doing his job. "Easy, boys," he drawled, all Texan polite. "You folks keep back, please. Thank you. Back a little more." There was just a hint of roughness to his voice that spoke of his cat, and the desire to slash with claws. I hoped that his eyes weren't glowing golden. The churchmen would get all riled if they knew a werecat, a devil creature, was giving them orders.

Without taking his eyes from the crowd, he added to Mama, "Just keep rubbing her fingers and hands to get the blood flowing, Mrs. Nicholson."

Mama rubbed harder and the pins and needles worsened. I hoped that was a good thing. "Did you'un make the vines grow here?" she whispered to me. "Did you'un make the tree attack Larry?"

I chuckled sourly. "No. It did that on its own."

"Devil tree," she muttered.

"Could be," I muttered back, "but it saved me."

I looked up as Occam walked to the other side of the small area, toward where Daddy and the Adens and the other two mamas stood. His hand dropped from his weapon and his posture relaxed, letting me know that the human was fully in charge, getting ready to confront my daddy, who knew he was a wereleopard. A wereleopard who'd just had his hands all over me. Church courting etiquette placed that kind of touching as a claiming, as proof of an intimate relationship. *Oh . . . dear.* I didn't know what Daddy or Occam was about to say or do, and they were too far away for me to hear.

An ambulance showed up on scene, and while Mama continued chafing my hands and arms, a paramedic cleaned up my head wound and argued with me about seeing a doctor for my concussion symptoms and finally muttered something about compartment syndrome and stupid cops. I didn't tell her my reasons for not going to the hospital, and, with Occam having cut away my leaves, she had no point of reference for why I refused an MRI or CT scan. For the most part, I looked human. I'd have to think about that when my brain was working right again.

For now, I listened in on the chatter about which agencies should be called to investigate my kidnapping and charge Larry Aden. Since I was relatively unharmed, I hadn't been missing for long, and the kidnapper hadn't crossed state lines, the lead agency was up for grabs. Someone called the FBI, but for reasons not discussed with me, they declined to make an appearance.

As the discussions went on, the anger of the older members of the crowd began to diminish and the evidence gathering of the investigation into the kidnapping of a federal agent began. The cops took my story and, at Occam's suggestion, questioned Sam. After that, things de-escalated rapidly. Fortunately, because the church had installed motion sensor cameras to protect themselves from outside attack and influence, one camera had caught Larry's arrival and my removal from the trunk. Also fortunately, the camera had shut off after thirty seconds and hadn't captured the growing of the vines and thorns and leaves. I had to wonder if that had been Sam's action, if he had been watching the cameras when Larry drove up and that was why he got to me so fast. Sam didn't volunteer the information and no one in my hearing asked for it. But once Sam brought out the video, everyone was more willing to talk, and seeing the footage went a long way to convince the cops that Larry was working alone and even further to convince the churchmen that Larry had been doing something criminal. Two of the churchmen told me they were sorry. Others backed away. Their attitudes were improbably respectful, unexpected for churchmen.

I realized that for most of the churchmen, I was no longer viewed as a runaway churchwoman. I was recognized by most as a federal law enforcement officer. Technically, I was no longer "fair game." That understanding caused a curious heat to pulse through me, part shock, part something unknown.

JoJo, back at HQ, sent the footage of the attack in the PsyLED parking lot to the unit's cell phones, adding to the evidence that Larry had been working alone, which meant that

the zip-stripped men were released and none of them had to
be brought in for official questioning. When things had settled, Sam came by and whispered to Mama and me that, based
on the evidence, Brother Aden was planning to call for formal
banishment of his son. Mama's head dropped lower, and I realized that she hadn't met my eyes, not once. Was Mama
afraid of me? I couldn't figure out how to ask that and Sam
moved away.

As the discussions between law enforcement and the churchmen took place, and the tensions continued to decrease, my
headache subsided to bearable. I drank the water Mama
brought and when I could hold the bottle by myself, she announced that my hands were now fine. My fingers were indeed
pink and much less painful, and Mama patted them before
leaving me to wander around, listening and taking in the gossip. I knew that, later, she and the other mamas would have a
long gossipfest and compare notes on the happenings of today.

In the back of the crowd, I spotted Esther, my sister, the
one I thought might be a plant-person, like me. She was staring at the odd clusters of leaves and thorns in the parking area,
clusters that hadn't been there an hour ago. Her hand slid up
to her hairline as she stole through the gathering. It was the
same gesture I made when I was feeling to see if my leaves
had grown. Without speaking to me, she slipped away.

With the approval of the churchmen who had gathered to
watch the proceedings, Larry was strapped to a gurney, hauled
off in the ambulance to the hospital, and then to jail, in custody of the sheriff. He was still unconscious, but would be
charged with kidnapping and violent assault on a federal officer, both potential federal crimes, and a host of other, lesser
charges.

I was in a daze still, but I gave select members of the
church the stink-eye as the ambulance rolled out of sight. My
expression promised retribution the minute anyone looked at
me or Mud. A couple of the Jackson cadre looked back with
hatred and a promise of their own to get even, and I committed
the names and faces to memory. As for Larry, I'd tasted his
blood like a vampire. It was on my clothing. In my hair. If he
came to my farm again, he would nourish Soulwood just fine,
and something in my demeanor must have communicated my

intent and willingness to do violence, because all the church-men stepped back.

Yes, I thought at them. *I am an officer of the law. But I'm more than that. And you best remember.*

Communicating threats and promises through body language and expressions cost me in terms of the headache, and when tears gathered in my eyes, it was apparent that I needed contact with Soulwood sooner rather than later. I sat back and asked to go home.

My coworkers divvied up vehicles so that Occam could drive Mud and me home in Rick's car, which seated more than two, while T. Laine and Rick took the other cars. I was pretty useless and didn't argue. And didn't remember how I got to my house, into my jammies, and on a blanket in the backyard, my hands in contact with the ground. But I guessed it was thanks to my baby sister and my cat-man.

I woke in midafternoon, pain free, to a scent that had to come straight out of heaven. It turned out to be venison stew from my freezer, and commercial, boxed, dried pasta heated in the microwave. There wasn't a better smell in the world. I trudged inside to the long kitchen table and took my place, letting Mud serve me. We sat silent and I closed my eyes, the peace of Soulwood flowing up through the floorboards, through my bare feet, and into my bones. Through the soles of my feet, I felt Occam in cat form patrolling the church side of my property lines, keeping us safe while I slept. I called him to join us for dinner, knowing we'd be through before he got there.

Mud, seeing my eyes closed, took my hand and offered thanks in a traditional church prayer. "We thank thee for mercies great and small and for this food. And for Mama, who come—*came*—to help me cook it."

I smiled slowly and said, "Amen."

Twenty-five minutes later, Occam was at the door. Any upset he might have experienced from my kidnapping and rescue was gone. He'd shifted and run and killed and eaten a turkey. He had lain on Soulwood and let the land soothe his soul. In human form, silent and tranquil, he ate microwaved leftovers from a good stoneware plate, squeezed my fingers, and took off in Rick's vehicle, leaving us alone, all without a word spoken.

Mud and I spent the rest of the afternoon upstairs in her room in the eaves, in front of the air conditioner, putting together outfits she would wear to school soon and adding to the list of clothing, supplies, and other purchases she would need in order to become Cedar Bluff Middle School's newest green tree Giant. Even with the AC, it was hot, sweaty work, and I remembered sleeping on the second-story landing in the summers, my cot close to the top of the stairs so I could hear Leah—John's first wife—if she called out as her illness took her slowly away from us. And then, later, so I could have privacy from John. The fans that turned continuously on both floors did little to move around the cooler air between floors, and had Mud not come from the church, she might not have been able to bear it. Churchwomen were sturdy stock and Mud seemed not to notice the trickles of sweat and the clothes that stuck to us.

As we worked, we talked about Larry, the kidnapping, his arrest, and Mud's questions about what Larry had planned to do to me. It seemed to help us cope with the trauma of the day. When we had it all out in the open, we fell silent, working together. It was serene and quiet, a peaceful discourse.

When the clothes were put away, I took another nap, what the townies called a power nap, and I called a cat nap, for a lot of reasons. When I woke, I discovered that I had missed a visit with Occam.

Mud said, "Mr. LaFleur and Occam brung—brought—your truck back." She added, "They was in a hurry and Occam said I wasn't to wake you since you was asleep. Should I have waked you up anyway?"

Disappointment scurried through me on little mouse feet, but I shoved it away. "No. It's all right. He knows his time limits. But the proper verb forms are, They *were* in a hurry and Occam said I wasn't to wake you since you *were* asleep."

Mud repeated me. "Townie English is hard. Can we look at the house plans?"

Carrying a tape measure, we walked through the entire upper floor, looking at the huge storage space at the top of the stairs that might become the bathroom, discussing where the fixtures would go if bathroom plumbing could be worked out. The upstairs was composed of multiple large spaces. There were two big bedrooms with low vaulted ceilings and dormers facing the front and the back of the house. On either end of the house, on the far sides of the bedrooms, were large, unfinished spaces, kept closed year-round, each with a dormer, both hotter than the armpits of hell. Currently, the unfinished space on the east side of the house held old furniture and antique chests full of John's family's belongings; the space on the west side was used for the solar batteries. It was a big house. It had been built for multiple wives and lots of children. With a little elbow grease, wallboard, paint, and added dormers, the rooms could become additional bedrooms. We were dreaming about spending a lot of my as-yet-unearned money, which made my belly ache just thinking about it. The unaccustomed stress of entering the modern world of debt was offset by the happiness of Mud possibly living with me.

Still dreaming, we stripped her bed and put on fresh sheets. Mud was stuffing a pillow into a pillowcase, her back to me, when she said, "Soooo . . . Mama met Occam."

I dropped onto her bed, rumpling the smooth summer bedspread. "What?"

"She likes him, even though he's a werecat." Mud shot me a playful look. "She done invited him to church on Sunday. She quoted scripture to him and he quoted some back. Didju'un know he was the son of a preacher?"

"Yes," I said softly. I'd heard Occam's story, or as much as he would tell. My family knew that Occam was a werecat, and Mama had seen Occam rubbing my arms, the claiming-type touching on the church grounds. My brain waffled back and forth in near panic. I wasn't a churchwoman anymore to be courted and claimed and treated like property by a man. But I wanted Occam. Mama would have kittens. That thought made everything inside me come to a screeching, flustered halt and I smiled. *Mama would have kittens.*

"Mama . . . *liiikes* him." Mud drew out the word.

That snapped me back to the conversation and Mud's laughing, knowing eyes. "Oh dear."

"Uh-huh. She likes him a lot. He knows the Bible. He called her ma'am and called Daddy sir. He was polite. And he kept Sam outta jail. Mama'll be matchmaking soon."

"Oh dear," I repeated.

"Him being a werecat ain't no problem, not when Mama's got love in her eyes."

I suddenly understood JoJo's actions the one time I'd seen her banging her head on her desk. "Ummm . . ." I started and floundered. I broke out into a sweat that had nothing to do with the temperature.

"And you like him too. I seen the way you look at him."

"I have seen, or I saw," I corrected, trying to figure out how to deflect this conversation.

"Right. Seen you looking at him like you like him. You gonna marry him?" Mud dropped onto her newly made bed and crossed her legs. She was wearing cotton pants and her hair was down, but her manner was all churchwoman in a matchmaking, gossiping mood. "I think the mamas would like it if you was married, even if it's to a townie, but I ain't sure about you being married to a cat-man."

"Oh dear." It sounded like a terrified moan. "Mud—"

"Have you'uns had sex yet?"

"Oh . . ." I flushed from my toes to the top of my red hair, though Mud wouldn't be able to see it, beneath my woody coloration. "No. Mud—"

"When you'uns have sex, will you have kittens? Or plant-babies? Seeds with cat faces and fur?"

I blinked. "You're teasing me."

Mud burst out laughing. "You shoulda seen your face." But then she went on, "That's okay. You ain't got to tell me. Mr. LaFleur said you'uns—you—shouldn't come in to work tonight 'lessen you feel like it. You going in to work?"

I was happy to have a break in the bombardment of questions about my romantic life and I could hear the restrained excitement in her voice. Mud liked it when she could camp out in PsyLED HQ while I did database research and paperwork, a temporary situation until I settled on child-care arrangements. "Maybe. Let's see how I feel after a shower and getting dressed. Maybe we could do some of your shopping on the way in."

Mud smiled, her face lighting up. "I'll clean up the lunch dishes. You shower." She was trying to sound blasé about the trip into town, but I knew that my sister had developed a love of shopping for store-bought clothes.

"Deal."

Before I could get to my feet Mud leaned across the mattress and threw her arms around me. "Thank you," she said, hugging me tight.

I patted her shoulders uncertainly. There was no blazing insight to her emotional state when we touched. But I was no longer accustomed to spontaneous displays of church-style affection, so I was still uncomfortable. "For what?" I asked.

"Thank you for not getting killed today. For not getting punished by Larry. For lettin' me live here. For letting me have a room all to *myself. Mine. My* space. Not shared with three or five true sibs and half sibs and—" She stopped. "And for making sure I get to learn. Get to go to school. Get to choose for myself who I'm gonna be. Get to not be burned at the stake if I grow leaves. For keeping me *safe*," she finished.

Tears prickled under my lids and I hugged her tightly back. Voice thick, I managed, "Sister mine, it is totally, completely, full-to-the-top, my pleasure." Gently I eased back so we could see each other, both of us teary eyed. "And you need a shower too. And use some of that deodorant I made us. As a woman grown, your body's starting to change and you need to change hygiene habits."

Mud's nose wrinkled up. "You'rn one to talk. Take a whiff of yourself."

In my best PsyLED accent, I said, "Duly noted."

I was dressed and we were ready to head to Walmart and Kohl's when I felt a vehicle turn onto my road and begin the climb up the mountain. At the same time, my phone dinged with a text from Margot Racer, special agent with the FBI. Mud read it aloud to me as she passed me the cell. " 'You home? Am in the neighborhood. On my way up your little mountain.' " Mud looked skeptical. "Is that a lie? About being in the neighborhood?"

"Most likely." I took the cell and texted back. *Come on up.*

"Is this about the cops and the dustup at the church this morning and you getting hurt?"

"Dustup. Yeah. And probably. The kidnapping of a federal law enforcement officer and raid on the church compound probably hit the news. And maybe she's heard about the witch circles and did some digging. Maybe she's responding to the report that KPD and the sheriff's department didn't share info with us about paranormal reports. Either way, this is official business, not tea and cookies."

Mud crossed her arms over her chest and her face took on a mulish expression, mouth firm, eyes narrowed. "I ain't going upstairs and twiddle my thumbs."

"Is this one of those lifestyle things we're working through?" I asked. "Like, how our living arrangements will work when I go into the field? Because if you think a social services worker will be okay with you being present during discussions about official police business, then let me tell you, you're wrong."

"I'm staying some nights at PsyLED HQ. That's full of police business."

"You'll be there while I'm doing paperwork, *not* in the middle of a debrief or with me in the field or at a crime scene—and only until I get child care worked out."

"I don't need no dagnab babysitter."

"We will talk later. Now scoot. Take your tablet upstairs and practice."

"This ain't fair."

"This *isn't* fair."

"That's what I said. Not fair." Mud snatched up her tablet and stomped up the stairs.

"Ha-ha," I muttered, grinding my teeth. I put my gobags together and started a half pot of coffee. Mud was twelve, a grown-up woman ready for marriage according to some in the church, but just entering her teenage years. God help me.

Margot walked up the steps to my porch. She was tall, lean, with broad shoulders and her hair buzzed short enough to see her scalp, a perfect do for the weather. I shoved my own red locks away from my sweaty face and dreamed of central air-conditioning. It had to be in the high nineties in the shade and nearly that inside the house, even with the window unit going full blast. Normal for late July.

I opened the door and studied her, even as Margot studied me back. She was wearing her badge and weapon in plain view. She might have implied that this was a friendly little chat, but she was on the job. That hurt my feelings, but I shoved it down inside and stepped back from the door. "Welcome to my home. Hospitality and safety while you're here." It was a God's Cloud of Glory greeting and promise. "Come on in."

Margot said, "I'm honored to accept your hospitality." That was one of the proper church responses and I tilted my head in surprise. "I'm one of the few special agents who've bothered to learn the proper responses for the church." She stepped inside. "Dang, girl, I thought you left that 'suffer for the sake of your soul' stuff behind. It's hot as hades in here."

"Mm-hm," I said. "Coffee?"

"Sure. Let's make the unholy hell of this furnace room hotter."

"I got ice cubes if you want."

"Iced coffee? That sounds like a little bit of heaven."

I led her to the kitchen and she leaned on the counter, seemingly content and comfortable in my home. I took a tray of ice cubes and felt her looking around, taking inventory. The first time a cop had done that I had accused him of wanting to steal my belongings. Now I knew that cops were just notoriously nosy.

"Where's your sister?" Margot had indeed been snooping.

I didn't answer and she said, "I can't see any court not wanting Mindy to live here. If you need a reference, I'll happily provide one."

A spurt of anger shot through me. The fact that Mud was living here off and on and I was trying to get custody of her wasn't widely known. Margot had been spying into my court records. "You been keeping better track of me and mine than is common even for cops," I said, maybe a mite too calm. "Want to tell me why?"

Margot stood and went to the wood-burning stove, inspecting it as if she had never seen one before. She held a hand over it as if testing to see if it was being used in the overheated house. She said, "You knew my secret. I expected you to out me and you didn't. I was curious."

I made a sound in the back of my throat that might have meant anything from agreement to a question. I could feel her eyes land on me, but went back to the task at hand, making iced coffee. I got out sugar and creamer. Found a pretty, hand-thrown mug with a soft greenish glaze. Tried to figure out how to temper it for hot and cold together. I didn't want to crack my mug. "I did tell my boss," I said. "Internal eyes only. If you have a problem or need help, you can ask and receive. Sugar and cream?"

Margot nodded slowly. "Both when it's iced."

I found an old Pyrex measuring cup in the pantry and dumped in cream and sugar, poured in the hot coffee. Stirred. Added the ice cubes, which made happy little crackling/popping sounds as they exploded under the change in temperature. Carefully, I transferred the mixture to the pretty mug, which did not crack or shatter. I gave the mug to my . . . guest.

Margot wandered some more, pausing to stroke Cello, who was lying across the back of the old couch. The cat sprang away and raced up the stairs. Margot sipped. "Word came to my SAC from high up in PsyLED that there've been black-magic witch circles in Knox County, circles not reported to PsyLED."

High up in PsyLED meant Soul or the new man, FireWind. "Oh?"

"She asked me to do a little digging. As you know, I keep a watch on everything witchy in the county for familial reasons, so I take a lot of work home. I didn't like what I discovered. Then you sent me a message. And then you got yourself abducted."

She was laying out a timeline for some reason, but I had no idea why. I had discovered that when someone made an incoherent interrogative sound, people kept talking. "Mm-mm?"

"I had a meeting with the sheriff earlier today. He was busy, but he made time for me." She meant that he was busy because of me, but made time for the FBI. It was a faint, professional dig. I didn't react and Margot went on. "Seems there's a young, para-hating detective who tried an end run around Unit Eighteen, not reporting magic and sacrifice. The sheriff called him into his office and took his badge, informing him and me that, pending an internal investigation, Detective Steff is on administrative leave. I don't expect the investigation to result in Steff being dismissed, but it does place a black mark on his record."

She tilted her nearly bald head to me and smiled. "FBI confiscated the detective's official and personal computers, laptops, and tablets." By her tone, I knew Margot meant she had done that in person. "I made copies of everything on external hard drives and transported the contents to PsyLED. Jones was overjoyed. That woman is a serious risk to PsyLED security, isn't she?"

I looked at Margot innocently. "Beg pardon?"

"Right." She didn't roll her eyes, but I knew I wasn't fooling her. In the church, her attitude would have been considered rude and antagonistic. In the world of law enforcement, it was just the way cops did things when they were fishing. "She was a known and respected force in the hacking world. That's no secret. It's also no secret that hacking is addictive to certain types of personalities."

I didn't know where Margot was going with this, but I was having trouble keeping innocence on my face and honesty in my heart. I was also truly impressed with the speed, breadth, and depth of her investigative work.

"If Jones happened to be drawn back into that world, she could be blackmailed, or her own hacking could expose her to other hackers who could then follow her trail back into PsyLED's electronic systems. And through PsyLED into other government systems."

A hollow place in my belly opened up, like a tunnel into darkness. The tunnel pathway Margot was drawing was scary.

"Last, but not least, if Jones gets caught dipping her toes into the hacking world, she can go to jail."

I thought about trees and Soulwood and managed to keep my face at least semitranquil. Was Margot still fishing? Did she know things? Or was this a threat against JoJo?

"Anyway," she said, "I downloaded everything into a dedicated system, so now she and I are on the same page as to the witch circles and the lack of reporting."

Her meaning sank into me. She wasn't going to tell on JoJo. Tension eased out of my body. "I thank you."

"You're welcome. I'd like to request liaison with PsyLED on the witch circle investigation. Do you think LaFleur or Soul would be willing to put in an official request?"

"I'm still a probie and just back from leave, so I don't know how much it'll help, but I can ask."

Margot grinned at me. "You're a troublemaker. I like troublemakers. We get things done way faster and more efficiently than the fence-sitters and scared-to-be-noticed agents."

"Troublemakers. Hmmm. I reckon we're talking about this morning now. How much do you know?"

"Girl, everybody in the state heard about this morning. You look pretty good for a woman with a concussion who refused to go to the hospital."

I gave her a hesitant smile and pointed to myself. "Not human. Hospitals can't help me."

"Because you're a one-off." I had heard Rick use that term and understood it in general, but didn't know how it applied to me. At my blank look she said, "A one-of-a-kind. As in, they broke the mold after they pulled you out."

I thought I might have heard a gasp from upstairs. Little Big Ears was listening. And Margot had figured out a lot about me. "Pretty much."

"Hmmm. You just told me an untruth, Nell Nicholson Ingram."

"Not really. I told you what I hope, not what I fear." Truth. No one in my family had grown leaves yet. So far as I knew. I hoped they never did. I feared they might.

"Okay. Copy that. Thanks for the coffee. Let me know when Unit Eighteen posts the liaison request so I can push it through." She walked by me and rinsed her coffee cup, placed it in the sink, and moved toward the door. Just as she reached it she called out, "You have any problem in public school, Mindy Nicholson, you let me know. I have friends in places both high and low."

"Thank you," Mud shouted.

Margot winked at me and went out the front door into the heat of the day.

We got to HQ near dark and, together, carted Mud's purchases up the steep stairs and dropped them in my cubicle. I refused to think about how much it cost to send a child to *free* public school, but I felt horrible for all the people who had multiple children and insufficient money. Mud started sticking her fingers into the soil of my plants. "When you get finished with the plants, check in with JoJo or Tandy," I said. "Then take your tablet back and read your books. Last time I looked you still had three books for summer reading."

"Finished 'em," Mud said absently. "So I started on the required reading for eighth grade. They talk a lot about sex."

"Oh." I studied her from the corners of my eyes. "Does that bother you?"

"Nope. I think people are silly when it comes to sex."

I wasn't sure what to say to that so I settled on, "You have a point." Leaving her at my desk, I went through the office, ostensibly searching for Rick LaFleur, but also looking for Occam, whose office cubicle was dark, though whether he was off work or on a case, I didn't know. I found Rick sitting at his desk, his face green in the light of his laptop. He looked twitchy, tense, and very tired. I tapped on the doorjamb. "Got a minute?"

He glanced up and back down at his screen. "Maybe one. I just approved a request from the feds to have Margot Racer liaise with us on the situation involving Sheriff's Detective Steff not following protocol. And since she managed to dig him out, I'm approving her request. We had a long conversation and I read her in on the circles, including my part in it. She wants to see all the circles ASAP and we need eyes on the ground, even though most of the circles are old and were worked up by the locals. You up for that?"

Margot had moved fast. So much for needing my input and my request. I wanted to read the ground at each of the witch circle sites for maggots, so yes, but I wasn't the most important PsyLED agent for that job. "Why isn't T. Laine going?"

"Kent is going out later with Tandy or Occam to do a full

workup. I want you with the feeb. Your best pal. Chat her up. Bond." Rick's eyes were on the screen, not on me, and I frowned, not sure what he thought I was supposed to do.

"Fine, but Mud is here. Is it okay to leave her?"

Rick looked up. "You're going to have to deal with child care. Soon. For now, make sure the weapons locker is secured." His dark eyes returned to his screen. "T. Laine is working late and Tandy will be in the office all night trying to get caught up on the missing reports and doing research on the similar witch circles here, and some more that Racer found and sent us. Seems as though there were similar circles down south and one in Asheville." A hint too casually, he added, "T. Laine will also be talking to the NOLA coven and the Asheville coven."

I put the locations together with Rick's personal history. The Asheville coven was predominately the Everhart coven. The Everharts were Jane Yellowrock's friends. Jane Yellowrock was the Dark Queen of the Mithrans and Rick's ex, and she had spent a lot of time in both New Orleans and Asheville. That explained why he seemed twitchier. "Okay. Interesting," I said. According to the rumor mill, things had ended badly for them on a dance floor (thanks to Paka) and then ended badly again in a permanent way while I was a tree. I didn't have an emotional context for Rick's life, though I'd been brought up to speed on the facts of the breakup. My question toneless, I asked, "Is Yellowrock involved?"

Rick stared at his laptop, his hair glowing black and silver in the screen lights. When he answered his tone was lifeless. "Not that I know."

I took a slow breath, fighting any kind of tentativeness. "Shall I find out?"

"If the case leads you to look for that information." He sat back in his chair and met my eyes, his skin lined and sallow. "Ingram, Jane and I ended months ago. I'm good. I am not, and I don't want to appear to be, stalking her. She has enough problems without having to worry about me. If you need to call her, call her. You don't have to run it by me. Copy?"

"Copy that," I said softly.

"And Nell?" A faint smile curved Rick's lips, making him

look younger and less sharp-edged. "Your official vehicle is on the way. I'll let you know when the delivery date is confirmed."

My mouth opened and closed. Opened again. "Oh. Thank you." I stood there a moment longer before spinning around and nearly skipping back to my cubicle to talk to Mud. I was getting a car! And Rick was sending me out in the field again. I was still a probie but not such a newbie that I was useless.

"Rick is an interesting man," Margot said.

I slanted my eyes at her. Margot was staring out the windshield at the night, hands light on the wheel, guiding her official vehicle. If you call a man who had been driven to the edge of insanity by kidnapping, torture, and his were-creature interesting. Strong, determined, gritty, and maybe a mite crazy might be better terms, wrapped up in a man carrying the magical equivalent of an incurable, infectious disease, but I didn't say that to the special agent, settling on, "Mm-hm."

"It's got to be heartbreaking to be a wereleopard and have no females around. Unless he and Occam are together."

I managed to hold in my yelp of shocked laughter. To give myself thinking time, I adjusted the air-conditioner vent. Then I readjusted it. The FBI had access to personnel files on PsyLED. There was no reason to suppose Margot hadn't simply gone through official channels to learn about us all, and no reason to suppose she had anything negative in mind for us. She was just nosy, and not very delicate about her nosiness. Or she had orders to chat me up, orders similar to my own. I couldn't think of a way to deflect her comments or ignore them, so I just put my head down and bulled through it. "That was a leading question, Special Agent Racer. And kinda personal to them both. Where's this going? Is the FBI collecting data on my team?"

"What? No." Margot shrugged, her wrists rising and falling on the wheel. "Rick's managed to make a life and move up in a federal agency despite his para state. He's got that bad-boy-tamed-and-suffering thing going, and he can't do anything about normal human desires now that the wereleopard

Paka is no longer part of your team, and missing in action. Neither can Occam and he was gorgeous before his accident. A regular vampire chick magnet."

Occam had me. The notion was just *there* in my brain, like being stabbed by a pitchfork, impaled on the thought. *Occam had me.*

And then several things hit me: Margot knew something about Paka, from the *missing in action* comment; some of her questions were personal on a sexual level; and some were professional law enforcement. They could also be construed as asking if Rick was a liability and security risk. Which he was. Which we all were, and which we never put into reports.

Except she'd said that Occam had been a vampire chick magnet.

I stuffed my reaction to the Occam part of her comments down deep inside for now, so I could concentrate on the other things. But I felt it there, under my skin all crawly. I couldn't lie to Margot and get away with it. I didn't know what to say to both protect my team and remind Margot that we knew the were-taint was contagious. "Ummm. Well. They aren't gay. They don't date each other, not that it's your business, Racer. And we have grindylows on-site to keep the populace safe, just in case anyone doesn't follow protocol to keep from spreading the were-taint."

"Prickly," she said of my tone. "And put in my place with pure truth. Okay." She sent me an amused look.

The crawly feeling under my skin got worse, but I pushed on. "Special Agent Racer, I'm sure that every single human on the planet is aware that were-taint is spread by blood sharing, saliva in cuts and bites, and sex. We know, and Rick knows, that any of the above means a death sentence for any were-creature who bites, or has sex with, someone who can contract the taint—and for his partner if the grindys decide so. He's careful." I wanted to add, *And alone,* but I didn't.

She brought the conversation back to the witch circles. "Site of the oldest Knoxville witch circle is just ahead. The circle was discovered by a local teen. It was fairly fresh at the time and I'm putting its tentative date of construction and activation just before the new moon, or waning sickle moon in May. The witch circle was cold and dead and there was no sacrifice present on the site when the circle was reported. There was also no blood when the deputies checked it out, though we have to consider the activity of scavengers carrying away any sacrifice and the spell itself taking away any blood. How close to the river are we?"

Back to business. A wave of relief flushed through me. Margot's hands tightened on the wheel, as if she felt my reaction. I said, "GPS says two hundred feet to the river. Then down a ways to the actual water."

Margot parked near a copse of trees and we got out, switched on flashlights, and started to the site, my gobag over my shoulder. There was nothing left of the circle except shallow trenches here and there. With a little imagination I could create a spoked circle out of them, but it was hard in the dark and with the passage of time and early summer rains. I had already calibrated the psy-meter 2.0 and done QC on it by reading everyone in the office. I laid my blanket on the ground and measured the circle's levels. There was nothing left of magic in the ground. But when I surreptitiously touched the soil with a fingertip, I got a hint of maggots. I didn't share that with Margot yet. Not until Rick gave me permission to read her in to everything.

Silent, I packed up and we went back to the car, where Margot marked her map with a green star. There were other stars, three now green, the rest yellow. She put the tablet down and started the car. "What kind of witch is doing the circles?"

"Our first thought was a single moon witch sitting at north, but T. Laine pointed out that moon witches always practice their workings at the three days of the full moon, to make better use of the moon's entire power, so we changed it to a water witch working alone because of the river locations. Looking over your shoulder at the map of the witch circles—those stars are the witch circles, aren't they?" I interrupted myself.

Margot nodded.

"Then I'd say we have a water witch. We're not ruling out a second witch. We're not even ruling out a moon witch." I frowned. "We're not ruling out anything at this point."

"I think that's wise. So maybe two witches," Margot said. "Or a single really powerful witch who has a secondary affinity for the moon. Or . . . I hate guessing." She started the car and we motored on to the next-closest site. And then the next. By midnight we had visited five sites and I had tested each with the psy-meter and a fingertip. I felt maggots at almost all the sites and magic at one—levels one and four. Vampires were part of this—whatever this was. Or maybe even witch-vamps. Was the witch also a vampire? I had a lot to talk about to the team, and since Margot was driving, I typed out the bones of an outline for a report. Ninety-nine percent of my job was paperwork. I had always been good at it and I was getting better.

We brought hot Krispy Kreme donuts back to HQ, where I found my sister watching a horror movie on the biggest screen in the conference room, sitting with Tandy, earbuds in her ears. Mud's eyes were wide and her knees were drawn up under her chin. When she saw me she pointed at the screen and shouted, "*Aliens!* There's such a thing as *aliens!*"

I was surprised that Tandy would watch a horror film, but he seemed fine with Mud's emotion. He paused the film and Mud tugged out her earbuds. I said, "You had to start her out with *Aliens*? Why not *Attack of the Killer Tomatoes* or *Snakes on a Plane*?"

"*Creature from the Black Lagoon*," Margot suggested, sliding the donut box across the large table and plopping her gobag onto a chair. "*Killer Clowns from Outer Space*."

Mud's eyes went wider than I had ever seen them. "Really? Clowns are from space?"

"No. Not really," I said severely. "These are movies, not reality. And my coworker—the empath—should have known better."

"The empath"—he pointed at himself—"did know exactly what she needed to see. Something horrific that could be overcome. But no clowns. Never clowns."

"Wimp. Scaredy-cat," T. Laine said, coming back into the office.

"The weres may be scaredy-cats," Tandy said. "I am not."

"Right," Margot said. "The weres. I need to use the ladies' and stuff a few things in a locker. Who do I see about getting one?"

"Pick a locker with no lock and nothing inside," T. Laine

said. "Locker room is near the stairs you just came up. Sign on it says 'Locker Room.'"

"Har-har." Margot picked up her gear and headed back the way we came.

I pointed to the earbuds and Mud put them back in. The movie restarted. Quickly I updated them, saying softly, "Circles were all constructed in the waning moon. Maggots were at half of the sites. Vamps and witch are absolutely working together."

T. Laine asked, "Any reason why we're not telling our new feeb?"

I didn't know why I hadn't told Margot about the maggots. But . . . she had indicated a strange interest in Occam and Rick and the werecats' sexual habits. It had felt oddly predatory and had aroused a protective instinct in me. I glanced at Mud, who was staring at the big screen as an alien burst out of a stomach cavity in an explosion of blood and goo. "No real reason," I hedged.

Tandy looked at Mud and stood, stretching. "Come on, Mud," he said, pausing the film. "I have a window that needs a window box with herbs. You can give me some suggestions. Then I think your sister will say it's your bedtime."

They left together. To our resident witch, I quickly detailed Margot's odd interest in the werecats and shared her specific questions about Rick and Occam. T. Laine listened with narrowed eyes and a deep-rooted sense of suspicion. Then I added a few more details on the maggots, vamps, sacrifices, and the witch circles.

T. Laine said, "Noted. While you were gone, I think I put the runes together with the different sacrifices. The working where the white rats died had a single rune in an inner, tiny circle just big enough for the rats and the rune. Nauthiz. This one was the only rune not reversed. Nauthiz symbolizes distress, confusion, conflict, and the power of will and magic to overcome them. It's both a recognition of one's fate and an indication of self-initiated change. I think she's using this circle to heal herself from something painful at the same time that she's getting revenge. Or more clearly, using the revenge to heal herself."

"Okay," I said, glancing up the hallway. "What about the ones with the black cats?"

"They have Nauthiz merkstave, or upside down. That's the curse part, intended to constrain freedom, bring distress and hard work that results in nothing. It's intended for the recipient of the curse to feel deprivation, starvation, poverty, and extreme emotional emptiness and hunger. I think the spells start off without a cat in the middle and actually call black cats to the site to be used as sacrifice. If that's so, then maybe Rick got caught in a calling. He's experiencing some behavior changes that coincide with the black cat circles, but that doesn't mean he's the intended recipient. Or maybe I'm just in denial. I admit I'm guessing at a lot of it." I didn't reply and she went on. "It could be a kid trying to kill her bullies, or get back at an ex boyfriend. Maybe someone hates a football team that has a black cat for a mascot. It could be anything."

"Let's say you're right and Rick isn't the intended victim. What would happen if the witch caught Rick? Would Rick become the sacrificial victim?" I asked.

"I don't know. And that scares me, which is why I've recommended that he play that infernal woodwind music twenty-four/seven."

"Hard to do," I said, "in a restaurant, in the shower, in meetings with the powers that be."

"JoJo has requested a newfangled earbud that will work directly off his cell. Top-of-the-line Spook School device."

"And Occam?" I asked.

"Occam is a spotted cat. He hasn't been called. Either he isn't as susceptible to the working or the curse, or spotted cats weren't summoned. I'll send a note to have him play the anti-shape-changing music just in case. Have you had a chance to talk to Rick about his tats?"

Margot came down the hallway and she had obviously heard the question. I stuffed a donut into my mouth and busied myself making coffee. I don't think I fooled Margot at all.

The clock read two a.m. I pushed away from my desk in my cubicle and went to the sleep room. I had confiscated Mud's tablet when I put her on the mattress in the back room where agents crashed when we were working twenty-plus-hour days. She was asleep, curled around a small clay pot of basil. Some girls would curl around a doll or stuffed animal. My sister chose a plant. I smiled in the dark and tiptoed toward the conference room.

T. Laine looked up from her laptop as I entered. I carried the old pot of coffee dregs to the break room and poured out the sludge before starting a new pot. No one had ever said that pots were to be started by the newest person in a room; it was more an unwritten rule.

As I worked T. Laine said, "I'm worried. Or may be worried. Might be."

"Okay." I added grounds and said, "You want to brainstorm?"

"Now that Margot's gone, yes."

I glanced at the unit's witch, curiosity in my expression. "Oh?"

"Yeah. You aren't the only one with odd feelings about the special agent. Tandy is getting something too. There's something she hasn't said. It's possible that she's here in order to get info on Unit Eighteen, maybe because we took down the Knoxville FBI director. Or because we discovered the devil dogs that they all missed. All that must have left a bad taste in the mouths of the local feebs."

"Or we're all paranoid," I said. "But I sent you a report on the things she talked about on the drive tonight."

"I got it. That was screwy," T. Laine said. "Rick's problem with his cat is incredibly complicated magic-wise and it started long before he got the were-taint, back when the tattoo spell was first applied. Vampire blood was inserted under his skin as part of the spells. Cat blood too. The torture he experienced then and when he was a prisoner of the werewolf pack and they were trying to gnaw off the tats may have changed them. All the choices he made under duress and undercover may have changed things. Acquiring were-taint affected all the existing magic in his flesh. And then Paka's magic and the times she tried to force him to shift into his cat. The magic in his flesh is fu—*messed* up."

"That makes sense," I said as I rinsed out my metal cup painted with leaves, ignoring her almost cussing.

"I sent hand drawings of the circles with the runes, the rats, and the black cat in them to three covens right away. They all called me back and told me not to contact them again."

"That's . . . strange?" I asked.

"That's what has me worried. An hour ago, the local witch coven messengered over a charm they say might help protect Rick, but they refuse other help. They say something evil is brewing in Knoxville and they're battening down the hatches. They invited me to come hunker down with them." T. Laine stared across the table at me, her eyes a deeper brown with worry. "When witches run, that's a very bad sign."

Mouth dry, I asked, "What do you think they're running from?" A chill raced through me, dread shaped by a childhood full of dark tales of evil things that attack people.

"I don't know, but yeah. Something big. I've sent word to Soul and FireWind, and LaFleur. For now, they're using the meetings in town at FBI headquarters as a way to get all the agencies up to speed and ready to lock everything down."

"Why does magical crazy stuff keep happening here?" Was it my fault? I had changed things, fighting a magic creature who flung energy around and skipped off the magma deep in the earth. Our battle had bounced energy into the ley lines. That easily qualified as a "disturbance in the force." There had been so much energy pumped through the liminal system it was possible that I had opened a path and made a weak spot for the magma to push up through. The salamanders—who had likely been using hot springs as an entry way—had found an easier way up through the magma, and had used it to their own purposes.

I started to say all this, but T. Laine spoke first.

"Honestly? I'm afraid it's still all tied into something happening in Secret City. Maybe something else is being tested, something we haven't found yet. Maybe something that's a mixture of tech and magic again, or more spells gone bad. LaFleur looked into it. I looked into it. But no one is admitting anything."

I thought about my land and the church. People I loved. "Is this—?" I stopped.

"Public? No. Not yet. You want to know if you can call your family and warn them that something's coming. No."

"Oh."

T. Laine looked at me hard. "You call them, what are they going to do, Nell? Go hide in the caves on church land? What if something is reaching toward Knoxville and is coming through local cave systems?"

They could pray, I thought.

"So keep the info to yourself." She looked back at her screens. "The charm for Rick got here just a bit ago. It's an onyx amulet in the shape of a black cat, spelled for protection. It passed my examination. It's safe and it might help. Who knows?"

"That's why you're working after hours, isn't it? To make sure Rick gets the amulet."

"Yeah. And I hope it's enough."

SEVEN

An hour later we got a call on the official line, which came over the speakers in the conference room. It was Rick. And he was growling.

"Rick?" T. Laine said, startled.

"Grindy with . . . In trouble." His next words were garbled and Tandy appeared in the doorway, his eyes wide and skin too dull, as if all the blood had left his flesh and coagulated in his core.

". . . driving. Close now . . . Null . . . ," he growled, the sound less human. "Open . . . doors . . ."

"LaFleur," Lainie demanded.

"Rick's near here. He's in trouble," Tandy whispered.

" 'Open doors,' " I repeated. "He wants us to open the outer doors. The grindy is with him so he's a danger to humans. His cat's trying to shift."

"Null room. Move!" T. Laine said.

Tandy and I raced down the hallway. Tandy grabbed up a chair and I took my service weapon in one hand and a potted plant in the other. T. Laine shoved the null room door open behind us, activating the strongest antimagic we could access. She locked it in place, groaning in pain as the null magic that stopped magical workings washed over her. She stumbled back to the conference room. Rick's antishift music blasted over the speakers.

I blocked open the stairwell door at the top with the pot. Tandy raced downstairs and into the night, blocking the outer door open with the chair. He was going to wait on Rick outside. Dangerous. Very dangerous.

I placed myself in front of Mud's room and drew my

weapon. If I had to shoot my boss to protect my sister I would. The enormity of having her here while I worked fell on me like an avalanche. Saving her from my family had put her in danger. Mud couldn't stay here.

I heard the sound of a car stopping, tires screeching. A door opening but not closing.

Rick hissed. I heard him stumble at the entrance and I looked down the stairs. My boss's body was silhouetted in the entrance, his shoulders hunched, only his hands visible where they gripped the metal doorjamb. They were covered in black hair, fingertips clawed and gouging into the paint. He was caught in a partial shift, fighting it. This wasn't a full moon shift, but Rick wasn't shifting by choice. This had to be the result of being called to a witch circle.

"Hurry," Rick growled. "Hurry. Null . . . room. Now." But his feet didn't move. He was caught in a stasis of misery in the outer doorway, panting in pain, fighting what was happening.

Tandy said something, his voice soft. Soothing. I could help him to pacify Rick. I slipped off my shoe and touched a toe to the potted plant I had brought to hold open the door. Tentatively, I reached for Soulwood, drawing its calm to me. I had claimed Rick for my land to save his life, and I sought that part of him. Pressed Soulwood's peace into him. He gasped. Looked up the stairs at me. His eyes were glowing green. His shoulders writhed and the hunched shape resolved into a neon green grindylow. Her claws were out too and they were pressed against Rick's throat. Because Tandy was right there. In danger.

Grabbing my shoe, I backed away as Rick started up the stairs, his movements unexpectedly lithe and supple, graceful as a cat in the night. He moved up, step by step, his silver hair glistening in the overheads. He reached the top of the stairs and started toward the null room just ahead.

From the stairway entrance a woman emerged. Margot. She was following Rick.

As if he was stepping into hell, my boss stepped inside the null door. T. Laine tossed me something on a chain and said, "Inside with him." I caught the thing—dark stone, hanging on a leather thong—and tossed it inside the null room to the floor. It skittered across the room and when it stopped spinning, I saw it was a carved stone black cat. The amulet sent by the local witches. We hadn't tested it. We didn't know what it did. Rick whirled to me, claws at his fingertips. I shoved the door shut. Through the layers of steel, I heard Rick scream. I slid on my shoe and turned to the woman who had followed him.

Margot was dressed in jeans and a tank, her dark skin glistening with a faint sheen. Her eyes were heavily made up with black liner and mascara; she looked fabulous and . . . sexy. As if she was on a date, or wanted to be. Had she been with Rick when he was spell-called? She wore earrings and a necklace with an unpolished moonstone on it. The stone was carved in the rough likeness of a sleeping cat and . . . it was glowing. A moonstone. A magical amulet. And she was still following Rick. I put my body in front of the null room door to stop her.

T. Laine said, "What the hell." She practically flew down the hall, throwing out her hand. A wallop of magic slapped Margot into a corner and Lainie was on her. Our witch lifted the necklace from the feeb's neck. "What are you doing wearing a magical cat amulet?"

"It's not magical. And get your hands off it. And off me."

"It is magical. I feel the working in it." T. Laine dropped the cat and backed away. "Forgive me if I say so, Special Agent Racer, but your appearance here when LaFleur is caught in a calling/curse working by a black-magic witch, while wearing a magical amulet in the shape of a cat, is disturbing and too coincidental to be ignored."

"It. Isn't. Magic," she pronounced, her voice a snarl. "You can grill me later. For now, I can help LaFleur."

"No."

"I was helping him all the way here," she said. "I can help now."

"Is she a witch?" T. Laine asked. "She isn't in my database."

I hadn't included Margot's family line in my official report, only the report to Rick. I sighed out the words, "No. Not exactly."

Margot's head came up and her dark eyes bored into me. "You said you hadn't included it in your report, but I got a jolt of untruth from you. I assumed you were prevaricating."

"No. I told Rick verbally. We kept it out of the reports for your privacy, because I didn't know how it fit in your personnel records."

"Damn," she huffed. For an FBI agent, Margot had very expressive eyes, and I could see things passing through their depths. "Cat's out of the bag now, pardon the pun." She met T. Laine's accusing gaze. "The only witch in the family was my grandmother. My mother has some minor talent."

"And you?" T. Laine asked.

"I can tell when people are lying."

Tandy said gently, "She believes what she's saying."

"The child of a witch family didn't know she was wearing a renewable amulet?"

"Not—" Margot stopped, one hand sliding around the charm, her face going through an even faster series of thoughts and emotions. "My grandmother was a lapidary. She gave me this in her will. She gave me dozens. I didn't know."

"True," Tandy said. "But you still haven't addressed the rest of it."

She took off the necklace and gripped it in a fist. "I called Rick to ask about the circles." She leaned in and glared at us all. "He answered from Bistro at the Bijou, where he was replacing the band's sax player. Last-minute gig. It sounded like fun, so my date and I decided to eat there and take in the show."

Rick played saxophone? Had I known that? "Date?" I said.

"I ditched him when Rick took off like a cat with his tail on fire. I followed and talked Rick down from driving away *and* from shifting. I put his music on despite the fact that it was *awful* to listen to." She swallowed and forced back what looked like fury and helplessness. "I helped him stay human, per his request, but he was in a lot of pain. Pain *caused by illegal and immoral use of magic*." She stopped and took a deep breath, running a hand over her nearly bald head. It was a strangely masculine gesture and it looked exasperated and confused. She was giving a lot away. Or she was becoming an empath, which I had once thought about her. Or she was a really good actor. "He was being spelled." Her glare deepened. "Not. On. *My*. Watch. No one suffers from black magic on *my* watch. You understand?" she demanded. "I drove him here. In pain. And now I'm responsible for helping him through the rest of it."

"What happened to the date?" I asked, because while it made sense, it was also too coincidental to be real.

"Gah!" she screamed in frustration, throwing back her head. "You people! My date came after me and found me sitting in the car with LaFleur, holding his hand, talking him down. Stupid man got pissed and took off without me. I have a feeling that relationship is over before it ever got started."

T. Laine frowned but backed down the hallway with Margot following, as if the feeb was about to attack her. Margot glanced at the door behind me as she passed, seeing the words *Null Room* on it. "Damn," she cussed again. "That's why he wanted to come here."

In the conference room T. Laine opened a mic into the null room. "Rick. Talk to me. You still human?"

"Yes," he said, his voice gravelly. "But, God. It's bad."

Her hand hovered over the camera controls, but she left them off. "There's an amulet in there, sent by the local coven. Hold it. Better?"

"Maybe . . . a little. Yeah. Turn up the music."

T. Laine turned off the antishift music in the rest of HQ but increased the volume in the null room. "How can a summoning spell reach him through the null room?"

No one replied.

"Put your hand on the speaker," she directed Rick. "The music magic should work on you even there."

We heard stumbling through the system, perhaps the sound of a chair turning over. Then Rick groaned out a note of relief.

Margot cocked her head and muttered, "That's why he was playing that awful music." She leaned over the table and said into the mic, "Hey, LaFleur. Stop being such a pussy."

I stepped back in surprise at the crudity. Rick laughed, the sound shocked but less pained and more human.

"Don't ask me to feel sorry for you," she said into the mic, as she took a seat. "Injuries are part of the job."

"True dat," Rick said, a New Orleans cadence strong in his pain.

"But since I have you as a captive—pardon the pun—

audience, I'll finish the update and debrief your unit. I've been going over NCIC files looking for spell/animal-sacrifice sites and crimes and tracking them back for twenty-four months. You were right. Some found in Louisiana eighteen to twenty-four months ago."

"Year and a half?" T. Laine said. "Two years? Rick was in NOLA then."

"Yes. And the circles look odd," Margot said. "I sent photos of the Louisiana ones to the coven leader of NOLA, Lachish Dutillet. She says that some of the early ones look like summoning workings, the kind lonely women do to call a man to their side, except more. More intricate and more vicious, a summoning combined with a curse. It's peculiar."

"You know Lachish?" T. Laine asked.

"Not personally," Margot said. "But her grandmother knew my grandmother. She's been helpful. So I know stuff. Like despite the fact that Lachish is scared spitless of this circle, not that she said so. You still with us, LaFleur?"

"Yeah. Tell me more," Rick said, his voice breathy and harsh. "Cuss a lot. Be callous. I'll try not to be such a wimp."

"Good. Nothing worse than a whiny-ass man. Survive childbirth and then tell me about pain."

"You had a baby?" Rick asked.

"Yeah. I was sixteen. Baby didn't make it."

"That's terrible." Rick stopped. "I'm sorry."

"Me too. So, if someone will get my laptop out of Rick's car, I can sync my system with yours and we can update data." Which would give Margot Racer complete access to all our files. Not what we had planned.

Rick, sounding more like himself, asked, "Why did the FBI want a liaison on this case? A case with no crime and no victim except me? And that might be accidental."

"I don't think it's accidental," Margot said. "The bureau wanted what I wanted—to get me on the inside of PsyLED. Except they want info on the paras you keep track of. I want access to your people to keep paras safe." Like her witchy family.

No one spoke or moved, and finally Tandy said, "I'll get the laptop." Which meant the empath had just approved of Margot Racer and her motivations for liaising with PsyLED.

And just that fast, Special Agent Racer's transition to a provisional part of the team was complete. We wouldn't trust her with everything, but we wouldn't treat her like a potential enemy either.

"What about demon summoning as the motivation for the circles?" Rick asked. "I've seen two demons, one that was willingly working with a black-witch and eating her friends, and one that had been summoned in concentric *hedge of thorns* workings, trapped in a reversed *hedge*, and was eating the sacrifices."

"That had to suck. None of the circles I've seen have centered, reversed *hedge of thorns*," Margot said, "and no halfway competent witch would summon a demon into a circle with her. The demon would eat her, use her blood and body to disrupt the circle and get free. Waste of time and good protein."

Rick made a chuffing cat sound of laughter, probably at the waste-of-protein comment.

T. Laine said, "I'm going to try and scry for a witch circle or a magical working. See if I can spot the calling. I'll be outside."

"Take your weapon," Tandy said. "Keep comms open."

"Yeah, yeah," she said, waving the words at us. "Roger that."

I had heard only bits and pieces about the cases Rick described and went back to my cubicle to research it all, still not satisfied. But Tandy was the motivational and emotional gatekeeper of the unit and he approved of the special agent, so my misgivings weren't significant.

I pulled up the reports Margot had compiled and studied the witch circles in Louisiana as well as here. Some of the early circles overlapped with Rick's travel itinerary. Margot hypothesized that the caster had been tracking and calling Rick specifically. Rick had been the PsyLED special agent in charge of the Southeast region—five states—for less than a year, with Knoxville as his home base. Before that he was working as a detective with NOPD, and even before that, he'd been undercover with NOPD. His itinerary up on my laptop, I compared the circles with Rick's whereabouts. Some matched. Some didn't. But *something* had happened to Rick tonight. It was the waning moon. If someone was trying to call Rick—specifically call Rick, not a coincidence—to use him in a sacrifice or to harm him, that made this a crime against a federal agent. That made this an investigation, not just an inquiry.

I added Margot's research to mine and, using her search parameters and language, broadened my own search pattern much further back. I found a witch circle in New York State, near a small town called Aurora, on the bank of Cayuga Lake. This one was from over five years ago, and though it had no runes, it had an odd, six-sectioned wheel-spoke form, no dead animal in the center. In a report from six months later, I found another circle documented on the same lake but farther south, close to Ithaca, centered with a single rune. Nauthiz. In Arizona, where Margot had found one witch circle in the desert, I discovered another one on the bank of the Salt River, near Apache Lake Marina and Resort. It was the oldest one yet, the circle smaller, no runes at all, and only a cross pattern instead of the twelve spaced spokes. But there was a dead rattlesnake coiled in the center.

Rick had been nowhere near New York or Arizona on the dates the circles were found. He had never worked or lived in either state.

I thought it unlikely that Nauthiz and the odd circles would be coincidental with the circles found here, though I couldn't prove it, and the distance between all the places suggested it was different witches or witch factions. Maybe several witches, all members of different covens. Or isolated witches with no covens nearby. Or outcasts, banned from their covens for doing evil, who met on the Internet. That sounded possible. Likely even. Did covens have Internet gossip boards or pages? Would word of outcasts have made it out of the covens and into witch gossip? What if a cadre of black-magic witches, keeping in touch over the Internet, were trying to refine a spell of some kind? That made even better sense. There was nothing to tie the early circles to Rick. He wasn't summoned then. Everything about this summoning seemed coincidental. But I kept working on the case/inquiry, just in case. I sent a note to T. Laine asking all my spell-type, coven-type questions and turned my attention to more mundane possibilities.

Over the years, Rick had arrested or been involved with the

arrests of seventy-four people. Of that number, some were witches, one was a vampire down in New Orleans. Then there were the werewolves who had died or who were in permanent custody in silver cages because of him. Large numbers of *gwyllgi*—devil dogs—had died here in Knoxville, and the rest had been shipped out. Maybe we had missed some? All the recent cases involving paranormals had been high profile, and Rick was quickly becoming a high-profile para in Knoxville law enforcement. He had enemies who might pay a witch for revenge. Maybe a witch had honed a curse spell and was selling it?

I expanded my criteria. On the personal side, Unit Eighteen needed to talk to old girlfriends, like Jane Yellowrock and Paka, and recent enemies, like members of the Party of African Weres and the president of the International Association of Weres, Raymond Micheika. Rick and Jane Yellowrock had made a lot of people mad while I was busy being a tree, and Jane had instigated legal action to keep Raymond out of the United States. The Dark Queen had taken possession of some African were-lion cubs when the pride alphas died. She hadn't given them back to Micheika.

Rick was, in effect, the second-ranking were-creature in the country, both as Jane's beta and by being a part of Clan Yellowrock. He had come to that position in the Party of African Weres through some arcane machinations by Jane. What any of us knew about that situation was limited, and there was nothing in the databases detailing how his promotion came about. Rick was also chief cat over a leap of black were-leopards somewhere in Africa. Rick was, or could be, politically powerful. His cat was cat-dominance-powerful.

But . . .

I stopped. My thoughts were treading off in a dangerous direction. I had an in with Jane's business partners. Admittedly, I hadn't talked to them in a long time, seeing as how trees were seldom verbal. Instead of a phone call, I sent a text to Yellowrock Securities. That seemed easier, though it may have been social reluctance, aka cowardice.

I hauled my thoughts back to things I could delve into tonight—all those situations and cases. They made Rick a target to bad guys and government spooks alike. In one criminal

investigation recently, there had been indications that someone in the CIA had been passing along classified info to a
para-hating homegrown terrorist group. He or she had to be
high up, maybe an overseer, as no busywork agent would have
had access to all the info. The responsible person or people at
the CIA had never been identified, and so they were still out
there, and they might still be unhappy with Rick and other
paras guarding Secret City. But since hunting federal agents
would require a higher security clearance than a probie had, I
passed the overseer concept up to JoJo, who could use her
hacking skills to find out more than I could. I'd have to concentrate on criminals.

A short time later I had lists for all the people Rick had
arrested, human and otherwise: either out on bail, on parole,
still incarcerated, or having served their full sentences and
released from incarceration. Most were easy to locate and I
started a search to verify the location of each one. I made a
call to find that the witches were still being held in witch
jail—null rooms run by witches. They were accounted for. I
made a note for JoJo to check out the vampire. A significant
number of the case notes on the Mithran were redacted, showing that even this was over my pay grade.

I needed to also consider any NOLA and local vampires
Rick might have irritated.

There were hints that Rick was related to a very important
vampire Blood Master, perhaps Katie Fonteneau, the Master
of the City of Atlanta. Katie's enemies might be Rick's enemies, and if the circles were indeed targeting Rick, that would
go a long way to explaining the maggoty feeling at the circles.
But all I had so far were questions and not very good questions
either. I kept coming back to Tandy's suggestion that I talk to
Rick.

I tracked the waning arc of the moon on a lunar calendar
on the Internet. It wouldn't set until afternoon but Rick was no
longer in pain, and back in his office. Margot was in the break
room. It was as if the episode in the dark of the night had never
happened. But I still remembered the pained moans of my
boss as a spell reached him. In the null room. Where no spell
should reach. Ever.

I was finished at five, before sunrise, and I could have left, but I didn't, pecking out my summation report, blaming my dawdling on not wanting to wake Mud. But I knew that I was waiting for the day shift to arrive. Occam in particular, since I was determined to be honest with myself. I didn't have anything to tell him, but I just wanted to . . . see him. It was an attitude I'd noted in the church while growing up, women or men loitering in a place they had no real reason to be, until someone else showed up. It was courting behavior. I wasn't sure I liked seeing that emotionally needy part of myself, but there it was. I was waiting on Occam.

Minutes ticked by, the sky graying. I watched as Margot and Rick left. Together. Of course, Margot didn't have a car here, having arrived with Rick, so maybe that made sense. A grindy sat on Rick's shoulder, the neon green cute-as-a-button killer nuzzling his shoulder. The boss looked tired, dark circles under his eyes, sweat stains on his shirt, and his hair hanging lank. Fighting turning had been hard on him. Being in the null room was hard too, the antimagic in the walls twisting all other magic into knots and making it unworkable— except for the summoning that had been trying to force him into his cat. If not for the music spell, Rick would have gone catty and fled.

T. Laine leaned out and watched as they left, coming to my cubicle as they disappeared and the door to the stairway closed. "What do you think, Nell?" she asked. "Can Rick restrain himself with a woman? I'd hate to be called to a scene to find my boss naked and dead at the claws of a grindylow and Margot bitten."

"He never bit Jane and they dated for a while even after he was turned."

Occam walked up the stairs and closed the door. "Somebody want to tell me what's going on? I just passed Rick and he stank of moon magic. And Margot is all over him." He was holding two paper cups of gourmet coffee from Coffee's On, the scent strong, and he placed one on my desk. It had my name on it. "Your usual," he muttered, his eyes on Rick and Margot on the parking lot camera screen. T. Laine looked at me with a *You go, girl* expression and I ducked my head.

Occam's cell dinged and he glanced at the screen. His face

blanched and he walked away, fast. T. Laine said, "That was rude. And weird."

Yes. It was. It almost looked like guilt. "See you later," I said and slipped past our witch and down the hallway to the sleeping room. I woke my sister and drove us home. Mud never truly woke, and I was tired down to my bones. But as we bumped over the entrance of the drive, I spotted a stack of very large boxes on the front porch. Boxes that hadn't been there when we left. "Stay here," I said to Mud. She woke up fast, reaching for the door handle. "No. Stay here. Keep down."

I slid from the truck cab and drew my weapon. Moved around the house to check the back door, which was secure, and the small locked shed, also secure. Carefully I eased back around front and climbed the steps, halfway to the porch. The front door was still secure, no indication of breaking and entering. The windows were all intact. The boxes appeared to have packing slips on them and were securely taped shut. But I had felt no one walk onto my land.

I moved down and back to the truck, holstered my weapon, and grabbed my one-day gobag from the truck cab. Searched through it.

"What is it?" Mud asked. "Is it a body in a box? Is there blood all over it?" Curiosity and desire to take part in whatever was happening practically vibrated the air around her.

"No body. No blood, Mud. Stay put a bit longer, though."

"But—"

"Stay put." I climbed the steps. Removed the pocket-sized psy-meter 1.0 from my gobag. I hadn't looked at it in forever, but it still had a charge. I crouched, so I could inspect the boxes.

Now that I was close enough, I saw that two of the large boxes were clearly marked as solar panels. A smaller one was marked as a battery, one designed to make the best use of captured but unused solar energy. The markings on the other boxes were less obvious, except for the one marked as an 18,000 BTU window-unit air conditioner and heater, suitable for a thousand square feet of space. Strangely, they were all brands I used and was familiar with, but I hadn't ordered them.

I eased closer and saw my name and address on the boxes. The packaging slips looked real. This was neither a bomb nor a mistaken delivery. I holstered my weapon, feeling a little foolish, but I wasn't used to getting packages. Then it hit me.

Someone who knew me well—Sam? Daddy? Occam?—had ordered all this stuff for me. That someone had taken over my decision-making power and done what Occam might call an end run around me.

I heard the truck door open and shut softly.

Mud said, "Oh. Ummm. It came early."

I swiveled on the balls of my feet to see Mud on the steps. She was wearing her new jeans, a T-shirt, and sneakers, her hair down in a long tail and her tablet clutched in her hand. Her face wore an expression that was defiance with a little bit of guilt. "Came early?" I asked.

The defiance grew stronger. "Daddy told me he'd give me a dowry as good as yours when I got married or the cash now. He said I could use it for school or my wedding or however I wanted. I ain't planning on a wedding and I can get financial aid at school, so I took the cash now."

"I didn't get—" I stopped. John had never told me there had been a dowry. But then, I had never asked. Seems that my daddy and my husband had handled things without the input of the daughter and wife, just like the churchmen always had, which should make me mad now that I knew it. But Daddy had let Mud make her own decision like a woman grown, so maybe Daddy had changed.

"I done all this behind your'n back, before we had that negotiation about working together." She hunched her shoulders and hugged the tablet to her chest. "I seen where—I saw where you kept the papers on the brands and the models. Sam helped me order 'em online and I talked to your friend Brother Thad at Rankin Replacements and Repairs about the cost to put them in. It was supposed to be a surprise. But if'n I'm honest, it was also to get my way. Since we talked I been scared to tell you."

I stood and studied the stack of boxes, remembering Thad's hesitation when he talked about my solar array. "Well. Did Brother Thad give you a ballpark figure for installation?"

"He said he'd talk to you about it, but it'd be in range with the last upgrade. You ain't mad?"

"If you had to do it over again would you talk to me about it first?"

"Yep."

I shifted my eyes to my younger sister. "This must have cost several thousand dollars. Where did Daddy get that much money? He doesn't even own his own land."

"Six thousand, seven hundred dollars and forty-six cents after taxes and shipping and handling. And Daddy's got money. The church sets up commercial greenhouses and windmill pumps for cattle and horses. Your'n windmill is a church product. They used to make a fortune growing and harvesting trees for the paper mill industry. That income stream started dying 'bout twenty years ago, but wood still brings in some cash. Daddy's got investments. Mosta the churchmen got investments. And useta be, there was all the money the mamas brung in."

"What did you say?" I asked, startled. "The money the mamas bring in?"

"The mamas," she said, as if I was stupid. I just looked at her, confused. "The state put an end to their moneymaking after the raid. The one where them vampire hunters done come across your land."

"What money?" I stood, feeling the sweat trickling down my spine.

"They's poor and unmarried and they useta get medical care from the state and money each month for each young'un. It ain't that much per young'un, but they gots lots of them. Daddy useta put some a that money aside each month in an account for college and for dowry."

"Daddy and the mamas—" I stopped cold. That was why none of them had been legally married to Daddy until recently. They spent decades complaining about the government interfering in their lifestyle and they had been taking money from the state? I was pretty sure that was welfare fraud. "Used to take money?"

"The social services people put a stop to it after they raided the church," Mud said, matter-of-factly.

That meant I had been indirectly responsible for the

church's loss of income when I let the raid start from across my land. Another reason for the church to hate me. Like a hammer of doom, all the personal implications hit me. I hadn't been legally married to John until I was fifteen. Had John and Leah earned money off of me while I lived with them? I'd had Medicaid? Welfare? Medical attention I never used or never thought about? All behind my back. Or had Daddy kept getting the money when I went to John?

A tiny barb of anger lodged itself in my chest, prickly and painful. I had a bad feeling that poisonous spine was gonna grow until I had this out with Daddy. It was hypocrisy of the highest order and I wanted to throw things. Maybe break things. "Why do you say they *used to* make money?"

"They had to settle with the state. Pay 'em some back and not take money the way they useta. Social services people make sure it's done right now."

Instead of screaming, I took another breath and said, "This AC will *eat* power. Are you willing to go back to using lanterns an hour or two earlier in the summer? Because we'll be out of light that much sooner."

"But we'll be cooler. I done decided I'm gonna be a townie girl real soon. Townies don't sweat all summer and freeze all winter." She paused, as if reconsidering. "Well. I'm gonna be a townie girl with a greenhouse and plants and a business selling my veggies and suchlike."

"Hmmm." I walked to the wide grouping of potted flowers and herbs on the far end of the porch and tilted one over to retrieve the key I had left there. There was a note beside the key, which I opened and read. It was from Brother Thad. I said to Mud, "Brother Thad says he's adjusting his bid for the upgrades we talked about." I looked at my sister, who still seemed a little on the defensive side. I keyed open the door and led the way inside. It was still cool enough, the night air chilled by the small air conditioning unit. It wouldn't last long. A new AC unit would be nice. "A townie, huh?"

Mud followed me in. "Pretty much."

I walked through the house and opened the back door, letting the cats inside. "According to my note"—I waggled it at her—"Brother Thad will be sending me an e-mail this morning. The second-story walk-in closet is more than a closet. At some point before I came to live here, maybe before John's second and third wives divorced him because he couldn't give them children, that space was roughed in for bathroom plumbing. I never knew. Putting in a small bath for you may not be as expensive as we'd feared."

Delight flashed across my sister's face. "I'm gonna have my own bathroom?"

"Maybe. We're going to get prices for a new bathroom and all the remodel, including installing your solar upgrades. But don't think it's a done deal. The money for the custody court costs is not something I'm willing to touch. If we can't afford all the construction, we'll have to pick and choose. It might, come down to a bathroom upstairs or a greenhouse."

Mud let out a whoop that echoed in the rafters and the bedrooms upstairs.

EIGHT

I needed a nap, but that wasn't going to happen. Just as I crawled into bed, newly showered and wearing a cropped pair of John's old boxers and a tank top, my cell buzzed with a text. It was a message from Ming of Glass, the new, first-ever, Master of the City of Knoxville. The MOC was demanding my presence at her clan home. Now. After sunrise. In the daylight. Vampires slept by day. Ordinary vampires. I didn't know about a Master of a City.

The text had come from Yummy's number and I knew for certain that Yummy wasn't old enough to be awake. The text had also gone to Rick. I wondered if the MOC had gone into the sleeping lair of her bodyguard and used Yummy's dead-by-day finger to open her phone and send the message. Had the MOC known how to do all that?

My cell rang and I answered, "LaFleur. I see it."

"We aren't usually subjected to a command performance," he said. "Part of me wants to refuse on general principle—law enforcement doesn't act at the behest of fangheads—but the realistic part of me knows we should go. You up for the drive or should I send someone to pick you up?"

"I'll drive. What does she mean when she says, 'Ming of Glass and Knoxville demands the attention and assistance of PsyLED. We have been physically and electronically attacked. Two blood-servants are missing.'"

"We'll find out when we get there."

"Copy that." I hit end. "You're a big help," I accused the phone.

Mud stuck her head in the doorway. "I can go to Mama. The womenfolk is canning tomatoes and making basil vinegar and pesto today. I can grab some a our'ns and add to the mix in exchange for some jars."

"Hurry and get some picked. And be careful of the roots. They need rain. We leave in twenty minutes."

Mud raced to the garden, urging the cats out with her. I considered work clothes in the closet. Instead, I fingered a pair of jeans and a T-shirt and spotted a lightweight cropped jacket. "Demand my presence?" I stripped and dressed. "Get me off duty?" I sniped. "Just be glad I ain't showing up to your au*gust* presence in bib overalls and work boots."

I frowned at the world. I had started talking to inanimate objects and the air. Being a special agent was making me crazy as a bedbug.

I dropped Mud off at Mama's, the smell of garlic and basil and tomatoes making my mouth water, and took off for the clan home of Ming of Glass. In the middle of the morning.

I beat PsyLED SAC Rick LaFleur there, so I drove by the house, which was off Kingston Pike, on Cherokee Boulevard, in the fancy part of town. I pulled over, turned off the truck, and lowered the window, taking the spare time while I waited on my boss to Google the address and go through county records. Every Tennessee county kept building records on deeds, titles, land boundaries, and most everything else. I extended my search into the county building inspectors, looking into plumbing, electrical, security, and everything else I could find.

The house was within spitting distance of the Confederate Memorial Hall, and probably had a view of the Tennessee River. Seen from above, it had a huge footprint. According to county records it was nearly twelve thousand square feet and had an attached six-car garage, a full, newly upgraded security system, a sprinkler system, a slate roof, a swimming pool, a tennis court, and a three-hole putting green. There was what looked like a brand-new greenhouse on the far side of the house. The barn and five-board fencing had a new coat of paint since the last satellite pictures, and the jump rings set up on the pasture seemed to get a lot of usage. The grounds were attractively landscaped with local flora and had dozens of mature oak trees that provided shade to the horses I could smell

on the hot summer air. I noted that the security upgrades had
been done by Yellowrock Securities, Jane Yellowrock's company. Rick's ex had her tentacles in every vampire clan home
in the Southeast. I checked for a text reply. Nothing yet.

The entrance to the address was protected with a reinforced iron pole gate. Nothing but a small tank or someone on
foot was getting through. I'd spotted a camera and a small
speaker at the entrance as I drove by, and other cameras followed the fencing, with what might have been motion detec-
tors and low-light and infrared monitors.

Rick—LaFleur for this interview—cruised up beside me,
lowered his window, puffed out cigar smoke in a little ring,
and smiled. Cigar smoke had been used for decades as a way
to mask scent patterns from vampires and he would reek of it.
His silver and black hair was brushed back; he was wearing a
white dress shirt and a tie. For a para who had spent the night
in the null room, he looked pretty good. "You up for this, Ingram?"

"They'll call me Maggot."

"They might. But how long they do that is up to you."

I tilted my head. Up to me? I wasn't sure what he meant by
that, but he didn't give me a chance to question him. "Leave
your window down," he said. "Show your ID to the camera and
wait until they give you permission to enter. Follow me in.
Leave your weapons locked in the truck." He made a U-turn; I
followed him up to the gate, waited my turn, and showed my ID.

The first quivers of nervousness raced through me on tiny
little spider feet. I swallowed the nerves down. According to
Spook School, vampires could smell nervousness and it activated their predatory instincts. I didn't know if I could protect
myself from a vampire. Didn't know if I could drain them into
the earth if they should attack. I didn't know if the earth would
spit them back out or entrap them as it had Brother Ephraim.
Leaving my weapon in the truck felt stupid. Taking it with me
felt more stupid. I wished I had bought a silver cross. Silver
stakes. Something.

Ming of Glass owed me a boon. Boons were important
things to vampires and that boon was worth much more now
that Ming was an MOC. Did that give me protection and bargaining power? Was that what Rick meant? Then again, being

called Maggot or Maggoty might be endearing, and might therefore give me the power to manipulate them without them knowing I was doing so. Churchwomen were excellent manipulators, and while I wasn't near as good or as sneaky as one of the mamas, I was still pretty good. To be Maggot or not to be Maggot. It was a conundrum.

The driveway was long and winding, made of pressed and painted concrete that looked like cobbles; visitor parking was a wide area to the right of the house. I parked beside LaFleur's official vehicle and took in the armed human guards patrolling, working with dogs. I made a point to step out of my truck where one of the guards could see me and remove my weapons, leaving only my ID and badge in view as I moved with false confidence toward the front entrance.

The house was made of dull brown river rock and a similar color brick. The wood trim was painted in three tones of cool browns and the working shutters were painted steel. I knew a lot about Ming of Glass, but a lot of what I thought I knew was from my church upbringing. The vampire was often used as a threat against unruly children. "You'un be good or Ming of Glass will snatch you'un outta your'n bed and turn you into a demon."

The door was open, ice-cold air billowing out, when we reached it. A man wearing a dove gray suit with a scarlet pocket hankie bowed us in and I realized the suit was a tuxedo and the man had to be a butler. He was about five feet, six inches tall, clean shaven, and he was wearing white gloves even in the heat.

"Master of the City Ming of Glass welcomes you to her clan home. Please accept refreshment. I'll inform the master that you have arrived." He bowed again and swept an arm toward a fancy room, what might be called a parlor. A maid, wearing the same color scheme, ushered us in and offered us iced black tea with lemon or mint.

Rick said, "Thank you. We'd love some. With lemon for me."

The offer was not something I should ignore or refuse even though I was already shivering as the sweat chilled on my body. But I didn't want cold tea. "Thank you," I said. "But if it would be possible I'd like a cup of hot tea?" And a blanket, which I did not say aloud. Ming's lair was cold.

The maid opened her mouth and closed it, glanced at the doorway and the butler who was standing in the opening. Something passed between them and was gone. "Of course, miss. It will be just a moment longer."

Rick's lemony tea appeared in about ten seconds, the dark liquid in a cut crystal glass, carried in on a silver tray. I knew very little about really good crystal or silver, but this was heavy, the glass faceted like diamonds. Rick sat on the small sofa and took his glass in hand. He was all elegant and upper class and . . . Why wasn't Rick a vampire chick magnet? He fit right in. That was strange.

Two minutes later, the maid reappeared with a teapot and a pretty teacup and saucer on a wooden tray. Two strings hung outside the teapot lid. I stared at the strings. I'd read a library book back when I wasn't working for PsyLED. It was a novel about a modern girl from China and her very old grandmother. The young girl had made tea from loose leaves for the older woman as a sign of respect. In the novel, giving guests tea from tea bags was an insult. Ming was Asian, an old, *old* Asian. Tea in the China of her day would probably have been nearly sacred. While icing tea could be considered a way to blend into local culture, serving it steeped from a tea bag was probably like thumbing her nose at us. I didn't know enough to do more than guess that Ming was offering a sly disrespect.

I debated trying the tea. Uncertain, I took my place on a leather chair with carved swan-neck arms, touching the wood surreptitiously, and looked over the large room. It had a high ceiling, attic fans, and stiff-looking furniture. I surveyed the room, looking for the most likely hiding places for the security cameras, just like the nosy cop I was becoming. I figured that a room this large would have at least four cameras, and decided that they were on the bookshelf, on the mantel, over the entrance door, and at the smaller door to the side where the maid had emerged.

I also decided to not drink the tea just yet. I kept the fingers of my left hand on the wood of the swan-necked chair arm. It was fine wood, tightly grained cherry, from a local forest. I liked it. And it offered me a connection to the land.

From the doorway I was facing, a black-suited man I identified as Ming's primo human blood servant—Cai, no last

name on file anywhere—and Ming's vampire security special-
ist, Heyda Cohen, entered. Cai was about my height, slender,
and though there was no data on file about his fighting abilities, I got the distinct impression that he was deadly. He moved
like a hunting cat, perfectly balanced, fluid. Rick watched him
move and placed his glass to the side as if to free his hands.
Heyda was tiny, of Middle Eastern or East Asian descent and
very beautiful. She was also awake in the daylight, and though
she looked as if she could fall asleep in a heartbeat, being
awake by day meant she was quite powerful. A vampire war
against God's Cloud of Glory Church had been fought over
her, and I had been partly responsible for her rescue from the
churchmen. It was the occasion when I first met Jane Yellowrock, and . . .

I took a slow, steadying breath. In many ways, Heyda was
responsible for all the changes in my life. Heyda's eyes were
sharp when they landed on me and she nodded solemnly, as if
in recognition of me as something or someone important. In
her eyes I might be. I had been involved in other ways with the
protection of the vamps in Knoxville, including the return of
Mira Clayton's adopted, nonhuman child. That rescue was the
source of the boon between her boss and me. And yet, Ming
offered questionable tea. I could be reading the situation
wrong.

The maid reentered behind Heyda, carrying another tray
with tiny scalloped toast points topped with what looked like
raw meat, and cucumber sandwiches on white bread. *Raw
meat?* Another subtle insult, this one directed to the cat-man?
I inhaled, trying to catch the scent, and thought it might be
smoked salmon. That was expensive and so . . . no insult? I
wished I knew more about manners outside of the church. The
servant set the tray on a tea table, poured tea into my cup, and
departed, the butler following her out, leaving Heyda and Cai
behind. The two stood at what looked like parade rest, facing
the main entrance to the parlor.

When Rick put down his glass and stood, I followed suit,
though I heard and smelled nothing. The Master of the City,
Ming Zhane of Glass, entered slowly, her power zipping over
my skin like a swarm of ladybugs had landed on me. Ming
was dressed in a black silk robe over a scarlet gown, the exact

shade as her lips and the same shade as fresh blood. A gold chain hung around her neck, with a ruby pendant the size of a robin's egg. She was Asian, petite, with almond-shaped eyes of an odd dark honey shade. Her black hair was long, up in a bun just like every other time I'd seen her. Her skin was smooth and pale as ivory, and her lips were painted scarlet.

The last time I met her, Ming had been only a clan Blood Master. Now she was a great deal more. She exuded all the power, elegance, and lethal intent of an apex predator. She looked totally at ease. And she was up, in control, and alert in the middle of the morning, which told us how powerful she was.

She would squash us like rats if we let her. I knew. I'd dealt with Ming before and she liked messing with humans and paras she considered beneath her. Like us.

Cai said softly, "The Master of the City of Knoxville and Tennessee hunting grounds, and Blood Master of Clan Glass, Ming Zhane, welcomes the special agents of Knoxville PsyLED Unit Eighteen to her clan home."

Ming had said this visit was urgent, but clearly *urgent* did not negate protocol or the vampire social niceties when dealing with human law enforcement. Realizing that every word spoken today would have much more meaning than appeared on the surface, I ran the primo's words through my mind.

Technically, Ming was her family name and Zhane her given name. She should have changed her family name to Glass when she defeated the clan founder a hundred-plus years ago, but she hadn't. Keeping her own name, in the Asian manner, stated to the vampire world that she wasn't one to abide by Mithran or human rules unless she wanted to, and that she was powerful enough to get away with anything she wanted. And the words *Tennessee hunting grounds* meant something more than being MOC. Ming was claiming the entire state of Tennessee as hunting territory. With Leo Pellissier true-dead and in the grave—or so they said—and Jane Yellowrock, the Dark Queen, in hiding, Ming was stretching her power and influence. Ming might be playing with us like a cat with mice.

Ming knew us, but Rick introduced us anyway, title to title. "Rick LaFleur, special agent in charge of Unit Eighteen of PsyLED, and Special Agent Nell Ingram. What can we do for you, Ming of Glass, Master of the City of Knoxville?"

I noticed he didn't say anything about his werecat titles. And he didn't mention the Tennessee hunting grounds. That was interesting.

Instead of answering, Ming sat and gestured us to sit as well. We did, on the edges of our seats. I pressed my left fingers against the wood again and watched as Ming smoothed her silk robe. She said, "I hope the refreshment is to your satisfaction."

Rick looked nonplussed at the deflection, but I was ready for it. I lifted my cup and sipped, saying, "The refreshment offered by Ming of Glass is welcome, especially as the Mithran Master of the City is in such penury."

Ming lifted a brow in what might be amusement. "Penury?"

I set down the cup and nudged the tea-bag string with a knuckle. "I know about whole leaves being preferred over the tea dust in tea bags." I gave a smile as faint as her own and added a bit of church to my accent. "I ain't a connoisseur of anything except vegetables, but I know my manners. And serving iced tea and store-bought tea-bag tea to a guest is an insult. Right? And Ming of Glass would never insult a guest. So Ming of Glass must be broke."

"Broke?" Ming blinked. "Vegetables?"

"I've been told that I grow the finest vegetables in the state," I said.

Rick looked at the sweating glass in his hand. He might know all about vamps, but he didn't know about a woman's insults. "We're here for—" Rick started.

Ming's hand flew up in a cutting gesture as she interrupted, "My finances are not an appropriate topic of discussion. You will try the cucumber sandwiches." She indicated the plate of sandwiches. "I should like your opinion."

"Oh, I'd never compare my cukes to anyone else's," I said. "That would be too unkind of me, would reek of hubris and ego and disrespect to my host."

Ming's deep brown eyes sparkled in amusement. She knew I was insulting her not-so-subtly in return for the tea insult and she was enjoying herself. "But I insist," she said, her tone dropping into vampire compulsion that felt like warmth and heat and drugged happiness.

Except it didn't work on me, especially with my hands on

wood. "In that case, I'll do Ming of Glass the favor of taste-testing her veggies." I took a sandwich, bit, and chewed. Rick's face went bland as a vampire's face, as he caught up with the deeper potential meanings of the preceding conversation. The rest of the room awaited my judgment in fascinated interest. I swallowed and sipped the now-tepid tea in my cup. Set down the cup. Making her wait. I was channeling the mamas' careful social interactions with the wives of other churchmen. There was an elusive line I shouldn't cross.

"It's quite nice," I said, staring at the small sandwich in my hand.

"Only *nice*?" Ming asked.

"I've always found that lemon cucumbers need a bit more organic material in the soil to give them that zing. The soil you used is just right for Mexican sour gherkins, though."

"Organic material?"

"Dead things," I said. Rick made a soft grunt of air, Ming's eyebrows went up, and the room went frozen, offended, silent. I just smiled the sweet kind of smile a churchwoman uses when she's about to offer a kind, syrupy, polite insult. "Maggots know all about dead things. They make good eatin'."

The silence went harder and colder and deadly. A good three seconds later, Ming burst out laughing. Well, it was a little titter of sound, but for her I reckon it was like a belly laugh for ordinary folks. "Mexican sour gherkins," she repeated. "These are good cucumbers?"

"They're actually not a cucumber or melon at all." I scrunched up my face, trying to remember. "I think they are in the *Melothria* genus. A little sharper lemon taste. Fewer seeds. A little more . . . tart maybe? But really good with mayo and sourdough bread, which, when made right, has bigger holes than the white bread your cook is using. The holes let the flavors mix better. I have some Mexican sour gherkin seeds I'd be happy to have delivered to Ming of Glass for her gardener to try. It's a little late in the season to plant outside, but they'll do okay in a greenhouse. With the right amount of organic material."

Amused, Ming sipped her tea. "Would Special Agent Maggot be willing to test our organic mixture and recommend the perfect addition of . . . dead things . . . to improve our vegetables? We expect the Dark Queen to visit us when she goes on progression."

"Progression?" Rick asked.

"To visit her far-flung subjects."

Rick said nothing, but Ming's nostrils fluttered and she smiled slightly. Despite the cigar smoke, she had smelled his reaction to the discussion of Jane Yellowrock—the Dark Queen of vampires, who was not going on any kind of trip that I knew of. Ming was playing games with us, slashing at Rick's emotions, trying to put us where she wanted us. Ming wanted a favor but didn't want to be beholden to cops. She shifted her attention to Rick. He set his glass aside. I followed their lead and put down my tiny sandwich. Niceties were over. And I knew without looking that Rick was ticked off with me. There might be words about my taking lead on the social portion of this discussion. I wasn't planning on backing down.

Carefully, Ming said, "We have a legal conundrum and wish advice upon how to proceed."

Rick nodded once and glanced at me, but when he spoke it was to the Master of the City. "Ming of Glass, I hear, but need to clarify. Do you wish to make an official police report?"

"What are her options?" Heyda asked.

Rick considered, leaning forward and clasping his fingers together between his knees. "If Ming of Glass wishes to file a report, she will be speaking to the SAC of Knoxville. Every detail will be entered into a database that might be read by many people in law enforcement."

"Ming does not wish her words to be made known to others," Heyda said. "This will not be an official report."

Rick nodded his understanding. While he didn't seem to comprehend the niceties and backstabbing of Ming's chitchat, my boss did appreciate the vampire mind-set when it came to power plays. He took off his badge and placed it on the table. I followed suit. Now I was just Maggot, and Rick was just Rick. Not cops.

"Rick LaFleur hears Ming of Glass."

"Rick LaFleur the human? Or the wereleopard, the cat who is second in the leap of the Dark Queen? And first in Gabon, in Africa."

I stiffened in surprise. Ming was really well informed and

she was getting a lot of mileage out of this meeting and this problem. Or she needed help of a different nature.

"I am many things," Rick said evenly. I wondered if Rick was really this calm or if his old undercover reflexes were kicking in.

"It is to the Dark Queen's leopard I will speak," Ming said with a mean little smile.

Rick didn't react visibly, but I had a feeling his scent changed enough for the fading cigar smoke to no longer hide it. He hadn't talked to Jane Yellowrock in months. He had no power in the leap and no permission to speak for Jane, but he was over a barrel. "The beta cat of Yellowrock leap hears."

Ming said, "We were attacked last night, our land and holdings and humans. Two humans have been turned or they would have died. Two Mithrans are injured and sleeping with my blood in their veins to heal."

"Would Ming of Glass specify what kind of attack?"

Humans hadn't died, so we could keep this unofficial, but Ming was pacing a narrow path.

"It was magical," Ming said, with distaste.

Heyda said, "We defeated the attack and strengthened our defenses, but to know such a thing was possible would be a gift to our enemies and an indication that Ming was less powerful than she clearly is."

I understood. The vampires were awake in the daytime, which was an indication of might. But they had been successfully attacked.

"This magical attack," Rick said. "Please clarify."

"A spell of calling was issued, a magical summons," Ming said. "Two of our number attempted to leave the grounds and their humans endeavored to stop them."

Rick's body tightened and his eyes glowed a slight green with his cat. He leaned now toward Heyda. He said, "Tell me about this calling."

Heyda said, "After midnight, two of our number stood and walked to the doors, moving as if automatons, as if not hearing the calls of their humans, as if they were spelled. The humans tried to intervene and the Mithrans killed their own blood-servants. I was able to stake the Mithrans and thus stop their actions. Ming and I were able to turn the humans. The spell was strong, lasting for hours, during which time other Mithrans fought to remain in their lairs, fought to not answer the calling. Altogether eleven Mithrans were staked. Only two of us resisted the spell used against us.

That meant that Yummy had been called too. Yummy was the closest thing I had to a vamp friend. But I couldn't ask about her right now. I firmed my lips, stopping my words.

"How many times has this calling happened?" Rick asked.

"Why do you ask this?" Ming asked. "How do you know this attack has occurred more than the once of which we speak?"

"Because I have been called to my leopard and once ended up on a riverbank in cat form, near a witch's circle. A circle of cursing and summoning, one that showed evidence of the presence of Mithrans. I was called last night, and resisted the spell."

"A witch curses both were-creatures and Mithrans?" Ming said, her eyes flashing. "What do the local spell casters say to this? We have tried to contact them to negotiate that they cease such attacks. They do not reply to us."

Softly, Heyda said, "Ming is ready to go to war with the spell casters. She has called for the assistance of Lincoln Shaddock. He and his people will travel here during the night."

Shaddock was the new MOC of Asheville. That meant a lot more vampires in Knoxville than normal and tensions might flare. A war between the paranormal creatures was a very bad thing and to be avoided at all costs.

Rick held up a hand in a gesture for peace. "The witches are not your enemies. One of the city's PsyLED special agents is a witch and she is as baffled and concerned as we are. She spoke with the local coven leader. They don't know anything about the circles and they're . . ." He paused. "Not fearful, but wary. Worried. They say the witch circles are a dangerous and forbidden magic and they refuse to help us apprehend the witch who is casting this curse. They say it's an outside witch, not one of their own."

"And you believe them?" Heyda asked, skeptical.

"Yes. Both as a law enforcement officer and as a were-leopard."

"Are the witches also under the summoning?"

Rick shook his head. "I don't think so. But they're casting auguries for the future and reading the cards. They told our agent that all the readings so far point to 'grave danger.'"

"How many circles?"

"Twelve," Rick said, "over the three moon cycles."

Ming's lips tilted slightly down and she said, "Maggot. You have read the land at the circles of summoning?"

"I have. Mithrans were there, either before or after the summonings were cast."

Ming's eyes tightened, her white-powdered face giving little away. "My clan is spread about the city. Only a few lair here. None have reported such a summoning. Heyda, you will contact the ones who lair otherwhere to see if they have been called and did not report it."

Heyda murmured, "Yes, my mistress."

Rick asked, "Why wouldn't they have already contacted the Master of the City if they've had problems?"

I was looking at Heyda when he spoke and I caught the barest flinch in the skin around her eyes. I knew that look. Fear. Ming's people were afraid of her, and Heyda couldn't say that. But I could. "You rule your people with an iron hand, don'tcha?" I felt the brush of Ming's magic. I dug my fingernails into the wood before it got too strong and I forgot what I wanted to say. "People, even blood-sucking people, don't look for help to the ones who show no mercy."

Ming speared me with a look and I almost reared back, losing face, in vampire terms. Almost. Instead, I pressed my nails into her chair arm so hard that I damaged the shiny finish, the bare wood beneath soothing. After a space of time, Ming's eyes narrowed. Stiffly she said, "Will you read my property to see if the summoning is in the land?"

And now we knew the real reason we had been commanded to visit the clan home of the Master of the City of Knoxville. Ming wanted another favor, without us understanding that it was a favor. I had been setting and keeping careful boundaries in this meeting, boundaries that established who was head honcho, who was alpha. That alpha person was my boss. Pointedly, I looked at Rick. I was being deliberately heavy-handed enough that Ming was certain to pick up on all my clues. "I have my blanket in the truck. I can do that *favor* for Ming of Glass now, if *you* like." I put careful emphasis on the word *you*.

"Yes," Ming said, answering for him.

"Special Agent Ingram, you have my permission," Rick said at the same time.

I replied to Rick in the vernacular of Unit Eighteen. "Boss, it's unlikely that I'll note anything except the sensation of Mithrans on this land."

"You will sense maggots," Ming said. This time there was no playfulness in her tone.

I took my badge and closed my fist around it, keeping it out of sight so Ming would know that I was speaking as Nell, not a cop. "Ming of Glass did not kill her *guests* when we placed ourselves at her mercy by answering her *invitation*. I will read her land for her as a favor and a kindness." I left the room for the front of the house and the door, hearing the softly indrawn breath of Heyda. Yes, I thought. Think on that. You don't want to make it official? Then it's tit-for-tat and quid pro quo. Now Ming owed me a boon *and* a favor.

On first read, I got nothing on the land except the crawly sensation I associated with vampires and dead things. Then I pushed into the earth with my consciousness, calling on Soulwood, and the earth opened up around me, colors sparking and tumbling and full of power. Ming's land was more active than my own, the energy lively and youthful. I realized that, in some way, Ming had sealed this land to herself and fed it for decades. She called it her hunting grounds. I wondered briefly if she had spilled human blood on it in sacrifice to claim it, but I was pretty sure that spilling blood for the land was an ancient European custom, not Asian. If Ming spilled blood it was her dinner, not a sacrifice, though the land might not know the difference.

I studied the earth all around and decided that no witch magic had penetrated the ground itself. Nothing in the trees. Whatever the attack had been, it left no trace. Withdrawing, I stood and carried my blanket to the truck.

Rick was leaning against his vehicle, sunglasses over his

eyes, his silvered hair swept back, ankles crossed, one hand dangling from his pocket, the other rubbing his mangled tattoo. "Ingram."

I gave him a nod and opened the truck door. Heat billowed out. I had forgotten to leave the windows open an inch. I tossed the blanket inside to the passenger seat.

"You did good catching the thing about tea. I've visited at the Glass Clan Home before and been offered tea, always iced."

"It might notta been an insult. What's polite in one culture—Southerners drink a lot of iced tea in summer—is an insult in another. Ming's an old vampire. She's adapted, but I bet not enough to offer a respected guest tea from commercially packaged tea bags. When someone she respects is a guest, they probably get the good tea, something loose leaf from a single estate."

He gave a faint smile. "I'm guessing she's starting to respect you." He shifted slightly and changed the subject. "What did you find in the earth?"

I leaned into the heated cab and found a water bottle. It was an old one I had filled with Soulwood water and, though it was disgustingly warm, I opened it and drank it anyway. The taste of Soulwood was a refreshment I couldn't explain to anyone. I capped the empty and tossed it back in the truck to refill later. "Nothing useful. The witch magic didn't soak into the land. The property itself wasn't compromised. I'm guessing it was a calling, just like what you're getting. I also have a feeling that when she talks to the vampires who lair off-site, she'll find they've had issues that they didn't report."

Rick nodded slowly. "You did good, Ingram. Go home. Get some sleep."

I was exhausted. I waved to the humans guarding the grounds, climbed into the heated cab, and drove home. With Mud at Mama's I didn't have to be alert. I slept like a log, which was still funny in all sorts of ways.

NINE

I woke to the sound of someone knocking on my door and the sensation of my land in happy welcome. *Occam is here.* I crawled out of bed, sweaty, sticky, and summer-miserable, and checked the time to discover that I'd slept a whole four hours. I shoved my arms into a robe and passed the cheval mirror to see a leafy woman with green eyes and very bad bed-head. I tried to tame the crazy, damp ringlets, but it was like yanking on kudzu vine—a study in wasted effort. I twisted the tangled mess up in a bun, stuck a long bobby pin in it, and went to the door.

Occam stood on the other side, leaning a shoulder on one of the porch posts. His face was in shadow, arms crossed, muscles bulging at the T-shirt sleeves. The scars on the side of his head appeared less rough and his ear actually had a curve of cartilage, a bit more healed than when I'd looked last. There was even a fresh spot of hair sprouting on his scalp where there had been only white scars before. Shifting was speeding his healing. Shifting on Soulwood was maybe speeding it even more. There were two brown paper grocery store bags at his flip-flop-clad feet, which were scar free, with rounded nails. Surprised to see him, I opened the door and stared at my— *the*—cat-man.

I said, "You're supposed to be working, twelve on, twelve off, day shift."

"Afternoon, Nell, sugar," he said, his voice low and gravelly. "You look pretty as a picture."

A before picture in one of those beauty magazines, I thought, but since Occam looked a lot like the boogeyman in an old Grimm fairy tale, I didn't say it.

"Rick gave me the afternoon off, putting me on split shift today. He wants me there at moonrise, which will be close to two a.m."

To keep Rick safe, to help him not shift and race off to be slaughtered by a blood witch. I held the door wide. "Come on in. Hospitality and safety," I said, paraphrasing from my church days. "I need to clean up, but I'll be with you in a bit."

"I'll make us breakfast," he said. "Eggs and ham in the microwave, some juice. I'd do banana pancakes except for the fact that you don't use your stove in summer and it's too hot to use the brazier in back."

It was afternoon and it wasn't too hot for the brazier, or not too hot for a churchwoman, but I wasn't going to argue with a man who was gonna fix me a late breakfast. I dragged myself to the shower and cleaned up fast in the cool-to-tepid water from the cistern. As I showered, I mentally went over my long-term and short-term to-do list and added to it. The windmill that pumped my water into the cistern needed its semi-annual mechanical inspection and maintenance. The old pump needed lubricating on a regular basis and that had been ignored while I was a tree. I also needed to figure out what to do about providing hot water to the upstairs bathroom. The little hot water heater on the back of the wood-burning stove was fine for the small downstairs bath but was insufficient for adding an upstairs shower. That meant buying a hot water heater and more energy usage. Coming into the twenty-first century and letting Mud be a townie girl was going to be expensive.

I dressed in the jeans and tee from Ming's and twisted my freshly washed, overly curly hair into clips off my face. I opened the door and the smell of sizzling ham in the main room whooshed into the bedroom and woke up my hungries. It was only microwave ham and eggs, but any pig-based meat was good meat. I stopped in the doorway to catch a view of Occam bent over my sofa, tucking something up under the cloth bottom. "Got a mouse?" I asked.

Occam jerked upright and spun around. And looked guilty. I frowned at him. "Occam?"

He chuffed a breath, sounding very catty. "You caught me."

"Doing what?"

He reached under the sofa and tugged something out,

scratching sofa and wood floor in a muffled scraping sound. It was a small gobag. He looked sheepish. "I've been keeping a bag of clothes here in case I needed to shift and change and didn't have anything in the car. You know. Emergency supplies. Toothbrush. Soap. Just in case."

"Whyn't you just put it on the shelves?" I pointed to the wall with my few books and lots of Leah's and John's old things.

"Because it was . . . invasive?"

"And hiding things isn't?"

"I didn't want you to think that I thought I was living here."

I opened my mouth, but nothing came out. I closed it. *Living here?* Oh. *Like living in sin here.* I started to grin but squashed it. Occam was trying to be nice, not realizing that the church's idea of living in sin was vastly different from the rest of America's ideas. Concubinage and polygamous marriages were normal where I grew up. As a church widderwoman, I could take up with an unmarried man if I wanted to and if my daddy didn't object. As a *former* church widderwoman, I could do what I wanted and not ask my daddy. "You can put the bag in the bedroom at the top of the stairs, across from Mud's room. There's a closet with a bunch of John's old things that I never got around to throwing out."

"Oh." Occam looked as if he didn't know what to do with his hands and he finally tossed the bag on the sofa. "Okay. So. Um. So we should talk."

I narrowed my eyes at him. In the church a woman said, "We should talk," when there was trouble brewing and she wanted to head it off at the pass. Or when she was feeling neglected in some way. Or when the children had a problem. A man never said that. A man said, "I'm calling a family meeting," at which point he laid down a new rule or law. This was odd. And interesting.

"I'm listening," I said. But I didn't sit down, and I put my shoulders back and my fists on my hips. I had learned that posture in the body language class during Interrogation 101 at Spook School. It meant, I'm not afraid and I'll fight back if you try something I don't like. It was an alpha-woman move.

Occam looked away and then back at me quickly, as if he'd caught himself doing something he hadn't intended. "You know I was out of the country while I was healing and you were on disability."

"I was a tree," I said distinctly. "But go on."

Occam hesitated, not even breathing for a bit too long, processing my words and my stance. I waited, face tight.

"I went to Gabon. In Africa."

"Uh-huh. I know that."

"To heal."

"I understand that. You died. I brought you back and healed you where I could. You're still scarred up and the two fingers you lost are still stiff and useless. Your ear is a mess but getting slowly better. You won't take off your shirt so I can see what still needs to be done to heal you."

"There's things you don't know. Things I haven't told you. Not to keep them a secret, or because of anything . . ." He stopped. Started again. "After the fight when I was burned, I was . . . a gibbering, screaming half cat." He studied me, adding slowly, "I had third-degree burns over seventy percent of my body. My lungs were damaged. My esophagus and trachea were mostly gone. When Soul came back to her senses, she put me back in a silver-lined cage and T. Laine spelled me to sleep, hoping I'd heal."

I hadn't known all that. There was probably a lot of stuff I had never known. But it's hard to know things when no one wants to tell the truth, when they want to spare you from the painful things in life. Or when they just don't think it matters and therefore don't tell you stuff that might be important later on.

"Rick was a lot better off than I was and he flew to Gabon soon after the fight, to look for a healer capable of working with weres. He found a clan of wereleopards with a werehealer willing to help us heal. He flew back and packed me up and brought me to Gabon with him."

"I know that."

"The healer was a . . . like a tribal shaman, I guess. He spoke only French and the tribal language, one of the Bantu languages, and Rick left me with him and came back to the States. I understood some things by hand gestures and there were enough similarities with Spanish that I could follow other things, but I was alone."

This stuff was new. Stuff I didn't know. "Okay," I said, my ire slipping away.

"There were a lot of ceremonies and a lot of horrible stuff to drink. Strange things to eat. They put me in moving water to debride the burns, and the children born into the black leopard clan kept watch over me to make sure the crocs didn't find me and attack." As he talked, Occam's eyes had begun to glow golden. His voice had dropped to a growly note of cat. "Believe it or not, the pain of healing was a hell of a lot worse than the burns themselves because the nerves in the burned tissue were burned dead, but when the water ripped the dead tissue away, it exposed the nerves and . . . no one can ever believe that level of pain unless they've been burned like that."

"I'm so sorry," I whispered. If I hadn't been a tree, I might have helped him.

He shrugged slightly, more a tip of his head than anything defined. "I got better. The pain got less. I came back to help you de-tree."

I smiled at his choice of words.

"However, while I was healing alone in Gabon and while you were a tree, the Dark Queen and the New Orleans fangheads killed a lot of European vamps. They also killed a mess of were-creatures, including some African werelions and Kemnebi, Rick's black wereleopard alpha."

I had read the reports—every special agent in PsyLED had read the reports—but I had a feeling Occam's monologue was leading to something that I didn't know, so I didn't react. I waited. Occam didn't respond agreeably to a woman just standing there, waiting, restrained, silent. I had to wonder if his mama or some woman in his past used to throw things. Pots. Dishes.

"This part isn't in the official reports. And I don't know the details. But somehow Jane, the Dark Queen, made Rick her beta and somehow, through the Merged Laws of the Cursed of Artemis, Rick inherited Kemnebi's property." He smiled slightly. "And ended up with Kem's family. Four wives and their kids."

"Rick . . ." I stopped. I didn't know where this speech was going, but I didn't like it. "Okay. Rick has four wives. Like the church."

"He offered them annulment. Or divorce. But they won't go." Occam's eyes went the nervous bright gold of his cat. He scrubbed his hands on his jeans; his palms were sweating. "Together as a leap, with Rick as their off-site alpha, they have a strong pack magic and have managed to repel all the males who might want to take over. They like things the way they are. No male on-site."

"Okay. I'm'a be honest here, Occam. You're rambling." But Occam seemed to have reached the end of his ability to communicate. Or the look on my face had stopped him. Or my scent, which must be communicating my reaction even better than my words or expression. "Occam, what are you trying to tell me? Spit it out."

"I slept with the leap of leopards, all in a pile, as part of a healing." Occam turned a darker shade of red. If his color was an indication, he was about to die from apoplexy. "And I had to be naked. That's the first thing."

I had heard of pack magic for helping injured were-creatures to heal. I didn't know if it was real power or something like a sugar pill, but Occam didn't have a family or a pack or anything except Rick, and Rick had saved him when I couldn't by sharing his new family. I reckoned that meant I owed Rick something, except that would mean that Occam and I were a . . . *thing*. But he had used the words *slept with* and *naked*. "Occam, are you trying to tell me that you had sexual relations with one or more of Rick's wives?"

"No! Slept as in slumber, not as in sex." He waved his hands in front of me as if he was wiping away something in the air between us. "No sex."

"Are you trying to tell me that you had sexual relations with one of Rick's children by marriage?"

Occam stepped back fast. "No. *Hell* no."

"Are you trying to tell me you had sexual relations with Rick?"

"Holy shit, woman. No."

"I don't rightly think God shits. Jesus, now, he probably had to go."

Occam made a sound that was part splutter, part gasp at my blasphemy. "How did we get on the subject of Jesus' bowel movements?"

"You said holy shit."

"Oh. I'm sorry. I . . . Yes, I cussed." He wiped his palms on his jeans and ran his disfigured hand and fused fingers through his hair and over the bald, scarred areas of scalp. He had broken out in a sweat that stained the underarms of his T-shirt. "I needed you to know that I was naked during the healing."

"Okay."

"Because there was talk about the wives coming here someday and they might meet you."

"Okay." I was fighting a grin. "And you drove all the way out here and woke me up to tell me about something that happened months ago? In Gabon?"

Occam blinked once at that. "But I didn't have sex with anyone while I was in Gabon. Or anywhere else since I met you. Even with Yummy, who offered to heal me with her blood if I slept with her. If I had sexual relations with her. Last night. I mean, she offered that last night. This morning actually. Just after I got to the office." He held out his cell phone as proof. There were texts on the screen.

Ahhh. Understanding bloomed through me like a flower opening. This was why he was so odd this morning. This had been the text that sent him walking away from me after bringing me coffee.

I didn't look at the cell, keeping my eyes on Occam. "Why not?" When he looked confused I asked, "Why didn't you have sex with anyone?"

"Because I'm . . ." He shook his head, befuddled. Which was a much better word than confused. "Because I was waiting on you, Nell, sugar."

"You were waiting on me to *have sex with*?" I asked, my irritated amusement taking a hard turn into a new causation. "Just to clarify."

"For someone who knows nothing about romance you sure do talk straight, Nell, sugar." Sweat had popped out on his face and I had a feeling it wasn't just the heat making that happen.

"You're right," I said. "I don't know nothing about romance, but I know a lot about sex and not much of it good. You gonna clarify?"

A strange expression flitted across Occam's face. It was part perplexity, part wonder, part uncertain discomfort, part embarrassment. Carefully, he said, "Nell, sugar. I'm not waiting to have sex with you."

I tilted my head. "That's what we're talking about, isn't it? Or talking around?"

"No. It isn't. Since the first moment I met you, I've been waiting to make love with you." When I didn't reply he added, softly, "I love you, Nell, sugar. And I have a feeling you never made love with someone who loves you to the full moon and back."

The anger and amusement drained out of me like water from a broken dam. My fists unclenched. My body felt heavy and tired and agitated all at the same time. Something I didn't understand pulsed through my body like . . . like the way heroin must feel when a junkie shoots up. Something good. Something addictive. The words *I've been waiting to make love with you* and *loves you to the full moon and back* ricocheted around in my brain box like balls on a billiards table. "Oh," I said.

Occam took a step closer. A sliding, muscular movement that was nothing a human can make. Silent. Hunting cat. "I love you, Nell, sugar. I love you with no demands. Nothing held back. I love you to the exclusion of all others. I love you now, when you are the most beautiful woman I've ever seen. I loved you when you were a tree. I will love you when you grow gray haired and your leaves are brittle and brown. I want to make love to you. When you happen to be ready. When you know you love me that exact same way."

"To the full moon and back?"

"Exactly that way."

"Are you courting me, Occam?"

"I am indeed, Nell, sugar. After Larry Aden abducted you, I informed your mama and your daddy that I was courting you."

He was close, so close I could feel his body heat through my clothes even in the stuffy house. "Oh?"

"Your mama seemed happy. Your daddy called me a devil cat. I told him this devil cat loved his plant-woman."

I didn't move.

"I told him all that, not to lay claim to you like a possession, but to provide you with what protection I could, from the men in the church who might still want to claim you and your land. And since we're looking for total clarity," he added, "I didn't ask his permission. I informed him. Just like I informed the vampire that I was not interested in being her dinner or her sex toy."

Occam lifted his hand and stroked his fingers along my jaw, soft as heated silk. I exhaled, the breath shuddering slightly. "Occam," I whispered, "you might not shoulda done that. Courting is for a permanent relationship. Marriage or concubinage."

"I was made fully aware of that by your daddy," he murmured.

His eyes were the bright, shining gold of his cat. He was standing so close that his breath teased across my shoulder and curled down my chest. His fingers slid along my nape and into my hair and tugged along my leaves sprouting there. They shivered and so did I.

"And?" I whispered. The word was almost silent, but his cat ears picked it up.

"And I told him that when you were ready you could ask me to marry you. Or ask me to become your concubine."

My mouth opened slightly. A male concubine? Oh. That was . . . new. And shocking. And—

"I told him I was yours and that if you'd have me, you were mine. I told him I'd kill any of his church people who harmed you or Mud. And because he's a man of the Word of God, I told him I was cleaving to you. And I also told him that if you sent me away, I'd go and give you whatever time or space you needed. But that I was yours. Forever."

"Oh . . ." I breathed out.

"Yes. Big-cats don't mate forever. Werecats don't either. But *I* do."

A quiet voice in the dark of my brain hoped his tie to Soulwood wasn't forcing this.

"I'm yours, Nell, whenever you want me."

That didn't sound like a Soulwood binding talking. But . . .

When I didn't reply, he said, "There's this line of dialogue in an old movie I watched when I was a kid. A knight or something like it telling his king, 'I am yours to command.' Nell, you're in charge of this thing we might have, like that king was. I am yours to command. *You are in charge*, Nell, sugar. Totally. In every way."

I swallowed, the sound dry and kinda rubbery. Occam's fingers smoothed the leaves in my hairline and I felt a tremor run through me, thick and heavy and all twisted with meaning. It was like vines crawling over and across one another, winding and curling together. *You are in charge, Nell, sugar. Totally. In every way* . . . Heck fire. I wasn't even in control of my own life yet and here was Occam pretty much giving me *his* life. It was a heady and terrifying feeling. I'd never had anyone give themselves to me before. "Oh," I managed again. Definitely not Soulwood. I could think of absolutely nothing to say. Nothing at all. Silence stretched between us like heated taffy.

Occam reached out and took my hand. And lifted it to his mouth. He pressed my woody nails against his lips in a kiss that heated all the way to my toes. "Nell, sugar? Let's eat."

I nodded and turned to the kitchen. My legs felt a little wobbly and my breath was coming a mite too fast. Helping get the food on the table eased my shock some, however, and we sat at one end, me at my place, where I had recently staked my claim to the head of the table, and Occam to my left. That was where Leah had sat when I was part of a polygamous household. It felt strange to have Occam there, after the conversation we'd just had. The cats leaped to the tabletop and Occam said, "Later you," as he put them down. "I got treats for you."

"You're spoiling my mousers."

He grinned and picked up a thin square of ham with his fingers and bit into the greasy goodness. I used a knife and fork. "I passed a guy cutting up a downed oak tree in town," he said, by way of conversation. "I stopped to talk and he'll give away the wood if you'll take care of delivery and splitting. You want it?"

"Some idiot's giving away free wood? Yes."

"He'll split it for thirty bucks a cord. You want it split?"

"I'm not paying some yahoo to split wood. Townies always leave it too thick and I have to split it again anyway."

"You got a good ax?"

"Yep." I had a good ax and a strong back, but I didn't say that.

"How many cords?"

"Whatever he'll let me have. I usually go through four cords each winter. Sometimes five. If the wood is too green, it'll have to dry this winter and I can use it next. I'll see if Sam will handle the delivery."

"I'll help Sam, if he wants," Occam said, casually.

I hesitated, feeling that there was something more than general kindness and neighborliness in his tone, but since I couldn't decipher what it might be I let it go. "You know Sam will likely have a brotherly talk with you, now that you talked with my daddy. It might contain threats of bodily harm should you beat me."

"I would certainly hope so, Nell, sugar."

I wasn't completely sure what he meant by that, but it didn't sound as if he intended to fight Sam. "Okay. Long as you're prepared for whatever Sam throws your way," I said.

"I give you my word of honor," Occam said, his face grave but his eyes alight with mischief, "that I will not eat your brother."

I burst out laughing, which he surely intended. I sobered quickly and said, "Sam knows you're a wereleopard. That means others in the church might. And some a them—some of *those*—others might want to hurt you."

"I'll be careful on all fronts."

Before I could figure out what to say next, our cells dinged with texts from JoJo. "This is getting to be a bad habit," Occam muttered, reading his aloud. "'Highway Patrol found Rick's car. Crashed. Rick not there. Get there ASAP.' There's a GPS and a map. It's close to Rick's house."

I read mine aloud, "'Get to Rick's house and see if he's there.' Ditto on the GPS and map." It was the first time ever that I had used the word *ditto*. It felt all modern and townie coming out of my mouth, but there wasn't time to enjoy it. It was still light out and too early for a summoning, but this accident of Rick's felt bad on multiple levels.

We dropped the dishes in the sink and raced outside, me grabbing my gear on the way. "Do you know if Rick was wearing the antimagic amulet made by the Knoxville coven?" I asked as we bounded down the steps.

"I never saw him put it on. Doesn't mean he didn't."

We roared out of the driveway, Occam in his fancy car and me a lot slower in my Chevy C10 truck.

It took more than half an hour to get there, and as I drove, I got word that Tandy would be joining me at Rick's place. Rick had moved recently to a rental house on Hunter's Trail, near a swatch of wooded land and a low ridge of hill marked by one of Knoxville's ubiquitous and overbuilt power lines. There were black walnut trees growing in the area, and I remembered the black walnut branch at the witch circle. I'd never been to Rick's and was surprised as I drove up the short drive. I had expected a bachelor pad and found instead a comfortable-looking family home with shutters and a small, covered front stoop. Tandy pulled in behind me and I followed him up the walkway to the porch. "Can you tell if he's here?" I asked.

Tandy stopped and looked around, or would have if his eyes were open. He turned in a circle with his eyes closed, as if seeing things I couldn't. "No," he said. "I don't sense his emotions in either form."

"His emotions are different in cat form?" I asked, surprised.

"Very. Rick is primitive, hungry, and violent when he's a cat. There's less disunion in Occam's human and cat sides, but he's been a cat for a long time and has managed to put himself back together emotionally."

"How?" I asked.

Tandy hesitated. "He hasn't told me, but I think Soul knows. I *think* Soul helped. Occam's emotions are very restrained, well-ordered, and structured. He's reserved and deliberate, and when he does lose control of his cat, he gets it back quickly. There are times when he has more difficulty than others, of course, but for the most part, Occam owns his emotions even when in leopard form. Rick loses command when he's a cat and has to fight to dominate his were-self. Sometimes he doesn't manage that."

"Oh." I didn't ask what areas Occam's cat had trouble with. That seemed too intrusive.

Tandy gave me a small smile. "You have no idea how important it was for Rick to fight off giving in to his cat last night. He's come a long way."

Our cells dinged and we had both received text photos of

Rick's car from Occam. The car had skidded off the road into the scrub and was wrapped around a small tree, the side bashed in where the tree had stopped its momentum and spin. At a glance I'd say the car was totaled. Flipping through the pictures, I noted that the interior was shredded by claws and his sliced and tattered clothes were in a heap. There was blood on the steering wheel and puddled in the seat. Occam's caption to the photos was a simple, *Be careful. He's cat.*

Both of our cells dinged again with, *No tracking dogs. Rick will kill anything that hunts him.*

"That would be bad," I said in response to the text. "Do we wait here?" I asked my partner.

"JoJo wants us to open the back door in case he comes home and needs to get in. Then she wants us to wait half an hour since the crash was so close by. I have the security code to the back door. Come on."

Inside, the kitchen was scrupulously clean, not a dirty dish anywhere. The main living space was dusty, but not terribly so. The house was modern and sleek, with a wood dining table and chairs in the dinette, an oak kitchen with stone cabinet tops, and comfortable, squishy furniture and a big-screen TV in the living area. The house was cold, the air-conditioning set at sixty-five. It was empty and had the feeling of having been empty for hours.

I couldn't help being snoopy. There was nothing in the small pantry except a half-empty box of rice, a bag of flour in a plastic ziplock bag, four extra-large cereal boxes, three cans of crushed tomatoes, and a bread bag with moldy bread heels in it. What Rick's house lost in the bachelor pad department, the refrigerator made up for in guy supplies. There was a carton of milk, take-out containers, and a pizza box with half a pie in it, the pizza dried out, wrinkled, and growing a spot of green fur. And beer. Four twelve-packs of local microbrewery beer. Beer had no effect on werecats unless they drank a gosh-awful lot of it. Rick had a gosh-awful lot of it.

I looked in the garbage and the recycling. There were a gosh-awful lot of empties too, and not much of anything else. Rick used to like to cook, but there was no indication that he had ever used the pots and pans. The dishes in the cupboard had a layer of pollen and dust on them.

The laundry nook had a basket that contained boxers and socks, another holding a set of sheets, and still another with outerwear clothes in it, some from the previous night. Everything stank of man and sweat except the outer clothes, which also stank of horse. I lifted the pair of jeans on top and studied the creases. Jeans creased according to the way they were worn, and dirty denim, especially *very* dirty denim, could tell a trained investigator how they were most commonly used. These had been worn sitting, straddling, the creases stretching from crotch to knees, and were worn on the bottom from sitting on a saddle. I was sorta surprised that horses didn't bolt when they smelled Rick. Mouser cats lived in barns, but werecats had to smell dangerous on an instinctive level. More bloody. I dropped the jeans and spotted a pair of low-heeled Frye western boots. They smelled of horse and hay and manure. I put the boots back, frowning. I hadn't known Rick rode, but clearly he did. I closed the laundry door, ignored Tandy's censoring stare as I snooped.

I found the stairs up and glanced into each of the two bedrooms up there. The one on the left was empty except for a sheetless air mattress. The one on the right was just empty. The bathroom was scrupulously clean, or maybe never-used clean.

Back downstairs, I found a neat half bath hidden under the stairs and then Rick's room in the rear of the house. This room was a disaster. The bed linens were rank and piled on the foot of the bed. There were piles of clothes everywhere, some folded in stacks, others clean but rumpled in baskets, and still others on the floor, obviously dirty. His en suite bath was filthy, mold growing on the shower tile, soap scum coating the sink. I backed out quickly, fearing I might actually catch something in there.

The only neat thing in the master suite was the bookcase on the wall across from the bed. On the shelves were dozens of books with topics ranging from music theory to the Merged Laws of the Cursed of Artemis, which was a book on werecreature law. Part of me wanted to open it and read, but there were scraps of paper sticking out like bookmarks, each with notes jotted on them, and that felt too much like prying. Which I was doing anyway. There were science books and a book called *Quantum Physics for Dummies*. There were books in French, and one in an African language I couldn't read and which I didn't know Rick could speak, or maybe just read. The other things on the shelves were small drums, some looking African or maybe New World tribal. A small collection of wood flutes nested in an oiled wood box that looked antique. There was a purple candle that had burned down into a puddle of wax on a tiny plate, and a black rock that was polished smooth on two sides, fractured and broken on the others. There was a small box with a drawing of a saxophone and the name *Vandoren* labeled on front. It was half-full of things that looked like small tongue depressors. Everything on the shelves, except the *Vandoren* box, was coated with a heavy layer of dust and pollen, suggesting that the room hadn't been cleaned since before spring.

There was a sound system on the middle shelf; it was dust free and probably hooked up to a house Wi-Fi system. I pressed the on button and a jazzy blues song came on. I hit off.

In the corner was a silver metal stand holding a brass saxophone. The sax wasn't dusty either, showing that, whatever was going on with Rick in terms of filth and cleanliness, and whatever that meant about his mental state, music and horses were a big part of his life. He seemed to be clinging to things that had kept him sane, things that had kept him human. The values and ideals that had made him the man he once was.

I wanted to hear him play, but I had a strange feeling that listening to him would make me sad. And I also knew that I was searching for something of the man Occam might be, in the things that made up Rick's life.

"Nell? Your emotions are all over the place today. You need to talk?"

I turned to Tandy, who stood in the master suite doorway, watching me. "No. I think . . . I think I'm okay." I looked around the clutter and organization, the filth and cleanliness. "I think I'm going to be fine."

"But you're sneaking around Rick's home. Why?"

Frowning, I turned in a circle, my hands on my hips. "I feel as if I'm missing something and . . ." Then it began to come clear. I spoke through it slowly. "The public part of the house is fine, if not immaculate. The private part is a disaster. Like

Rick's private life. This space proclaims that Rick is a slob. It shouts the fact that, unlike other bachelors, Rick can't have a woman over to spend the night"—I pointed to the bed—"so why have clean sheets and a clean bathroom, right? Why not let it go to ruin? And he did. Everything is messed up here except the books and the music and horses, as if only those things are keeping him sane. Someone needs to talk to Rick. You're a counselor of sorts, right?"

"Of sorts," Tandy said softly. He tilted his head toward the front of the house and led me back to the living area, speaking over his shoulder. "Rick may need more than I can offer."

"You won't know unless you try," I said to his back. "And being afraid of Rick's cat is not a good reason to abandon him."

"I'm not abandoning Rick." Tandy sat on the sofa and gestured me over. "Have you talked to him about the callings?"

I grimaced. "No fair throwing my words back on me." I took the opposite side, my back to the arm and my knees drawn up. That showed self-protective body language, so I swiveled around and sat with my feet on the floor. I was uncomfortable and didn't know why, except that I had a feeling Tandy was reading me and that made me feel violated. It wasn't lost on me that he was doing to me what I had been doing to Rick when I snooped. "Okay. Fair question. Go ahead."

"When I was first hit by lightning—"

"Three times in a row."

"Right. I had no idea what had happened to me, no idea that trauma could turn on the genes that make sensitives into empaths. There are so few empaths that I'd never heard of them. I had no way to process what was happening. I didn't realize that I was picking up the thoughts and feelings of the doctors and nurses and technicians who were taking care of me. I just thought I had brain damage and my own emotions were flying all over. Until my girlfriend came to see me in the hospital."

I stopped frowning and fidgeting. This was Tandy's story and I'd never heard it from his lips. "What happened?"

"At the time, I hadn't seen myself in a mirror." Tandy touched his face, the pale skin and the darker reddish Lichtenberg lines that traced across his flesh like the veins of leaves or the tributaries of rivers as seen from the skies. "The lights were off. She walked in and took my hand. She had been crying. She said, 'I thought you were dead. I was so worried.' A nurse followed her in and turned on the light. And I felt her reaction. I was the ugliest thing she had ever seen. She jerked away, with a little scream, and ran out of the room."

"Did you ever see her again?"

"Yes," Tandy said softly. "With her new boyfriend. We passed on opposite sides of the street. She pretended not to see me, but I knew her enough to feel her revulsion even across the lines of traffic."

"That stinks."

Tandy tilted his head as if agreeing.

"And yet you and JoJo are together," I said.

"Jo likes my skin. She thinks it's sexy." He gave me a grin showing his slightly yellowed teeth, even the enamel marred with fractures of Lichtenberg lines.

"That's good," I said, feeling out of my depth and uncertain.

Kindly, Tandy said, "It's time to go, Nell. JoJo wants us back at HQ."

I figured that meant the conversation was over. "Okay. By now, JoJo can probably monitor the place on Rick's security cameras. Talk about snooping."

Tandy chuckled softly. "Come on. We can leave the back door unlocked in case he comes back here."

"The doorknob is round. Cats can't handle round doorknobs."

"Rick's cat is smart. Let's go."

Unit Eighteen—JoJo, T. Laine, Tandy, Occam, and me, but still no Soul or FireWind and no Rick, who was presumably still a cat—had gathered around the conference room table, laptops and tablets open. On the overhead screens were the photos Occam had taken at Rick's accident scene. This was the official end-of-day summation, and Rick's vanishing act was now a matter of PsyLED record. He was in danger and was potentially a security risk. Even now, he might be a prisoner of the witch. Or dead. We had to find him fast and keep him safe until we caught the black-witch who was calling him, or he would end up on administrative leave with his job on the line. We still had no idea where Rick was or what he was doing, and T. Laine had not managed to scry the location of the working. The sun was setting and the moon wouldn't rise until around two in the morning. If the boss had been spelled and summoned so early, it was a good bet the spell would only get stronger as night deepened and the waning moon rose. It was shrinking each day, edging to the new moon, and tonight it would have a claw forming on either end.

Because this was official, Clementine was taking everything down in voice-to-text software. Clementine was much easier to say than CLMT2207, but no matter how cute the software's name was, we had to be careful or we might give away our personal secrets, and none of us wanted that.

Unfortunately, no one had any idea who was calling/cursing Rick, or why, or what the calling might have to do with vampires. We hadn't heard back from Ming about her far-flung scions being called. This was a case that had generated only a minor amount of evidence and no leads, a nice way of saying we had nothing.

Occam said, "JoJo—Jones—and I have determined no tracker dogs should be brought in for fear LaFleur in cat form would attack the dog and the handler. Cats in the wild do not like to be chased. I attempted to track by scent in human form, but I lost him. Soul, when she returned Jones' call, instructed us to let him go."

Tandy said, "You could chase him in cat form."

"I could. With a camera. And he might let me chase him. Or he could kill me. I'm more experienced, but I'd hold back in a fight because I don't want to kill him. I don't know what his cat wants and Rick doesn't dominate it very well in a fight."

"Never mind, then," Tandy said.

Occam ended his report summation with the words, "My final topic is Special Agent Margot Racer. She showed up at the car crash even though she was off duty. She stood around watching the accident investigators and me work. Spent a long time studying the skid marks on the road and searching through the inside of the car."

"What was she looking for?" Tandy asked.

"No idea, but she informed me that she didn't find the amulet necklace created for Rick by the local witches, so I assume Rick was wearing it." Occam rubbed his disfigured hand over his scarred scalp as if they both itched. "I'd judge Racer's emotional and mental state as calm but pensive, but next time you're around her, Tandy, get a read."

Our empath said, "Copy that."

Occam said to T. Laine, "Just so you know, Racer wasn't wearing the spelled cat necklace she had on before. Did you get a read on her amulet?"

"So far as I could tell it was a *protection* working. A charm a witch might give her child. I'm betting all her grandmother's gifts are charmed the same way. But we didn't know that at first. I may have overreacted."

Tandy said, "It was a magically charged situation. Additional energies might have been dangerous."

T. Laine twisted her hand open in a gesture of uncertainty.

JoJo asked, "Is that all?"

"Occam, end of report," he announced to Clementine.

JoJo said, "Jones reporting. As of the discovery of Rick's car and his disappearance, Soul made a personal call to PsyCSI and put the testing of the witch circle focals on the front burner. Ten minutes ago, I received a prelim report. We have fingerprints back from the focal objects found at the circle. Some older prints that are too badly smeared to have reliable markers. Also some clear prints. They've been run against every database we have and we got nada. No matches. The techs think they have some acceptable DNA from the golf ball and from the outside of a glass vial that contained black liquid. They've tested the substance inside the vial and determined it to be decomposed Mithran blood. It was too far gone to get DNA. However, the rotting scraps of gauze cloth were indeed stained with human blood, type A positive—which, by the way, matches Rick's—and it's currently being run for DNA comparison, along with fluid from the other vial. There was a trace of blood on the small steel paring knife, and it too is being run for comparison. This may or may not be important, but Rick always played golf with his dad when they were together, so it's possible—not likely, but possible—that the ball and tees were his. With his DNA. Which could have been used in a circle.

"The lab also ran mass spec on the clay sample from the circle. The biological and mineral markers put it as coming from the Tennessee River. Local clay. The black walnut tree was also likely local. So we finally are getting something to work on, people."

JoJo punched a key on her laptop. "Some really pixelated security camera video of the witch who is doing the spells, or someone who is helping her. These are from the pet supply store where our witch got the white rats and didn't pull a no-see-me spell over herself. Or her human helper. Whichever. Her face is hidden in the shadow of her hoodie, but she appears younger than T. Laine or I expected, moves like a teenager, eighteen at most. She has shoulder-length dark hair or wears a wig, and we can't see the face above the chin. Caucasian. All legs and long limbs. It's summer and she's in long sleeves and a hoodie. We're thinking a junkie, maybe? The clerk doesn't remember her at all."

"Ingram, you've got a strange look going on there." She made a circle in the air where my face was.

"What? I don't . . ." I stopped as it came to me. "Those are the same clothes worn by the subject who robbed the Pilot Gas and the pawn shop. But the body is different."

"Different how?"

I shook my head. "I don't know. I think she's . . . familiar? Maybe wearing a glamour that throws us off?"

"Which means we have no idea what she looks like," T. Laine said.

"Fine. Dyson"—Jo looked at Tandy—"I've printed stills of the few places we get a hint of the face, but I'm guessing that a glamour means there's no chance of a composite sketch?"

"It's unlikely," he said. "The best information we have from witnesses is a description of her chin."

"Occam," JoJo said, "if LaFleur comes back here in distress, we can use the null room again, yes?"

"If he's in human form, yes, if we have to," Occam said. "I don't think his cat will come here and I don't think the cat will go into a null room willingly. I suggest we set up a silver cage.

It's more painful than a silver bracelet or necklace, but more effective, and less likely to result in a fight that spreads were-taint. I have the feeling that a silver cage will stop any calling, even his own magic, because it stops the ability for a were to change shape. Two birds, one cage."

Occam had spent twenty years in a silvered cage. Occam knew what they *could* do and what they *might* be able to do.

"You got a cage, CC?"

Occam smiled at the Crispy Critter reference. "I do. La-Fleur's used it before. It's familiar, a safe place, so I think his cat would go into it. I can set it up in his office or the sleeping room."

Rick, in cat form, here. Having Mud at HQ when I was working was looking like a worse and worse idea. I needed to figure out child care now, not after the court gave me custody.

"LaFleur's office," T. Laine said. "That way he won't disturb us if he starts yowling."

We looked at her in disbelief. "Really?" JoJo said. "Yowl? You're talking about our boss."

"So? Cats yowl." T. Laine's face creased in a mischievous grin and she looked at Clementine's speaker in the middle of the table. "There was a feral cat who actually brought her boyfriends to my front porch and had relations one night. It was loud!"

Tandy and Occam snickered. I realized this was a joke that would be included in the day's record.

"Ingram," Jo said to me. "Report."

I filled them in on the vampire meeting and the few insights I had to offer. It wasn't much.

"EOD concluded. Clementine, cease recording," JoJo said, dumbfounded, shaking her head. A small red light I hadn't noticed on the mic went dark. "Dismissed. Be safe, people."

The team dispersed slowly, JoJo and Tandy going over the files and discussing what to do if Rick came back or called one of us or was spotted in cat form by the public. T. Laine said she was working on something and would be late in the morning. As he left the room, Occam pointed a finger at me, saying, "I'm running some errands, but I'll pick up dinner and bring it back."

My heart warmed at the thought that I'd get to see him

again. He walked from the room and my eyes followed him down the hallway, his body moving cat-like, graceful and smooth. It was good to see him being Occam again and not so badly burned and wounded. And my thoughts returned to his . . . not his proposal. He hadn't offered one. But he *had* said he loved me. Loved. Me. Leaves and all. Except that I didn't know how I felt about loving a man. About giving myself to him. I had done that once before out of desperation and the bargain had been worth it, but I didn't know if I wanted to bargain for my freedom again. Would that be what I was doing if I loved a man? Bargaining for my freedom? Did I even love Occam? I wasn't sure about that. The few romance books I had read suggested that love followed attraction and I certainly felt an attraction for Occam. But . . .

Brow furrowed, my brain thinking too many things on too many levels to really concentrate on just one—like work—I went to my cubicle. I started putting together a list of spells that had been used against vampires in the past, something akin to the spell that was calling them. I was still wearing jeans and the T-shirt I started the shift in, and since I'd be working in the office, I saw no reason to change just to do paperwork. I had a nicer pair of pants in the four-day gobag should I need them. I took the laptop to my cubicle and called Mama and then Mud, before I started in. Mud was planting herbs in good Soulwood soil and playing with her computer. "Don't be ordering any more electrical equipment," I warned.

Mud giggled. "Nope. Sam, Jedidiah, Daddy, and me are talking greenhouses."

"Tell them to not let you break my budget." My sister was safe with the Nicholsons tonight and I made arrangements to pick her up when I got off work. Unless Rick reappeared, it was shaping up to be a quiet night.

Two hours later, I heard the door from the stairway open, with a strange metallic banging clanging sound. I got up from my desk and stuck my head out in the hallway to see Occam wedging a stack of metal against the door to hold it open. He whirled and padded down the stairs again, his boots so soft on the steps I could barely hear them.

I went to the top of the stairs and inspected the flat metal, which turned out to be an easily assembled cage, steel walls and top with a removable, silver-plated steel bottom. Rick's cage. Occam came in again, this time carrying bags of hoagies and a plastic container of iced tea from Frussies Deli & Bakery on Gay Street. He grinned at me as the outer door closed. "I got a Dirty Bird, a Three Little Pigs, a Turkey Club, and a James Dick's Favorite. I—"

Something slammed into the outer door. Faster than I could follow, Occam set down the bag, drew his weapon, and raced back down the stairs. From the conference room JoJo shouted, "It's Rick's leopard!" The banging, slamming came again. Even though the outer door was reinforced to withstand a small bomb, I could see the edges give.

Occam's lips were bloodless in the harsh lighting. His eyes tense as he mentally ran through his options.

The banging came again. And again. I looked back at the window. It was dark out but the moon hadn't risen yet.

"A grindy is with him," JoJo shouted. "What do you want to do, CC?"

Occam, one shoulder against the wall, changed out magazines for silver ammo and said to me, "Set up the cage in Rick's office."

I grabbed the cage, which was heavier than I expected and bulky, and dragged it more than carried it to Rick's office. It was easy to assemble, with a tab that read, LIFT HERE. I lifted and the cage opened with relative ease. There were steel supports for each corner and for the top and bottom. I snapped them closed. No pawed creature could open them. It would require opposable thumbs. It took me maybe half a minute to set it up, and the booming continued as I worked. I opened the cage door. Satisfied, I raced back to the stairwell. "Got it."

"Close all the office doors but Rick's. Lock yourselves in the conference room," Occam said. His voice was calm, emotionless, steady.

Slamming doors behind me, I raced to the conference room. I locked Tandy, JoJo, and myself into safety. Turned and faced the room, my back to the door, so I could watch the camera feed overhead. One camera showed a black leopard throwing himself at the outer door. Another showed Occam slapping open a security baton. The volume was up on the speaker system and the sound of the baton opening was a *schink-snap*.

From the way it moved through the air I knew the baton was
heavy-weighted steel.

Occam braced himself behind the door and opened it. The
parking lot's lights blasted in.

Rick leaped inside, a black smear in the silvered lights.
White fangs bared. His snarl was a growl of menace. The
leopard twisted in midair, body lithe, supple, vicious. He
reached out with his front claws. Slashing for Occam.

TEN

My heart stopped.

As fast as Rick, Occam spun. Arm back like a batter's. Brought the baton down on Rick's front legs just above the paws. Reversed. Rapped Rick's skull. Fast low thumps while the cat was in midair.

The black leopard went down with a thud. Rick didn't move.

"Wow," I said. Blinked.

A grindy jumped from outside onto Occam's shoulder. Occam petted the grindy, a long swipe down its body. "Hey there, Pea. Or Bean. Whichever you are. We're all good."

Bending, Occam shoved Rick out of the doorway and closed the door. He closed the baton with a metallic click and placed the grindy on the step. Holstering his weapon, he bent and grabbed Rick's front legs near the chest. He heaved Rick up and over his shoulder, a black weight with front legs that hung at odd angles. Broken. He carried Rick up the steps. The amulet created by the local witches swung from its chain around his neck. I couldn't tell if it was working, but considering the shape Rick was in, I guessed not.

JoJo activated different security cams as they moved, allowing us to follow Occam as he carried Rick to the office. He bent and tossed Rick inside the cage in front of Rick's desk, banged the cage door shut, and secured it. He wasn't even breathing hard. Occam went back to the stairs and retrieved the sandwich bag and the gallon of tea, made sure the door to the stairs shut properly, and came to the conference room.

I opened the door. Behind me JoJo said, "My hero."

"Anything for the ladies. Hey, Nell, sugar. What sandwich you want?"

"Looking at her, I'd say to give her the Dick's Favorite," Jo said.

There was something in her tone that made me think she was saying something else, but it was something I had to ignore, mostly because I didn't know how to react to it. "I'd rather have the Three Little Pigs," I said. "And extra mayo if you have it."

Occam gave me a look that I couldn't interpret, but it might have been tenderness. Or possessiveness. Or neither. He unwrapped the sandwich and passed it to me, then handed out the rest of the food as the others requested. He passed around napkins and paper cups for the tea, which was sweating on the conference room table.

We ate in silence until JoJo spoke around a bite of meat and bread. "So you broke Rick's legs. That might piss him off."

"It might," Occam said, laconic, drawing out the last word as if he didn't care.

"This part of that dominance thing you two are always fighting through?"

"Rick and I don't fight."

"Uh-huh. Right." JoJo gave up and finished her sandwich. Overhead, on the screen from the camera situated outside of Rick's office, we watched as Rick twitched, spasmed, and made a mewling sound. He was in pain. JoJo turned off the speakers.

"We oughta do something for him," I said.

"No," Occam said. "He needs to dominate his cat better. Maybe the pain will drive the point home."

"Even if he was being spelled?" I asked.

"Especially then. If Rick can't control his cat, he'll lose his job."

And the job was all Rick had left. I remembered his house and the way Rick was living. I held in a sigh and took a big bite of pork sandwich. No one else spoke.

We had finished eating when T. Laine climbed the stairs carrying a bag from Firehouse Subs. She tossed the bag on the table and said, "Great minds and all that. What happened to the door? It looks like a truck hit it."

"Rick happened," JoJo said. "He's in cat form in a silvered cage. With two broken legs and probably a concussion."

"Dang," T. Laine said. "Was he wearing the amulet created by the local witches?"

"Yep," Occam said.

"I'm guessing it didn't work."

"Maybe it helped a little," Occam said. He sat back in his chair, his sandwich in front of him on its wrapper. "He was human enough to remember to come here. That isn't a cat's thought. Lemme eat and I'll see what's up with the boss."

T. Laine flopped in a chair and said, "I'm not quite done with it and it hasn't been tested, but I've devised a leather and black titanium collar for Rick, with GPS tracking, to track him when he shifts." She plucked a chain from her pocket and placed the necklace on the table. We passed it around as she said, "It's not too girly, not too disco or surfer boy. It can be worn with the witches' amulet without the workings going boom. The black titanium chain won't show in his cat coat, and it kinda looks like Rick."

It was a small rough nugget of stone, something with a crystalized shape that caught the light but diffused it in the thin linear crystals. It was wrapped with black metal and hooked to the chain, which closed with a lobster claw clasp on one of three rings, making it adjustable. Magic tingled all through the small stone, but muted, as if it was a passive working. "You can track him with it?" I asked, handing it on to Occam.

"Pretty much. Don't ask me how. It'll hurt your church-girl feelings, all black magic and stuff." Her tone was sarcastic but T. Laine's eyes were dancing with laughter as she bit into her sub. Chewing, she added, "Because he isn't in the null room, I can follow the magic in real time to test it out. Anyone thought to take the leopard a sandwich?"

"He'll be in too much pain to eat until after we let him out and let him shift," Occam said.

"You're gonna let him out?" JoJo asked.

Occam said, "As soon as he's fully shackled his cat, yeah."

"You can tell when he's in charge?"

"Scent never lies."

"He's hurting," I said softly. "Is it okay for me to pull on Soulwood to calm him and take away some of the pain?"

"Yes," Tandy said. "That would help."

I glanced from the screen that showed us Rick in his misery to Tandy. The empath was pale and sweating, reacting to the strongest emotion in the building. Rick's pain.

JoJo frowned and said, "Oh. Damn. I didn't realize—Fine. Go for it, Nell. Tandy, if you need to, go use the null room. If not, why not go lie down for a bit."

Tandy nodded and left the conference room for the break room, and the sofa there.

I went to my cubicle and stuck my fingers into the soil of a potted plant, hearing the unit talking about Margot Racer and how they should handle her. The dirt was Soulwood soil, and the farm answered my call instantly, coiling around me like a snake or a living vine. I reached out with the power of my land and found Rick, a familiar snarl of cat magics and new red pulses of energy that weren't there the last time I soothed him. I held back, studying the magics. Spook School classes had taught me that foreign magic wasn't something to be trifled with, and this was different from Rick's usual magic. This was a bright pulse of light with a braided luminescent tail. The pulses seemed to wrap around his heart and his brain and twine through his tattoos. I slipped in between the pulses and called on the magic that claimed Rick for my land. I drained off some of his pain and felt him chuff and settle.

An hour later, Occam opened the cage door and Rick crawled off the silver tray that was keeping him in cat form. He lay on the hallway floor, panting and mewling softly in pain, his legs still at odd angles, even with were-creature healing abilities. The breaks had been thorough. JoJo turned off the camera, giving Rick an illusion of privacy, and we waited, only Occam and T. Laine close to the cage when the boss shifted, Occam to stop Rick if he lost control, Lainie under a small of *hedge of thorns*, to evaluate the magic of the amulets and Rick's shifting.

I had hauled T. Laine aside and explained, verbal report only, what I had seen in Rick's magic and what I had done to calm him. "Not bad, Ingram," she'd said. "Good work."

The simple words made me feel as if I had contributed something important to the unit, more than filing reports, transcribing anything Clementine missed or messed up, and the occasional reading of the earth. Being useful felt good.

The shape-change took fifteen minutes, shorter than the last time I measured his shift. The camera came back on when Rick was human shaped and dressed in jeans, his hair longer, face with a silvered beard. He was still bare chested and the tattoos of cat eyes were glowing gold in a field of dark tattoo ink and scars and his olive-skinned chest. Occam handed him a T-shirt. Rick dragged it over his head and I heard T. Laine say, "Jo, don't turn on the antispell music yet. Thanks to Ingram's insights, I did a *scan* working and looked at Rick's magic. Someone's using the spelled tats to call him."

"Hurts like a mother," Rick said, his voice rough and pained. He rubbed the mauled tattoos on his shoulder and arm. "And the cat-tat eyes are burning hot. I need the music."

"Just gimme a minute," T. Laine said. "While you were shifting, I followed the magic calling you. It came from out toward the river. If you'll hold still I can try to get a more precise location and can pinpoint it with a scry."

"Hurry."

Rick stood still, half sitting on the cage that had held him, rubbing his arm, his body tense.

"Okay. Got it. Music."

A woodwind melody played by an air witch flowed through the speakers. A measure in, Rick released a pent breath, walked to the conference room, and took his place at the table. Occam gave him a cup of coffee and a paper-wrapped deli sandwich from the fridge. Rick said softly, "Thank you."

Occam nodded, his eyes kind. "When you're up to it, I need to ask you some questions."

"Okay. I'm good now that I got music," Rick said, biting into his hoagie. "Go ahead."

"Tell me where you were, what you were doing, and anything you remember."

"I was watching the game at a sports bar on State Street. It was midafternoon and the moon had been up for hours, but I wasn't thinking about it consciously. Why should I?" he asked, as if asking himself the question. "It was nowhere near full. Hell, it was nearly moonset. I was wearing the amulet. I should have been fine. But I felt the draw of the summoning. It started like a buzzing in my chest and my fingertips. I remember that I paid my bill. Got in my car. Somehow ended up here. I probably have all kinds of tickets coming from traffic cameras." He chuckled wryly. "Worse, I have to wonder how many security cameras got footage of a big black cat racing the streets."

T. Laine entered last and placed a paper map on the table, the creases worn. "I think I have the location of the witch circle, at least the general area. It's different from the last time. It's out off Alcoa, near the Woodson Drive exit, on the bank of Spring Creek. There's grassy areas and wooded areas there." She looked at Rick. "Do you want us to try and get there?"

"No point in running lights and sirens." His face wrenched down in banked rage. "It's starting to ease up. I think the witch is finished with the spelling. You can wait and check it out in daylight."

Occam leaned over the paper map. "As the crow files, that's more than five miles. Either she's getting better or she used a bigger sacrifice. And we still don't know if the effect on Rick is deliberate, coincidental, or incidental."

"The calling was drawing on Rick's tattoos," I said. "I saw it. It isn't coincidental."

No one replied.

"What does that do to any overlapping areas?" JoJo asked.

"Swings it all over the place," T. Laine said. "Why can't it be easy?"

"Why can't what be easy?" I asked, not understanding, frustrated.

"We were hoping that there would be overlapping areas of the spells that might lead to a narrow part of the city where the witch might be staying," Occam said. "No such luck."

"I have a thought," T. Laine said, her hair swinging forward to cover her face. She took a breath and pushed back her hair, holding up the titanium tracking necklace she had made. "We have the option of belling the cat with the tracker." She slid her eyes to Rick. "Next time, you could let go, let the spell take you, and we could follow."

Rick looked from T. Laine to each of us in turn.He drained his coffee cup and held the empty in his fingertips, tilting it. "What does Soul say about that possibility?"

"She finally called us back. She says it's stupid. Though she used more diplomatic wording."

"And FireWind?" he asked, an edge to his voice.

Occam sat, facing the window, his back to Rick, which I figured was a cat thing. "We thought it best not to contact him. He's still dealing with that black-magic case in Maine."

Rick made a hmmming sound that was close to a purr. He reached out and took T. Laine's necklace. "What's it do?"

"It's a black tourmaline. It's aligned to this one." She dug in a pocket and lifted up a similar stone. "It puts out a signal I can follow."

Rubbing his finger over the black amulet, Rick said, "Okay." Fingers moving quickly, he combined the two necklaces and settled both stones under his T-shirt. "If I get forced into the cat, you can track me."

The cat. Not *my cat.* Interesting. "Your shift was faster than from before I was a tree," I said.

Rick's face split in a grin at my tree comment and a breathy laugh followed. "Yeah. I haven't been a cat for long, but I'm getting the hang of it."

"Occam has a fluid shift from human to cat and back again," I said, "as if he shares the body of the cat, even with his scars. You're more binary—human or cat, with little of the cat in the human and little of the human in the cat, and both fighting for domination."

Rick narrowed his gaze on me, listening.

I let the magics I had sensed during his shift slide through my mind. "I've always thought that the mangled tattoo spell might be keeping the parts of you more separate than other weres and . . . I might be able to ease your pain during a shift and speed it up a bit. I'll watch next time you're on Soulwood and see if I can help. And you can also try to make friends with your cat-self." I took a breath. "And you can tell us about your tattoos. More than is in the official reports."

"You been reading my official reports, Ingram?" There was a soft menace in his tone.

"Yes," I said, calm in my own. "We all have. You were missing and in danger. You should expect a complete lack of privacy."

Suddenly the rest of the team was busy with chores or their tablets or laptops. Rick looked like he was about to get mad, so I said, "The unit wants to believe you aren't being personally targeted. But there's strange new magic in your tattoos. You're being called to sites of black magic. There's secrets and then there's stupid secrets."

Rick rubbed his shoulder, seemed to realize what he was doing, and stopped. He cursed once, hard and crude. "Early in my career undercover . . ." He stopped. Turned. Went to the coffeemaker and dumped used grounds and their filter into the garbage.

His back to us, his hands busy, he continued. "I was chatting up a vampire, Isleen, for information." He stopped, as if telling the story was painful. His hands started shaking, a delicate tremor. "She . . . She drugged me. I woke up chained to a black marble slab, in the center of an old witch circle, in a decrepit barn. She brought in a witch."

He hesitated, his voice sounding hoarse when he said, "Her name was Loriann." His head ducked forward at the name, like a twitch of pain. Rubbed his shoulder. "Before you ask, the circles are not Lori's handiwork."

Lori, I thought. And I wasn't the only one to notice the sweetness in the name.

"Isleen forced Loriann to ink me in a blood-magic tattoo of binding. The tattoo was intended to make me into a blood-slave, something Isleen hadn't been able to accomplish with her own blood. I don't know why. The tattoo inks were mixed with vampire blood. Cat blood. Gold foil. There was a blood-magic spell involved."

I noted the two names in my cell, spelling them phonetically.

Tandy asked softly, "A vamp forced the witch to ink you?"

I realized that this was the first time Rick had talked publicly with his unit about the event. He found a bag of his favorite dark roast Community Coffee in a drawer, opened it, and scooped out grounds. His movements were sluggish, as if he was moving in his sleep, the rich scent filling the room. When he spoke again, his voice sounded strangled, the words little more than a whisper, halting and slow.

"Isleen . . . had killed Loriann's grandmother while the

family watched. Had taken Loriann's . . . sibling. As hostage. Was forcibly drinking from . . ." Rick stopped. Cleared his throat. The grounds poured with a nearly silent shush. "Loriann had no choice. But she managed to . . . to get help." He folded the coffee bag up again and put it to the side. "Leo Pellissier . . . killed Isleen. The binding was never finished. It wasn't a problem for years, until I was bitten by a black wereleopard and then the werewolves . . . chewed on them."

He lifted the coffeemaker reservoir, turned on the tap, the water scudding into the bottom. We all waited. Silent. He replaced it and slid the coffeepot on the coffeemaker. Placed both hands on the counter, steady but paler than normal. He bent forward and his hair swung over his jaws, hiding more of his face.

JoJo said softly, "I'm guessing that the unfinished binding merged with werewolf saliva, fighting the black leopard weretaint."

Rick nodded once. "The combination damaged my weremagic. Kept me from shifting. Then Paka came, supposedly to help me."

He punched a button on the coffeemaker and turned to face us. His voice sounded stronger. "My tattoos were tested by a witch in Spook School. There was no breach, magical or otherwise, in them. Soul keeps an eye on them. No breach."

"That they noticed," T. Laine said. "Once there's a fissure, there's always a weak spot. And Soul isn't here now."

Rick nodded. "I've been feeling . . . odd. Restless. For the last few months, during the waning moon." He reached up and touched the scarred tats, his fingers uncertain. Then he smiled, his lips quirked up on one side, and he looked younger, less harried, and wry. "We'll assume for now that I'm a security risk." Rick's job, his career, was on the line. "Meanwhile"—he turned his dark gaze to me—"were the local vamps attacked by this spell?"

My mouth opened in an O and I punched my cell on again. There was nothing from the vampires on e-mail or text so I dialed Yummy.

"Maggot," she said by way of greeting. She was trying to be mean and I'd had just about enough of it.

"Yeah, Fanghead," I said.

Yummy laughed, a human kind of laugh, the kind that meant they were not thinking as blood-suckers but as the people they had once been.

"Did you guys get spell-called today?" I asked.

"No." Her tone sharpened and took on that faint Louisiana accent I heard from time to time. "Why? Did you all?"

"One of our cats, yes." I dragged the paper map to me and traced my finger across it. "And the spell was likely cast within two miles of your lair."

"Nothing. Not a thing. But if it was in daytime, we wouldn't have felt it once we were asleep."

"Okay. We'll talk later." I ended the call and reached for T. Laine's map. "The spell site was closer to the vamps than the night they were called. So either proximity wasn't a factor or daylight changed it. I think this is still a spell in the planning and designing stage."

"I agree. It feels different each time, but planning for what?" Rick asked. He drummed his fingers on the table and then said, "I'm not taking any chances. I'll be sleeping in HQ for the duration of the case."

"Good." JoJo pointed at a view from an outside camera and T. Laine power-walked to the door at the top of the stairs. "Margot's here and needs an update on Ming of Glass, the fact that we've made a report to the governor's office, Rick's new amulets, and his likelihood of being a security risk. All of which I can handle."

T. Laine called back to us, "I'll get her security codes and an ID for the doors."

"Great," JoJo yelled. Margot followed our witch inside, T. Laine giving her what she called a down-and-dirty debrief. She finished with, "If you're taking the night shift, we need someone to visit the scene of the spell casting and see if there are common areas, overlapping places where the witch might be staying."

Margot, dressed in business pants and jacket, settled into an empty chair at the conference table and when JoJo finished the recap, Margot said to the group, "Okay. I'm up to speed. I have additional info that falls under the umbrella of PsyLED, if it's true. The FBI just heard rumors that a small group of rogue vampires have established a hidden lair here in the

Knoxville vicinity. They want me with your unit until we de-termine what the vamps want and if the local witches and the vampires are working together."

"Local?" Rick asked softly. "The FBI thinks the *local* co-ven is involved? Vamps and witches generally hate each other and *we* have evidence of only one witch at the circles. And rogue vamps do not lair together. Ever. What evidence?"

Margot lifted her left hand and inspected her nails. They were painted green with sparkles in the polish. "Evidence? Not a damn thing."

"So why suggest that there might be a collusion of para ac-tivity against Knoxville citizens and PsyLED itself?" T. Laine asked, censure in her voice.

"Not me. The acting head drew all the conclusions and made the decision. I'm just passing along supposed CI info that might or might not be true."

The table went silent and still as we all processed her words. CI meant confidential informant. But it sounded as if Margot didn't believe it was true information so much as a big ol' lie.

Margot showed teeth in a smile worthy of any were-creature. "New vamps in town? That part's confirmed. My bosses are determined to make this a witch hunt. They don't know I come from witches. I am the perfect person to liaise because my agenda won't match theirs."

"Ohhh . . . ," I said, my disappointment easing away. "You're protecting the witches. And us too. That's why you were so insistent on being part of this team."

Margot flashed me a smile, brilliant in her dark-skinned face. "Witch hunts piss me off and I've been watching this one brewing for quite a while."

T. Laine said slowly, "You sneaky thing you. Humans are paranoid and nutso. And human law enforcement are even worse."

"Hey, human FBI agent here," Margot said.

Well, sort of human, I thought. My cell dinged and I an-swered, puzzled. "Yummy? What can I—"

"We need help! We're under attack!"

I hit the speaker button and the sound of gunfire was am-plified into the room. "We've called 911!" Yummy shouted into the cell, her voice high-pitched and panicked. "The police say we aren't in their jurisdiction. They refuse to send SWAT! The governor's not answering our calls!"

"Copy," I said. "You're on speaker. SAC LaFleur is here."

Rick pointed at Margot and she left the room for the hallway, where she started making calls, her voice toneless, steady, too low to hear.

Rick said to Yummy, "We need info. For starters, how many enemy attackers? Are they vamps or human? What weapons?"

More gunfire came over my cell. The sounds of shouting and screaming. Yummy didn't answer, but the background noise changed as if she was moving.

Rick said to Jo, "Get FireWind on the line, I don't care if he's neck deep in vampire guts at a crime scene. The rest of you grab your gear and get back here to gear up."

I raced to my cubicle, grabbed my two gobags, my weapon, and sped back. I dumped everything on the table and started checking my weapon. The others slammed their gear down too.

Rick said. "The vampire isn't responding. We don't have the training or the equipment to take on an armed attack without the backup of SWAT."

Over my cell, I could pick out semiautomatic weapon fire in three-burst patterns. The boom of what sounded like a shotgun. Or maybe even a small-bore cannon. More screams, human and the high-pitched screams of vampires, echoed.

The ambient noise of the cell changed again and we heard, "I can see maybe ten humans and pick out three Naturaleza by the scent patterns." Yummy's voice had steadied. She was breathing in a slow, regular rhythm, like a human who had taken control of herself. Yummy hadn't been a vampire for long. Under stress, she sometimes fell back into human reactions. Clicks and metallic sounds came over the speaker. She, or someone close by, was reloading. "There may be more coming in from downwind."

"Any magic like the summoning attack?" Rick asked.

The sound of a single shot overwhelmed the cell's mic and Yummy came back on in midsentence. "—that two. One down. Trying to avoid hitting the attacking humans. No magic." She cursed, hard, succinct. "They've put their own humans in front of them. They're using their cattle as shields." She cursed again, inventive and sexually explicit.

JoJo whispered, "Locals are calling 911. Multiple calls reporting gunfire."

To Yummy, Rick said, "Blood-servants are still counted as human in the current political climate. Using them as shields guarantees armed response, but it might be slow."

"We don't have time for slow! Our people are dying!" Two more shots followed.

I remembered the other vamps Ming had discussed. "How far out are Lincoln Shaddock and his crew?" I asked Yummy when I thought she could hear me.

"They're not answering our calls." Yummy fired again. Again. The cell went silent, as if I'd lost the signal. I strapped my vest in place, the Velcro loud in the tense silence. The vest was dark with the word *PsyLED* on the front and back in stark white, marking me as law enforcement, either someone to listen to or a target, depending on their intent.

"We're all geared up. Why aren't we on the way?" I demanded.

"When Ming became Master of the City and created a council chambers," Rick said, "she effectively created an ambassadorial residence under the auspices of the new European emperor and the Mithran Dark Queen. According to the current arrangements with the secretary of state, the diplomatic corps, and other agencies within the federal government, only federal agencies can respond to calls for assistance on the grounds, not local police unless there's a direct danger to the local populace." His voice was toneless, shut down, void of emotional entonations, yet his eyes were glowing green. He'd had a bad night and exhaustion had brought his cat close. "Access to vamp grounds is limited except by invitation of the MOC. Law enforcement response and presence, therefore, has to come from us or the FBI and I don't have the people to order armed response onto the grounds in the face of multiple armed attackers. We need SWAT."

JoJo added, "Only if a vamp is attacking humans away from council chambers can local law provide armed response."

"That's stupid," I said. And if I cussed, I'd be saying awful things right now.

When the mic began to work again, Yummy was screaming, the piercing ululation of the dying vampire. "I'm hit," she said. "Oh shit. I'm . . . hit . . ." The cell call ended.

Rick answered his cell, saying crisply, "Soul. We got problems."

I tuned him out and dialed Jane Yellowrock. The Dark Queen of the vampires had to have some authority over what was happening here. It went to voice mail. I dialed her business partners in New Orleans. Voice mail. I called the personal cell of Alex Younger. Voice mail. It was almost as if they were avoiding me. I dialed the Mithran Council Chambers of New Orleans. Voice mail. I left the same message on every line: "The MOC of Knoxville is under attack by unknown vampires. Please advise." But I was getting madder and madder, and I could feel leaves tickling at my neck as my anger made them grow and unfurl. I lugged the agency landline phone to me and dialed the NOLA number. When it went to voice mail, I knew that it wasn't just me who was currently persona non grata, it was PsyLED. Or they were under attack too. That seemed a stretch, but it wasn't impossible. Jane pretty much lived at war.

"Margot," Rick called out. "Soul gave us the go-ahead. Tell me you got armed response."

Margot stuck her head in the door. "I've got SWAT on the way," she said, "along with a small group of FBI under the command of the Knoxville acting SAC. Local cops will set up perimeters half a mile on either end of the road. Medic is on the way to their locations. But I gotta tell you, SWAT isn't overly motivated. There was chatter about letting them kill each other off."

"There always is," Rick snarled. "Vests and headsets, silver and standard ammo, flashbangs and smoke grenades. Occam, assault rifle. Let's go, people."

"On it, boss," Occam shouted from the weapons locker. Unit Eighteen had only one assault rifle and Occam was the only one qualified.

Not having a modern assault weapon suited me just fine. I had a shotgun in the truck and I had never been afraid to use it. I was shaky at the thought of a vampire fight and having trouble getting my breath, my Kevlar vest too tight. Adding new weapons would have made me shakier still.

Rick's cell rang and he glanced at the screen. To Jo, he said, "Call Soul. Update her." He took the call, and, from the tone, I guessed he was updating FireWind.

Jo touched her earpiece. T. Laine ran back to her desk for more amulets. I patted my vest and made sure I had extra magazines, the silver-lead composite rounds on one side, regular ammo on the other. Ran back to my cubicle for my field boots. And water. My mouth had gone dry as desert dirt. I could hear T. Laine muttering under her breath, yanking out null charms and attack amulets and healing amulets. Occam was inspecting the assault rifle, his scarred face tight, yellow-glowing eyes intent. Margot was reading a sat map.

My heart was slamming in my chest, an almost painful, hollow sensation. *Humans have hearts, plants don't.* A frenzied titter of laughter tickled in my chest.

Margot said, "Picking out a staging area from satellite maps."

"Comms on the para freq," JoJo said, "and on our own dedicated freq."

Rick snarled again, "Move!"

We piled into the hallway, moving fast.

"Not you, boss!" JoJo shouted.

We all stopped. Rick whirled on her, his black eyes glowing the green of his cat.

"Not you. What happens if you get spelled while your team is in the middle of a firefight?" JoJo asked.

I said, "I saw the magic in your tats. Jo is right. You can't go with us."

Rick cursed. Strapped on his vest. "I'm going."

A new voice came over the speaker system and flooded through HQ so we could hear as we geared up. "LaFleur, I've been kept apprised of your situation."

I looked up at the speaker over my cubicle, knowing this male voice had to belong to Ayatas FireWind, the new man over the eastern states. Rick cursed again and his eyes glowed greener.

"Jones has the right of it. You are to remain in HQ and

assist her," FireWind said, "until such time as you are urgently needed on scene. For the rest of you, SWAT has suddenly developed a keen interest. They are lead until the site is secured. If a breach is required or SWAT engages with the enemy, let them do their jobs and stay out of the way unless null magic is required. PsyLED will assume command only when the situation moves from potential armed combat to diplomatic exercises. This will occur once SWAT has secured and cleared the premises and the grounds."

Intense relief washed through me like a flood. Tears gathered in my eyes and I blinked them away. Suddenly I could breathe. We weren't going into a firefight alone. I didn't know who had forced a "keen interest" into SWAT, but I was grateful.

Rick started to argue. "This is my unit."

"Yes. It is," FireWind said, "and I understand your frustration. But this course of action and organizational command structure was agreed upon in joint meetings this week, with acting FBI SAC of Knoxville, Shultz, and the team leader of SWAT, Gonzales. Despite our differences, LaFleur, this is not a personal attack. Should the witch targeting you begin a working during a firefight, you might present a danger to yourself and others. You will *stand down*."

We had stopped dead in the hallway, halted by FireWind, his voice bare of regional accent, his words precise. "Cameras and headgear on everyone. Jones and LaFleur, I want access to all comms. Dyson, you are to stay in the unit's van unless accompanied by another agent until the site is secure."

"Yes, sir," Tandy said. Rick snarled again.

I threw my gobags over my shoulder and made sure I had my headset, vest camera, cell, and tablet. The address of the Master of the City of Knoxville backed up to the Tennessee River, within two miles of the general location of the witch circle T. Laine had scried for. It was smart to keep Rick here at HQ.

I headed out and Occam raced up behind me, fast. "My car," he said. "It's faster than your POS." I knew what a POS was and Occam had just insulted my truck. In other circumstances I'd have called him on it, but now I got out my shogun and two boxes of shells. I broke the shotgun open, securing it in Occam's car for safe travel, but put the gobags up front with me.

Occam slapped the emergency lights to the dash, locked the AR-15 into place behind the seats, and we slid in. The sports car roared to life and we shot out of the lot, headlights bouncing on the rough asphalt, while I was still buckling up. The siren was piercing. We were the first vehicle out, going from zero to eighty in seconds. Cars followed us out of the parking area but fell quickly behind.

"Comms check," JoJo said into my earbud.

"Occam. Check." He whipped the wheel and I let the seat belt catch me.

"Ingram. Check," I said, making sure I was on PsyLED's dedicated frequency. The rest of the team chimed in, voices strained and tense. We were all here, all on the proper freq.

Margot said, "I have the satellite photos of the local area up. I've marked two likely staging areas on either side of the MOC's property, with GPS coordinates and topography." We were going to plan an op on the fly. This was how people got killed. That thought settled me as Occam flew around night-time traffic.

"Got the sites up at HQ," JoJo said. "Rick?"

Rick said, "I like the southern site. Ingram, you and I were there most recently. Do you concur?"

"Affirmative," I said. "The slight ridge gives us protection from the estate and errant gunfire. But if we like it, then so might enemy vamps. What if they're already there?"

"We need to know what direction the attack came from," Occam said.

I was already dialing Yummy again. "Hello," a breathy voice answered. Relief surged through me. "Maggot," she said. "What's your ETA?"

I glanced at Occam. He said, "Ten if traffic is agreeable. SWAT will be at least thirty."

"We won't last thirty," Yummy said. I heard a voice in the background and Yummy's voice turned away from the cell. "No. You can't give any more. Get out of here. I'm healed enough and you're too much of a temptation. If you spot another human to feed me, send them my way. But protect Ming's back trail."

"Yes, my mistress," the voice said.

"Ming has a way out?" I asked.

Back into the cell, Yummy said, "No comment. They breached the main house. Ming is safe, but I don't know for how long."

"What direction did they come from?" I asked, strapping my low-light/infrared headset in place.

"The ones I saw came from the south."

"Nothing from Shaddock?" I asked. "Is he almost here?"

"Nothing. Not a word."

Rick said into my earpiece, "We just got word that the Master of the City of Asheville's clan home is under attack."

Yummy must have heard it. Vampire hearing was better than human. "Shaddock's home is under attack while he's here, helping Ming? That is not a fluke."

Into the earpiece, Margot said, "It may not be relevant, but I was just updated re the unconfirmed bureau reports on the invading rogue vampires. It suggests that over twenty vampires made their way ashore before, during, and after the Mithran change in leadership. LaFleur? Comments?"

Occam laid on the brakes as an ancient VW van coasted out of the way. We passed the rotting van at the speed of light. I yanked my seat belt tighter across my belly and wondered if prayer would keep me alive if we flipped at this speed.

"Similar intel came in earlier today," Rick said, "and I just now opened the reports. Possibility of a number of vamps making their way to Florida. Three unknown vamps were seen one night in Myrtle Beach, South Carolina. The next morning a dozen teenagers down for spring break disappeared. Their families have heard nothing from them. We assume they were rolled and carted away. No further word or sightings. Local clans denied all knowledge and were cooperative with authorities. No indication vamps came up from Louisiana to the Appalachians."

Margot and Rick had similar information. Maybe the FBI and PsyLED were sharing intel, finally. Looking into the darkness, I checked my headgear, twisting the knob back and forth, switching from the greenish illumination of low-light to infrared.

Occam took a hard turn that rocked the car. He said, "Lights and sirens off. Ingram and I are in the area of the clan home. Local marked units are stopping traffic behind us.

Make sure they know that the rest of our team needs to get in and tell them to turn off the blue lights. That makes them easy to target."

"Roger that," Rick said.

"Ingram and I'll take a leisurely drive to reconnoiter." Occam braked hard to a laid-back twenty-five miles an hour and rolled down his window. I followed suit and muggy summer air billowed in. I wasn't even under fire and I was cold and shaking. The heat felt good. I hadn't even noticed the air conditioner running.

"Hurry," Yummy said. "I've only got three rounds of ammo left and I've bled like a stuck pig. They can find me by the smell and I know they're inside."

"Where are you?" I asked. I took a breath and forced myself to calm. Took another. I began to steady. Began to ease. This was my job. I could do this.

"Over the garage," Yummy said. "Low-ceilinged crawl space. It's set for a secure sniper hide, but there's no protection for me from inside, once the defensive team is down and the house is penetrated."

We passed by the spot Margot wanted for a staging area. It was occupied by two vans, lights off, when there should have been nothing there but an empty lot. My heart thumped hard. *Fanghead vans?* I said, "Southern potential staging area is a no-go. Two twelve-person-sized panel vans are parked there. Nothing visible on low-light or IR. Kent, when you drive by, see if you can spot anything."

"Roger that," Lainie said.

"I see the clan home property," I said. "What I can make out from the street looks peaceful. No visible bodies on low-light or IR. However, the security lights are out and the grounds are dark."

"I smell blood," Occam said. "Vamp and human. A lot of it."

Rick said, "SWAT will take out the panel vans first. Set up staging area at the northern site."

"Northern site. Copy that," Occam said.

"Body!" I said, pointing. "Two o'clock." It was lying on the side of the road, in tall, decorative grass, and it wasn't showing much on IR. "Pull over and put the car between the house and me. I'll examine it."

Occam braked and backed up, cutting his lights. "Make it fast."

I opened the door and slid from the car, weapon in hand, a silver-lead round in the chamber. I switched on my tiny penlight and took in the body. "Female. Throat torn out." I bent closer and opened her mouth, looking for vamp fangs on their retractable hinges. "Human. Deceased. She's wearing pajamas, so she might be a local. Cool enough to have been here a while." I was proud that my words made sense and my voice was steady. Strangely, seeing the body had smothered my panic.

"They probably took over a house near Ming's and drained the inhabitants," Rick said.

I slid back into the car and closed the door. Buckled up. Occam looked at me, his lips asking silently, *You okay?*

I nodded. Lying. I wasn't panicky now, but I wasn't okay. Occam had to be able to smell my sweat but didn't say anything as he progressed along the road, one hand on the wheel. His weapon was on the edge of the open window, ready to fire with his maimed left hand. It would be an awkward shot, but better than nothing. "Northern staging area just ahead. Slowing," Occam said. "No sign of vehicles. Turning in. Tell SWAT we have an acceptable staging area, but there are three occupied homes between us and the target."

"Copy," Rick said.

Yummy whispered, "I hear footsteps. Too soft to be human. I count two Mithrans coming up the stairs."

"We can't wait," I said.

"Ingram and Occam. Stay put," FireWind said.

I wanted to scream. "Respectfully, sir, we just found a dead body," I said, hearing the fury and disagreement and fear in my words, "indicating imminent danger to human inhabitants." A thought hit me. "Send a unit by with lights and sirens. Maybe it'll startle them away."

"Negative," Rick said to me. "I will not endanger my team. Or the local LEOs."

"No time," Yummy whispered. I heard the cell placed down with a soft clatter.

"Passing the southern perimeter," T. Laine said. "No live or undead bodies at the panel vans per *seeing* working, but psy-meter shows presence of Mithran energies. Permission to disable the vans?"

"Arcane or mundane means?" FireWind asked.

"Either."

"Come on, come on, come on," I whispered to the night and to Yummy.

"If you can disable the vehicles without danger to yourselves, yes," Rick said.

"Okay, boss. Going in," Lainie said.

Over my cell I heard two shots fired, close up. The particular but distant ululation of a vamp dying. Thumping sounds. Shots fired from farther away. Then a final shot, Yummy's last round. Then nothing. I wanted to scream or throw things. *We were right here. We could have done something.*

A full minute later, her voice rasping from physical activity, T. Laine said, "Vans can still drive, but they won't track properly with multiple tires slashed in the sidewalls." Her car door closed softly in the background. "Drive," she finished.

Over the cell came a peculiar sound like a titter of drunken laughter. "Day-am. I'm a better shot than I thought," Yummy whispered.

Relief shook me like a child's rattle. Tears filled my eyes. *Thank you,* I mouthed to the night and to God. I was pretty sure I had been praying—for a vampire, of all the strange things in my life.

Yummy said, "I took their weapons and the last of their blood. I now have a total of six rounds and a measure of healing, but it's not enough. I'm leaking and we have more troubles coming. Humans on the way. And they are not friendlies." I heard shots in the distance over the cell, staccato. And the sound of voices pleading, barely heard. "They have our humans hostage. I'm going in."

Rick said, "Tell her no. SWAT is nearly there."

"I heard," Yummy whispered. "Rick LaFleur, if you can hear me, I'm not one of yours, but you can call this fanghead recon. I'm at the top of the stairs. I count ten human heartbeats and smell two enemy fangheads. Can't get any closer without them catching my scent or sound. Backing back to my sniper hole."

Rick cursed softly. Occam's hands tightened on the wheel. This passivity was probably making his cat crazy.

"Can you get out?" I asked. Occam's headlights illuminated a raccoon waddling in front of the car. Three juveniles gamboled behind the mother. They all disappeared.

"Not without walking through the hostages."

"Can you punch your way through the floor into the garage?" I asked.

There was a sharp silence on the cell. Then, "That, Maggot, is brilliant. It'll ruin my manicure, though."

"We all make sacrifices," I said. My sarcasm seemed to help because Yummy laughed.

Two cars and a SWAT van sped in behind us. Over the cell came the sounds of splintering wood. Shots fired as Yummy laid down cover fire. Then more splintering wood.

"I'm in the garage," she whispered. "I have two rounds left. Ming will kill me, but I'm taking her Mercedes limo. The armor will let me punch through the garage door. Tell your people I'm heading out."

"Copy that," Rick said over the earbud. "One nonhostile escaping." He gave details.

I heard a half dozen shots. Yummy grunted in pain. An engine roared to life, followed by a crash. And the sound of Yummy's laughter, a little more crazy than I might have hoped. "Hey, Maggot," she shouted. "I need blood. I got a couple more holes in me than just a minute past. Feed me, woman!"

"I'll stake you first," I said.

Yummy kept laughing. Her limo whipped into the small partially empty lot and up to Occam's car. "Hello, cat. Maggot," she said through her open window. There was blood on her clothing and in her pale hair, visible in the low glow created by multiple sets of headlights. Her skin was paper white and bloodless and she was vamped out. "I'm dying of thirst, but you can offer to be my hero later. What'll it take to get SWAT to breach now?"

"They would have to be killing the human hostages," Rick said into my earbud.

"I smelled dead and wounded humans," Yummy said. Vampire hearing had let her overhear Occam's and my comms. I'd have to remember that. "Two shot dead that I can account for. A lot . . . of human . . . blood," she added. She was breathing fast and sounded a little crazy. Or a lot hungry.

Rick said, over the para frequency, "Gonzales. We have reliable inside intel that the attacking vampires and their humans are killing the local humans. Do we have a go?"

"We have a go," FireWind said. Yummy laughed, a sound so far from human amusement that it made my hair stand up.

Gonzales said, "Douglas and Montgomery, take the back. Josephs and Avery, in through the garage door. I understand there's a car-sized hole in it now. Smith and Flint, you have perimeter. Matthews and I have the front. On my mark."

Yummy opened the limo door. Swiveled her body around until her feet were able to drop to the ground. Her blood splattered the earth only inches from Occam's car. Only feet from me. The soil soaked up the vampire blood. Bloodlust stirred. I forced my shoulders down and breathed through my nose, watching the blood trickle down Yummy's legs onto the ground, crimson in the headlights. "Hungry," she whispered, echoing the need of my land.

Seconds later I heard each of the teams report they were in position. Then the SWAT leader said, "On go. One. Two. Three. Gogogogogogo."

My heart leaped into my throat.

Yummy growled and leaned out of the limo. The sclera of her eyes was scarlet, her pupils dilated far wider than a human's. A wet breeze off the Tennessee River blew through, pressing the blood-wet dress against Yummy's body. She was naked beneath scarlet-soaked fabric. Her blood trickled onto the ground in a thin stream.

Over the earbud came the sound of crashing, splintering wood. Three shots. Then a lot of shots. People shouting. Cops shouting, "Down. Down on the ground." "Put the weapon down. Slowly." "Down. Hands behind your head." Then gunfire. And SWAT returning gunfire. "Multiple civilians down," Gonzales shouted. "Get me medic!"

"Clear the house," FireWind said.

Gonzales cursed. Sweat slimed down my back, sticking my clothes to the Kevlar vest. I blinked sweat out of my eyes. Yummy was watching Occam, her hunger with a target.

Seconds ticked away as his men cleared the house. "Clear." "Clear." "Clear." "Clear." The voices ran together in my brain, none of them familiar, none of them real to me. And all of them out of sight in a firefight.

Yummy grabbed the limo door. Her talons were pointed and sharp as knives in the faint illumination from inside the limo. My hands clenched into fists. I checked my weapon. Again. Silver-lead ammo. One in the chamber. Ready to fire.

"We got a runner," a SWAT team member said, then shouted, "Stop! Police!"

The sound of gunfire in measured bursts.

Yummy laughed. If Death himself could laugh, that would be the sound. "Huuuungry."

"One down," the same voice said. "Female vampire. Not true-dead. Took two torso rounds and staked in the abdomen."

"Give her to me," Yummy said, her voice a low snarl.

"Not happening," Occam said casually. His weapon was at ready. My cat-man wasn't casual at all.

"I am injured. Feed me, werecat."

"Not happening," Occam said.

"Clearing the southern side of the house," Gonzales said. Seconds later he said, "Main room. Clear. Multiple bodies, human and vamp. Some alive." His tone changed. *"Son of a bitch!"* Three shots fired. "Get medic in here *now*! And blood donors for the fangheads." He fired three more shots. And three more.

"Copy that," FireWind said. "LaFleur—" His voice disappeared beneath gunshots from the house.

Yummy stood slowly, dragging herself to her feet. Her dress had been gray. Or maybe green. There was so much blood on it the original color was hard to discern in the poor light. "Huuuungry," she whispered. Her blood formed a small pool on the soil. Soulwood opened inside of me. *Wanting.*

"Uh-oh," I said.

Occam raised his weapon and placed it on the window opening. "Nah-ah-*ah*," he said, almost playfully. "Keep it together, fanghead. I have silver-lead ammo."

"You would kill *me*?" she asked, a soft accent on the last word.

I raised a hand to my mic and shifted to a private channel. I whispered, "Jo. Yummy's hurt. Vamped. Get me a donor."

"Roger that," Jo said.

I switched back to para freq in time to hear Rick say, "Local LEOs have three limos full of Mithrans under gunpoint. Tennessee plates. Get someone to make sure it's Shaddock and convince the locals to let him and his people through. He has humans and vamps who can feed our wounded."

T. Laine said, "Kent here. Dyson and I can handle that." Their car spun out of the lot, throwing gravel in the glare of the headlights.

I hadn't even noticed that my teammates were onsite. Yummy didn't notice that they had left. Her black and scarlet eyes were focused solely on Occam. "Feed me and I will heal you," she whispered.

"Not. Happening."

In the earbud, Margot said, "If you need backup to get Shaddock free, let me know."

Gonzales shouted, "Where's medic? We have multiple injured. Two bodies in the shrubbery, condition unknown. More in the back bedroom. We need uniforms deployed to keep the house secure so we can expand our perimeter."

Rick said, "Officers on the way. Local LEOs are moving in to your location and encircling the location of the disabled panel vans in case the vamps show there."

More cars and vans began to pour in, both here and on the site of the shooting. News vans were being stopped at the perimeter. Yummy's talons were slowly piercing the steel of the limo door. She stepped from the limo, exposing her torso and abdomen. Occam swore.

Yummy had been shot multiple times, open wounds dripping. Her clothing was drenched scarlet in the glancing lights from the cars all around. She was staring at Occam and . . . smiling. It was enough to make me wither inside, even as I licked my lips in need. Occam said, "We need humans to feed an injured vampire, at my twenty, *now*!"

I focused on her neck wounds. Blood dribbled out, looking fresh, though I knew it was cold and watery. My body reacted to the blood on her clothes, the blood splattering on the ground. Bloodlust that had been a low, slow need rose and thrummed through me. It moved the way sound waves move along a stringed instrument, humming, a prolonged and varying noise of *need*.

I wanted to feed the earth. Soulwood was awake and needing.

"Huuunger," Yummy said.

Huuuunger, I thought.

"Shaddock's on the way," Rick said. "He's dropping off his people at the house and coming directly to your twenty. How badly is she injured?"

I swallowed down my hunger. "Bloody with open wounds. And vamped out."

"Feed me," she whispered, leaning toward Occam. Reaching.

"Can you contain her," Rick said. It wasn't exactly a question. *Contain. Not kill.*

I drew a stake. I had never staked a vampire. I'd been taught how at Spook School, but training and combat are very different things. I placed the stake in Occam's lap and opened my car door. Shoved the low-light/IR headgear off. Raced around Occam's car, knees bent, my service weapon at the ready. It was loaded with silver rounds. Yummy wasn't very old. Silver rounds might kill her. But regular rounds would only make her mad. Yummy was a friend. I might have to kill her.

She was focused on Occam, her pupils black and wide, the whites the color of blood. "Cat," she whispered. "I have missed the taste of your blood."

My hunger focused on the bloody vampire. "Hey, Yummy," I shouted. Her head whipped to me. Need ached through me. "You control yourself or you'll wish you had," I whispered.

"Maggot," she hissed.

"Yeah. I'll consume your dead flesh," I whispered, barely a breath of sound.

Yummy laughed, the laughter the devil might make while he tortured lost souls. She leaped. At Occam.

ELEVEN

My finger began to squeeze the trigger.

She was illuminated, leaping through the air. A pop of displaced air sounded. And she was gone. Just disappeared. Something thumped on the ground to my side in the dark.

The shock stole my need away. I released the trigger and whipped around, spotting a rolling, hissing, moaning *something* in the darkness. "What just happened?" I asked the empty space in front of us.

"Lincoln Shaddock happened," Occam said. "He tackled Yummy into the weeds. Saved our butts."

I sat down on the ground hard. And just breathed. Mosquitoes buzzed around me. If they had been here before, I hadn't noticed. I finally holstered my weapon, fighting tears and blood-lust. Occam squatted near me, his knees spread, his hands dangling between them. I could see officers in the dark staring at his scars, but he just looked like Occam to me. He handed me my stake and tapped off his mic. "Good move, Nell, sugar. You okay?"

"I'm just fine and dandy," I said. The dregs of my bloodlust wriggled deep inside.

"Liar."

"I am. I totally am." And I could deal with the comment about Yummy missing the taste of Occam's blood later. "We need to get into the house and render assistance."

"Yes, we do." He offered me a hand and I let him raise me to my feet. "Before I met you," Occam said to me. "Not since."

A mishmash of relief and happiness filled my chest and I grinned at my cat-man, who had read my mind. "Good." Together, we got in his car and sped up the street to Ming's battleground. Weapons ready to fire, held in two-hand grips, we jogged into the well-lit yard and drive at Ming's.

There were two pale humans lying, unmoving, on Ming's lawn. I provided cover while Occam checked pulse points on both victims. They were bloody and maimed, their throats and wrists and upper arms showing holes from multiple feedings. Naturaleza vampires drank from any pulse point on their cattle and I didn't want to know what other sites had been bitten as the humans were drained.

I started shaking, my fingers tingling. I was hyperventilating. I fought to slow my breathing, wishing I could touch the ground with a single fingertip. Wishing I could call on Soulwood, reaching through the earth to find calm. But the blood on the ground would be construed as sacrifice. I couldn't claim the victims and the earth for my own. Secrets. I had secrets to protect.

"Nell?" Occam asked.

"I'm good. Probie nerves," I lied and Occam knew it.

The front door was open, throwing a wedge of light into the darker yard. A familiar form stood there, slight, Asian. Composed as if he had gunfights on his property all the time. Cai, Ming's primo. He was wearing a headset and he bowed to us. It was a slight bow, but it was there just the same. I faltered, and followed Occam's return bow, my head not dipping quite as low as Cai's had.

"The council chambers of Ming of Glass, Master of the City of Knoxville, are secured," Cai said. "We have taken two living enemy Mithrans captive to learn what they know, but the human SWAT team will not allow us to interrogate the parasites."

"Not a problem," Occam said. "Does PsyLED have permission from the Master of the City to enter and to parley with the SWAT team? This must not be construed as opening diplomatic relations, as I don't have the authority for that."

Cai tilted his head slightly. "Your words negate permanent contact and communication between sovereign countries, parley that your Congress has not agreed upon between the United States of America and Mithrans. This is parley for emergency circumstances. Is this correct?"

"Correct," Rick said into my earbud.

Into the same earbud, FireWind said, "Let me speak to him."

"Call me on my cell," I said to my up-line bosses. To Cai, I said, "Ayatas FireWind, PsyLED special agent in charge of the eastern seaboard, is calling you on my cell phone. He is able to parley with you." My cell rang and I answered, "Ingram here."

"No," Cai said. "We will not speak to this wind of fire. Ming will parley at this time only with humans and creatures we know."

I felt Occam stiffen. In my earbud, Rick muttered. I figured he was talking to FireWind on a private channel. Silence stretched and I was pretty sure that Cai's face tightened, as if he was ready to hit us or to bolt. We needed him. And we couldn't wait on an off-site political decision.

"Fine," I said, speaking into my mic. "Everything is unofficial, then, to be handled only on a local level, with nothing of national or international consequence."

FireWind said, "Ingram!" He didn't sound happy. But he wasn't here, watching Cai.

"Such is acceptable to Ming of Glass and those who serve her," Cai said instantly.

"Does that put us in charge?" Occam asked.

"Yes. In the future," FireWind said, his words clipped, "probationary agents are to be seen, not heard."

I started to tell FireWind that he sounded like a churchman talking to one of his womenfolk, but Occam put a hand on my arm and mouthed, *Later*.

"Fine," I said to the boss's boss. To Cai I said, "We'll talk to SWAT and to Ming. I mean, my senior partner will talk."

Occam chuckled silently, cat chuffing. I narrowed my eyes at him and he smothered the soundless laughter. I ended the call without saying good-bye, holstered my weapon, and we followed Cai inside, into the light and frozen air of an overworked air-conditioning system. My sweat chilled and I shivered.

There were three bodies and pools of blood in the foyer. All human. All dead. Weapons at their sides. They had died fighting. I followed Occam past without looking. Much. Not seeing the difference between the blood of a threat and the blood of a victim, my land *wanted* the bodies. *Wanted* the blood.

No, I thought. *No.*

My stomach churned. I clenched my teeth and said nothing as we entered the main room. Medic raced in and started attending to the humans on the floor, checking for vitals. In a corner, two vampires were secured with silver cuffs, back to back. The reek of burning vampire flesh soured the air, coming from the silver wire wrapped around them. Both were bleeding and vamped out, struggling, burning. I wanted to draw my weapon and shoot them, I wanted to take their blood for the land, but I resisted. Everyone had vest cams.

I heard a soft pop of sound and flinched. Lincoln was standing beside me. Once again, he had moved with vamp speed, displacing air. Shaddock was long legged, a little rough around the edges, his shoulder-length dark hair swinging around his craggy face. He was wearing work boots, jeans, and a cotton button-down shirt splattered with a fine spray of blood. And he was carrying a single-bladed ax. Not what I expected in a vampire rescuer. More like a lumberjack on holiday. The tall, spare man nodded at me and at Occam and Cai, three small bobs of his head, in what felt like an old-timey greeting. Cai bowed back, a deep obeisance, before leading the way to the captive vampires and the SWAT team leader. Gonzales was standing in front of the prisoners, his weapon at the ready.

I stared around the room as the three men and Occam chatted about what was going to happen next, the administrative transfer of the premises, the occupants, and a lot of other legal stuff I needed to hear and would have found fascinating, if I hadn't been holding down my bloodlust. It wanted to feed the land. It *needed* . . .

When they had everything settled to their respective satisfactions, Cai knelt in front of the captive vamps, holding the gaze of the female. She was the older of the two, her fangs a good three inches long, curved, and thicker than most. And . . . she had upper and lower fangs, which I'd heard was common in one bloodline of European vampires. Cai *held her gaze.* I knew how hard that was. Nearly impossible for a human.

Occam touched my arm and we stepped to the side. Ming of Glass appeared and took our place. Her power filled the room and ached on my bare skin. I wanted to claw it off me, but that might be construed as an insult.

Shaddock dropped his head a bit lower to Ming than he had to the rest of us. "My old friend. I wish we had been here sooner. We will stay and heal your people."

Ming dropped her head, equally low, to Shaddock. "You are the balm of Gilead to me, my old friend. My companion in arms."

I blinked at the *balm of Gilead* comment. The balm was a medicinal perfume mentioned in the Bible, maybe from a camphor-smelling plant or the terebinth tree. That Ming would mention it was unexpected and jarring. Maybe for vampires, the balm was blood, or loyalty, or a combination of the two.

"We will fight together," Shaddock said, his voice soft and leisurely, an almost-familiar hill country accent. "I offer you my strength and my power to determine our mutual enemies."

Shaddock held out a hand and Ming took it. Holding it, she turned to the female captive. "The name of your master," she said softly, "or I shall drink you down and claim you as my own."

"You do not have the power to claim me," the female vampire said. "Even with the help of that bumpkin." The female had a foreign accent, one I couldn't place except that it wasn't from around here. Maybe someplace in Europe.

"I have far more power than your pitiful master ever imagined," Ming said. "Together, the Master of the City of Asheville and I are a force to be reckoned with." She lunged at the vampire. Grabbed her behind the head. Sank her teeth in at the female's neck.

I flinched, taking two steps back before I could stop myself. Ming lifted the other vamp and they settled to an ottoman. At her side, still holding her free hand, Lincoln withdrew a small blade from his boot and pricked Ming's pinkie finger. He put it in his mouth and sucked.

I frowned in confusion. Occam was watching the vampires, his attention on the bound male. "Don't try it," Occam advised. He raised his service weapon, aimed at the vampire. "I got silver rounds and no mores against using them to shoot out your knees. You'll limp forever."

Weapons ratcheted behind us. Occam turned slightly and raised his voice. "PsyLED! We got this."

"Don't look like you got shit, dude. Fangheads sucking on each other? You should let us take them in."

"You have jails that'll hold them?" Occam asked. "Lined in silver and secured from daylight? Something to feed them so they stay sane? No? Then let us do our job."

I heard feet shuffle away.

Occam said, "Ming of Glass, we are under local rules of parley. I surely do hope you plan to share whatever you learn. Oh. And don't kill the li'l vampire lady, okay? That might get my butt in a heap of trouble."

Her teeth still buried in the vampire's flesh, Ming shifted her eyes to him and smiled.

Twenty minutes later, Ming of Glass pushed away from the vampires she had been drinking down. She was flushed, full of blood, and healthy. Lincoln dropped her pinkie finger and hauled her to her feet, an arm around her waist. There was something sexual and passionate in the action and I felt my body react. Cai guided them both to a sofa, where the two master vampires sank down gracefully. I pretended not to notice that Ming ended up in Shaddock's lap and his arms closed about her. If I had to guess, the two had been lovers in the past. Maybe still were.

Ming said, "We have learned all they know about our attackers. And we have a name." She looked at me. "Maggoty. Have you or your people ever heard of Godfrey of Bouillon? In French, he is called Godefroi de Bouillon?"

I started searching on my cell, texting that name with possible spellings to JoJo and Rick. As I worked, Ming kept talking. "There is a vast power vacuum in the world of Mithran and Naturaleza politics since the two strongest of us—Titus, the emperor of Europe and Leo Pellissier of the United States—are dead and the Dark Queen has gone to ground. Many attempt to fill those voids. Godfrey is here to claim my city and all its cattle as his own."

"You got that, JoJo?" I muttered into my mic.

"Got it. Searching databases. Good guess on the spelling, Ingram."

Ming went on, "His people have attacked your lands tonight, my friend, Lincoln. He has claimed your clan home as his own. We do not know that the Dark Queen will fight him for this."

"We don't need her, Zhane," Shaddock said in a local accent. "We defeated his people here. As soon as things are secure here, we can take back my lands. We will exact revenge, my love."

"Yessss," Ming said. "And now we know where they laired the last nights. In this neighborhood, among my neighbors, draining them. This too will be avenged." Ming looked at me and then at Occam. "How long will this local parley last? Will PsyLED Unit Eighteen fight beside the Mithrans of Knoxville, or will you allow the city to fall into the hands of the Naturaleza of Europe, Godefroi de Bouillon?"

My cell rang, and the area code and number were both unfamiliar. I answered anyway. "Hello?"

"Give the cell to Ming of Glass," FireWind said.

I handed my cell to Ming. "It's my boss, Ayatas FireWind. He wants to parley with you."

"I do not know this name," Ming said, still refusing again to talk to people she didn't know.

"If he lies, you can take it out of my hide," I said quickly, stepping back, leaving the cell in her hands.

Ming took the cell and said into the microphone, "If you treat with us without honor, we will take the life of your Maggot."

Across the distance, I heard the voice of my newest boss say, "I always speak with honor and honesty, Ming of Glass."

Take the life of your Maggot . . . Ming had just threatened my life. Which meant she would kill me and also kill my family if it suited her. She thought I was important, of value, but powerless. Well. She was wrong on both counts. I had a feeling that I'd have to show Ming of Glass I wasn't someone to be trifled with, and soon. Shotguns wouldn't scare her. But Soulwood would.

Around four a.m., the moon hidden by trees or the hills ringing the plateau, the killing battleground had become a crime scene, with all the dead being carried off for postmortems and the living either healed or sent to area hospitals. Occam and I left the site of the battle between Ming of Glass and Godefroi de Bouillon, and went back to HQ to file reports. Rick gave Occam another assignment, leaving me on my own. By five twenty, I was on my way to God's Cloud of Glory Church to pick up my sister and to talk about child care. My bloodlust had gone unsatisfied but had at least quieted.

I sat in the truck for a bit, reading through my messages to see an update on Larry Aden. He was in jail, awaiting a bond hearing and a psych eval. That was good. I didn't want to have to shoot him this morning. It was Sunday and I was here for one of the sermons I had agreed to attend as part of getting custody of Mud, not murder.

I didn't knock, just slipped from the truck cab and in the door of the Nicholson house. No one noticed I had arrived and it gave me time to watch everything and everyone.

Sam, his heavily pregnant wife, SaraBell, my sister Esther and her husband, Jedidiah Whisnut, and Mud were all there, gathered around Daddy's rocker, chatting with him as the patriarch drank the first of what would be many cups of coffee today. Esther was my true sib, and I remembered her touching her hairline like I did. I studied her from my hidden position and thought her hair looked more red, like mine. Over the din I heard talk about greenhouses.

There were ten or twelve young'uns—some of them neighbor kids, I was certain—running around yelling some church song about Noah and the ark and the animals that came to him to be saved from the flood. If there was a tune, I couldn't discern it. I wasn't sure where they had heard about SpongeBob SquarePants, but I was pretty sure he hadn't been on the ark and I had no idea how he had been worked into the song.

A group of teens and preteens were sitting around a small table, sipping coffee and talking politics. It was boys on one side and many more girls on the other, but there was still some interplay between the disparate groups. Four older boys sat in the far corner, alone, with their heads together. They were dressed for outdoor work and had likely just finished chores. I knew

Zeke, Harry, and Rudolph, my half brothers, and one who was not a Nicholson boy. All four looked troubled. Resentful.

There were three girls in the kitchen with the mamas, cooking. One was making coffee in the ancient thirty-five-cup percolator. One was working dough in a huge wooden dough bowl. One was setting the table. The mamas were cooking bacon, eggs, grits, biscuits, and pancakes on the wood-burning stoves.

That many people in the Nicholson house, with the wood-stoves burning high, was unbearable hot, even with the summer fan in back dragging air through all the open windows and outside. I stood in the foyer of the big house, sweated, and watched the homey, happy commotion.

Sunday breakfast and lunch were a multifamily, multigenerational event in God's Cloud of Glory Church, and while I didn't agree with much of nothing the church taught, I did think getting together with family once a week was a pretty great thing. I didn't want to deprive my sister of the Nicholsons, of the love and social discourse and interaction that a huge family could provide. In the church, all the kids were well socialized. It was a survival necessity and a skill she needed, even in the townie world.

The women and girls were in summer wear: long bibbed dresses over loose cotton shirts and, oddly, cloth sneakers. That was new. Anything new in the church was a good sign, but seeing Mama in red sneakers was surprising. Mama Grace was wearing sunflower yellow sneakers that matched the yellow plaid in her bibbed dress, and Mama Carmel was wearing sturdy, dour, navy blue sneakers to match her navy dress.

Daddy looked quiet and happy. SaraBell was propped in a chair nearby, feet up, rubbing her belly in slow, steady circles, looking big enough to pop and utterly miserable. Her ankles were swollen and she seemed to be having trouble breathing deeply. I hadn't asked, but it was possible that she was having twins. Or maybe a litter.

Sam glanced questioningly at his wife, smiled at her so sweetly, so gently, a look so full of love that it made my heart clench. She shrugged. He turned back to Daddy and asked, "When are Ben and Bernice getting married?"

"My courtin's none a your'n beeswax," a girl setting the table yelled at him.

Bernice was one of my half sisters. She was sixteen and old enough to be considered a woman by the church and old enough to wed in Tennessee. The only churchman named Ben I knew, who was old enough to marry, was Ben Aden, a college-educated man who had courted me before I turned into a tree. Ben was blue eyed and dark haired and pretty as a model in a fashion magazine. We wouldn't have suited at all. But it was a surprise to hear he was courting my half sister. I didn't know how to react to it.

"Nell!" Mud flew across the room, arms outstretched. I caught her and nearly fell back against the door. She wasn't the skinny waif I had first seen only a few months past. Before she had become a woman grown, she had put on inches and height. But her hair was bunned up again. A tight, braided, twisted bun that had Mama's handiwork all over it.

For a good two seconds my brain struggled. I wanted to fight this. I wanted to make a scene and tell the Nicholsons that they had no right to bun up my sister, not even as a social consideration or to fight the heat. But I didn't have custody yet. They did. And if I wanted custody of Mud, then I needed to keep my blasted mouth shut and save this battle for another day.

I managed a slow breath. Then another. And gently set my sister aside with a slight smile and the words, "You look pretty." Because I'd be hog-tied and set on fire before I put her in the middle of a battle she was too young to comprehend fully.

Mud touched her slicked-back hair and asked, "You'un okay with this? It's hot."

I muttered, "'And damn'd be him that first cries, 'Hold, enough!'"

Mud's eyes went wide and she froze at my cussing.

"Shakespeare. I meant that we aren't finished fighting this battle. We'll pick our fights and now is not the time."

Mud grinned and leaned in closer, whispering. "I'm gonna cut my hair someday. 'When the hurly-burly's done/When the battle's lost and won.' I read some a your'n Shakespeare while you'un was a tree. He talks pretty and he's right smart."

Tears, totally unexpected, burned under my lids. "Yes. He was. And now we need to eat. Then I need to talk to Daddy and the mamas and Sam about a variety of things."

The meal was noisy and hot and I had no chance for a private conversation with anyone. When the family left for church, Mud and me in with a group of womenfolk, Mama looked at me askance, me still wearing jeans and work shoes. I hadn't kept a skirt at HQ. We filed into the Nicholson benches and I sat. This was the first time I'd been in the church since it had been shot up and Daddy and I had been mortally injured. I was a little uneasy being there, and found myself studying the wood pews for signs of bullet damage. I was glad that I had kept my weapon on me.

The song leader led three hymns. There was prayer and the Lord's supper. And then came time for the sermon. To my surprise, Sam stood up to speak. I had intended to zone out and not listen, but with Sam preaching that went out the window. My brother had a gift for talking, for leading a crowd through the scriptures, and today's scripture verses were based primarily on First Timothy, and he spent an hour suggesting, hinting, and implying that polygamy was not the Christian way.

I was delighted, though not everyone in the congregation was so impressed with the direction of the sermon. There were a number of men scowling, and an even greater number of women with their heads down. Being told the men were sinful for abusing women had to make the men mad. Being told that they were being treated like pieces of meat who had been forced into a sinful lifestyle couldn't be easy on the women. My brother never said any of that, of course, but the implication and the inferences were there.

I was proud of my brother. Prouder than I could say. Finally the ninety-minute service was over and I stood and moved to the back of the church, a hand on Mud's shoulder. Until the movement of the line stopped. Three men stood blocking the Nicholsons' way. Blocking the mamas. Blocking Daddy, who was still using a cane. Blocking Sam. And mostly, I feared, blocking me.

I recognized Judah and Daniel Jackson, the younger sons of Preacher Ernest Jackson. Jackson and his eldest son were men I had helped kill, if only indirectly. If I hadn't let Ming's scions and Jane Yellowrock cross my land to search for a missing vampire, the old man and Jackson Jr. might still be alive. Maybe. Or not. Either way, I had a feeling Jackson's younger sons were no better than their daddy or Jackie Jr.

Meshack Lambert was with Judah and Daniel, carrying a shotgun. Gad and Esau McCormick were carrying cudgels. Five against Sam and me. I slid my hand under my jacket to the holster.

Judah stuck out his chin and said to Sam, "You'un got no cause to impugn our way of life."

"You'un got no right to call our women harlots," Gad said.

"You'un got no right to bring your witchy sister here among God-fearing people," Esau said. "A witch dressed in pants like the whore of Babylon."

Anger flushed through me, but I kept my voice calm. "You need to learn your scripture. The whore of Babylon wore scarlet and purple. Not pants. And I'm not a witch." I chuckled low and added a social media quote that would go over their heads. "Mama had me tested."

"I will not speak to this whore and witch," Esau said, his face turned away from me. "I will not be led into temptation."

From the corner of my eye, I saw Daddy assist SaraBell and the mamas between two pews toward a different exit.

"She should be burned," Gad muttered of me. He slapped his truncheon into his palm with a soft smack. "Burned at the stake."

I was turned at slight angle from them, behind Sam, and I eased my weapon free. Dropped my hand, the Glock GDP-20 at my thigh, my hand comfortable on the grip, trigger finger on the slide. There was no round in the chamber. I needed to remedy that, except that would be obvious and right now we were teetering on the sharp edge of violence. Racking the slide might push us over into bloodshed.

Daniel, who bore a strong resemblance to his daddy, stepped closer to me. Unlike his brothers, he had no trouble looking me over. "There might not be a punishment house anymore," he muttered, "but I'm inventive. I'll take care of the whore."

Mama Grace and Mama Carmel shoved the young'uns down, where they crawled under the seats toward the door. The Nicholsons always had an exit plan.

"And then she'll be burned. Her and all her ilk," Judah said. "Her sisters and—"

I raised my weapon.

"That's enough, boys," Brother Aden said, stopping me before I fired. "There will be no talk of taking the law into our own hands. Vigilantism is outlawed by church charter."

Not to mention murder. But I didn't say it.

"Your'n son is in jail because of this whore!" Gad said.

"Larry is in jail because he kidnapped an officer of the law. I love my son, but he has shamed himself, his family, and this church." Brother Aden shook his head. "I brought my sons up to know better. To do better. I have offered up my son to the elders of the church for banishment."

The silence in the church was so thick I could have bounced on it like bouncing on a balloon. "Banishment?" Judah repeated. "But . . ."

"The scripture tells us to test the spirits," Sam said, "and that means to test ourselves, our elders and deacons, each other, and our understanding of scripture all the time. You want to teach a sermon on an opposing viewpoint, feel free next time your name comes up in rotation."

Sam took a step close to Judah and Gad, and the group of five moved back. Sam followed them and maneuvered his body between them and the rest of the Nicholsons. Without taking his gaze from the threats, he held out a hand, indicating that we should all go outside. I walked past, not making eye contact with the cadre of would-be attackers. At some point I might need to show some aggression, but not now while Sam's wife was still waddling down the stairs and the littlest young'uns were still escaping out the back pews into the safety of the day.

The adrenaline spike was long gone by the time the last of us got back to the Nicholson house. A teenaged boy was armed and watching out a front porch window, his face in shadow. The windows upstairs were open and I could see gun barrels resting on the sills. Inside, the young'uns had been sent to the third floor to play under the care of two girl children with unbunned hair.

Sam helped SaraBell into a rocker and propped her feet up, looking her over top to toes for problems. "I'm okay," she said softly, flapping a hand at him. "Go on. Take care a things."

He asked the teen boy at the window by the door, "Zeke. Placement of shooters?"

"Me on the lower floor. Harry on the third floor at the front. Rudolph at the back of the house on the upper floor."

"Barn?"

"Judith," Zeke said, "positioned to see the greenhouses. Bernice just checked in; girl shooters are in place, one at your'n place and one walking home with Esther and Jed. Four girls are in the storage caves. All quiet."

"Girl shooters?" I asked.

Daddy eased into his rocker with a breathy grunt. "You'un taught us our girls can fight. So Sam and the boys been teaching 'em to shoot. Mud too, if'n you'un approve."

"Yes," I said. *Girl shooters? In the church?*

Grimly, Sam said, "They wear handguns under their dresses at all times." He stared hard at me. "Things've been hard around here, Nellie."

"Anything I can bring charges against?"

"Nothing we can prove," he said. "Petty vandalism in the greenhouses. Theft from the storage caves. Accusations with no evidence."

I frowned. Theft and vandalism had never happened in all the years of the church. But Sam was preaching an end to polygamy, so . . . things were changing and there was always resistance to change. "You get witnesses or photos, you let me know."

"So far nothing on the cameras," he said, even more grimly. He led the way to the back of the house, to a closet once filled with baby clothes. The shelves had been cleaned off; instead of onesies, they now held a series of small computer screens and a piece of electronic equipment that handled all the camera input. There were twelve screens, each with multiple views showing from all the Nicholson clan houses, the storage caves where the church kept its supplies and seeds, the vampire tree, multiple views of the church and its parking area, the entrance, and the main roadways.

"Wow," I said. I didn't know what else to say. While the church freely used solar and wind power, they had previously not allowed TVs, computers, e-readers, or anything else of a worldly personal electronic nature. Now they had a security system and my brother was running it. I had known about it, but seeing it was disconcerting.

From the front of the house Zeke shouted, "Ben's here. So's Caleb, Fredi, and Priscilla. And Caleb's hurt."

Caleb Campbell was half carried into the house by Ben Aden. Caleb had been beaten; he had a black eye and a broken nose and was holding his ribs. Fredi, Caleb's senior wife, was big pregnant, maybe eight months along, with her third, and Priscilla, my eldest sister, was nursing her second. The three squalling toddlers were carried out of the big room by Mama Grace and my mama, and Priscilla threw herself into a chair. "This is your'n fault," Priss said to me, stern as a frozen ax.

"Priss. No," Caleb said softly. "Nell was a trigger, nothing else. The church has been heading down this path a long time."

"I ain't gonna let you divorce me," Priscilla said, sounding stubborn, as if this had been often discussed and debated.

Fredi, Priss' best friend, burst into tears. And that sparked SaraBell's tears. Pregnant and nursing hormones and emotional triggers were not a good mix.

Thankfully, Sam's cell phone rang. He spoke quietly for several minutes before saying into the phone, "Stand down. Everyone get home. We're going Tomatoes."

"Tomatoes?" I asked, confused.

"Today's password for all is good and we can relax," Zeke said. "I'll make the calls and get the shooters back here."

Just that fast, it was over. "Come on, Mud. We're going home."

Mama followed me to my truck and stood in the open truck door, blocking my exit, her face set and sad. "Mama?" I asked.

"You think I'm sinning being with your'n daddy." It was a statement, not a question.

"Mama, the church has never followed the laws of Tennessee. As to sinning, I went to a church in town. They got this plaque on the wall with the Commandments of Christianity. The first one is, 'Thou shalt not judge.' Only God can judge morality and whether someone is heaven bound or heading the other way. Whether you're sinning is between the Almighty and you, Mama."

The lines in Mama's face creased tight in some emotion I couldn't describe.

I touched her shoulder. "I was John's second wife, and if Leah had lived, that would have been a relationship I entered into, knowing exactly what it entailed. That said, my job is all about the laws the church ignores, and the law says you can't be legally married to Daddy because Mama Carmel married him."

Mama looked away, the frown lines beside her mouth deep grooves. "You'un gonna marry that Occam?" she asked, staring out over the trees.

"I ain't planning to marry at all, Mama. But if things change between Occam and me, you'll know it right away. I promise." I started the truck and Mama backed away so I could close the cab door. "We'll see you in a day or two," I promised, through the open window.

"I love you, baby girl."

"I love you too, Mama."

She whispered, "You'un take care of your'n sisters." And she walked away.

A chill in my soul, I drove out of the yard, down the gravel drive, past the vampire tree, and out the gate toward Soulwood. On the way home, I pulled over and texted Brother Thad. He wouldn't respond anytime soon, as his church services lasted from ten in the morning until two in the afternoon, with a break for lunch on the grounds. My text said, *I'm free tomorrow if you want to send me the cost of upgrades.* I had to get Mud away from the church. I had to push for custody.

Seemed like I'd be going into debt for sure.

TWELVE

While I slept, a heat wave from the Gulf swept through, with the accompanying thunderstorms, high winds, slashing rain, and temporary cool temps. I loved storms and so did Soulwood. The land enticed me deeply into sleep as the sky watered our leaves and roots.

The cool didn't last, and my sleep didn't either. The storms were followed by muggy, miserable heat and by late afternoon, I woke from confused dreams to find myself drenched in a soggy sweat. I twitched the sheets back to let them dry and dragged myself to the bathroom for a tepid shower. In the heat wave, I was almost ecstatic that my underground cistern kept my well water at a cool sixty degrees. It certainly woke me up fast. I dressed in cotton and followed the smell of coffee outside to the brazier, which had a percolator coffeepot on it. Two mugs were on the table nearby, and I fell into one of the two chairs someone had placed in the shade of the house.

I poured a cup and sipped, watching my sister as she measured out a potential area for the greenhouse. She was dressed in my old overalls and work boots, toiling in the heat, working up a sweat as she hammered stakes into the ground. Stakes she had made herself, if the pile of split wood was an indication.

Two of the cats lay in the garden beneath the bamboo-cane trellis, in the shade cast by leafy green bean vines. Torquil was lying at the edge of the woods at the base of a tree. All three cats were flat to the ground in the heat. "You're gonna get eaten by a hawk," I warned her. The cat ignored me.

"Ain't no hawk gonna eat the cats," Mud yelled, brandishing a mallet. "I'm too big and too mean and I scare them off." She stomped over and fell into the other chair. Sipped her coffee.

"When did you start drinking coffee?"

"While you were disabled. Mama says if you drink hot coffee on a hot day it'll cool you off. I think Mama's delusional, but let's keep that one between us."

"Yes," I said, smiling into my cup. "I think that would be wise."

"I got news about the church. It's dividing along the lines of multiple wives and pretty much all the Jackson side is ready to kill you and burn out the Nicholson side. There's been talk of the church splitting for nigh on a year now, and the lawyers is ready to fight it out in court."

"Oh. Lawyers, huh?"

"According to Sam, polygamy was designed by menfolk to get more sex," Mud said. "Is that what you think?"

I looked up at the sky and said, "Save me." God didn't. I had no idea how my sister and I ended up having part of the conversation that most church mamas had on the wedding day of their far-too-young daughters.

My cell rang and I thought, *Saved by the bell,* and answered without looking at the screen, because I needed to be saved, even if it was by a robocall. "Ingram."

"Yellowrock," the voice snarled. The connection was staticky, parts of words dropping out. "Why are you calling my people?"

I looked at the screen then and a jolt of a different sort went through me. "Jane? You sound . . . strange." I had almost said she sounded awful, like a sick, wet cat, but that wasn't smart.

I could hear her breath blow across the phone and she replied in a tone that was more diplomatic, if not serene. "Sorry. I've been . . . Never mind. What's up?" She sounded better, but the connection was still awful. I decided not to ask her to call me back over a different cell or landline. She might not bother or she might be on the progression—whatever that was—mentioned by Ming, and I'd lose this chance. And since I didn't know what Jane did or didn't know, I had to cover a lot of bases fast.

"A vampire named Godfrey of Bouillon, or Godefroi de Bouillon, attacked Ming of Glass, the MOC of Knoxville. Ming and her people won, but it was a narrow margin and there were a lot of injuries and deaths. The Shaddock Clan Home in Asheville was also attacked, and because Shaddock was in Knoxville helping Ming fight, he lost his lands and his people. Witches are attacking Ming too, possibly the same one who is attacking"—I almost said Rick but changed it—"our people, though that hasn't been verified."

I heard a voice in the background and realized I was on speakerphone. Alex said, "Lincoln Shaddock and Ming have some of the best fighters in the States. Your boss is Ayatas FireWind. Why do they need our help?"

Jane said, "There's nothing I can do that they can't."

"That's garbage." I scowled at the world and Mud's eyes went big. I flapped my hand at her and mouthed, *Not you.* To Jane I said, "You're the Dark Queen. You have resources."

Jane chuckled and the sound was different from her previous laughter, disheartened, maybe even depressed. "Yeah. The all-powerful Oz, that's me." She continued before I could respond. "This much I can do. Alex, will you chat with Unit Eighteen's Jones? See if you can send them some information on Godfrey."

"Sure," Alex said. "I like a woman with a rep. File will be prelim data and I'll send more later. Watch for a file named 'Godfrey of Bouillon One.'"

Alex was a former hacker and he knew about our Diamond Drill.

Jane went on, "If things get dire, I'll call the governor. I know you think I'm some kind of genie in a bottle, but I'm not. I can't fix Ming's problems, short of depriving her of her city and clan and taking over. And frankly, Ming would challenge me to a blood duel if I tried."

"I'm not—"

"I'm tired of killing, little *yinehi*," she said. "Take what you can get. And if you want a job with Clan Yellowrock, ask for it. I could always use a . . . a *gardener*." Her tone suggested that she knew I was far more lethal than an ordinary gardener. The call ended.

"Was that the vampire hunter?" Mud asked, her eyes still wide. "The demon one what killed a demon from hell and that old vampire? On the TV?"

"Yes. And no. That was Jane Yellowrock, but she isn't a demon. Demons don't fight demons. Remember your scripture."

"A house divided against itself will not stand, meaning demons don't fight demons. But Sam said—"

"Sam's wrong," I interrupted. "Jane is a shape-shifter. And that old vampire she killed on TV was the emperor of the European vampires, and he was gonna kill a lot of innocent humans just for spite. Killing him made Jane queen of all the vamps, one of the most powerful people among the vampires everywhere."

"*She* don't seem to think so."

"Something's wrong. I don't know what. But, you know how the church is dividing into factions? Well, the vampires are even worse. She's also Mr. LaFleur's ex-girlfriend. Things are complicated."

"I'm'a be a townie girl. Townies like complicated."

"Is that so?"

"Yep."

My cell dinged again and Mud arched her neck to read the screen. I read the text, holding the cell so my nosy true sib couldn't see it. The text was from T. Laine. *I might be able to break the black-magic calling Rick, but I can't do it alone. Rick tried again to get the local coven to help. Copied is their reply: NO!.*

The cell dinged again with a text from JoJo: *Heard from Alex Younger of Yellowrock Securities. He sent info and offered to provide assistance tracking the fangheads who attacked Ming. TY.*

"That was fast," I said. I texted back with an acknowledgment to both agents and laid the cell facedown.

"You got to go into work tonight, don'tcha?" Mud asked.

"Yes."

"I'll stay with Mama and Daddy tonight, okay? I got greenhouse stuff to do."

At which point I realized I hadn't discussed child care with Mama and Daddy while I was at the church. The threat of violence had driven it out of my mind. "Okay. I'll take you on the way in to work."

"I'll be working on my tablet. I think I'm gonna need me some tutoring in math. Okay if I look for one online?"

I grinned at her. "Female, with her own transportation and excellent references."

Mud grinned back.

I tugged my laptop to me and began to run a search for Isleen and Loriann, vampire and witch, last names unknown.

I was driving along Main Street in Oliver Springs at about five thirty, merging onto East Tri County Boulevard—officially Tennessee Highway 61—on my way into HQ when the cell dinged with a text. By feel, I found the cell and hit a button to have the phone read it to me. "Text from Jo Jones," the androgynous voice said. "Call to FBI tip line. Witness saw teenaged girl snatched out of her front yard. Caller said attack was inhumanly fast. Racer took call for FBI and PsyLED. Sending GPS and address. Get there ASAP."

I turned onto Strutt Street and into the parking lot of an empty building just as the cell dinged again with the information. I input the address, slapped the lights on top of the truck, engaged the siren, and pulled back into rush hour traffic, guided by the cell.

The address took me to an older, updated house on Panama Drive, in a well-established middle-class neighborhood. I whipped the wheel, turned off the lights and siren, put them away, reseated my weapon, and clipped my ID and badge in place as I looked the land over. It had likely been farmland once upon a time. Now it was detached housing with big lots, houses built in the seventies, older trees, outbuildings, trucks, manicured lawns, a news van, five police cars, and neighbors everywhere, milling around, some crying.

I studied the land, which looked tired, overfertilized, and underloved, showing a distinct lack of organic matter, companion plants, or complementary plantings. It was drab and not as green as it should have been this time of year. I shook my head at the sad state of the landscaping, and secured my hair in an elastic.

I drove back onto the street and up to the armed uniformed officer, showed him my ID, and parked where he pointed. It was after six and still hot as blue blazes when I exited the Chevy C10. The heat radiating off the blacktopped road, the stink of old tar, and the muggy temp still in the nineties slapped me in the face. The officer pointed at a two-story house. I lifted a hand in thanks and trudged beside the concrete drive, my field boots on the springy, too-long grass. It needed cutting and had browned slightly in the heat. The storm had missed this area and it needed rain. But it was okay. It was grass. It would survive. The oak trees in the yard were twenty-five or so years old and needed rain too, but there was nothing I could do about that.

Crime scene tape marked off the entire front yard and there was an additional square of tape about fifteen by fifteen near the mailbox. The place where the girl had been taken, I presumed. A crime scene tech was placing markers in the brittle grass.

"Ingram!"

The sound of my name shook me from my contemplation of the grass and trees and I spotted Margot on the porch. "What do we have?" I asked.

"FBI has lead on this one. A missing girl and a witness who gives me the creeps, the five minutes I spent with him in the victim's house. I want you to check him out, see if your church-dar sets you off."

"What?" I asked, confused.

"Church-dar. Like radar but for creepy old men." She pointed at the house across the street. "His name is Jim Paton, fifty-six, white, single. Talk. Then find me."

I was still confused, but maybe Margot wanted me that way. I had learned that probies were often sent into situations where they could see things with a fresh eye, or learn things the hard way. I went back across the too-hot asphalt and walked around the witness's one-story house. The front plantings—aged boxwoods and thirsty azaleas—were dry and sere, if neatly trimmed. The back was enclosed with a six-foot brick wall and secured with a sturdy padlocked wood gate. I leaned into the gate and put an eye to a crack to see a wonderland of raised beds and lush plantings, masculine garden furniture, a small garden house, a lovely fountain of a naked nymph pouring water from a jar on her shoulder, and a water feature that mimicked a mountain stream. It looked like up-scale commercial work, far too pretty for this neighborhood.

Back around front, a uniformed officer let me in and I chatted him up, taking in the front room. The house had been built in the seventies and not painted or updated since. The living room walls were a brownish gold, the trampled-down shag carpet a deeper version of the same shade. Matching couch and chairs were upholstered in floral fabric with big gold roses on each cushion. Matching vases of faded yellow roses rested beside matching lamps on matching end tables. A big-screen TV and a newish recliner sat front and center. A heavy layer of dust covered everything except the recliner. The place smelled of mold. There were cobwebs in the corners. Dry-rotted draperies covered the front windows, a paler gold than the walls, and were ruffled along all the seams and the hem. The room looked as if it had been decorated by two very different people, a woman who liked roses and, much later, a man who liked TV. I texted JoJo to see if Jim Paton was the original owner or if he was a newcomer, and if he'd been married or had a significant other in the past.

I followed voices to the kitchen, standing in the doorway, taking everything in before I was spotted. The kitchen was neat as a pin, gold-painted walls, gold-painted cabinets. No dust. No dirty dishes. Everything in its place, though way too much gold. Gold flooring, the kind that came in long rolls and was designed to remind people of tile but was really plasticized stuff. Gold stove and fridge. Gold tablecloth. At the small table was a uniformed officer and a man who did not fit the house. He was neither a decorator who liked roses nor a man who belonged in the comfortable recliner. Jim Paton was middle-aged, fit, with khakis and a dress shirt that had started out the day starched and pressed and still looked fresh. His hair was combed and neat, his shoes polished to a shine. Despite his athletic physique, he had plump cheeks, blue eyes, and what I mentally described as a benevolent face. When he smiled, his cheeks formed little cherubic balls of joy, his eyes twinkled, and the uniformed officer smiled with him. "Anything I can do," Paton said. "Raynay is such a sweet child. This breaks my heart. The world is so full of horrible people and our young are no longer cherished and protected."

I put a sweet look on my face and let my voice rise a little, more high-pitched than my normal tone, as I stepped in, interrupting the chitchat. "Mr. Paton, I'm probationary special agent Nell Ingram with PsyLED. I understand you saw the girl abducted?"

Paton turned to me, and I understood Margot's church-dar comment. Paton surveyed me in one swift glance, evaluating and categorizing me, my voice, body type, hair, shoes, and gun. It was fast, so fast I'd have missed it had I not been focused so tightly on him.

"Probationary? Such a sweet young woman for such a dangerous job." He shook his head. "I was just about to fix Officer Cobb a cup of coffee. Would you like one? Or maybe tea?"

"No, thank you," I said, my voice going a little more girlish. "I know you've already told your story several times, but can you tell me what you saw?"

"I came in from work, got a cola from the fridge"—he pointed at the gold antique—"and sat in my recliner. I looked out the front window and saw Raynay walking to the mailbox. A black panel van rolled up, braked, and I saw several pairs of feet moving faster than a human possibly can. The van sped off. Raynay was gone. I raced across the street, banged on the door, and told Lonie what I had seen. Lonie Blalock. That's Raynay's mother. We called the police together. They got here fast and said it sounded like a vampire kidnapping. Do you know anything new?"

"Did you see a license plate? Get a look at the driver?"

"The van was between Raynay and me." He put a hand over his heart, a gesture of commiseration, but . . . it looked off. Affected. *Fake.* My newly described church-dar for creepy old men was clanging loudly. "The windows were tinted," he continued. "It happened so fast. I didn't see anything else."

"I see," I said. "You were in the recliner? In the living room?"

Paton's face altered just a hint. Barest tightening of the creases around his smiling blue eyes. "That's what I said."

"The recliner in the *living room*?"

Paton said nothing.

"The recliner in the living room?" I repeated.

"Yes," Paton said, and he pasted a happy, innocent smile on his face.

"Thank you." I left the kitchen for the living room and stood near the recliner. The drapes were closed, but I couldn't rule out that Paton had closed them. I opened the drapes. A puff of dust filtered out. I retook my position at the recliner, looking out the front windows. I bent to where Paton's head would have been when he used the chair. Shifting back and forth, I considered his line of sight along the recline position. The draperies obscured most of the yard across the street. The area where the crime scene tech worked was hidden behind the trees. I opened the front door and studied Paton's house. There was one window that gave a clear line of sight to the place where the girl supposedly had been abducted. I texted Margot and JoJo on the same thread. *Witness lying. Margot, get over here. Jo, check databases for past domestic abuse or sexual assault allegations on Paton.*

Margot strode across the street to me. Jo texted back, *In process.* Margot called out, "What do we have?"

I shut the door to give us privacy. "Witness says he was in his recliner when he saw the girl abducted. He saw several pairs of feet beneath a van. You can't see the house from his chair. But there's a bedroom window that might work." I pointed. "And it's low enough that he might see feet."

Margot changed direction and walked to the window. She leaned in and made a circle of her hands against the screen, pressing her face close. "Gotcha, you lying son of a bitch." She raced to the porch, past me, and inside, one hand on her weapon. She looked heated and cold all at once, focused and scary. I followed her more slowly. "Mr. Paton," she said. "You've told us several times about seeing Raynay abducted. Tell me again. Starting with where you were when you saw the event. And this time? I want the truth."

"I'll be calling my lawyer," Paton said calmly.

"In that case I'll be taking you in for questioning." There was something gleeful in Margot's voice. "Read Mr. Paton his rights, Officer. Cuff him, and put him in my unit."

"Yes, ma'am," the cop said.

"Don't touch anything," she added. "I want a warrant for this one." Margot came back in the main room.

"Be sure to include the backyard in the warrant," I said softly for her ears only. "And his business office. And any

properties he might own or rent. And whatever he watches on
the TV in the main room."

"Why's that?" Margot asked.

"Church-dar. For creepy old men." For things that seem
wrong.

Back in the Blalock yard, I asked the crime scene tech to step
back and used the psy-meter 2.0, reading the spot where
Raynay disappeared. I caught a hint of vampire. Which was
strange because vampires in the daylight were impossible. But
Paton's description of the abduction sounded like the way
well-fed blood-servants moved—faster than normal. And pan-
eled vans with tinted windows were a common method of
transportation for vampires.

I looked back at the window of Paton's house that faced
this spot. Compared it to the front of the house where Raynay
lived. On a hunch I packed up the psy-meter, thanked the tech,
and made my way to the Blalock house. Quietly, I made my
way down the hall to the bedroom where two cops and a crime
scene tech were standing. Green walls and carpet. Unmade
bed. Clothes on the floor. High school banners hung on one
wall. The room of the abducted girl faced the front of the house,
overlooking Paton's house, with a clear view of the window
where Margot had said, *Gotcha, you lying son of a bitch.*
What had she seen?

My cell dinged. JoJo had sent a text to Margot and me.
*Found a Peeping Tom report from twenty years ago, and one
count of lewd behavior with a minor. Nothing since.*

Margot texted back, *He went underground.*

She meant that Paton was a sexual predator who had
learned to hide his activities enough to be considered safe
around neighbors. But why would a sexual predator claim he
had witnessed an abduction if he was the culprit? Why not just
remain silent? I thought about the sanctimonious predators at
the church and considered them in light of the evidence here.
I texted back, *I'll access all reports of missing girls when I get
back to HQ. But I think he really saw the girl abducted. It fits
the MO of a man hiding his own activities. In warrant, look
for child pornography.*

Margot texted back, *My money says we got him.*

I hoped her money was right, but just in case, I sent a text to Yummy that said, *Can vampires smell other vampires and their blood-servants? If so, when you wake and get this, I'd like you to take a sniff at the abduction site of a human teenager.* Then I sent a shorter text, *Please.*

Because a child was missing, Margot got her paper in record time. I spent the next hours working on my search on Isleen and Loriann, running back and forth between Paton's house and the Blalock home, updating people at HQ, and keeping my nose in everything important.

In the middle of the running around, my laptop dinged. I took it to the truck and plugged it in to charge while I looked at the results of my search. I sat for a while, sweating, my fingers on the keyboard, limp, as I stared at the results. Then I called JoJo on her cell.

"Jones," she said.

"I may have found Loriann, Rick's ink blood-magic witch."

"Go, probie!"

"Not really. Things are convoluted. There's an NOPD complication from the two years after Rick was inked." I told what I had discovered.

Jo listened and then said softly, "I'll do some more research and then call Soul."

"Copy that." I ended the call. If I was right about what I had discovered, Rick had been hiding things from his unit.

Two hours after the call had first come in, we had significant evidence against Jim Paton for possessing child pornography and for watching Raynay Blalock through her window with a telescope that was usually set up on a tripod in his bedroom. The scope was found under the bed, but the feet of the stand had made indentations in the carpet that were impossible to explain away. Jim claimed he had nothing to do with Raynay's kidnapping, but he was in deep trouble and his lawyer was trying to arrange bail and a safe place for the man to stay. So far no judge was willing to consider letting him out on personal recognizance, and Jim wasn't going to be safe in his own house anymore, not since word had gotten out to his neighbors that he was into abuse of children.

But. Raynay was still missing. Margot and another FBI agent I didn't know had spent hours with the mother of the missing girl, but she knew nothing. I still didn't think Paton had anything to do with the kidnapping.

It was finally dark and Yummy was on her way over to add more evidence. Waiting on her, I sat in the overheated truck cab, windows open, sweating, making cell phone calls and typing up reports, my skin coated with that oily, greasy sweat that results from high humidity and midsummer heat. The temps were making me gripey and impatient and I was hungry and thirsty and I had forgotten to refill my water bottle, which meant I'd had to refill with city water from the Blalock kitchen tap. The taste was chlorinated and awful. And Yummy was late.

That thought was still echoing in my brain when the truck rocked and a fanged face slashed at my windshield. I had drawn my weapon and aimed before I realized it was Yummy. False vamp laughter, mocking and insulting, echoed down the street. Playing a vamp game. My heart was stuttering around one-eighty, and my breathing was still trying to catch up. Knowing she would hear me through the open window, I muttered, "I'm loaded with silver-lead ammo. Be glad I didn't fire."

"Maggoty Nell would make me true-dead?" she asked through the glass, still laughing. But it was now human laughter and her fangs snapped back into place in the roof of her mouth as her eyes bled back to human.

I reseated my weapon and opened the door, sliding out of the seat. "Thanks for coming."

"The news media is all over this like white on rice. If my assistance will stick Jim Paton behind bars and recover the missing girl, then I'm happy to oblige." The edge in her voice convinced me she was more than willing to help this once, with no quid pro quo to balance the account between us.

I inclined my head toward the crime scene tape and together we ambled over, unconsciously keeping the cruisers between the news van cameras and ourselves. Softly, so no one with a parabolic mic or something even fancier could overhear me, I said, "I don't think Paton took Raynay. I think he'll go to jail for child pornography, but I think blood-servants took the girl. I got a reading that suggested vampires took her in broad daylight, and since that's not likely, I'm thinking blood-servants who have been drinking a lot of vampire blood—enough to make them read a little like vamps—took her."

"You are not accusing Ming's people," Yummy said, half question, half assertion.

"No. But you tell me."

We had reached the fifteen-foot-wide square of lawn marked off by yellow crime scene tape. The tech was long gone. Yummy looked at me as if asking if she could cross the tape. I shook my head. "Do the best you can from here."

Yummy dropped into a squat, one knee on the ground. She was wearing tight Lycra running pants and still wasn't sweating. I didn't envy the whole blood-drinking thing, but I did envy the vampire not-sweating thing. She leaned forward and sniffed several times. Then sat back on her haunches. She said softly, "The human girl was frozen in panic. The ones who took her are the same blood clan as the Naturaleza who attacked the council chambers of Ming of Glass." Yummy's blond hair shifted and fell across one shoulder as she angled her head up to see me. "They're Ming's enemies. The enemies of all the Mithrans of Knoxville. When we find the location of their lair, we'll kill them all. But we'll be mindful of prisoners."

I frowned. "Don't you think it would be better to get PsyLED to take down a lair?"

"No."

That was succinct. "Okay then. Thank you for coming."

"One thing." Yummy rose to stand beside me. "I also smell magic on them. Perhaps not enough to register on your machine, but enough to make them dangerous. Be careful. They might have powerful amulets."

"Okay. Hey." I stopped, thought it through, and asked, "You ever hear of a vampire named Isleen?"

"Yes. She is true-dead. If you have further questions, ask your LaFleur." Yummy faded into the night.

I went back to my truck and called HQ, filling them in on the information Yummy had given me about the kidnapped girl, calling her a confidential informant. It wouldn't fool any-one at HQ, but it did keep Yummy's name off my reports.

When I explained my blood-servant-kidnapper theory, JoJo said, "So you think we have three cases. A kidnapping involv-ing the vampires who also attacked Ming of Glass, a witch creating a circle to curse Rick, and Paton with his child porn addiction."

"Yes. Or maybe overlapping cases," I said. "And if the vam-pires need blood, they'll be taking more people off the streets."

"Why is nothing ever easy?" she muttered and ended the call.

I was back at HQ when the case turned itself on its head, and because I was the probie taking calls on the night shift, I got the news first. "PsyLED Unit Eighteen, Special Agent Nell Ingram," I said, answering the official line.

"I'd like to speak with Rick LaFleur," a female voice said.

"Special Agent LaFleur isn't in right now," I said, as I pe-rused the list of missing teenaged girls within a ten-mile ra-dius of Paton's house. There had been seven in the last twenty years, three returned safely, four never found. That seemed like a lot. Distracted, I said, "Can I help you or do you want his voice mail?"

"Will you call his cell and tell him to call Loriann Ethier at New Orleans Police Department, CLE. It's urgent." She gave me a number, pronounced and spelled her last name, which didn't match at all, and hung up.

Loriann. Rick's Loriann. And she had just called PsyLED from NOPD. I sat at my desk, not sure what to do. I finally called JoJo on her cell so I could speak privately.

"This is weird, probie," she answered. "I can see you from here."

"Loriann Ethier just called HQ. She wants me to have Rick call her at NOPD CLE, whatever CLE is. Can you track it back?"

"I'm in the system. Hang on." She repeated the number back to me. Then, "Dang, probie. You're batting a thousand. You were right. The witch who spelled and inked Rick cur-rently works for the New Orleans Police Department."

Rick had to know Loriann worked at NOPD. Boss man had been keeping secrets. "Rick was going to stick around HQ until the witch circles stopped. But he's not in-house. What do I do?"

"Call his cell. Pass along the message. I'll notify Soul."

I dialed Rick's cell and opened with, "A woman wants you to call her. Her name is Loriann E-t-h-i-e-r," I spelled out, "pronounced 'Etta.'" His reaction was so intense it shivered through the silence on the cell. I stilled, feeling his shock through my bones and through my connection to Soulwood. Whatever it was, it was something with power, with magic, and it had hit Rick. Or come from him. "She's the witch who inked you, isn't she?"

Reluctant, hesitant, he said, "Yes. Loriann Ethier is the witch who . . . tattooed me . . . with a blood-magic . . . spell." He growled out the last words as if they ached.

Magic. I'd been right. "Do you think she's the one who's cursing—"

"I'm not speculating. Occam and I dropped by my house to pack more clothes and I'm on my way back. I'll make the call from HQ. ETA eight minutes." He ended the call.

I gathered up my tablets and the note with the name and number and walked into the conference room. In the darkened space JoJo and Tandy were both poring over laptops and multiple tablets. "Rick's on the way in to call her back. He says she's the witch who gave him his tats."

JoJo suggested that someone have sexual relations with her and scrubbed her hands over her turban. Tandy laughed. "We've already amassed a lot of research on her," Tandy said.

Jo dropped her hands. "Yeah. With our combined talents, we pretty much know where Loriann is, where she gets her hair done, what her pets' names are, what medicines she takes, and how she likes her steak cooked. All in fifteen minutes' work. All we needed was a last name. Which Rick never gave us."

I didn't envy Loriann the loss of personal privacy. As we waited on Rick, I gave attention to my plants, sliding sturdy leaves through fingers and thumbs, thinking, trying to make the investigation fit together. Nothing fit. Parts of the puzzle were missing. Or I was blind to them. Probably that. But I did

know that Rick should have told us about Loriann, that she
worked for the New Orleans Police Department, because many
of the witch circles had been found in Louisiana. No matter
what she was today, this witch had done evil to Rick once. She
should have been on a list of suspects from day one. And Rick
hadn't told us about her.

Rick blew into HQ like a storm, his eyes glowing the green of
his cat, his black and silver hair flying around his head and
shoulders as if caught up in a wind. He dropped his gobags
and took his place at the conference table. Occam wasn't with
him, and I felt a shaft of disappointment. "I assume you're all
up to speed on Loriann," he snapped. When Tandy and JoJo
nodded, he said, "Fill me in."

Crisply, JoJo said, "She's twenty-seven years old, lives in
New Orleans on the second floor of a two-bed, one-bath,
Victorian-style two-story duplex just outside the Garden District." She pointed to a photo of a house on the screen overhead. "She owns the house and two others, courtesy of her
grandmother's will. She's single, has two cats, and works for
NOPD Crime Lab and Evidence. She rents out the lower floor
of her home to a doctor of paranormal species at Tulane Medical. She has a brother with a drug problem. She reported him
missing twelve months ago. The number she gave us is the
CLE direct number, but it's possible that your call will be di-
verted elsewhere. This"—a second photo popped up on the big
screen over the windows—"is from her most recent driver's
license, and the one beside it is from her NOPD ID."

The woman had dark brown eyes and pale skin. She wore
her brown hair parted down the middle and hanging close to
her face in the driver's license. In the NOPD photo, her hair
was back in a tail, exposing her ears. Ear cartilage, shape, and
placement on the head were better identification markers than
facial markers, which could easily be changed by surgery. In
both photos, she was unsmiling. I got the impression of heavy
burdens and years of sadness from the photographs.

"She stopped dying her hair," Rick said, his voice going
soft. He cleared his throat as if something clogged it, and I
remembered that odd sound when he told us about the ink

spell earlier. "After I was rescued, Katie Fonteneau, once number two in the Pellissier vampire clan of New Orleans, and who is now Master of the City of Atlanta, saved Lori."

"Why would a vampire help a witch?" Tandy asked.

His voice hoarse, Rick said, "Isleen was Katie's scion—her blood-made vampire child. Isleen was also a psycho fanghead. Katie felt responsible for everything done to Loriann. And to me, I think."

A vampire had to have known that her scion was insane.

Rick put his hand on his throat. Coffee gurgled into the pot behind him. Raspy, he said, "I helped Loriann get a job as a consultant at Crime Lab and Evidence. She did good work for a couple of years. Then she vanished. I haven't had contact with her since."

Jo said, "She was rehired by CLE this past January when the European Mithrans tried to take over. She's full-time now, instead of the former consultancy. Her six-month evaluation was excellent."

"Has she been researching something in private?" Rick asked softly.

"I can't tell," Jo said. "Her work computer files are encrypted and her personal system is set up to give an alarm if anything tries to read it. I can't get in easily, if at all."

"Really?" he said, as if he found that interesting. "Okay. Let's do this. Clementine," he said to the voice-to-text software, "record. Rick LaFleur, Jo Jones, Tandy Dyson, Nell Ingram, on conference call to Loriann Ethier"—he spelled it out—"currently of NOPD CLE."

"CLMT2207 recording," the system said.

He gave the date and time and punched in the phone number.

It rang once. "Crime lab. Loriann Ethier. How may I help you?"

Rick's mouth opened. Nothing came out. I felt an odd, tugging sensation on Soulwood. "Rick LaFleur," he said, sounding calmer than he looked. "How are you, Loriann?"

"You've had fifteen minutes, you and Diamond Drill. I'm sure you know everything about me."

Jo's head snapped to Rick at the use of her old hacker name. Loriann had been researching us, it seemed.

Loriann continued. "How are *you*? Since the *calling* started, I mean."

Jo tapped on her laptop so fast it was a tiny little burr of sound. Tandy focused on the far wall, as if blocking out everything except the voices.

"How do you know about the calling?" Rick asked. I'd have thought him steady, uninvolved, except for the brightening green glow of his black eyes.

"Your tats are being pulled on. I can feel the magic attacking them. So I did a little research."

Tension shot through me. Loriann knew something about the magic in Rick's tats, and not just from the original inking. Could Loriann be the witch cursing Rick? It made sense, except for the logistics. She wasn't in Knoxville. But . . . she knew too much and there was no reason why she should know. Unless she had left a backdoor into Rick's magic tats. I sent that possibility to Jo, who shot me a startled look.

Tandy scribbled something and passed the note to Rick. It read, *Too far away to be sure, but I think she's half lying.*

Rick rubbed his eyes and temples as if his head hurt. "Go on," he said, sounding a lot more cop-like than he currently looked.

"I heard about the Knox vamps being attacked and the witch who's casting a curse there."

"Who is the witch?" Rick asked. "What is she casting?"

Loriann said, "I got a look at the photos of the circles and they look a lot like ones I saw on the bank of the Mississippi last December, a month or so before the European vampires were destroyed." Her voice took on an intensity that sharpened her sibilants, making her next words almost hiss. "Three circles. All created to be cast on the three days of the new moon. The spells are called Circle of the Moon-Cursed, or Circle of the Curse, or more commonly, Circle of the Moon."

"Ohhh," I whispered as something seemed to fall into place in my brain. As a curse, it would be cast as a *new* moon circle. Curses and new moons had been taught in Spook School, but the course info had been sparse. Curses were rare, against witch law. We had already considered that this spell was brand-new, experimental. If this was the testing phase, then it worked like a pulse of magic and then stopped. Was that why Rick was aging slowly—a pulse at a time? If so, then the final, full curse was still to come. It all made sense, but my knowledge of magic lore wasn't extensive. I pulled my laptop to me and sent my info to the unit. JoJo's system pinged softly and she shot me a look, nodding once to say she agreed.

I had missed something and looked back up to see Rick's hand drop. "You know what the spells are," he said softly to Loriann. Because until now, we hadn't fully known how to classify them.

"Yes. Maybe. I think so. I don't know for sure. But I think I can help. I've requested to be assigned to Knoxville to assist you. My boss said there's no crossover with NOPD and KPD or PsyLED Knoxville. But if PsyLED DC asked for me, and offered to pay my salary while I'm there, he would let me go."

The home office of the Psychometry Law Enforcement Division of Homeland Security was located near the District of Columbia. She was asking for help from the main PsyLED office. She had already worked out the knots in her request. "Go on," Rick said.

"Soul could ask," Loriann said. "And I'd be there to help Tammie Laine Kent if you needed spell casting. Since the local coven has gone in hiding."

Loriann knew a *lot* about what was happening in Knoxville. A lot about our agents. She'd had access through NOPD CLE channels and she hadn't wasted the opportunities. She'd done her research. I wondered if she had gotten all that from our employee sleeves or was a hacker like JoJo. Of if she had a contact in Knoxville. And who that might be. Perhaps Margot Racer?

Working at PsyLED had made me a suspicious woman.

I didn't like that about myself.

Rick promised to talk to Soul, though he didn't promise to request that Loriann be loaned to the Knoxville PsyLED field office, an oversight I caught even if Loriann didn't. After the call ended, we sat around the table, three of us silent and thinking, JoJo tapping away like a madwoman, jerking on her earrings between attacks on the tablets and laptop. Rick watched us, the green glow in his eyes diminishing slowly. I caught him reaching up, several times, to rub the mangled tattoos, to touch the amulets hanging around his neck, to rub his throat, and I wondered if he was aware of the gestures. Abruptly, he turned and went to his office.

Softly, I said, "She has access to the magic in Rick's tattoos."

No one responded.

I excused myself and went to my cubicle, where I stuck my fingers into the soil of the plants in the window boxes, trying to decide how I'd research curse circles, tattoo magic, and my boss. Because no matter how much we hid it from ourselves, Rick LaFleur could be a security risk. A big one. Propped against a basil was a small envelope. I tore it open to read a note from Occam. *Nell, sugar, no matter what time you read this, you should know I'm missing you something fierce.* An unfamiliar emotion, soft yet intense, swept through me, and I tucked the note in my gobag to take home.

THIRTEEN

I didn't really know what I was looking for, so I started with Rick's NOPD sleeve, the parts that my clearance level allowed. This was not the same as a personnel folder, but the kind of information that other law enforcement officials had access to. A lot was redacted, but I refreshed my memory on his history.

Richard LaFleur graduated from high school in three years, started university at seventeen in prelaw, and got his degree in criminal justice in two years. He was spotted early on, recruited and fast-tracked into undercover, researching the New Orleans vampires, which was where he met Isleen and Loriann Ethier. At the age of twenty-one he started living on the dark side, where he stayed for nine years, far longer than the one or two years for most undercover operatives. He had been in the public, visible side of law enforcement for only about three years, since he was bitten. His long history undercover explained his willingness to accept JoJo's less-than-lawful talents. And perhaps my own, much darker, gifts.

I buried myself in research on curse spells, on blood-magic bindings and tattoo magic, and into Loriann Ethier, digging as deep as I could, saving reports to study later. Sadly, the magic stuff looked apocryphal, like boogeyman stories, not like reality. Loriann's sleeve and social media presence were sparse to nonexistent. I was getting nowhere.

JoJo left to sleep, giving me a wave of her hand on the way past. Rick went into his cage soon after, taking a mattress and a fluffy comforter. The office went quiet. Lights low.

At three a.m. Tandy buzzed my desk phone. "What's up, Tandy?"

"Get up here. I just heard a report on official police radio frequencies that the body of a young girl has been found in a ditch. Passing motorist, grisly crime scene, according to the chatter."

I raced to the conference room. "We've got voice-to-text," Tandy said, pointing to a screen that had text across the bottom, dedicating it to KCLE—Knox County law enforcement.

"Is it the Blalock girl?"

Tandy shook his head, his pale skin and Lichtenberg lines picking up the glow from the screens in the darkened conference room. "I don't know."

I got coffee for us and waited with him, the volume on the radio chatter turned low, watching the screen. We sipped, listened, read as things were updated, Tandy still tapping away on his tablet, his body mechanics currently a lot like JoJo's. It made me wonder if he was picking up more than just an intro into information gathering—hacking—from JoJo, but also taking on her personality and habits. I wondered if that meant the empath was losing bits of himself, of his own personality. Taking on bits of everyone else. Wondered if that was common to all empaths or something peculiar to Tandy.

Most of what Margot had put together about missing girls and our suspect would be incorrect if the body was ID'd as Raynay Blalock. There was no way creepy Jim Paton could have taken her, stashed her, banged on her mother's door, and killed her. The timeline was impossible. And Paton was in custody now. He wasn't the killer.

Within half an hour, we saw text from the investigator who had taken over the scene, calling for the chief forensic pathologist and the chief medical examiner of Knox County.

Tandy muttered, "Odd that both were called."

Having both the forensic pathologist and the ME on-site was a rare event under any circumstances, TV and films notwithstanding. "What does it mean?"

"At a guess, it implies that the crime scene is so bad, or so weird, that the top brass are needed personally to handle the body at the scene and direct the evidence collection."

"If it's weird, then PsyLED should be there," I said. But the phones didn't ring.

I drank too much coffee and ingested too much chatter that told me nothing, but in my rooty gut I had a feeling that the girl—the body—was Raynay Blalock.

The coroner's van arrived. KPD set up a live-feed camera and Tandy put it up on the screens. More lights lit the scenes.

A woman in a white Tyvek uni with mask and gloves stepped into a ditch. We got a view of the body from the camera on her suit. I looked away.

"Someone from PsyLED needs to be there," Tandy said.

"Yes," I said. "And the officers at the scene had to know that. They didn't contact us."

"I've got their names and the name of the investigator who showed up first. Detective Emery Hamm."

He punched in a number on the official line and Occam answered, "What's up?" his voice carrying over the speakers in the conference room. He sounded groggy. Voice rough. The way a man did when he was waked from a deep sleep. Something warmed in me at the sound and Tandy sent me a look that said he had picked up on my reaction. I looked back at the screens, finding them suddenly fascinating.

"Hate to wake you, Occam," Tandy said. "We have an incident. Deceased human female, vamp bites, and no one in PsyLED was notified. Nell shouldn't handle it alone. Rick's in his cage."

"Is it the girl who went missing today?"

"Unknown."

"Is Margot Racer on scene?" Occam asked. "She was in charge of the abduction earlier," the werecat said, suddenly sounding alert.

"No. So far as we've been able to detect, she wasn't notified either."

"Already tarred with the brush. I'll call her. Send the particulars to my cell. I'm on my way in five."

"Copy that. Info going out now." The connection ended and Tandy activated additional screens overhead as the officers and investigators on scene sent active video to their headquarters, something that would not have happened only a year past. Tech was making everything at crime scenes an instantaneous matter of record. Because of the same changes in tech, Tandy was also able to put up shots of the crime scene as they were uploaded to the coroner's files and local law enforcement. All of which was supposed to be "eyes only" and encrypted.

I didn't ask how Tandy got access to all the info. I also didn't study anything too carefully. There were parts of being an investigator that I would never get used to, and seeing crime scenes involving children, even children who were seventeen and older, children I had once been accustomed to viewing as adults of marriageable age, was one of them.

Within an hour, Occam and Margot Racer were an active part of the investigation, though the conversation when the two special agents met with Detective Hamm was off the record. Hamm left the scene; minutes later a tentative ID went on record. The body was believed to be that of Raynay Blalock. Preliminary COD was exsanguination. She had been drained of blood from multiple vampire bites. PsyLED and the FBI were now lead on the case.

I wanted to contact Yummy. I wanted to track down every single aligned and rogue vampire in Knox County and fill them with silver, but I was bound by laws and protocol and, as probie, governed by Tandy, who levered a look at me each time I thought about investigating on my own or contacting Knoxville's vampires. He was right. I wasn't a private citizen, so I stayed put until I received orders otherwise. If a Knoxville vamp killed the girl, if that was even halfway provable, that vampire would be judged and punished by Ming. *Punished* in this case being a vamp euphemism meaning killed true-dead. If the vampire or vampires who had killed Blalock were Ming's enemies, then . . . I didn't know what happened in that case, but it still wouldn't be me who dealt with it. Occam called in to HQ and discussed the lack of official communication with Tandy, who called the sheriff and complained. Again.

At four thirty, I peeked in on Rick, who was sleeping too hard, his breathing fast, too deep, his chest heaving up and down, as if he was chasing prey or racing for his life. The moon had risen around three a.m., and I wondered if the moon had affected his sleep. I decided that waking him would be dangerous and left him sleeping. I checked my plants again, this time looking for dead leaves, letting my mind wander through bits and pieces of information and memories, alighting on this or that, to no specific purpose.

As daybreak began to gray the world outside, a white female walked up to the exterior door and knocked. Tandy adjusted the camera to get a good look at her face. It was Loriann Ethier. From New Orleans. Tandy's hands flew over the keys as he determined how she'd gotten here, and he said, "She took a red-eye direct. Go wake up Rick. Occam's on his way. The others will be here in half an hour."

"What about *her*?" I asked, staring at the screen with Loriann's face on it.

"She can wait until Rick says to invite her up."

Almost as if she had heard the words, Loriann looked into the camera, pointed to the side, and walked into the coffee shop that had opened at five for the morning's business. Coffee's On had the best coffee in the city, though I might be prejudiced. I was a regular. The security video from Coffee's On appeared on the next screen. I looked at Tandy, who wore a defiant expression. "JoJo's work. We have an in for Yoshi's Deli's security cameras too. In case someone goes after the neighbors."

"And do they know we've invaded their privacy?"

Tandy might have flushed just a bit, though it was hard to tell in the darkened room.

"We're too kind," I murmured, indulging in unfamiliar sarcasm. I shook my head and went to wake Rick, who was sleeping better as dawn approached. With a thick, darker-than-once-before fingernail, I tapped on the cage, the tone both woody and metallic. Rick rolled over, the motion all cat, lithe and languid, in contrast to his wrinkled clothing and scruffy, unshaven human face. "Nell," he said. He seemed in control.

I unlatched the cage and said, "You have a visitor. Loriann Ethier is in Coffee's On."

Thoughts and reactions crossed Rick's face. He rolled to his feet and stretched. "She didn't wait to be invited." He raised an arm, sniffed, and made an awful face.

"Shall I go let her in?"

He reached around his cage, grabbing his four-day gobag from the corner. "I need to shower."

"What if you get called to your cat while we make her wait?"

He grimaced. "If I meet her looking like this, the initial interview shifts in her favor. Remember your Reid method. I'll lock myself in and I'll be fast."

The Reid interrogation technique was a method that got subjects to talk, and included a behavior analysis interview. Rick needed to be dominant to use Reid against a potential danger.

Back in the conference room, I made a pot of coffee and opened the box of Krispy Kremes that an early arrival had left on the table. The box contained eleven donuts and appeared to be half lemon-filled and half raspberry-filled. I left a five and two ones, because I'd have more than one, chose a lemon, and bit in. It was scrumptious.

Occam came in behind me, walked to the tinted windows, and stared out at the sky. His eyes were hollow and dark with visions of the crime scene. He didn't speak, but stood so still he might have been a vampire. Something about him suggested restrained violence, a need to break something . . . or kill someone. I started to reach out to him, but Tandy shook his head, eyes wide, telling me to leave Occam alone. I dropped my hand and walked from the conference room.

I stayed in my cubicle, finishing up my EOB—end-of-business—report and snipping dead leaves out of my hairline, listening to the soft murmur of voices as Tandy guided Occam to talk and they caught up on the night's events. I heard enough to know that Occam was talking about the crime scene, and though I wanted to know everything, there was pathos in his tone. Occam needed this time with the empath. When he had talked himself out, I went back to the conference room, passing Rick in the hallway. He was dressed in clean black slacks, starched white shirt, cuffs folded up, and black shoes. Fancier than the usual casual black he normally wore. He was freshly shaved, his hair wet and slicked back. His badge and ID were clipped at his waist and he was wearing a shoulder harness with his Glock GDP-20 in its Kydex holster. I had expected him to look tired or upset, but he looked steady and oddly excited.

"Call her," he said to Tandy as he strode into the conference room. "Tell her to come on up."

"Call who?" JoJo asked. She was standing in the middle of the hallway, vibrant in orange and purple, hues that looked perfect on her.

"Loriann Ethier," Rick said. "She's in Coffee's On, having a croissant and a cup of coffee." He tilted his head at the screen.

"Well. That's ballsy," she said, skirts swirling as she whirled into the conference room.

Tandy dialed and held out the office phone to Rick. The boss shook his head and Tandy shrugged, saying into the phone, his tone emotionless, "Someone will meet you at the door."

Rick made a slashing motion across his own throat and Tandy ended the call. Quickly, Rick gave us instructions.

"I'll let T. Laine know." Tandy rose from his chair and went to the door, down the steps, his fingers texting as he moved. JoJo took his place and shifted the overhead screens until we could watch as Loriann exited the coffee shop and entered the door Tandy held open. Rick sat, taking his usual chair at the head of the room. He was a silhouette in the brightening windows, the overhead lights still in nighttime mode. Occam placed a cup of coffee in front of him and put the box of donuts aside, clearing the expanse of table. "Sit," Rick ordered. "Face the entrance."

Occam, JoJo, and I sat, spinning our chairs to face the doorway, our cells where we could see them but no one else could. T. Laine appeared from the locker room, glanced at the overhead screens, cursed succinctly, and took her seat, aligning her chair like ours, to face the door. She placed three pens on the table. Working for the cops, Loriann would surely know what they were. A threat.

We were going for impact. For first impressions.

The mamas talked about starting out as you intend to go forward. That discussion had been about marriage and the heady, frightening, upsetting, exciting days of a new marriage. Loriann was like a new wife entering an established home. Margot's presence had done the same thing but without the bleakness I sensed in the room today. I guessed that the FBI agent was still at the crime scene, but that thought was for later.

Together Loriann and Tandy climbed the steps, Loriann

talking about her flight. About the weather, which was "as hot as New Orleans, though not as humid." I might have expected her to sound nervous, but she didn't. She sounded . . . not exactly arrogant. She sounded what the mamas in the church referred to as disagreeable, which was a combination of pushy, opinionated, and thoughtless. The kind of person who would say things just to cause trouble. Which was a really terrible thing for me to think of a woman I hadn't met yet.

And then Loriann was inside, walking down the brightly lit hallway, Tandy leading her. He entered the unlit room and took his seat, his chair facing the doorway, and held his cell in his lap where it couldn't be seen. Loriann stopped, standing in the doorway, facing the unlit room. She looked from silhouette to silhouette, though it was clear she couldn't really see us. No one spoke. Loriann's eyes adjusted and she focused on Rick, the silver of his hair shining bright in the stark light of the screens, his eyes glowing cat-green.

There was no reason for it, but I did not like Loriann Ethier.

Rick watched her, letting the silence swell, an uncomfortable stillness that built and intensified, growing so thick it had weight and mass and density. Finally, his voice a low purr, he said, "Loriann. It's been a long time. You look well."

It was so quiet I could hear her breath when Loriann drew it in to speak. "You look old." She blinked, as if surprised to hear her words.

Following Rick's fast orders, Tandy tapped one finger on his cell. *True,* appeared on my cell phone screen and on all the others in the room.

A twisted smile settled itself on Rick's face. "Yeah. My father went silver in his thirties. Why are you here?"

"I think if I go to the sites, I might be able to ID the witch by magical signature."

On my cell screen appeared a one-word text. *True.*

"But I need to read the actual sites of the black magic to be sure."

Lie.

Rick said, "Your liaison position hasn't been approved."

"No. It hasn't. But it will be."

A single word appeared on my screen. *Uncertain.* That

meant either that she was uncertain of the truth, or Tandy was uncertain. Rick hadn't had time to finesse the communications with our resident lie detector.

A quote from Shakespeare rose in my brain. *'Tis best to weigh the enemy more mighty than he seems.* There was nothing about Loriann that looked dangerous, but Loriann had multiple motives and lots of secrets. I looked at the faces around the table. The unit knew that.

"Tell me what you know about the witch circle," Rick said.

"Black witches commonly use Circle of the Moon workings three days of the full moon. The workings are a curse. From the photos, it's one of the most complicated circles I've ever seen. It's not only a curse, it's a summons. It has properties of binding to it. And even though I don't know all it does, I'm pretty sure if it's invoked on the dark of the moon, all hell will break loose."

True. Beneath it appeared the word *Uncertain.* Mixed messages from Tandy, resulting from mixed messages from Loriann. She was still standing in the doorway like a supplicant. This didn't feel like the Reid interrogation technique. It felt like something else.

"Summons?" Rick asked. "For what?"

"I don't know."

Lie. Uncertain.

"T. Laine?" Rick asked. "Evaluate."

"Nonspecific," T. Laine said in her best cop voice. "Ambiguous. And comprising little we don't already know. Who will be cursed? Who will be summoned? Who will be bound? And what part of hell will break loose?"

"I don't know." Loriann's fists bunched.

Lie.

Loriann knew a lot more than she was telling us.

"We don't need you here for this," T. Laine said, her tone insolent, a shade from insulting.

"You do. You're a lone witch. You need a coven to fight this, even if it's only a small coven. A coven of two is better than none."

True.

Rick said, "Step out into the hallway. Close the door. Wait."

Loriann opened her mouth to argue, closed it. Followed
orders. The door shut with a soft snap. "Secure us," he said to
T. Laine and JoJo. Our witch nodded, withdrew a small moonstone from a pocket, and tapped it three times on the table. A
small *hedge of thorns* leaped up around us, tingling on my
skin. The *hedge* made sure our magical visitor couldn't hear.
JoJo switched off Clementine so there was no recording.

"I don't know if she can be believed about *anything* relat-
ing to this case." Rick sat back in his chair, relaxing for the
first time since he woke. Thoughtfully, he shifted his eyes
around the table. "Assessment. Kent?"

"If it was up to me, I'd set her tail on fire and put her on a
flight back to New Orleans," T. Laine said.

"I'm not rich, but I'll pay her way myself," JoJo grumped.
"That girl sets my teeth on edge."

"Occam?" Rick asked.

The werecat shook his head, his eyes still haunted. "We got
some bad stuff happening, boss. Too much bad stuff. If she has
a snowball's chance in hell of helping out on even a portion of
it, then let her stay."

"Tandy?" Rick asked.

"Loriann Ethier is lying. She is so full of anger, guilt, and
jealousy that the emotions swirl around her like a slow-moving,
dark tornado. But—" Tandy looked at JoJo, and she nodded at
him to continue, as if there had been some silent communication between them, question and answer. "But I think the tornado is destroying her inside, rather than a landscape outside
of herself. I think she's profoundly self-destructive and utterly,
dreadfully dangerous."

Rick nodded slowly, his head moving against the windows.
"Yes. Yes. She has always carried those emotions, always been
turned against herself. I think it started when she couldn't protect her family from Isleen. Nell?"

"If she stays, someone has to watch her. And I don't want
her at Soulwood."

"Why?" Rick asked.

Because the land will view her as a threat and eat her. But
I didn't say those words. Instead I said, "Because Soulwood
will magnify everything she's feeling and it will affect everything that we do."

A single word appeared on my cell phone. *True*.

I looked at Tandy. "Stop assessing me."

Tandy tilted his head in a tiny shrug.

Rick sighed and said, "Open the door, please."

I was closest so I stood and opened the door. Loriann stepped from the hallway lights into the darkness of the unlit room, blinking.

"You have a car?" Rick asked her.

Loriann bobbed her head. "Yes. Rental."

"If a liaison position is approved, you can stay," Rick said. "JoJo, you have her number. Make a hotel reservation and text her the particulars." To Loriann, he added, "We'll see you at four p.m. For now"—he gave her a heartless, unamused smile and rested his arms on the chair arms, a king at ease—"you are dismissed."

I held in my grin. Rick had learned a thing or two from vampires and dismissing a lesser being was one of them. It put Loriann in her place. She frowned at us, whirled away, and left the building.

Rick's shoulders relaxed as he looked us over. "Well done." Everyone blew out a breath and the overhead lights came on, making us all squint into the brightness. Rick stood and slid the donut box around the table. The others tossed in a few dollars and took a donut.

I took another of the fantastic pastries and bit in, studying Rick even as he studied us. The vampire kidnapping and murder had to be triggering memories. Loriann's reappearance had to be triggering memories. Occam's distress had to be affecting his cat. Yet the boss didn't look freaked out. He met my eyes and gave me a twisted smile. He tapped his ear, and said, "Music. It helps." I realized he was listening to the spell music, which was why he was okay.

The day shift poured coffee. I took a water bottle from the fridge, the label marked with an *X* and my name. It was a re-used bottle filled with Soulwood water. When we were all settled again, Rick said, "JoJo, track Loriann's cell phone."

JoJo's eyebrows went up. "Can do. But do you want a warrant first?"

"Soul is getting papers. Once you get the cell tracking, I also want the photos of the circles enhanced and enlarged as much as you possibly can. T. Laine, I want you to search the photos of the enhanced circles again, looking for anything we might have missed. Anything, no matter how small. And when Loriann joins us, someone needs to take her to the most recent sites and observe her. Whatever she's hiding, it's at the circles." The IT tech and the witch both agreed. "Occam," Rick said. "You went to a crime scene. Report."

Occam was on the phone to someone in local law enforcement. He looked tired, despondent, and sounded frustrated. He was focused on his call and lifted a hand to me when I came by, but didn't try to flag me down. I got a small potted rosemary plant from my cubicle and brought it to him. I placed it on his desk and when he looked up at me, quizzically, listening to the masculine voice on the other end of the phone, I captured his fused fingers and guided them to the soil. Soulwood soil.

Occam took a slow breath and blew it out. He focused on me as if he had never seen me before and said, "Hold on." He tapped his cell, set it down, and reached for me. I placed my fingers into his unscarred hand and he closed it around mine. He was werecat-warm. "That's . . . Thank you."

I bobbed my head, slid my fingers free, and left him to his call, satisfied that I had helped.

I was late leaving work and Margot Racer drove up just as I got into my C10. She lowered the window of her car and waved a listless hand at me. I was pretty sure she was wearing the same shirt from the day before.

I walked over. "You just left the Blalock girl's crime scene?"

"Yeah. It was bad. Crimes against children always are. Now I'm heading to talk to Jim Paton again, after letting him stew in a cell all night."

"He was watching the girl?"

She nodded. "There was a lot of porn on his PC, and a lot of it was photos of young girls he had taken himself." A look of sly, repressed fury settled on her face. "Then someone took her."

"She was *his*," I said softly. "He couldn't stand that. That's why he got involved. Why he reported it."

"Yeah. I can't see any evidence that he physically abused

girls since the one time he was caught, but I'm still on him. If he has secrets, I'll find them. And I'll find the vamps who killed Raynay Blalock." Margot sped away, her tires screeching on the pavement. I wasn't sure why she had come by, or why she hadn't gone inside HQ. Unless she had been looking for me. Like a friend might. That made me feel oddly warm inside.

I went home to a house that was already miserably hot. Mud was staying with her half sibs and true sibs, these last weeks before school started. Knowing I wouldn't be interrupted, I took a short shower and fell into bed. But sleep was elusive so I grabbed the computer and stretched out on the hammock on the back porch. It was stiff and covered in cat hair, but the porch was cooler than the stuffy house. I made a few calls to my local bank and started filing information online for a loan, for what turned out to be a line of credit on the house and land. When I was done, I closed my eyes. I was turning into a townie. Mud and me together. Sleep took its own good time finding me.

To make up for the two donuts, I made a sizable fresh veggie and greens salad from the garden, enough to share, if a certain cat-man happened to stay over for a while after he got off work. I got to work early and put the salad in the break room fridge, beneath Rick's takeout and on top of a pizza box. The entire second floor stank of fast food, and the sound of voices, both from video footage and from the office cubicles, was everywhere. I locked up my gobags and my weapon and eased into my seat for the end-of-day debriefing, listening to catch up on where everyone was.

Occam slid into his chair, cat-fast, finishing off a burger. Rick's hair was tangled and flyaway and his clothes were wrinkled. He looked tired and poorly groomed and irritable again. Everyone took places for the meeting except for Loriann Ethier and Margot Racer. Loriann was due in an hour. Margot was busy with the Blalock investigation. Rick pointed to the overhead screens and I saw footage of Margot and the sheriff giving a news conference on the body they had found. There was no mention of vampires as the killers. Not yet.

Rick said, "Clementine, record." He gave a list of the
agents present and then said, "Occam, report."

"At some point, Nell should talk to Ming of Glass in person, since I can't get past the human security team without
Maggot." He grinned at me, teasing. I tried an eye roll and
wasn't sure how successful I was. It wasn't a gesture I'd grown
up making, since it showed a lack of respect. He went on. "For
now, the humans at her compound say that Ming and her fangheads did not leave their lair yesterday or last night. After the
attack at her council chambers I tend to believe them. Ming's
had all the locals locked down tighter than a drum, to keep
them safe.

"We do have an update on the van used in the kidnapping.
Local sheriff's deputies—who are going to be calling us personally in the future with anything paranormal related—found
the van in a drugstore parking lot between Kingston Pike and
Old Kingston Pike. They found Raynay Blalock's sneakers in
it. It was a bloody mess and it'll take time to process all the
blood spatter.

"One of the local 'humans only' hate groups has promised
lethal retribution to the local vamps. Other right-wing wack-
job hate groups are joining in. It ain't pretty. Seems Detective
Hamm—former detective Hamm—was a member in good
standing with one. His face was plastered all over social media
today, attending a meeting. It cost him his job."

"We'll send flowers," T. Laine muttered.

I raised my hand, more to get attention than to ask permission to speak. "Ming of Glass has people looking for Godefroi
de Bouillon." I stumbled over the foreign pronunciation. "His
humans could be, possibly, the ones who took the Blalock girl. A
source identified that the people who took the Blalock girl
smelled like Ming's enemies," I said, speaking of Yummy's
reading of the abduction site. "I've texted Ming's security, requesting that they send us all the info they acquire on invading
vampires and the location of their lair when and if they discover it. I told Yummy that if the local vamps take out the attacking European vampires, it will be the word of one vampire
trying to convince the public that the bad guy is down, but that
if SWAT and PsyLED take them down, it will be believable. I
haven't heard back."

"Good move, Ingram," Rick said. "Let's hope Ming agrees. Jones, Kent, bring us up to date on the circles and Loriann Ethier. What did you find?"

JoJo said, "Circles first. Nothing on the photos. Once I got them big enough to see small things they were too pixilated. But when Lainie went back to the most recent circle"—Jo's lips widened into a grin that somehow said *gotcha*—"she found something."

T. Laine leaned in and took over. "Kent here. The storm that came through was spotty and didn't affect it, and the dry weather is good for preserving evidence. There are . . . let's call them slits in the soil, narrow, hair-thin slots or slashes beside every single rune, so small they aren't visible without getting on my knees, my nose a foot from the soil. I stepped on some doing the workups, but most are still there. The slits are uniform in size, and in the same placement in regard to the runes. I'm theorizing that they held something the witch took from the circles when she left, something more important than the focals and runes in the circle."

"Which leads us to Loriann," Rick said, sounding grim.

"I took Loriann to one of the circles," T. Laine said, "without telling her about the slits. And she got on her knees. She was looking for the slits. She's paler than a vamp to start with, but she visibly paled when she saw them. And then she acted as if nothing was there. Said not one word about them."

"So, she knows more than she's saying," I said.

"Correctamundo," Tandy said. He glanced up at me. "Old, out-of-date slang for 'that's a big yes.'" To the group he continued, "After T. Laine let her off at her hotel, Loriann drove to three other sites, locations listed on the sheriff's reports. And then she went to the medical examiner's office and had a long discussion with the forensic pathologist who was working up Blalock's body. She asked some very pointed questions, and the main one was, 'Were the vamps who attacked the Blalock girl feeding responsibly or in a feeding frenzy?' She explained the difference to the ME and even provided photos of a victim dead from a feeding frenzy."

"Photos we did not have in our database," JoJo said, "until the ME sent them to us. It's pretty graphic. On screen three." She punched a button and a photo of a body appeared on the screen. It had been ripped to shreds, almost as if the body had been attacked by wild animals. But his face looked peaceful and happy. Vamps could mesmerize. Vamp saliva took pain away.

"Did the Blalock girl's face look so peaceful?" I asked.

"Yeah. But her body wasn't torn to ribbons, just well bitten," JoJo said, her voice hard.

Rick brought it all together for us. "Early on, we knew that vampires were being called to the circles at some point in the working. It seems that Loriann drew that same conclusion, but based on the slits in the soil, instead of a maggoty feeling." He looked at me and took a slow breath. The lines in his face grooved deep, as if carved by a steel chisel. "The spell Loriann used to ink me . . ." He stopped, as if saying the words hurt. "The spell—" His words cut off. When he tried to speak again, his voice was raspy, and pained.

Occam sniffed as if there was something wrong with Rick's scent. Tandy watched them both, his face lined with worry and what I thought was compassion.

Rick swallowed painfully and went on, his voice harsh. "The spell relied heavily on the presence of a special deck of tarot. One that had been in her family for generations. It's possible that it was an original Blood Tarot deck." Rick looked down at his hands, which were folded on the table, fingers laced together.

"Blood Tarot?" I asked. "What's that?"

"Halfway mythical decks created with blood sacrifices and black magic, the ink in the drawings made with the blood of witches, were-creatures, humans, and vampires, long before the general public knew that paras existed," T. Laine said. "Among witches there's oral history about the tarot decks, claiming the cards contain long-forgotten workings and spells and curses in the artwork. In this century, covens have been searching for old magical relics, icons, and amulets, along with any remaining Blood Tarot decks."

"Why remaining?" I asked. "Were they destroyed?"

"There were claims that the decks had been confiscated in the Inquisition and used by Grand Inquisitor Tomás de Torquemada, to lead his assault against Jews, Muslims, witches, pagans, were-creatures, and other paranormals and ethnicities."

"And anyone who owned property he could confiscate in the name of the Roman Catholic Church," I said. T. Laine looked surprised. "I know my church history, especially the evils done in the name of God." God's Cloud of Glory Church had been eager to share with its conservative congregation the "evils" of other religions, without looking at the sins perpetrated by its own members and lifestyles. I frowned. "The leader of the Inquisition used black magic to track down light-magic users? That sounds like fighting a campfire with a wild-fire."

"The oral histories suggest he was using magical amulets and other items, yes, and that most of the items he confiscated are still stored in the Vatican," T. Laine said. "It's also suggested that the apparent psychopathy he presented was demon based."

I thought about the summoning part of the witch circles. "A witch summoned a demon?"

"No one really knows except the Vatican, but we know he tortured witches and there are reports that sound as if he got his claws into some vampires and were-creatures too. And he got their estates. Ergo, he got magical grimoires and amulets and blood from paras." She punched a button on her laptop and said, "And there are some reports that suggest he became a vamp himself."

I frowned, pulling up a Wikipedia entry and memories gained by the education provided by the church. Thomas Torquemada had been a Castilian Dominican friar, and the first grand inquisitor of the Spanish Inquisition, established in 1478 by Ferdinand and Isabella, the Catholic monarchs of Castile. Thomas had started out a perfectly normal priest of his time but quickly developed a psychopathology that was deeply steeped in torture and death. Because his methods had enriched the Catholic church and the ruling monarchs of Europe, the church itself had embraced the cruelty and barbarism. If Thomas had been using magic and had taken vampire blood, then he might even still be alive.

T. Laine looked up from her tablet and said, "I've done a search on Blood Tarot decks. I'll have to talk to some coven leaders to affirm it, but a few histories indicate that three of the decks still survive."

Tandy asked, "What would it mean if the witch who is working the Circle of the Moon is using a Blood Tarot deck?"

Rick made a small sound and closed his eyes. One hand massaged his tattooed shoulder as if reliving the pain. I looked away. It was impossible to watch.

T. Laine tapped the table with a fingernail. Quietly, she said, "Nothing about Blood Tarot would be good. But that would explain why the calling on Rick is so specific and so powerful. He was tattooed with a tarot working. With a Blood Tarot, a witch could probably easily cast a curse, maybe something worse, maybe several somethings all at once. That would explain why the local coven has run like scared cats. Pardon the pun."

"What about . . ." I stopped, knowing I was drawing on church scary-tales from when I was a child. "Someone mentioned a demon? Summoning a demon?"

T. Laine's forehead wrinkled into horizontal lines and her lips pursed as she thought. "We read the circles with the psy-meter 2.0. We got one and four. So far as we know, no one has ever actually read a demon with the updated psy-meter model—only the space a trapped demon occupied before he was banished. We don't know what a new psy-meter reading would show. Maybe it's a one and four. Maybe not."

The churchwoman in me shivered. "According to Spook School gossip, PsyLED's got a demon in a containment vessel."

T. Laine swiveled her head to Rick. "I heard that too. Some say that Rick LaFleur was in school when the demon was called. And was part of the crew who captured it."

I had heard gossip about my boss at Spook School. I'd also heard about the demon that had been summoned on school grounds and had been fed students as dinner and sacrifice. It was redacted in his sleeve. No one here had mentioned it and so I had thought it was rumor.

Rick pinched the bridge of his nose with finger and thumb and laughed, a cynical, injured, grieved sound that spoke of old wounds that still bled, though the roughness of his voice had eased. He dropped his hand. "Yeah. I was involved. But I only saw it feeding, and this looks nothing like that. I was also there when the demon was contained. But that's it. And this is not then."

"Can the psy-meter 2.0 read a demon through a containment vessel?" I asked.

"Not that I've ever heard," Rick said.

T. Laine shook her head, her eyes on Rick. "I've never heard either. There's only one person who might know the answer to that. Soul. She was a teacher at Spook School when you were there. Her meeting you is the reason she left teaching and went back to fieldwork. And before you say it, no. I am not going to talk to her about a demon. That's your job," she said to Rick.

We had watched Rick as we discussed the possibilities directly involving his past and present. He looked despondent. Grief stricken. But he wasn't totally down and out. His voice heavy and coarse, he said, "I didn't know much about . . . tarot when I was inked, but I researched after I got free. I think the cards Loriann used were ancient. Something special. *If* Loriann used a Blood Tarot deck on me," he said, addressing the pink elephant in the room, "and *if* the witch calling and cursing me now is using a Blood Tarot deck . . ."

He fell silent for several breaths and the lines in his face deepened, dark grooves of pain. He stared at his hands as if they contained all the wisdom he needed in life but he couldn't reach it without cutting them off. "Because the decks are so rare," he said, his voice gravelly and hoarse, "then it's *possible*, even likely, that it's the same deck used on me when I was inked." He looked up from his hands, to each of us around the table, and back down. "Loriann knows more than she's telling us. Which means she's hiding information necessary to a law enforcement investigation. Even before I knew all this, I'd spoken to Soul and FireWind. We got our warrant. When Loriann arrives, she'll be stripped of all her amulets."

T. Laine's head came up. "And how do you want that accomplished?"

"When she gets here, she'll be taken into the null room," Rick said. "I'll be waiting for her there. If she wants to work with us, she'll agree to having her bags and her person searched. She'll answer our questions with full transparency."

"But why the null room?" T. Laine asked.

Rick said, "I want her in a position where she can't use magic of any kind. And I want to make sure that anyone who is tracking her can't find her."

"You think she's being monitored? Tracked magically?" Tandy's mouth opened in a faint O. "You think she's the witch cursing you?"

"Not Lori. But I have a guess. No evidence to back it up." Rick didn't look up from his hands, grief and resolution warring on his face. "If I'm right, I want to make sure that witch can't hear us."

Ruminating, I said softly, "You forgave Loriann for inking you. For spelling you. You got her a job in law enforcement. But . . . The witch trait runs in families, an X-linked genetic trait. Her grandmother, who was killed by the vampire, was a witch. And another family member was being forcibly drank from by the vampire. Who was that? You never said."

T. Laine had placed her moonstone bear amulet on the table and was watching Rick with an active *seeing* working. Occam was leaning forward, his body tense, as if he was about to leap into battle over territory. Something was happening and I didn't understand.

Rick's hands tensed tight, forming fists. He was staring at them as if he was afraid they'd be stolen if he looked away. He took shallow breaths and finally managed, "Isleen killed Loriann's witch grandmother."

Leaning forward, reaching out a hand to Rick, I said, "You think Loriann's sister is the witch cursing you. She's here in Knoxville. Loriann's sister is targeting you?"

"Not her sister," Rick said, choking. "Her . . . her brother, Jason."

"Brother," I whispered. A *brother*, who, if he had magic, was a sorcerer. Things began to fall into place, as if shattered crystal tinkled to the conference room table before me. Gently, I asked, "Loriann had a *brother* who was kidnapped and drank from by a vampire as a child? Abused by an insane vamp?" Vamp blood and saliva did sexual things to the person being drained. "The boy was physically and sexually abused?"

Rick didn't look up from his hands. They were fisted so tight they looked bloodless.

"Boy witches grow up fighting cancer all their lives."

"Nell," Tandy said, the word sounding like a warning.

I held up a hand at him, stopping him. "The homeless thief

at the Pilot gas station, the one who disappeared behind the Walmart, near the circle we found, looked sick. The person who bought the white rats wasn't a skinny female under a glamour, wasn't Loriann herself, or someone she was working with, but was a very skinny, possibly sick, teenaged boy. He was Jason, wasn't he?" I studied Rick, his pale skin, the deep lines in his face, his silver hair. His pain. Why hadn't he told us? Asked us to look into this possibility?

Rick put a hand to his throat. "It didn't occur to me . . . until Loriann showed up. But yes. Possibly."

"And Loriann possibly inked you with a Blood Tarot?" T. Laine asked.

"Her grandmother was the owner of a very old, very special deck of tarot, used in my inking, in the spell Loriann cast to try to bind me to Isleen."

I said, "Clementine. Stop recording." The mic light went off. "Boss, I know you have a right to privacy, but if we had known about the brother, we could have raided the homeless tent camp the night I found the circle and maybe caught him."

"Yes." The word was rough, full of regret and pain. He rubbed his shoulder as if it ached. "Yes. I know. I should have told everyone. But . . . I—" His words stopped as if cut by a knife.

"Son of a witch on a switch," T. Laine cursed. "That's what I'm seeing. Loriann included a nondisclosure spell in your inking."

Rick's whole body tightened. "Is that what this is?" He gripped his shoulder. "I thought it was PTSD . . . a heart attack. That's the reason my chest and shoulder and arm ache when I try to talk about it?"

"Coercion spell," Occam said, "keeping you from understanding or speaking it."

"Witch bitch," T. Laine said, her own face hard and cold.

Rick's eyes went wide and greenish as he considered the effects of this revelation on his security clearance and his future in law enforcement. "That's why you shut down Clementine," he said, his voice easier.

"Yes. Oh," I said, as something occurred to me. "That was why you weren't spell-called the night I was behind Walmart.

The witch was still setting it up. He heard me arrive and he grabbed what he could and took off. If he had stayed around and seen you—" I stopped.

Rick nodded, the motion jerky, sending silver-black strands flying.

"A coven of two is better than none," I quoted. "She was talking about her brother and her. Loriann taught him all she knew about spell casting and he refined it. Now he's coming for you. Why?"

Rick said, "I honestly don't know. I let his sister ink a bonding into my flesh to keep him safe. There's no reason for him to hate me."

"He may not know the true story," I said. "Sometimes people leave things out, thinking that it will be easier for the victim to be kept in the dark."

"Personal experience?" Rick asked, his lips twisted into a wounded smile.

"Yes." I thought about the welfare fraud and the money paid to John for my dowry. "Secrets are stupid and evil." *Except my own, of course.* I refrained from saying that.

Rick nodded. "Yes." He looked up at the screen. "Loriann is here. Are we all agreed? The null room?"

"Yes," T. Laine said, grim. "Loriann's been holding out on us to protect her brother. That's gone on long enough. If we can't find him, we can't help him. And if we *can* help her brother, she might help get rid of the messed up spells in your tattoos."

Rick sent her a quick, fierce smile, all teeth, like a snarling cat. He gave quick directions and we moved into place. "JoJo," he said when we were all in position, "get her computer. Crack it. See if she has photos of witch circles on it."

"And photos of Jason," I suggested.

"Yes," Rick said, sounding more like the boss I knew. "Photos of the little bugger would be nice."

FOURTEEN

I stood out of the way, in the opening of my cubicle, watching. Holding a plant, my fingers in the soil of Soulwood. Not that I had any idea what to do if Loriann started throwing around *wyrds* of power or hitting people with magic.

Tandy led Loriann up the stairs, their feet muffled and yet sharp in the enclosed space. Rick stood in the hallway, the open null room door between the witch and him, the cold, deadening energies spilling from the room. T. Laine stood down the hall, hidden by the open stairway door, her null pens ready to throw and a *wyrd* spell of sleep, ready to speak. JoJo was in the conference room, monitoring everything on the screens. Tandy reached the top and stepped to the side, as if waiting on Loriann.

I watched as the pale woman reached the hallway and stepped toward Tandy.

Occam shut the stairway door and leaned against it. Loriann came to a complete stop, looking around fast. Seeing the trap. Some emotion combined of numbness and terror carved its way onto her expression. Her hands rose as if to grab something at her waist.

Rick said, "Wait. Please." Loriann hesitated and he went on. "I have approval from NOPD CLE for you to work with us on this case. But we need to talk, one on one, about your personal involvement. About Jason."

"Dear God," she whispered. She closed her eyes and her hands fell to her sides. "I knew you were going to figure it out. I knew it. I had to be here to keep you from . . . from hurting him."

"I'd never hurt Jason, Lori. You know that. You made sure

of that, didn't you? You inked his survival into my flesh. You put something in my tattoos to force me to protect him. And to make it difficult for me to talk about him."

She opened her dark eyes and said fiercely, "You won't hurt him. I made sure of that. But your team is a different matter." Lori looked at T. Laine and then to the null room. "I guess this isn't a weak threat. That you've contacted the U.S. witch enclave for permission to put me in a null room."

Rick stared at her, waiting.

T. Laine said nothing, though there hadn't been time to get permission to use the null room on Loriann.

"I've never been in one of those. Is it going to hurt?"

"Every second," T. Laine said. "For all of us."

"Shit," she whispered.

Rick held out a hand and said, "Your electronics."

Loriann's mouth curled in distaste, but she dug into her bag and handed over a small stack of electronics—laptop, tablet, and cell phone—to Rick, who passed them to Occam.

Loriann squared her shoulders and walked into the null room. Rick, Tandy, and T. Laine walked in after. The door closed, cutting off the miserable energies.

The rest of us went to the conference room, where we could watch everything on the screens from the cameras in the room, filming every angle, every nuance of speech, tone, and body language for later analysis. JoJo plugged Loriann's laptop into a special system she kept for just such purposes. The host system promptly began to mine Loriann's.

Rick told Loriann to remove all her weapons, magical and mundane. Loriann placed her satchel on the table. "My weapon's in there. And I have these, which will do me no good whatsoever in here." She slid off a ring I hadn't noticed and placed it on the table. Beside it she added a bracelet, a pair of what looked like reading glasses, and small things from her pockets. She took the seat Rick pointed to and sat. Looking around at the windowless room, she hugged herself, shivering, and not just from the air-conditioning temps.

"Tell me about Jason," Rick said. Loriann looked down, her mouth tight with bitterness and grief. She seemed to be thinking through what she might be willing to say. "Lori?" Rick pushed.

"I'll tell you what *I* have on Jason," JoJo said to Occam and me, muting the volume. "The kid vanished off social media over a year ago. Wiped his accounts, not that he used them much except for searching witch sites and black-magic chat rooms. His sister reported him missing within a week of him wiping the accounts and no one has seen hide nor hair of him. Prior to that, he was in and out of the juvenile system for years, and ended up in therapy mandated by the state, which usually means some fresh-faced counselor just out of school."

"We should have had prints from the focals," I said.

"His records were sealed when he turned eighteen. I'm trying to get them, but that can be harder than you think." Her fingers were flying over her keyboard as she spoke, and files began to pop up on the screens overhead. "Jason ended up with a Dr. Robert Perkins, a well-respected psychologist in New Orleans. Looks like payments went through the state and all overages were paid by a . . ." JoJo stopped and yanked on her earrings. It looked painful. "Isleen was Katie Fonteneau's scion, and Fonteneau paid the overages, until Jason went missing. As an aside, seven or so months ago is when Katie left New Orleans and took over as Master of the City of Atlanta."

I said, "I'm starting an Internet search on public events that took place twelve months ago, something, anything that might have set Jason off."

"Is Perkins alive?" Occam asked. "Patients who go off the deep end sometimes try to kill the therapist. And what can you tell us about Perkins' therapy files?"

"Alive and well. Old money. I'll never get into the doctor's accounts, not from here, and maybe not even if I was in the office. He has a nice firewall or three and the files may be encrypted. I'll come back to it." She put something else up on the screen. "Ah! Got something. Hang on." A moment later she said, "Pictures of Jason, one from only two years ago. Aaaaand, Nell guessed right. According to the state's records, Jason was sexually abused by a vampire. Because he was so young, he developed an addiction to vamp blood."

"He was a *child*," Occam growled, repressed fury in his voice. The memory of his cage glowed in his eyes.

I glanced at him and back to my laptop, thinking about the churchmen. Tender youth was a turn-on to pedophiles. My computer screen showed multiple news articles. "I found something," I said. "Twelve months ago in New Orleans, a single vampire killed more than fifty people in a dancehall bar and sexually assaulted some of them. It was all over the news, twenty-four/seven. That might have brought it all back to Jason. Might have been the tipping point."

"I remember that," Jo said. "Good work."

"Listen," Occam said, pointing to the screen with the null room video.

Jo hit a key and the speakers came on again.

"Jason stole my grandmother's tarot deck," Loriann said to Rick. "And yes, it was the same deck I used on you. He stole all the gauze and things I collected from the barn where I inked you."

"You kept some of the gauze with my blood on it. You were planning on . . . what? Finishing the working? Binding me to yourself?"

"No, I—I don't know why I didn't burn everything. I wasn't *planning* on anything. I swear."

Surprise in his tone, Occam murmured, "I sniffed the gauze and I didn't recognize Rick's scent, because he wasn't infected with were-taint when it was collected. His scent's different."

"And that's not the point," Loriann said to her interrogators. "The *point* is that *Jason has your blood* even if it isn't your werecat blood, it's still yours. When he calls you, he can get you." She looked around at the walls. "Unless you're in here. God, this place makes me want to puke."

"Yeah," T. Laine said. "Cry me a river. Tell me about the working. What part does the tarot deck play?"

"From what I could tell, he was using a combination of the Celtic Cross spread and, beside it, what might have been an Angels and Demons spread, with other cards at each spoke of the circle. It's a complicated working and he's been refining it for years, no matter where we've lived or vacationed. He's obsessed." She raised her gaze to Rick, something of guilt in them. "And he wants you dead."

"Why?" Tandy asked her.

"I have no idea," Loriann said.

Tandy's finger touched his cell. My cell screen brightened. So did Occam's and JoJo's. A single word appeared on the screens. *Lie*.

"Tandy's magic works inside the null room," I said softly.

"Not well, but well enough," Occam said.

"Tell me about the tarot deck itself," T. Laine said. "It was a . . . *very special* deck, yes?"

Loriann blanched. She was a pale woman to start with, but she went vampire-pale. "So I guess you know it was a Blood Tarot deck. It had been in the family for generations."

"Yes," T. Laine said, showing no satisfaction at having elicited the information.

I touched my laptop and looked up the cities where the witch circles had been reported. Had Jason created all of them? New York? Arizona? I began a search for Jason's next of kin, other than Loriann. I quickly found a paternal grandmother in New York and, shortly after, a vacation rental in Arizona, about five miles from the witch circles found there. Jason had been working on the spell for a long, long, *long* time. Loriann had known. Loriann had been hiding it or hiding from it. I sent the info to JoJo and to T. Laine in the null room.

A bit more work proved Loriann had witches on both sides of her family. The maternal grandmother killed by Isleen and the paternal grandmother Jason and Loriann vacationed with were both witches, according to PsyLED files. That was rare. I began a search to find out if the paternal grandmother was a member of a coven. Instead I got a hit on an obituary. I said, "The paternal grandmother died a little over a year ago, about the time Jason started having problems. The mother and father are both deceased."

"Sending that info to Rick, T. Laine, and Tandy," Jo said.

Overhead, I heard Loriann say, "Yes. I came to Knoxville to find Jason."

True.

"And how did you intend to do that?" Rick asked, his voice too soft, too gentle. It was his good-cop voice, one he used when he was about to get someone to say something they hadn't intended to say. "You were going to use me, weren't

you? And the binding you inked into my skin." Rick leaned
toward Loriann. His face looked sad, like a TV father disappointed in his child.

JoJo whispered someone should have sex with her again.
We were all focused on the screen.

"How did you figure that out?" Loriann whispered. Rick
didn't answer.

"Yeah. How did you?" Jo muttered. "Been nice to know
that too."

"He's guessing," Occam stated, reading body language
with cat communication skills.

Loriann reached for the ring that was no longer on her finger. She made little turning motions where it used to lie, as if
she twisted the ring. "During the original ink-spell casting?"
she said, as if reminding Rick of the torture but not having the
guts to call it what it was. "I put . . . bindings into your ink. A
binding to keep you from talking. A binding to Jason. To protect him if he ever needed it. To save him. But I didn't have
any of Jason's blood to create a link to find him through you.
So no."

Tandy texted *Uncertain*.

"Why bind me?" Rick asked, as if unsurprised.

"I had to. In case I was killed before Jason was freed, and
you managed to get away. I had to make sure you would save
Jason."

"You could have asked," Rick said, in that same quiet tone.
"Said please. I'd have protected your brother even without a
spell forcing me."

"Right. But I didn't know anything about you then. All I
knew was that I might die and someone had to save my
brother." Loriann lifted dark eyes to Rick. "Then it was over
and Jason was safe and . . . I didn't need the bindings. And I
didn't know of a way to undo them."

Tandy texted a single word. *Lie*. That was interesting.

"And now?"

"And now, you have a blood tie to Jason," she said fiercely.
"When he calls you, you have to answer. And you won't be
able to hurt him, no matter what he's done or what he's doing
when you find him. No matter what he does to you. And I can
follow you to him."

True.

JoJo was cursing steadily under her breath. Occam's eyes glowed cat-gold. He was silent, that deadly stillness of the predator waiting to pounce. I just sat, thinking of what I might do, what legal and illegal boundaries and rules I might push or break, if I was trying to protect Mud. I would never have done what Loriann Ethier had done. But I understood.

On the screens, Rick left the null room and disappeared into the dark of the building. Tandy raced to the conference room. He shook his head at JoJo's questions and said to Occam, "He needs you." Occam took off after Rick, moving in a burst of were-speed. To me Tandy said, "I had to get out of there. And I think I can read her from here." He dropped into a chair and pulled his cell, watching the screen. "She's wide open. No shields at all." He shivered with leftover null-effects and glanced at the coffee pot. "Please?" he asked. I got up to make a pot. "Thanks," he said.

In the null room, T. Laine took over the interrogation, concentrating on the spell Jason was using to call Rick and the spell Loriann had inked into Rick's flesh, and how they interacted. She was getting the particulars, the nitty-gritty. It was a magic/mathematics dialogue on a level I couldn't follow, about workings with energy. There were phrases like "potential energy versus kinetic," which I Googled to refresh my stagnant brain. I'd had magical energy classes in Spook School, but it had been a while. Potential energy is stored energy, like chemical, gravitational, mechanical, and nuclear. Kinetic energy is doing work—like electrical, heat, light, motion, sound, magical, gravitational, or mechanical energy. Kinetic energy is all about movement. In magical workings, forms of energy can be transferred and transformed between one another and between matter. I understood only enough to know that if a witch mixed the wrong kind of energies together things could explode, or transform in the wrong ways. There had been horror stories, which I hoped were apocryphal.

As the conversation turned even more theoretical, Jo and Tandy worked on traffic cameras from the day the Blalock girl was kidnapped, trying to find and track the van. I hid in my cubicle and called the Nicholson house. I needed to talk to my mother, which almost never happened. Needed to think for just a minute that normal, whatever normal was, might be part of my life someday. Instead, Mama was busy putting the little'uns to bed and handed off the cell to Mud.

"Hey, Nellie," Mud said. "Sam done offered to give me a puppy. And before you'un say no, she's a twelve-week-old, house-trained springer that some townie done gave to Sam, but he don't want her. Can I have her? Please, please, please?"

Mud had lapsed back into church-speak in the time she had been with the family, and that would make it hard for her to fit in at school, but dialects and teen angst would have to wait. I tilted the cell to the side so she couldn't hear my sigh. My vampire tree had killed Mud's last puppy. I waited for Mud to use that to get her way, but all she said was, "I think you'un should let me keep her. You'un always know when company's coming up the road, but I don't. If I'm gonna be a latchkey kid, I'll need protection when I'm there alone. If'n I have a dog, I'll be safer."

"I'll think about it," I said, knowing I was already lost. And knowing that Mud would need child care, that she wasn't safe on the farm alone. Knowing that Larry Aden and his kind would always come hunting us.

"Her name is Charade. Cherry for short. She's a tricolor and she'll be getting spots on her nose. And she loves me already."

"Springers have to be exercised. A lot. They're high-energy dogs."

"I can set me up an agility course out back a the house. And she can run with the werecats!"

"The werecats might eat her," I teased.

"You tell Occam I'll hit him with a rolled-up magazine if'n he hurts my dog."

I chuckled at that image. I'd felt the same way before. "When I get some time off, we'll bring her home for a few days and see how she does. But if she's not really house-trained or can't get along with the cats, including our friends, we'll have to take her back or find her a new home."

"Friends?" The silence was so intense that I thought the call had been dropped, and then she said, as if figuring it all out, "Wereleopards. Deal!"

"I'll see you as soon as this case is over," I promised.

"I forgot to say! SaraBell's in labor. Love you!" She ended the call.

"Love you too," I said to the empty air. SaraBell's in labor. Sam was getting ready to be a daddy. I was getting ready to be an aunt. A small smile formed as it hit me. SaraBell didn't want a dog around her new baby. I had just been backed into a corner by a preteen manipulator. "You little scamp."

"Nell!" Tandy shouted. "Get in here! We got the van!"

I sped into the conference room to see photos on the screens overhead. On one was grainy security camera video. It was the van that been stolen to pick up the Blalock girl.

"They trolled the streets in neighborhoods all around, looking for prey. We have multiple sightings from those doorbell security cameras," Jo said. "Those devices are ridiculously easy to hack. A tech-savvy burglar's wet—Ummm. Sorry."

I didn't know what she had been about to say and I didn't ask.

Tandy said, "According to the crime techs, the AC in the van wasn't working and at some point, it got hot inside and the window went down. And we got this."

The security footage began to move. Leaning from the passenger seat was a young man. "Who?" I asked.

"This is from Loriann's laptop," JoJo said, putting up another photo. "Jason Ethier. He was in the van with the group of nonlocal vampires. Maybe was with them from the beginning. I'm sending this to Occam and Rick. They need to know it. And to T. Laine," JoJo said.

"Tell her to hold it," I suggested. "Don't share it with Loriann. We might need all this later. Or . . . she might not know her brother is vamp-ridden."

"Vamp-ridden?" Jo asked.

"A church term. It's one they use for blood-slaves, and it's based on spiritual possession, like demon-ridden."

"The church of God's Glory does exorcisms?" Jo asked softly.

"A few. And no. Never on me. I left the church before I'd

have been old enough to see or participate in one. But I've
heard tales."

Overhead, JoJo, tech whiz extraordinaire, followed the van
through the neighborhoods near where Raynay was taken. The
unit had received more files via e-mail from Alex Younger and
I put them on the screen. They were titled Godfrey of Bouil-
lon_1, Godfrey of Bouillon_2, Godfrey of Bouillon_3, and
Godfrey of Bouillon_4.

I opened the files to the overhead screen and began scrolling through the information, which was presented in bullet
points with footnotes and links to more information on the
Internet.

- Godfrey of Bouillon, aka Godefroi de Bouillon in
  French, Gottfried von Bouillon in German, Godefridus
  Bullionensis from Wiki, and Godefridi Bullonensis in
  some other language I didn't speak

- Born on September 18, 1060

- As a young human he was a Frankish knight—Lord of
  Bouillon

- A leader of the First Crusade

- Later became known as the Duke of Lower Lorraine

I figured that Lower Lorraine was someplace in France.
The church taught a lot about the valiant knights of Western
Christianity who went to free the Holy Lands from satanic
rule, but my own research had led me to understand that the
Crusades were more along the lines of torture, rape, theft,
murder, and genocide. The next part of Alex's information
suggested that was more true than I had ever known.

- In 1099, Godfrey laid siege to Jerusalem

- His goal: to wipe out all Jewish people in vengeance for
  the death of the Christ

- Charged into Jerusalem and killed anyone who didn't
  leave

- Destroyed holy sites of three religions

- Soldiers, citizens, Jews, Muslims, and Christians who opposed him were killed

- Victims were burned or sliced open and left to bleed out

- Surviving Jews fled to a synagogue; Godfrey burned it down

- Ordered his men to hunt down and kill all survivors

- According to records, no one survived

- Piles of hands, feet, and heads were scattered throughout the city

- Godfrey is said to have stripped to his undergarments and walked barefoot through the blood, which reached to his ankles

- 70,000 Muslims were killed there

- Became the first ruler of the Kingdom of Jerusalem, though he called himself Advocate of the Holy Sepulcher or Baron of the Holy Sepulcher, not king; others of his time called him the Crusader King

- He never married

- Pedophile and sexual predator

- He died from "plague"—was turned on July 19, 1100

Godfrey sounded like the perfect Naturaleza: a warped vampire psychopath with no morals of any kind. As a human he'd used religion to hurt who he wanted and to steal what he wanted. He was like the churchmen of God's Cloud of Glory Church, who put their wants and beliefs and political values before the scriptures themselves.

Godfrey and his vampires were in town, attacking Ming, kidnapping a teenaged girl. We had Jason, who had been drank from as a child and sexually abused by Isleen, an insane vampire. A sexually abused teen in cahoots with—not in bed with, that was hitting too close to the truth—Godfrey. And

Rick and Ming were targets. Had Jason gone to Godfrey willingly? Or had Jason used black-magic circles to call Godfrey to use him?

Jason was awfully young to be so devious.

As I considered the list, the historical files that followed, and Alex's documentation, JoJo turned up the null room speakers again. T. Laine said, "You have to realize that the others can't trust you. You might be influencing Rick through his tats."

I spun my chair to face the null room screen. T. Laine sat forward, intent on Loriann, leaning across the table that stretched between them. Our witch had one hand lightly clenched on the tabletop. She looked kind, understanding, even gentle, unlike the plainspoken, straight-talking witch I knew.

"Loriann, I can't see you being able to work with Rick or this team. We can't trust you."

Loriann's face hardened. "But without me, you can't find Jason."

"Maybe. Maybe not. He was chased off one of his last circles. Unit Eighteen has physical evidence. Stuff that hasn't been entered into NCIC yet."

"I don't believe you."

Slowly, T. Laine opened her clenched fist to reveal the wooden golf tee we had taken from the circle. Or one just like it, which was more likely. T. Laine wouldn't touch real evidence, not with her bare hand.

Loriann's eyes locked on to the wooden tee. Her jaw came forward and her nostrils flared in surprise.

"You should," Lainie said. "You need a friend. I'm a witch. I might understand when no one else in the entire city might."

"Oh God." Loriann's eyes filled with tears.

"Yeah. Microscopic traces of DNA stuck on a golf tee, after a hot and sweaty round in NOLA heat, can be used in workings and curses by witches and covens. Rick never played golf except with his dad, and not for years now. He didn't know that Jason was following him around New Orleans, stealing personal things, did he?"

Loriann rocked forward and back in her hard chair. Rocking, she raked her hair from her face in a gesture that looked as if she was tearing it out. We three watched her, no longer scrolling through Alex's information on Godfrey, no longer talking. The NOLA witch looked defeated. Paler than when she arrived. She tried to speak, and the sound stopped in her throat, choked off by emotion. She went still and tried again, her words strangled. "It was three weeks after Rick and after the vampires, Leo Pellissier, and Katie Fonteneau rescued Jason." Her eyes filled with tears and she pressed the back of her wrist against one and then the other to catch the tears. Her mascara stained the wrist feathery black. "He was playing golf with his father. I was . . . I was playing in the group behind them."

"Ahhh," T. Laine said. "*You* were stalking Rick. To help Jason, right? If I'd been blessed with a sorcerer brother, it's what *I* would have done. Protect him. Family comes first."

"Yes," Loriann said, sounding relieved that Lainie understood.

Shifting subtly, Lainie mimicked her body posture until they were almost mirrored. It was standard Reid interrogation technique, but Lainie didn't touch the witch, not even in the safety of the null room.

"Everything I did was for Jason," Loriann said. "Always."

T. Laine's eyes shifted to the small mic on the table. Carefully, she covered it with her empty hand. "I get that. I do," she whispered. "But you have to understand that the others, they won't. Witches, witches stand together. But the mundane, they just don't get it."

Loriann's gaze swung from the covered mic to the tee in T. Laine's fingers, her tears flowing freely now.

"You've been alone, fighting to keep Jason safe all these years. Now you have help," T. Laine whispered. "You're not alone."

Loriann broke down in sobs, her head on the table, her shoulders shuddering. As Rick had said, Loriann was wracked with guilt and anger, but also with loneliness. On some level, I understood that kind of loneliness. I'd been alone for a long time too.

"And that," Tandy said, satisfaction in his tone, "is how you turn a suspect. At least until she realizes she's been messed with."

Gently, T. Laine added, "And then Jason disappeared, taking away all the items you had collected with Rick's DNA on them."

"I didn't know. I swear, I didn't know."

"Lie," Tandy whispered softly. "Lie."

"Added that information to the file," JoJo said.

In the null room, the interrogation of Loriann Ethier was ongoing, both witches sitting up now, and the mic uncovered. T. Laine's cell was on the table beside her and by her next sentence I knew she had checked her messages and was up to date on everything we knew. "Your brother, Jason, tracked Rick to the Appalachians. Did you know he also joined with a vampire named Godfrey of Bouillon?"

Loriann looked confused. "Vampire?"

"Godfrey is a known pedophile. He or his people kidnapped a teenaged girl and killed her. And Jason was in the van when she was taken."

Loriann slapped the table hard, coming up out of her chair. "No. No, that isn't true."

On her cell phone, T. Laine showed her the doorbell security system photo of the van with Jason's face visible. Loriann wilted in her chair. T. Laine swiped the cell screen to show the photos of the girl on the side of the road. Loriann, who had to have seen worse photos as a crime scene tech at NOLA CLE, looked away.

"Jason is a blood junkie," T. Laine said, her tone changing from understanding to inexorable. "He's a witch." Her tone went harder and firmer. "He's a teenager. He may be sick from one of the cancers that male witches are prone to." Her tone grew in volume. "You knew all this. And Jason is here in Knoxville. And he's with vampires who have *killed a human*. Now. How are we going to find him, stop him from using the Circle of the Moon curse on Rick, and get Jason help?"

Loriann began rocking again. "The bond I put into Rick's skin works both ways."

JoJo said, "Both ways. That's not what she said before. Not bad, Lainie girl."

"Rick has to come to Jason if Jason calls," Loriann said. "Jason can feel Rick's location if he tries. I meant it when

I said I can track my brother through Rick's tattoos. If he'll let me."

"I see," T. Laine said. She turned her head, breaking eye contact, staring at the wall. "I'll talk to Rick about this. Maybe he'll agree. Maybe he won't. I wouldn't let *my* torturer at me a second time if I had a choice."

Loriann flinched at the word *torturer*.

"One thing bothers me," T. Laine said. "Why does Jason hate Rick? Rick let you torture him to keep Jason alive. Why hate him?"

Loriann looked to the side and when she spoke, her voice was faintly different. "Jason blames Rick for not rescuing him in time. For letting him be tortured by Isleen."

"Even though Rick had no way to save him?" Lainie clarified. "That doesn't make sense. Come on. I know you're leaving out things, Lori. If you want me to help you find Jason before Godfrey drinks him down, you have to tell me everything. I won't put the team at risk over lies or inadequate information."

Loriann's eyes filled with tears again. There were black smudges beneath them from rubbing her tear-wet mascara. "I . . . I'm not proud of it. I'm not," she said fiercely.

"Okay. We all do things we're ashamed of from time to time. Let me help you make it right."

Loriann tilted her head in acquiescence and breathed out slowly. "I couldn't tell my brother everything about his rescue. Or what happened while he was held captive by the crazy-assed vamp. I didn't mean for it to happen, but somehow I told him enough that he believes that the cop with the tattoos didn't want to save him. That I had to use my magic to . . . to *force* Rick to save him."

"Witch bitch," JoJo muttered. "You selfish witch bitch. And now you want us to fix your stupid mistake."

"I don't understand," I said.

In the null room, T. Laine said, sorrowfully, "Oh, Lori. You took the glory of the rescue yourself."

"Not on purpose."

"Maybe not," T. Laine said. "But you gave Rick's name to Jason. And when you figured out Jason was blaming Rick, you didn't fix it. Even after Rick was out from undercover and living as a cop in the real world. You let your brother keep thinking *you* had rescued him, not Rick, because it made you look important. And Rick became what? The bad guy?"

Loriann didn't deny it. "I didn't think it was a problem. It was me and him against the world. It gave me some control when he wanted to drink vampire blood again. He was an addict, and the fact that I saved him, *me*, not Rick, was a . . . a bond of sorts."

"But . . . ," T. Laine encouraged.

"When Jason got old enough, he started following Rick as best he could. Rick's social media presence was minuscule early on. Music stuff from where Rick played in bands. He eventually discovered Rick was related to Tom, Katie Fonteneau's primo. Katie was the vampire who made Isleen and let her loose into the world before she was sane," Loriann explained. T. Laine didn't tell Loriann she already knew that information. She let Loriann talk. "Things only got worse when Jason did Rick's family timeline back. He discovered Katie Fonteneau was Rick's way-back ancestor through a child before she was turned."

I barely managed to hold in my gasp at that one. How had Jason found that out? All we had were rumors. T. Laine didn't react, but I had a feeling it was a near thing. Lainie said, "Because of Katie's decision to let Isleen live, Jason developed post-traumatic stress syndrome. Yes?"

Loriann nodded. "With emotional and mental problems. That crazy fanghead kidnapped him, drank from him, and forced him to drink her blood. He was a blood addict. He developed paranoia, and he started to believe Rick LaFleur was part of a conspiracy to hurt him."

Loriann leaned in, suppliant, trying to create a relationship that was slipping away. "Once I figured out he was going after Rick, I tried to set the record straight. I *did*. But Jason wouldn't believe me. He thought I was just protecting Rick and that got me tossed into the paranoid mix too. Jason blames Rick for his captivity. He blames Rick and me for everything else."

"Telling Rick he had a teenaged stalker would have been nice," T. Laine said. "He could have protected himself."

"What would I have told Rick? That my brother is mentally

ill and fixated on him? I had Jason in therapy and . . . I thought he was getting better."

"Until he left twelve months ago. He's a blood junkie, Loriann," T. Laine said gently. The words hung in the air like a note tapped on a warped brass bell, ugly and flat. "A magical blood-junkie who has created a spell for things we can only imagine. All of them bad. His magic involves Blood Tarot, just like yours does. And Jason's been tracking Rick, showing up on the banks of rivers, laying a blood-magic curse on Rick. *Rick*. Who saved him. A federal officer. Creating a spell that calls Rick and then leaving before Rick arrives, which we don't yet understand."

Loriann gave a tiny shrug. "Jason's deepening the blood bond in the tattoos until he's ready to use it." Loriann waved that away as if it was unimportant. "I know PsyLED is the agency that will find Jason and stop him. That's why I'm here. To help you bring him in. Alive. That's the price of my assistance." Loriann's face took on a hard cast, demanding, "I want my brother alive."

Rick and Occam appeared behind us, silhouetted by the hallway lights. I didn't know where they had gone, but I was glad they were back. Occam flashed his cell at me and I realized that JoJo had sent the live feed to Occam's cell and the two cat-men had been following along. Smart move. Rick said, "Jason is a sick little fucker."

It was coarse language, words that made me cringe, but he was right. I turned my chair to study him standing in the doorway. Occam stood behind Rick, not touching, but close, like a mouser cat offering comfort, and maybe using his cat magic to keep Rick calm.

I said, "So is Loriann."

"Yeah. She is," Rick said shortly. "I never saw it. I never realized any of this."

JoJo said, "Jason's eighteen. He's a legal adult. He's already helped vampires kidnap, torture, and drain a teenaged girl. There's no way to return him to his sister. She knows that. No matter what happens, Jason goes into a null room for decades. If he survives the vampires."

"So we get him first," Rick said. "We get him help."

JoJo shook her head. "Do-gooder."

Rick smiled slightly. "Yeah. I'm trying to be."

"Is it the tats talking?"

Rick shrugged. "I'm not sure it matters at this point."

On the screen, T. Laine said, "That's not all, is it?" Loriann's eyes flashed down, hiding her expression. "Tell me the rest," Lainie said.

Loriann dropped her head, hiding her eyes and her expression. "I had to protect Jason, even from Rick," she whispered.

"While you were being forced to ink Rick with a binding to a vampire, you also, voluntarily, inked a restraining order and a protection order into Rick's flesh," T. Laine clarified.

JoJo said to Rick, "No wonder you had such trouble talking about the tats and the Ethier sibs. You were bound against testifying."

On-screen, it looked as if steam was coming out of T. Laine's ears, but she forced it down. Her face smoothed and she said, "Tell me about the curse spell Jason is using. What effect is the curse having on Rick?"

"I don't know. The circle is Jason's design and he never talked to me about it. But I think . . . I think Jason is stealing Rick's years. Using his life force to power a multipurpose working."

"So you think the curse part is secondary to whatever the circle's real purposes are."

Loriann didn't answer, still keeping her head down. I glanced at Rick, who was now sitting in his chair. He had gone still as stone, his silver hair bright against the black strands in the overhead lights. Jason. Jason was responsible for Rick's aging.

"Okay. I'm taking a break," T. Laine said. "I'll see you get coffee and a bathroom break in a bit." Without waiting for a reply, T. Laine rose and walked from the room, shutting the door and securing it with the numeric punch code. She laid her head on the wall and cursed softly, over and over again.

"Get in here!" JoJo called to her.

T. Laine's movements were stiff as she covered the distance to the conference room and practically fell into her chair. I poured her a fresh coffee and JoJo pointed up, saying, "We have an incident. City cops are on scene now and uploaded a vid to us."

On the screen overhead was footage of a vehicle, similar to the one the vamp's humans used to kidnap Raynay Blalock. The van was turning into a convenience store, parking beneath a high, flat-topped, metal roof. The passenger door opened and Jason Ethier stepped out. The sliding side door opened too. The footage was grainy and coarse and there was no audio, but the man with Jason was, without a doubt, a vampire. He was vamped out, his eyes flashing black, his fangs long and curved, his skin pasty, glaring white. This was the first time I'd seen a modern photo of Godfrey, who wore dark pants and a light-colored shirt. And he was walking outside. In daylight. The old and powerful ones, like Ming, could stay awake in their lairs in daylight. But this was something more. Way more.

It had been posited that the very old ones could go about in daylight if they had heavy oxidized zinc or titanium oxide sunscreen on and stayed out of direct sunlight. Now we had proof of that.

I watched as the vampire and Jason entered the store. Jason walked up to the clerk at the checkout counter, and they seemed to be speaking. Godfrey walked around the long counter and behind it. Up to the clerk.

She was a pretty woman, African-American, well rounded in all the right places. She smiled at Godfrey as he walked to her. He bent her head to the side and casually ripped out her throat. Blood shot out everywhere. Godfrey unhinged his jaw, the way the old ones do, and placed his mouth over the pulsing wound. And drank. Jason went to the cash register and emptied it of cash. He also picked up a six-pack of beer and some Slim Jims. Godfrey dropped the woman. The two walked away and got into the black vehicle. Shut the doors. It drove away.

In sunlight. My mouth was so dry I couldn't swallow.

Jo said, "I can guarantee we just got leeway to take out that son of a bitch. With prejudice."

T. Laine turned and walked away. Moments later PsyLED received a message on the public info e-mail. It included a video that JoJo put on the overhead screen, a video of Jason. "Hey, PsyLED, see this?" He angled the cell phone away and we saw a vampire behind him, dancing with a naked, limp, human teenager, holding the boy up, drinking from him. It was Godefroi de Bouillon. He was killing the teenaged boy.

The reaction washed through HQ and through all of us. Horror. Shock. Fury. Helplessness.

Jason said, "Tell Ricky-Bo LaFleur that his cowardice did this. And that when he's mine, he'll suffer like I did. Like this boy did." The video ended.

I watched the footage again. And again.

Before I left to get some sleep, I read the EOD and SOD reports, paying close attention to everyone's summations. Tandy's read: *Through the witch Loriann Ethier, the two different aspects of our case have collided: LaFleur and vampires and the eighteen-year-old male witch Jason Ethier. We need teams tracking each group. I recommend Jones and myself track Jason. LaFleur and Occam track the movements of the European vampires and Godfrey of Bouillon, while staying close to the silvered cage in case Rick is called again. I also recommend Loriann be kept in the null room until Jason is in custody or otherwise neutralized.*

The words *otherwise neutralized* sent a chill up my spine. They meant dead. And keeping the witch in a null room when she had not been convicted of a crime, was illegal, a painful punishment.

JoJo had created a file on Jason Ethier's backstory and her summation read: *At seven years of age, he went into therapy. He was diagnosed with cancer—acute leukemia—at age nine due to the fact that he was a male witch. Loriann went to Katie Fonteneau (whose scion drank from the child and sexually abused him), and Loriann pressured Katie into saving her brother from the cancer. But Jason's vision of vamps was blood and sex and this treatment set his addiction deeper— blood and sex and violation, blood and healing, both felt good. Jason, in therapy, was fine for a while. It didn't last.* In her "Comments" section, JoJo had written two things: *How did Jason find Godfrey?* and *LaFleur deserves a commendation for maintaining security and confidentiality protocols while under a working.*

T. Laine had already typed in a comment. *There is a work-*

ing for vampires. It isn't very specific, but if you have a little vampire blood you can search for it.

T. Laine submitted her summation as I was reading the others: *Jason and magic. Blood Tarot magic was part of the Ethier family. Loriann had her grandmother's deck, said to have been owned by Torquemada himself. Per Loriann Ethier, Jason stole the rare deck. Using tarot, Jason practiced the Circle of the Moon and ways to alter it for unknown purpose. Note: Blood Tarot decks can be used in demon worship and demon summoning. Note: LaFleur's binding likely contained what witches sometimes refer to as a confidentiality clause, keeping him from talking about the tats or the experience. The working might have even kept him from remembering much of his experience. I'll be turning this all over to the witch council for evaluation and judgment. Loriann deliberately put a protection order and a restraining order against speech into the flesh of a human being, neither of which was part of the working she was forced to ink by the vampire Isleen. She did that of her own volition. And her brother is now, possibly, summoning vampires, which may be how he ended up with Godfrey.*

T. Laine's summation ended with two conclusions, *Jason's one goal seems to be to find and kill Rick LaFleur, who—according to his sister's lies—didn't want to save him, or was willing to sacrifice Loriann and Jason to save himself.* And, *Now that Rick has learned he had a* mute *compulsion inked into his skin, he seems to be able to force himself to speak through it. I hold out hopes that he can overcome the other bindings too. I see no indication of security breach in La-Fleur.*

My teammates were working to protect their boss and his job.

Here, just like in the church, everything evil seemed to have its feet planted in secrets and lies, control and abuse.

FIFTEEN

I went home, got some rest. When I woke, Sam was at the door with Mud and Brother Thad, the boxes of equipment behind them. I wrapped a robe around myself and opened it. "Hey. Is it a party?" I asked.

"Nope," Mud said. "I'm here for the next two nights, me and Cherry. I got nowhere else to stay." Mud seemed awfully pleased about that.

I spotted the dog in the yard on a long leash, racing back and forth and up and down, smelling everything, peeing and marking territory everywhere the leash would reach. I hadn't had a dog since the churchmen had shot and killed my three. A strange thrill raced through me at the sight, not one I'd have predicted. I was unexpectedly happy to have a dog here again. Cherry was long-haired, liver, white, and tan, as agile and fast as a racing dog. I turned my gaze back to Mud, who was not mine yet, according to the courts. "You can't stay here, sister mine. I don't have anyone to stay at the house with you yet."

Sam pushed Mud through the door. "At the Nicholson house, Mama and Mama Grace've got the stomach bug, along with five of the littles. Projectile vomiting. It's spreadin' like wildfire. Esther and Jed have it too."

"And I can't stay with Sam on account of SaraBell jist gave him a boy."

"You're a father?" I squealed and grabbed Sam, hugging him, the first time I'd hugged my brother since before I left the house at age twelve.

Sam laughed in delight and hugged me back, his blue eyes

sparkling. "Eight pounds, seven ounces and a head full of dark hair. SaraBell named him Sam Junior."

"But Mud can't stay here."

"Sam Junior is too little to be exposed. SaraBell has him in quarantine. And Mama Carmel's got her hands full. Sorry, Nell, but you'un get her back."

"I'm a big girl," Mud said. "And now that I got me a watchdog, I'll be right as rain here alone."

Mud could not stay here alone, but I wasn't going to argue in front of guests. "And Brother Thad?" I asked.

Brother Thad held out a hand to Sam and introduced himself. I had a feeling that Sam hadn't known that the Brother Thad I talked about being my friend and who had asked me to attend his church was a black man. "Pleasure to meet you, Sam. Nell says kind things about her brother."

"Mr. Rankin," Sam said.

Brother Thad dropped Sam's hand and extended a folded sheet of paper to me. "Your estimate, with breakdowns. There's one for the upstairs bathroom and water heater, a separate estimate for a redesign of the downstairs bath, and a third detailed estimate of central heat and air. There's a labor quote at the bottom to install the solar panels. If you do all the upgrades, there's a discount, but the estimate doesn't take into account any problems we might find when we tear into the walls and plumbing."

"And there's always problems," Sam said. "Nell, Mr. Rankin, I'd love to stay, but I need to get home. Nell, let me know if you want me to look over the numbers."

"I'm pretty capable of looking over numbers on my own, brother mine, despite being female and too dumb to understand basic math."

Sam caught the sarcasm. "Not what I meant, Nellie."

"Hmmm," I said, wrenching my robe tighter. "All I need from you is the cost of the supplies to build the greenhouse Mud asked you about. Then I can go to the bank."

"Mindy has the estimate of the construction materials in her bag," Sam said. "I gotta go. You'uns have a good night. Mr. Rankin, nice to meet you."

"Mud can't stay here alone and PsyLED isn't safe right now," I said.

"Not my problem. The mamas said to bring her." Sam
waved me away and thumped down the steps, the rubber
treads of his summer work boots echoing under the porch.

The mamas said to bring her. Pushing me back into a traditional female churchwoman role? Or showing me how hard
my plan to keep Mud would really be? No. They knew Mud
would always be in danger on church lands. This was exactly
what it appeared to be. A kerfuffle.

Brother Thad followed, saying over his shoulder, "You call
me when you know something, Nell."

I stared after them as Brother Thad followed Sam down the
steps and the two trucks went down the hill in line. I looked at
the dog. And my sister. Thought about a blood-witch in the
null room. Wondered if the vampire tree would make an acceptable babysitter.

And hoped Rick LaFleur wouldn't get all picky about a dog
in the workplace. I had to figure this situation out. Soon.

The three of us got to HQ before the start of my shift, when
the sun was still high but the daytime moon, invisible at this
part of the lunar cycle anyway, had set. The dog was a maniac,
racing up the stairs on her adjustable leash. Springers were
never yappy dogs, but Cherry was even more silent than most.
She was all nosy, nose to the stairs and then the door, sniffing,
racing back and forth, up and down, trying to get *all* the
smells. Her nails clicked and her tail wagged like mad, the
long tail hair, called feathers, whisking the air.

My arms loaded with my gobags and dog supplies, I used
my ID card to open the door at the top of the stairs. As the
door opened, Mud dropped Cherry's leash. I lunged for the
strap, but she rushed through like a tricolor whirlwind, dash-
ing silently down the hall. And leaped high into the air, onto
Rick LaFleur's chest.

My boss caught her, his eyes going wide. Cherry wrapped
her legs around his neck like a human would and hugged him,
that tail still flapping madly, her entire back half a crazy wag-
gle. The dog clearly had no problem with cat scent. Rick's eyes
went soft and he knelt so he could support the dog and pet her
too. "Well. Hey there," he said quietly, one hand stroking her

back. Cherry slobbered a half dozen dog kisses over his face and Rick started laughing. "Okay, okay. I love you too."

Something about the scenario seemed a bit . . . off as it replayed through my mind. And then it hit me. Mud had dropped the leash on purpose.

Mud raced after and took Cherry from Rick. "Sorry, Mr. Rick," Mud said. "She's a little excited." To the dog, she said, sternly, "Cherry, you behave."

"It's . . . okay," he said, sounding surprised and pleased all at once, scratching the dog behind the ears. "Cherry?" Cherry shoved her snout into his ear. Rick laughed and rearranged, so he could stroke the dog again.

I explained about the dog gift and the stomach bug on church grounds and Mud being with me for the next few days. Rick said, "I don't like it, Nell. Jason presents a dangerous situation and I'm not so sure that his sister isn't just as big a threat, and she's on premises. And a wereleopard might think Cherry looks tasty. I wouldn't want her hurt."

"Me neither, 'cause then we'd haveta shoot you," Mud said.

Rick spluttered, laughing.

"No one is shooting the boss. I'm sorry," I said, apologizing for my sister and for me.

Deliberately obscure in front of Mud, he added to me, "Time's getting close."

To the new moon. I understood that, but I didn't know what else to do with my sister. I put Mud in my office and arranged my window plants around the desk to keep her company. Cherry curled up at her feet on a dog bed I brought from the truck. I found a bowl for water and another for dog food. I had forgotten how expensive dogs were. When I had my sister settled, I gave the puppy an oversized, soft Nylabone to chew and went looking for the rest of the crew, none of whom were present except for Rick, who was in his office, the silvered cage in the corner.

"I'm sorry about Mud and the dog," I said. "I can't leave her at the church."

My boss gave me a tired, backhand wave as if it was just another awful on top of a truckload of awful. Rick was distracted, one hand on the amulets at his neck, his fingers worrying them like worry beads or one of those spinner things people use. If I listened closely I could hear a few notes of his woodwind antimagic music playing in his newfangled earbud. It ran on Wi-Fi, was powered by a new generation of batteries, and was smaller than a hearing aid.

Without looking at me, Rick said, "I want you to read and collate all the files on this case. See if we missed anything. Then at dusk, call your fanged friend at the clan home of the MOC and see if she knows anything new."

"Files I can do. And talk to Yummy." Since there was a dog and a little girl at my desk, I took my laptop and tablets to the conference room and opened up multiple screens. Instantly, I discovered that Loriann had been released from the null room and sent to her hotel to get some rest. Leaving the witch in pain, without charging her, would have been illegal according to witch law. I figured someone was watching her, either through arcane or mundane means.

I found a note from Occam, which said simply, *I wanted to stay and see you, Nell, sugar, but I'm tuckered out. I'll come in early and bring breakfast.* It wasn't much, but it warmed me inside and out, and made my assigned job seem a little less tedious. Not everything in police work is high-speed car chases or shoot-outs. Most of it is boring paperwork. Very boring. Even with the sun still bright through the western-facing windows, I had to take quick breaks to stay alert, so I checked on Mud and her dog several times, taking the dog out twice to potty, just to have something active to do. Once I caught Rick kneeling at my cubicle, petting the dog, and I remembered the barrenness of Rick's home. Rick seemed like the kind of man who would have pets, but only cats could survive his hours.

Around eight p.m., which was close to sunset in July, I was standing at the opening of my cubicle while Mud was in the locker room taking a potty break of her own. I automatically reached for the plants on the desk as I waited, and studied the dog, trying to see if she needed to go for a potty break again too. Her tail slapped the floor and her entire body wriggled under my scrutiny. More likely, she needed a run.

My fingers were in Soulwood soil. Touching a small rosemary plant.

I felt the sunset happen, up through my bones. I blinked. I had never—

Through the soil, the earth *moved*. I tilted, nearly fell, landing hard against the padded edge of the cubicle half-wall. *Earthquake?* Except the immediate sensation rising into my bones was filth. Foul. Something bad. On/in/through the soil.

Everything happened fast, overlapping. I wasn't sure, later, in what order it all occurred.

Mud screamed, "Nell!"

Soulwood *reached* for me through the earth. Wrapped itself around me, much like Cherry had wrapped her legs around Rick. Or like roots wrapped around a rock in the earth. *Danger*, came from Soulwood. The communication wasn't a word. It was more like lightning striking or rain flooding or wildfire roaring—

Rick, I thought. *In his office. Not in his cage. With Mud here. My sister, in danger.* I turned, dropping the plant. Running. Drawing my weapon. Knowing regular ammo would do nothing against a wereleopard. Hearing the pot shatter behind me.

A grindylow sped down the hallway from nowhere, sliced the air near my face. I dodged out of its way. It dove into Rick's office. Screams of the two shattered the air.

Someone—Jason—was working the Circle of the Moon. Even with the moon below the horizon.

"Blood!" Mud shouted, staggering into the hallway. "Lots of blood!"

I recognized it then too, and would have sooner but my first thought had been Rick. Someone, somewhere, was pouring a blood sacrifice onto the earth. A huge one.

In Rick's office, just ahead, out of sight, fresh blood flew, splattering on the walls.

I knew it. I felt it. Bloodlust woke in me. I stumbled toward the blood.

Want . . . It rose in me like water in a well. *Want . . .* I *wanted* to feed Rick to the earth. *Wanted* to help the blood-witch feed the earth. I wanted—Mud tore up the hallway after me, Cherry at her side. The dog was terrified, which I didn't understand. So was Mud, also not something I understood. Except that Soulwood might have claimed my sister too.

"Get in the locker room and lock the door!" I commanded Mud. "Now!"

I didn't look to see if she obeyed. She was church trained.
She would hide. Sprinting the last steps to Rick's office, I
readied my weapon, held it in a two-hand grip, a round in the
chamber, my finger on the trigger. If Rick had shifted, I'd need
to shoot fast, empty the clip and hope I slowed him enough to
get to safety. From the office came a strange sound, like cloth
and rubber and metal rubbing together. And a soft, almost silent whine. And panting. I slammed my back to the wall and
edged closer. *Feeling* the blood on the walls.

A metallic clang echoed through HQ. Rick's cage door,
shutting.

I whirled into the office doorway, weapon first. Feet planted.
Took everything in fast.

Rick was in his cage. With the neon green grindylow.
Rick's fingers still holding the cage door he had, somehow,
managed to shut.

My boss was a tangle of skin, human hands covered with
black fur, cat legs, and bloody clothes. Blood splattered the
walls in three long sweeps, like a crime scene. *Blood . . .
Want . . .*

"No," I whispered to myself and to my land. "No."

I forced the want down. Away. Studied the scene in the office more thoroughly.

Rick's hand fell off the door and his fingers made little
crackly sounds as they tried to become paws. He was in half
shift. Inside a silver cage. That was supposed to be impossible.
Jason's calling was stronger than silver.

Rick's bones shattered and ground together, the sound pop-
ping and cracking and splintering. He was bleeding from his
mouth and nose. It looked messy. And painful. The grindy,
Bean, I thought, hissed at me and flashed her claws, telling me
something. She looked at the padlock.

"Oh." Rick could still get out if he wanted. He still had
fingers on one hand. "Right. Right," I said. "Yeah. Ummm . . ."

I didn't want to move closer. I couldn't catch were-taint, but
I *could* be killed and eaten. If wereleopards ate plants. A hys-
terical laugh burbled in some crazy part of my brain.

I eased closer, hesitating before I holstered my weapon. I
needed two hands.

Breath coming fast, my mouth dry, I stretched, reaching to the cage, and latched the padlock.

I backed from the office and closed Rick's door. It wasn't enough. I sped to Occam's cubicle because it was closest and began to drag his desk out, intending to ram it up against Rick's door. Which was stupid because the door opened inward. I stopped and repositioned the desk. Leaned on it and let myself breathe.

"Nell!" Mud. Screaming. Her voice muffled behind the locker room door. My sister didn't know I was safe. She was terrified that I was going to be hurt.

I shook myself like Cherry might and put my shoulders back. And went to tell my sister everything was okay. But it wasn't. I still felt Soulwood's bloodlust. And my own. If I was a cursing woman, I'd be repeating JoJo's words about sex. Saying them over and over.

I pushed on the locker room door, but it didn't give. I wondered what Mud had dragged up against it, just as I had tried to do with the desk. Sisters, well trained to protect ourselves and others. I knocked, saying, "It's me. You can open the door."

"What if Rick has claws to your'n throat making you say that?" she said through the door.

A laugh stuttered in my chest. "I promise I'm good. On the soul of my land."

I heard something heavy being slid across the floor. The door cracked open. A dog snout stuck through, then Mud's right eye. The door went all the way open and Mud and the dog threw themselves at me, Cherry running in circles, wrapping us both in her leash. There was a line of benches stretching from the door to the wall opposite.

"I was scared," Mud said into my shoulder. Into my *shoulder*. With her head ducked. She was growing so fast. Not a little girl, no matter how I still thought of her.

"It's . . . not good. But it's okay," I said. "We'd make tea in the break room, but something's happening. I need to get to work."

"Something bad. I know." She eased away and met my eyes, our eyes nearly on a level. "If it's okay with you'un—with

you—I'll be in the sleeping room with Cherry with the door
locked."

"That's good. Drag in a desk and a chair and anything else
you need. I love you, sister mine."

"Barricade. Yeah. I can do that. I love you too. Be careful."
My sister raced to my office, taking whatever she needed to
be safe in the makeshift sleeping room. I went to the conference room and logged on to the communications channel of
PsyLED. There were messages already waiting. I opened the
one from the local witches, who had been avoiding this case
and Unit Eighteen as if we had the plague. The greeting was
to T. Laine, but the e-mail had gone to the PsyLED address
available to the general public. It read:

Tammie Laine Kent,
A demon is being summoned.
The Knoxville Coven of Witches

I sent the message out as an emergency text to the cells
of every PsyLED member, which was the easiest part of the
communications I needed to transmit. I then sent them a text
about Rick and the grindy, which was a little more complicated. If someone was listening in or reading the text, I had
to make sure they understood that Rick had gone into the
cage voluntarily, not been forced into his cage by the grindy.
Then I had to tell the unit about Soulwood's reaction, the
most tricky part. I hadn't exactly told them that my land was
semisentient or that it wanted to be fed blood. I wasn't going
to tell them that now, either. I reread the last part twice before
I sent it. It said simply, *I felt it through the earth. A large blood*
sacrifice. I may be able to track it but need protection. I didn't
add that I needed protection from roots trying to grow into
me. Or that the blood was still flowing. Or that Soulwood was
awakening, reaching toward the blood. So many things I
couldn't add.

In less than thirty seconds I had replies from Tandy and T.
Laine and the rest of the team. They were in vehicles, coming
to HQ. Coming to me. Then a text came from JoJo, private, to
me. *Call FireWind. We need him.*

I was shaking, so I made a pot of Community Coffee, which
was all the unit drank, wondering why Jo didn't call our new
boss. I poured a cup. Added milk and a lot of sugar to combat

my shakes. I ate the last donut in the box, and it was stale and crumbly and it wasn't the blood my land wanted, but it settled my stomach. I drank down the coffee for the caffeine.

Ayatas FireWind's number was in my cell. We all had his number. I punched it. He answered.

"FireWind. Nell Ingram, right?"

"Yes." I stopped.

"Ingram?"

I was shaking again, not sure why talking to the boss I hadn't yet met was making me so shaky. "Are you in Knoxville?" I managed.

"Yes. I just checked in to my hotel."

"You might want to come to HQ. The . . ." I hesitated and found the proper term in my memory of Spook School classes. Remembering it settled me. I could do this. Steadily I briefed FireWind. "The blood sorcerer has begun a major sacrifice. He's using a *lot* of blood. Rick was called to his cat and climbed into a silvered cage with a grindy before he shifted. The team is on the way in. I'm going to read the earth and see if I can locate the sacrifice site. If I can, we might need you for backup since mundane cops won't be any help." We didn't know what effect the curse would have on humans. FireWind wasn't human, and the effect on his species was in doubt too, but I didn't say that.

From Rick's office I heard a heavy body hitting metal. The cage rattled hard. Rocked up, slamming down. I peeked through the glass office wall and saw a black leopard in a cage. The calling/curse spell had forced my boss into his cat, inside of silver. That might have forced Rick-the-human to sleep and allowed the wereleopard to take over. And the leopard was trying to get out of his cage. Ramming the walls. The grindy screamed. I felt more blood.

"Is LaFleur being summoned?" FireWind asked.

"Yes." I wanted to see if I could calm Rick, but the blood sacrifice that was attracting Soulwood's attention might make things worse.

My cell buzzed and I glanced at the screen. Yummy. Dagnabbit. The vampires might be feeling the spell too.

"On my way. ETA fifteen," FireWind said. "I'll bring Loriann Ethier." The call ended.

I answered Yummy's call but no one was there. No voice mail. I sent a fast text. *Spell of calling. You okay?*

I realized that Loriann was likely staying in the same hotel as FireWind. The curse and the blood pulled at me. I *wanted*. I swallowed. Groaned. Sat down. Missed my chair, spilling the last sip of my coffee from my mug. I leaned my back and head against the wall. Time passed.

And then Occam was kneeling beside me. He murmured, "Nell, sugar. I'm here." He touched my shoulder.

I threw myself into his arms. And burst into tears.

The spell of childish tears didn't last long, but it was enough to ease my misery. It helped that Occam was murmuring sweet nothings into my ear, his jaw by my temple, his chin bristly with scruff. He was sitting on the floor with me, holding me. "I gotcha, Nell, sugar. You done good. It's okay."

"Not really," I said. "I tried to drag your desk in front of Rick's door."

Occam chuckled. It sounded growly through his chest.

"FireWind is on the way in," I said. "He's bringing Loriann. And Mud is barricaded in the sleeping room. Is FireWind gonna be mad that she's here?"

"Do we care?" my cat growled.

I thought about that. "Not really."

Occam stood and hauled me to my feet as the outer door opened. I smoothed my clothes and said, "Thank you. I feel better." And I did. Soulwood wasn't yanking on my brain so much. I found my chair and this time managed to sit in it. Occam told Mud I was okay, then cleaned up the coffee mess I had made, rinsed out my metal mug, and poured me a fresh cup. JoJo and T. Laine came in from dropping things off in their office cubicles. Rick slammed against his cage again. The grindy chittered in anger. Tandy came in, carrying a bowl of fresh fruit. My coworkers poured coffee. Took their seats. Tandy passed the bowl around and I took a banana. Peeled it. Everyone looked exhausted. I had waked some of them up after too few hours of sleep. The schedule was getting to all of us.

"I'm thinking I can read the land through the soil on the roof," I said to them.

Occam stilled, thinking. "How?"

"You and Rick put Soulwood soil there for me to plant things in. The soil is touching the roof. The roof is touching the earth through the three stories and the foundation. So maybe I can read the earth and track the blood without accidently getting rooted, since there aren't any roots in the dirt."

"Or maybe the earth will send up magic-roots and swallow the whole building trying to get to you," T. Laine said, sounding grumpy.

I gave our witch a small smile. "Soulwood soil will protect me from other pieces of the earth trying to claim me."

"Is that what the roots are trying to do when they grow into you, Nell, sugar?" Occam asked. "Claim you?"

"Or merge with you and with Soulwood," T. Laine said.

It was a possibility that had already occurred to me. I didn't know what would happen if I once again communed too long with land that grew roots into me. I might lose myself, might become a tree for real and forever. I took a breath that showed nothing of my apprehension, but Occam touched my shoulder again and I knew he could smell the anxiety coursing through my veins.

Suddenly talking fast, T. Laine said, "FireWind's here, and he's got Loriann Ethier with him. Tandy, open the null room door. Nell, are you going to be okay with him observing?"

"Oh," I said. *Not really. No. Make him stay away.* "Sure," I lied. Because I had no choice. I had called FireWind in. He was here.

I heard the upstairs door open and swiveled in my chair to see two figures enter and one disappear into the null room. It didn't appear to be voluntary. The door closed and Ayatas FireWind walked up the hallway. He was half a foot or so taller than Tandy, taller even than Occam or Rick, maybe six feet three or four. Rangy. His stride was long and purposeful and smooth, as if he walked barefoot. Long hair flowed behind him in an ebony wave. He was dressed in black jeans and a white shirt that contrasted with his coppery golden skin. A strong nose. Black hawk-wing brows. He was Cherokee; I remembered that.

The rest of the unit had worked with him. I hadn't even met him.

FireWind paused in the doorway, his eyes on me. He was sniffing the air. And . . . Ayatas FireWind had yellow irises. No one had mentioned that. I took another breath, this one less steady. I didn't know what to do. How to react. I knew what yellow eyes meant. "Skinwalker," I whispered. I had known that Ayatas FireWind was an unspecified paranormal, but not a skinwalker. That had to be need to know. Or need to figure out. But Rick knew. He had to.

Suddenly all sorts of things made sense. Thoughts raced through me, tiny pieces of puzzles I hadn't known were even in play slipping into place. His official history was full of holes. He was Cherokee and looked like Jane Yellowrock, who was a skinwalker. And I had just outted him.

FireWind dipped his head at me. It wasn't quite a bow. More in the nature of a formal greeting. And he didn't smile. Not. At. All. My blood froze through me like ice water, chilling me from top to toes.

"It is true," he said. "You scent of *yinehi*."

"How do you know that?" I asked. "Nothing like a fairy or elf or troll has come out of the paranormal closet."

FireWind smiled slightly. Finally. It was like watching an iceberg thaw. "The little people are said to smell of oak and running water, sweetgrass and white sage. And just a little of the blood of the earth."

Occam poured himself a coffee, scrutinizing our new boss, now that the skinwalker was out of the closet. He nodded thoughtfully as if what he now knew agreed with what his nose had been telling him about FireWind.

"The children of our family were taught that the little people would steal us and eat us if we were not careful. They were the boogeymen of the forest, used as a warning and a punishment if we were bad. Though no one I knew ever saw one, we were trained to be aware and to run back home if we smelled them." His smile fell away. "Mine was the last generation to be taught to smell out the little people, as there were none where I grew up."

"I don't eat people." *My land does.* Had my species once eaten *children*? My stomach did a little rolling flip of nausea.

"So I have been informed," he said solemnly, "and I am grateful."

"Jane Yellowrock is your sister," I said baldly.

Tandy's head jerked up. JoJo slid her eyes to me. "Need to know, probie," she said. Meaning that I should have kept my big mouth shut.

"Yes," FireWind said softly. He didn't sound angry. His expression didn't change.

"Does Rick know?" I asked.

"LaFleur knows almost everything."

"Well. Okay then. I'm going onto the roof to read the land." I got up and walked from the room, FireWind stepping aside in time for me to not bowl him over on the way.

I had seen the square of wood planks that held the fifty gallons of Soulwood dirt. I had come up once and looked at it. It still bothered me, though saying why was beyond me. Maybe because the dirt was piled in a rough wood cage or low fence atop a flat-roofed, three-story building when it should be attached to my land. I knew that the high-in-the-sky part didn't really matter, but it just felt wrong.

Dirt in a pot or on the flat, smooth roof, it didn't matter. The soil knew Soulwood, was a part of Soulwood, and was therefore part of me. The mineral-based, modified bitumen surface could be easier to work around, or through, than old-fashioned tar.

The dark of early night grayed everything, and my eyes began adjusting to the lack of light. The door opened and shut slowly, on its own gravity power, and I watched as Occam peeled back a tarp, revealing the soil. The air was heavy and muggy and my skin was already slick with sweat in the heat. Lightning flickered on the horizon, and I hoped that might mean rain soon and cooler temps.

I kicked off my shoes and blew out a hard breath. The pale gray-white roof felt odd and sort of slick beneath my bare feet, still warm from the day, and nasty. The roofing material was a modified bituminous membrane roofing. The name sounded like pure minerals, but the bitumen was contained in atactic polypropylene, a chemical that I was pretty sure was toxic to plant-people. I could feel my body fighting off the chemicals and curled my fingers under, hoping I didn't grow leaves while up here, as part of my body's immune response. I didn't want the new boss to see them. He might know some things about me from reports, but that was a lot different from seeing me grow leaves. That felt oddly personal and intimate for a relationship that didn't exist yet.

I stepped onto the dirt. It too was warm from the summer sun, and I wriggled my bare toes into the soil, sighing in happiness this time. I was *home*. I let go of all the tension that had squeezed my chest and hunched my shoulders and accepted the faded pink blanket Occam extended. I hadn't thought about the blanket in my truck. I used the blanket when I read the land, and though I could likely read the land just fine without it, it was comforting to have. I dropped it and plopped to my backside on it. The loose soil gave and I sank farther before it compacted and I stabilized. I shuffled my hands beneath the surface of the dirt. Occam knelt beside me in the dark, his blade exposed and ready to cut me free.

Ayatas FireWind exited the door from the third floor, arriving last, probably after inspecting Rick and giving orders to the rest of the team. He took up a place behind me, his back to the waist-high wall that protected us from accidently falling and landing on the concrete below.

I closed my eyes and reached slowly for Soulwood. The land was *here*. And there. I merged myself from here into my land and followed it down and down, through the brick and steel and mortar and deep under the foundation. And out, seeking. There was broken rock to one side, a ridge of hills over there, and deep alluvial soil in the Tennessee River valley, left from ancient floods. There were buildings that had been dug deep, many stories down. Power plants that thrummed into the earth. Dams and tributaries and islands in the water.

Soulwood *reached* for the blood that was still being poured onto the land, an elastic and thirsty yearning. The blood-sorcerer sacrifice was still taking place. *There*. I was ready for it this time and I shoved down on the bloodlust that tried to grab me, tracking the blood. *There*. Only a few miles away. I was grateful for Occam's presence. He seemed to mute the effect of the bloodlust. I could search in safety.

Something else, something darker than my land, reached

out. Fast. Latched on to me. I knew it. The vampire tree. It too was sensing the blood from the sacrifice. It too felt a rising bloodlust. The tree sent its vision of the Green Knight into my mind, its armor made of metal in the shape of overlapping leaves. A crusading tree. And now there were two of us searching for the witch circle, which made it simultaneously easier to find and harder to resist. The witch circle was . . . there.

"Occam," I whispered, a mere breath of sound.

I felt him sit behind me, encircling me with his arms, his legs out around mine. I leaned back against him, feeling his magic wrap around me, sigh through me. His magic was tied to Soulwood. Was tied to me. It hugged me like a warm blanket in winter.

There was a time when this type of contact would have been unpleasant, would have been a reminder of John and other things best forgotten. But it wasn't, not any longer.

"Do I need to cut you free, Nell, sugar?"

"Not . . . yet," I whispered.

"In that case, I need you to breathe."

I took a breath, long and slow, and realized I hadn't taken one in a while. Too long. I followed the blood, resting in Occam's embrace, not giving in to the bloodlust that would make me claim the sacrifice for the land and then claim the earth there itself. And . . . thereby claim the curse for myself. *Oh . . . that was possible. Care and care and greater care,* I thought.

I placed the river bends. The direction of the flow. The position of the moon, still below the horizon. The hydroelectric power plants. The Watts Bar nuclear power plant, not so very far away, a beacon of heat and light. I also located the places where the earth was poisoned with radiation from the power plant and the testing at Oak Ridge. Classified places of poison and death and secrets. Secrets I could never share because there was no way I should know about them.

I let myself be drawn back to the sacrifice. To the blood.

And maggots.

SIXTEEN

"Vampires are being called," I muttered. "Yummy hasn't called me. Someone needs to contact the Master of the City. See if they're being summoned this time too."

I heard FireWind's voice on his comms system, relaying the message.

"Occam," I whispered, "I need a map of Knoxville. A paper map." I meant most anything nondigital that magic wouldn't ruin, remembering the paper map T. Laine had shown us once. Occam said something to FireWind and I felt more than heard his steps move away. Occam kept his arms around me.

Softly, his lips at my ear, he said, "What do you think Jason used as sacrifice?" He was asking if a human had been killed.

"I don't know." But mostly I just didn't want to guess. Not yet. Minutes passed.

"Is he still at the curse circle?" Occam asked.

Bloodlust shuddered through me, but leaning against Occam eased the power of the spell. "Yes. He's killing another . . . something. Someone?"

I hadn't heard anyone return, but the quiet, crinkly sounds of a map being unfolded pushed back the silence. I opened my eyes and tugged one hand from the soil. I had slumped against Occam and he pressed on my spine, helping me sit up.

FireWind knelt on one knee and offered me T. Laine's map of Knoxville. I thought about the rivers and the tributaries, the moon and attraction of magnetic north, which I could feel as a deep steady draw in the earth. I turned the map and placed a finger on the paper. It landed on Mascot Road in a bend of the Holston River. "Around here? Is there someplace he could use here?"

"Lot of places," Occam said. "This area isn't heavily populated. But it's a lot farther out than before. Are you sure?"

"Yes." There was no doubt.

"What do you feel, Ingram?" FireWind asked.

"Blood. A lot of blood. He's sacrificing. I can't say what's dying. But he's using the life force to call something . . ." I hesitated. "*Filthy* isn't the right word. Neither is *evil*. But it's maybe both and neither. The spell is calling vampires and Rick and *it*. And *it's* trapped in the earth."

"Demon?" FireWind asked, his voice a whisper of sound.

"I don't know. The witches said a demon was being summoned, but it isn't deep. Not hell deep." And not as deep as magma, which was a lot closer than it used to be, thanks to lots of things, not the least Soulwood's interference in the geology of Knoxville while helping me.

"Hell?" FireWind asked, surprised.

I knew, intellectually, that the hell where demons were imprisoned wasn't under the earth, as in a physical place. But it was possible that some demons were tied to fire or attracted to fire, and that kind might associate with magma. When summoned, that kind might use the energies stored in the crust's molten core to rise. The salamanders had done so, but this wasn't a salamander. Was this thing a fire demon? I shrugged.

"To clarify," FireWind said quietly, "you are stipulating that the sacrificial blood is being used to summon an intelligence or an entity up through the earth."

"Just a minute." I eased back into the earth, deeper, straight down through soil and broken granite, through layers of rotting limestone, and deeper still to bedrock. And deeper. I searched, moving slowly, sensing ahead, finding the sleeping *presence* deep in the earth. What I thought might actually be the soul of the Tennessee River valley. It was resting, somnolent, though not so torpid as it might have been a hundred years in the past, when white men began to dam the rivers and build power plants. But *that* presence was not being called.

Before I could poke or prod the presence, even unintentionally, I eased away from the surface of the sentience. Back to my job. Back to the rooftop of the PsyLED building.

I looked at the new boss. I didn't know why I was predisposed to dislike him. He had done nothing bad to me. He hadn't fired me or even said anything about a dog or a teen-aged girl at HQ, though he had to be able to smell them both with his skinwalker senses. Maybe it was the deeply self-contained, reserved aspect of his nature. The sense that he was aloof, unapproachable, and arrogant. Arrogant, superior, *righteous* men were irritating.

I dipped my head and thought carefully about my words. As a Cherokee, he might know things about the spirit of the land that white men didn't. "The spirit that guards the earth is well. The thing that is rising through the crust of the earth doesn't belong there. I can't think of anything natural that might make the earth shudder with revulsion. It feels nasty but sentient. It doesn't feel anything like salamanders. I think it's something intelligent. Maybe a Power or a Principality." I didn't know his religious background so I added, "Powers and Principalities are how the Christian Bible refers to spiritual entities and authorities other than God or angels." I watched his face in the night, as he processed my statements. Seconds passed as I measured the rising speed of the filthy thing, my hands buried in Soulwood soil.

"How long before this demon reaches the surface?" he asked.

I drew a sharp breath at the term *demon*. "I don't know. But the more blood Jason uses, the more likely the filth is to break free. I think. I'm not really sure."

"Thank you, Ingram." FireWind had been leaning against the low wall. He pushed off and went back down the stairs, silent on the night, leaving Occam and me sitting on my pink blanket, wrapped around each other on the roof in the muggy heat.

"You okay to get up, Nell, sugar?"

"I'm just great," I lied.

Occam chuckled and said, "I know you're fabricatin' here, but it does feel good to not have to cut you free of roots and vines and branches and trim your bushels of leaves."

"I never had bushels of leaves, not even in autumn. I think I'm more of an evergreen, and evergreens don't shed."

Occam snickered at my seasonal leaf joke. "Come on, Nell, sugar. Let me help you find your sea legs."

* * *

We parked in front of the Knoxville Livestock Center on Mascot Road. The stockyard was miles out of the city limits, in a farming area with lots of acreage dedicated to crops and sparsely populated by houses. On satellite maps, the stockyard itself was a large square of land, marked by unpaved roads and unpaved parking, a few corrals, outbuildings, some scattered farm equipment, a large roofed area, and a few acres of pasture. In person, the place was hot and stank of manure, cows, horses, and maybe chickens and goats, the mixed scents strong, even from the road in front.

There wasn't time to reconnoiter, not with someone or some things dying, and the unit's small drone was out of order, waiting on a replacement rotor. Op planning was supposed to include strategic, operational, and tactical elements. Ours was pretty simple. Move in. Locate the witch circle. Throw a massive null spell at the working. Take down Jason. Without backup. Not because we were all macho or full of hubris, but because humans were no match against witches and other paras, so local law backup was useless and probably presented more danger than assistance.

On the way, in the unit's van, we had geared up in vests and completed weapons checks. FireWind had assigned clock positions to the entire property, based on the satellite map. The entrance was six, the main roofed structures were at the center of the clock, and some structures of some kind at the back of the cleared area were twelve. The hours were less assigned than general placement based on the fixed points. That was all we had in terms of strategy.

"Comms check," FireWind said.

We all called off and Jo, back at headquarters said, "Clementine is recording. Head and vest cams recording. All go."

The security lights were off. All the buildings were black-on-black, and with the moon still below the horizon, the property was unrelieved dark, darker than the armpit of hell, as John used to say.

My husband had a lot of pithy sayings. If he could see me now, he'd be telling me to get my backside home. But I wasn't a wife anymore. I was an officer of the law, a federal agent, in a Kevlar and Dyneema vest, weapon drawn, wearing night-vision headgear.

We raced forward, scanning the property and buildings. Bloodlust hit me again, seductive as a ball-peen hammer. It shuddered through me.

"Blood," Occam said, his voice in my earbud. "I smell a lot of blood." His eyes were glowing gold, and he and FireWind were advancing like hunting cats, all caution and excitement and careful forward progression.

My breath came fast.

We proceeded along the dirt entry road to the wall-less, roofed area. Courtesy of the new boss, I had my own head-gear, instead of having to share one set with the others. FireWind had brought all sorts of toys from PsyLED main HQ to the unit, which meant the world wasn't black as pitch, but glowed green in the low-light-vision goggles. Stalls, pens, but nothing moving. When I flipped the switch to infrared, there were animals lying everywhere. There must be a livestock sale tomorrow. Or today. But nothing moved. The pens and stalls were full of animals, all dead, all drenched in blood. I didn't switch off the headgear and shine my small flash as FireWind did, to get a better view. What I could make out in the green glow was bad enough. What I felt in the land was worse, a vile sickness that washed up and over everything. Sick, sick, sick. Illness and death. My bloodlust died.

"Is the circle under the covered area, Ingram?" FireWind asked.

Even through my field boots I knew it was farther back. "No," I said and pointed deeper into the property, into the darkness. "The Holston River is that way. The circle is close to the bank of the river." And the sacrifice. And the closer we got, the more I knew for certain what Jason had used. I could feel it, even through the soles of my boots.

"Moon witches want the open sky overhead," T. Laine confirmed. "And what I've learned suggests that this *curse* working needs open, empty sky."

"Then why the dead animals?" FireWind asked.

"I think the dead animals are secondary to the main sacrifice," T. Laine said shortly. "Their throats aren't slit. They just sponeaneously bled out. Like magical Ebola or something."

"I smell fangheads," Occam growled, "and their blood. A *lot* of blood."

T. Laine raced forward several steps and stopped. Her body quivered like a live wire. "The curse circle working just ended. Jason has to still be here, somewhere on the property. We don't have much time."

Knees bent, weapons pointing down in front, in two-hand grips, we sprinted in the direction I had indicated, beyond the covered holding pens into the open area, a place with no cover.

"I don't see anything," Occam said. "But I smell the blood. And cattle. And death."

I swallowed hard. *Hunger . . .*

FireWind said, "Spread out. Take it slow. Move into cover where you can. Dyson, take a position between the stalls and the road, in the trees at five o'clock."

Tandy turned and melted back the way we had come.

We moved across the property, past the covered sheds and a Quonset hut–like building, toward the river, leaving behind the dirt road for a grassy area that might once have been used as pasture. Ahead was a line of trees and a road, then more trees and the Holston. The smell of magic grew on the air, tingling and foul, making me want to sneeze.

"Fangheads," Occam growled. "Fanghead blood."

And now I was sure. Jason's attack used a vampire as sacrifice. Vampires. At least two of them.

On the road beyond the grassy space, a vehicle sped up. Braked. A door closed, a sliding door, like on a van or panel truck. The vehicle raced away. The decision to not have human law enforcement backup on-site came back to bite us. There was no one to give chase, and any local law meant the sheriff's deputies who covered many square miles of territory and were likely twenty minutes away, running lights and sirens. The van sped away, into the night.

"He's gone," T. Laine said, sounding frustrated. "It doesn't make sense. The summoning is over and nothing was called."

FireWind cursed. "We lost him. Hold your positions. Cover me." He dashed ahead, across the open area. He stopped so suddenly it was like watching an animated film. "Staggered approach," he said through the earbuds. "There's a line of dead cattle and then a circle." A small flash aimed at the earth for a half second, illuminating his field boots and something white on the ground. "Move carefully. Do not disturb the circle. I think it's a reversed *hedge of thorns*, blood activated. We do not, repeat, do *not* want to disturb it."

I moved through the shin-high grass toward the left of the bright green of Ayatas FireWind visible in low-light goggles, standing alone, in the open area. Occam moved to my side. T. Laine, laden with a backpack of witchy supplies, took FireWind's path.

"I smell Rick's blood," Occam muttered.

Not possible, I thought. Rick wasn't here. Even with the headgear, I nearly stumbled over a dead animal lying in the grass. I drew a flash and looked it over. It was a young steer, throat slit, blood all over the ground. I was shaking.

Hunger . . .

"No," I whispered. I shoved my bloodlust deep inside, tied it down and locked it away in the deeps of me. I could still feel it. Impossible not to with this much blood. Three young steers. All dead. Sacrificed. This was the first time Jason had sacrificed such large creatures. And so many. All outside the circle. *Why?* I moved on.

"*Hedge of thorns,*" T. Laine said, "still active, double layered, one on the outside of a talcum powder ring to keep people out, one on the inside to keep . . . the sacrifices in."

Sacrifices. People.

Even without the warning, I'd have seen the circle. A wagon wheel of twelve spokes, with pale things half-buried in each wedge opening. There was a pile of bodies in the center, at least three, visible in the low-light-vision headgear, naked so far as I could tell. Fear shot through me like being drenched with icy water. *Rick's blood? Rick is back at HQ.* I switched to infrared to see the bodies were cold, nothing warmer than the ambient temp, except for a small blot of red on top, fresh and warm-blooded. A *death* working? I had heard of them in Spook School. Humans were no good for such a sacrifice. But vampires would be just dandy.

"Vampires," FireWind said. "Jason Ethier sacrificed vampires."

"Except for the warm-blooded thing on the top of the pile," T. Laine said. "That's a black cat."

Rick had been tattooed with vampire blood. And cat blood.

A demon was being summoned. Rick was being used in the curse. Was Rick's part of the curse simply that he would die? And the sorcerer raced away because . . . I looked at the sky. No moon, not until nearly dawn. The timing didn't feel right.

I focused on the pieces of white tissue buried in the earth in the space of each spoke. I remembered the sight of Rick's crashed car. And the blood on the seats. Easy enough to have someone follow the car and, as soon as Rick left it, collect samples. "Dagnabbit," I muttered.

"Ingram? Explain," FireWind said.

I explained about the blood, and Occam said, "It's possible. I was first PsyLED on scene but not the first law enforcement or civilian. The blood was fresh enough for some to have been swabbed out from the puddles in the upholstery without leaving evidence of it."

"Kent. Can you close the circle and stop the curse?"

"Not alone. Even with a full coven, this is gonna make a mess."

"What kind of *mess*?" FireWind sounded amused at her choice of words.

"Livestock center could explode. Witches hurt, maybe second-degree burns, hair loss, damaged lungs. That sort of thing. Alone, I'd die."

"I see. I'll handle contacting the local coven. Jones, please see that the contact information is sent to my cell phone. And see that the sheriff's department sets a perimeter around the property. Ethier got away, but something still feels wrong about this place."

"It's the demon," I said. "It's close. It's clawing up here. Right there." I pointed. "In the center of the circle."

"How long?" FireWind asked.

I hesitated and when I spoke there was no certainty in my voice. "Tomorrow night? The next?"

FireWind said, "Jones, update the APB on an armed and

dangerous paranormal. Do not approach. If possible tag and monitor."

"Got it," JoJo said, sounding slightly tinny through the ear-piece. "Going out in ten."

"How is LaFleur?" he asked.

"Cat. Out cold. Bloodied and burned at jaw and claws from scratching and chewing on the silver. The grindy's curled up sleeping on Rick's ass."

I smiled at the visual.

"Margot Racer just drove up," she said. "From the look on her face, she knows about the op, and she knows that she wasn't asked to join. I gotta wonder how she knows. You folks be safe. I'll put on fresh coffee."

"Withdraw. Keep your eyes open," FireWind said. "We'll discuss this at HQ."

We backed away slowly, retracing our trails through the tall grass.

Back at HQ, my weapons were secured, my body and clothes picked clean of ticks, and I had looked in on Mud, who was sound asleep in the sleeping room with Cherry curled up be-side her. No one was shot, no one was injured, no one was missing, Rick was human again, and the demon was still trapped in the earth. We didn't have the bad guy yet, and the demon was still a threat, but it wasn't an awful ending to a nighttime op.

JoJo, however, was ticked off at having to babysit Margot. And Margot, standing at the top of the stairs, was livid. "You will never leave me behind on an op. Do you understand?" she spat at me.

I pointed to FireWind. "Talk to the boss."

FireWind jutted his chin to the side, indicating Rick's office. "Some jurisdictional discussion is in order. LaFleur? Join us?"

Margot's eyes flashed with ire, and I was glad I didn't have to be part of that discussion. It would be worse than a senior wife laying down the law to a younger one. I had never wit-nessed it myself, but church gossip suggested that could be unpleasant. They went to the office and FireWind closed the door, and the blinds over the wall windows.

In the conference room with the rest of the team, Tandy poured coffee for us, passing around our mugs and a small tray with sugar, cream, and plastic spoons. We were exhausted and despondent and worried about Rick and demons and crazy, revenge-obsessed witches.

I took my coffee in my leaf-painted metal mug and added both sugar and cream. Occam passed me the box of pizza. Coffee with pizza sounded awful, but I took a cold slice and passed the box on. We ate. Wrote reports in our laptops. No one talked. Loriann had been in the null room for hours. I took her to the ladies room and gave her a cup of coffee, a bottle of water, and a left over barbeque sandwich. Minutes passed.

"Okay," FireWind said, returning to the conference room, Margot and Rick on his heels. Neither one looked happy, but there was no blood so I figured that things were okay. "Clementine, record," FireWind said. "Date is—"

My cell dinged. It was Yummy, the screen presenting a photo of the vamp, her head on a sunrise background. I reckoned it to be a vamp joke. I showed the cell to FireWind, who nodded that I should take it, and said, "Speaker."

I frowned at him. "No. It might be personal."

"No?"

I had a feeling that few people said no to Mr. Flames and Hot Air. "Ingram. How can I help you, Yummy?"

"You could come feed me, but I have a feeling your blood won't do me much good. I need human juice to heal, not plant juice."

"Heal?"

"We've been attacked. Again."

"Okay if I put you on speaker?"

"With who?"

"HQ. The team plus the special agent in charge of the eastern seaboard, Ayatas FireWind."

"Him, I'd drink from."

"Going live," I said, so she wouldn't say anything over the speakers about my new boss.

"Hey there, FireWind," Yummy said. "I've seen your photos and read your sheet. You interested in a little slap and tickle, you let me know. Your blood should be tasty."

I wasn't sure, but judging from the team's muffled, horrified, and frozen reactions, and FireWind's amused smile, *slap and tickle* was probably about sex. "Thank you for the . . . proposition," he said, sounding almost vampire-formal and exceptionally polite. "You are injured?"

"Yes. Not as bad as the last time, but bad enough. Hurts like silver," she added, using a term I figured was a vampire colloquialism. "Nice strong bloooood would help," she nearly purred, her Louisiana accent far stronger than usual, "and the werecat is not interested in my . . . slap and tickle."

I frowned at the cell. "Yummy, are you blood-drunk?"

"Dreadfully, honey chile. It took the combined offerings of Ming of Glass, the Master of the City of Asheville, and three humans to bring me back. I was nearly cut in half," she said, sounding far too giggly for the bald statements. "And I'm still hungry."

"Cut in half," I said, appalled. "What happened?"

FireWind muted my cell and said softly, "Clementine, cease recording. Jones, pull up the security history at Ming's. And don't tell me you can't. I know about Alex Younger's security system." JoJo froze, looking down at her fingers on her keyboard. Her head was bent, her dark-skinned face looking stressed in the screen lights. She reached up and yanked on her earrings as if thinking, and then punched several keys, clacking fast.

I was left wondering what Alex Younger's security system was all about.

FireWind said, "Clementine, record."

On the screen overhead, we watched as vampires burst from Ming's house, pursued by six humans. The humans were carrying stakes and, in what looked like a well-choreographed act, they tackled their own vamps and staked them. The vamps had been spell-called. Stopped by their own humans. Then Cai and Yummy practically flew from the house and down the driveway, out of sight. They were both carrying swords. Ming of Glass and Lincoln Shaddock raced behind them, also armed with swords, and all four vanished, that faster-than-the-eye-can-follow speed of the vampire. There was no audio, just the video, the silence oddly unnerving.

On my cell, Yummy said, "Magic *called* our Mithrans. The local coven had messengered over some protective amulets as an indication of goodwill, but there weren't enough of them." Her voice lowered as if to keep others from hearing. "We have important guests." Her volume returned to normal, "So when the magic began, some of us were wearing amulets but not all of us. Our humans took down the ones who tried to go over. And those of us with amulets raced into the darkness where Mithrans were attacking."

On the screen, fighting figures danced back into the camera range, pushed back by the attackers, black in the darkness except for the flash of steel. Long, moving shadows striped the pale driveway. I counted ten figures, which made it four against six.

Humans with handguns, ten of them, rushed out of the trees, around the fighters, and attacked the humans and the vampires on the ground near the front door. There was no sound. But there was a hail of weapon fire. Ming's humans tried to get away. Fell. Blood ran across the pale drive. In the background, two of the attacking vampires were down. Then Yummy fell. Cai, Ming's human primo, was a whirling dervish, taking out three Mithrans. The last one raced away as Cai dropped to the ground. Badly injured.

The attacking humans grabbed up two of Ming's staked vampires and two injured humans and sped into the dark, dragging the victims. No one followed. Humans and vampires flooded out of the house to feed and heal and apply pressure to wounds and, in one case, do chest compressions.

"Cai is grievously wounded and close to death. He might be brought over before dawn," Yummy said. Her voice changed as if she was no longer speaking into a cell, the words sounding vicious and accusatory. "I hope his sacrifice was worth it to you."

I had a feeling that Yummy was talking to someone else. Maybe Ming, since she was blood-drunk enough to say too much. Overhead, we watched the fight from a different angle.

Her voice returned to the phone. "Two other humans are dead. Others are in healing. Two Mithrans were taken by the invaders. Two humans as well." Her words slurred slightly.

FireWind caught my eye and held up his tablet. On it was written the words, *Ask her what she wants.*

I nodded, realizing that Yummy had to want something. "Why did you call?" I asked.

Yummy laughed and then hissed as if her laughter hurt. "Cai's plan. He had it aaaall ready."

She fell silent, blood-drunk. I feared Yummy had fallen asleep. Unit Eighteen was tired enough to doze off too. Ayatas FireWind looked fresh as a daisy, but T. Laine looked scared, her face drawn with tension. Occam was stretched out in his chair, his long legs in front and crossed at the ankles, his hands laced across his stomach, his head resting back. He was watching me with cat-like intensity—though not in a predatory way. More of a sleepy cat way. I had seen that exact expression on my mousers' faces. Tandy was sitting with his chin in hand, his eyes heavy lidded. JoJo was staring at the screens overhead, loaded with security cameras, some inside Ming's clan home, which was a gross violation of official PsyLED protocols. FireWind's comment about Alex Younger, together with the video on the screens, came clear. Alex was Jane Yellowrock's IT, security, and electronic network partner, and had been Leo Pellissier's security guy. I realized that Alex must have hacked into—or created a backdoor into—the security systems of his own loyal vampires. And JoJo knew all about it. JoJo knew Alex's work. Had she burrowed in? Hacked in? Or had she gotten access during the time Occam and I were inside Ming's house, after the previous attack? I had seen no footage from that attack, so I guessed so.

The silence had stretched too long. "Yummy?" I asked. "What do you want?"

"Sex, blood, and rock and roll."

I smiled because even a church girl knew that phrase. "No. I mean what do you want with me? Which means no sex, no blood, and no Beatles music."

"Party pooper. Yeah, yeah, yeah, I'm getting to it. Cai's plan was his sacrifice. He had captured one of their humans from the previous attack and Ming rolled him. We knew what they wanted, which was some of us, though our talkative little rabbit didn't say why. We let them attack, and take our people. All of whom were wearing trackers. And still are. We know where they are, within twenty yards or so. We're going after our people and we're going to kill the invading Mithrans. And we wanted you to know there might be human casualties."

FireWind's eyes snapped to me. The others sat up straight,

except for Occam, whose mouth lifted on one side in a half smile.

"You might need to have ambulances nearby. Traffic control. At dusk tomorrow. I'll text the address." The call ended.

"The vampires at the demon circle weren't wearing trackers," T. Laine said. "They weren't Ming's. So who were they?"

The HQ security alarm went off. We all jumped. Tiny red flashing lights and a roar of sound, steady though soft, filled the entire floor. Overhead, a view of the parking lot replaced the view of Ming's clan home. Everything happened so fast it seemed to overlap.

The outer door blew open, banged back. Swung on one hinge, hanging. Smoke blew inward. On the camera screens, Jason Ethier stalked toward the building, stopped in the center of the parking lot, arms raised, a sorcerer in a hoodie and jeans.

Occam leaped across the table and down the hall.

FireWind pointed at Rick. "Into your cage!" Rick snarled but complied.

FireWind shouted, "Weapons!"

T. Laine cursed foully and rushed to her cubicle, even as FireWind said, "Kent! Every null tool at your disposal. Now! The rest of you, assault weapons. Into position here and there"—he pointed—"at the inner turn of the hallway."

"We have exactly one assault rifle in the weapons locker," Occam said, striding back up the hallway.

"Say what?" FireWind looked nonplussed.

Occam growled, "One. I'm certified." He held up the weapon, the matte black gun looking efficient and deadly. "Silver-lead ammo loaded. You're giving him access to the premises?"

"Yes," FireWind said. "He's here. We need to contain him. Take him alive. Find a way to get to Godfrey."

I raced to the sleeping room and tapped once on the door, hard. "Mud. Open." I hadn't wanted my sister here. I had known it was a bad idea. But my family, and the danger posed by the churchmen, had left me no choice. They never did.

The latches clicked. Mud stuck her face into the crack, her eyes wide, excited. "What is it? I heard the alarms."

"The blood witch," I said grimly. "Lock the door. Put

mattresses over the doorway and shove the desk up against it. Fast!" I rushed to my cubby and grabbed my weapon out of the upper drawer. Behind me I heard the door snap closed and the sounds of Mud obeying. I sprinted back to FireWind, readying my weapon for fire, already latching down on any stray blood-lust that might think to rise.

T. Laine called out, "He's using the tattoo magic to track Rick." From Rick's cage, a scream echoed. Cat scream of rage. The cage rocked and thumped and rattled as Rick threw himself at the walls. Shifting fast. Forced into his cat.

"He called Rick at every cat circle. At the stockyard. Why didn't he wait for Rick to arrive?" I asked. No one answered. Maybe Jason had been practicing. Maybe he was just trying to locate Rick. Maybe he had been gathering power for this moment. Or maybe he had multiple ends in mind.

Ahead of me JoJo said, "The null room is secured. Loriann can't get out or be freed from outside without the security code."

On the screens overhead, Jason Ethier entered the stair-well.

Margot said, "I'm with Rick. Last ditch if he gets by you all. I got a little something the FBI has been wanting to try." That sounded ominous, but there was no time to ask questions.

"We'll let Ethier open the door at the top of the stairs. Let him get here"—FireWind pointed—"and Kent will hit him with everything she has."

"If that doesn't stop him?" Occam asked.

FireWind flashed us the first real smile I'd seen, one full of joy. "Then I will." His expression held something like the ex-ultation of battle. Delight, fierce and brutal. FireWind *wanted* to fight the black-witch. He was an idiot. Jason had a lot of power. *A lot.* Unless we were very lucky, he would soon have even more, thanks to the thing below the ground.

A boom sounded. The building shook. The hallway door rammed open. Jason, reed thin, dressed in black, his black hair flying, stepped into the hallway. He was outlined by the door for a half second. FireWind shouted, "Kent! Now!"

T. Laine threw . . . something. A black, sparkling net of magic shot out. Visible even to human eyes. Filling the hall-way. Obscuring the witch at the end. We heard a thump and my heart stuck in the top of my throat. *Is it going to be that easy?*

Jason laughed.

T. Laine cursed.

Jason strode out of the fog. He shouted, *"Fulmen!"* and threw something at our witch.

T. Laine collapsed, her body jolting as if she was having a seizure. FireWind dropped beside Lainie, his body twitching like hers. A sensation of sleet slammed into me. My fingers clenched on my weapon, but I couldn't fire. My fingers were frozen. The team simply dropped to the floor, the others shaking and twitching, though not as bad as T. Laine and FireWind, who were struggling even to breathe. Slowly, I fell.

I realized that those of us at the back of the hallway had absorbed less of the magic. I could think, I could breathe, but I was lying, immobilized. My body had fallen in an odd position, twisted. I could see Jason's passage. He smelled like fire as he passed by me, the fire of a burning house, of burning garbage, burning filth. He was wearing three bracelets on his bare lower left arm, wide silver cuffs or bracers set with blackened stones. They glowed.

He reached Rick's office and raised his cuffed wrist. Margot threw something at him. It hit Jason. He staggered back. Screamed a wordless challenge. He drew a gun from a pocket and fired, multiple shots, fast, frenzied, ripping all sound from the air.

Margot did not return fire. Jason took a step into the office. Moving fast, he bent and opened Rick's cage. Leaned in and shoved his arm at the wereleopard. Rick was farther away from the source of the spell, not so deeply affected. He tried to pull away. Jason cut his arm on the leopard's teeth. On purpose. He then raked the wound against Rick's bloodied side. Infecting himself with the were-taint.

I struggled to grip my weapon. It felt like frozen steel in my bloodless hands. But I got my fingers around the butt. Lifted the muzzle from the floor. The weapon was shaking like a leaf in a winter wind.

Loriann threw herself down the short hallway. Leaped at her brother. Trying to stop him. In midair she shouted, *"Quiesco!"*

Jason whirled at the sound, weapon up. Firing.

Loriann fell.

Jason screamed. Reached for her.

"Run," Loriann said, her lips moving in the single word, the sound buried beneath the weapon-fire deafness.

Jason stepped back, eyes wide.

Two grindylows flew down the hallway. They attacked Jason. Which made no sense. Except Jason had infected himself, given himself the were-taint, which was a killing offense for grindys.

Jason flinched. Raised his cuffs at the grindys. He shouted a *wyrd*. *"Admordeo!"*

The grindys hit . . . something. It sliced into them, spilling their blood. Jason reached out a finger and wiped up the grindy blood, then smeared it across the black stones on his cuffs.

My body weighed a ton. But . . . I tightened my hands on the grip. Steadied my weapon. Squeezed the trigger. The ten-millimeter bucked slightly and my hands dropped to the floor.

Power exploded into the hallway. Jason disappeared.

Like magic.

Loriann fell back against the wall. Blood pulsed through her clothes. She dropped next to me, and even over the deafness caused by the gunfire, I half heard her say, "Transport spell. He did it. He really did it. Oh shit. He shot me."

And I had shot Jason. As my body returned to my control, I felt his blood on the floor.

FireWind sucked in a breath and said the words again, words that might have been cursing, or maybe angry prayer. He shoved to his feet and stumbled down the hallway, glancing at Loriann, stepping over the injured grindylows. Disappearing into Rick's office. I wondered fleetingly how FireWind and I were able to breathe on our own.

I struggled up. Couldn't find a way to make my hands holster my weapon. I didn't have that much finesse yet, so I carried it with me to T. Laine, where I placed it on the floor. Lainie was still not breathing. She was turning blue. I rolled her to her side and slapped her on the back. With each slap, a sensation of icicle electricity rocketed through my hand, up my arm, and down my spine. It *hurt*.

On the third slap, T. Laine sucked in a breath that was part scream, part moan, and all pain. I made it to Occam and slapped him too. Then Tandy, and last I slapped JoJo, who cursed long and foul as she caught her first breath. Then I remembered the training I got at Spook School, to help someone breathe—to make a fist and rub their sternum, in the upper center of their chest. Too late now. I picked up my weapon, holstered it, and fumbled my way to Rick's office.

I passed T. Laine, who had scrambled on all fours to kneel beside Loriann, opening a first-aid kit. She pressed a wad of gauze against the wound on the other witch's chest. JoJo was calling for backup and medic for "multiple victims with GSWs." GSWs. *Gunshot wounds.* Occam and Tandy were clearing the floor, weapons out, ready to fire, to make sure Jason was really gone, and not hiding.

I picked up a wad of bloody gauze from Loriann's side and put it in a pocket. If I needed it, if I needed to feed her to the land . . . I stopped that thought and went to the opening to Rick's office.

Rick was out of his cage and shifting back to human. He was naked, his lower half cat, his upper half human, and he was whispering, "Nononononono, sweet Mary, Mother of God, nononono," in a steady lament. I didn't think werecreatures shifted halfway. It looked painful and anatomically impossible, but it was perhaps due to the wound in his human-shaped shoulder. It looked like a half-healed gunshot. The werecat would heal.

Margot was frozen in place. Hunched in the small space behind Rick's desk and his cage. She had a GSW too. FireWind was bent over her and looked fierce. An expression I couldn't have described except for intense, inscrutable, and detached—vibrantly emotionless. He was sniffing Margot's arm wound, the action dog-like. He eased back and pressed a handkerchief to the bloody place, which looked like a long graze. Margot looked . . . horrified.

FireWind murmured, "It make not take. There may not have been enough." Margot sobbed once, the sound arid and petrified. Rick continued his dirge.

I didn't understand what was going on. Her wound wasn't that bad.

I swiveled and saw the grindylows, curled up together like

neon green kittens against the wall. *Grindylows.* Something stirred in the back of my brain. Grindys were the judges and executioners of the were world, and though there had been no grindylows in the Western Hemisphere until the last few years, it was thought that a litter had been born in the United States. The fuzzy little green killers were now changing the way were-creatures passed along the taint. When a were shared the were-taint, the grindys appeared and executed the offender. Not always and not always right away. There had been tales of times when the grindys hadn't shown up at all.

Two grindys had attacked Jason. Two. One would have been enough. *Why two?*

I looked back at Rick's office. Rick was shot. Margot was . . . The evidence settled in my mind, blooming, unfolding, revealing itself to me. Jason had fired at Rick. The round had passed through him, in cat form, picking up his blood, and wounded Margot. Margot stood a chance of going furry at the next full moon. Rick had infected her. And Jason had intentionally infected himself with Rick's blood. Two evils. Jason was a witch; he might be able to hide himself from grindylows hunting him to pass judgment and kill him. But Rick was a dead cat walking if the grindys decided to pass judgment on him.

Quietly, I told Ayatas, Rick, and Margot what Jason had done. How Rick's blood had been used to try to give himself the were-taint. This was why Rick had been targeted. So that Jason might infect himself. I went to the sleeping room, passing the null room on the way. It had been jimmied open, Loriann having used brute force and intellect where magic wouldn't work.

I tapped on the sleeping room door. "Mud? It's over."

The door wrenched open and Mud threw herself at me, grabbed me. Cherry was barking like a maniac, jumping all over me, racing up the hallway and back. Mud held me away. Her eyes searching me. "Are you'un all right? Are you shot? Turn around." She shoved me around and back. And yanked me into a hug. "I was scared as a deer chased by coyotes." She shoved me back and said, "Cherry, come. Stay." The dog ignored her and I caught the small springer by the collar. Mud demanded, "I want me a gun."

I was befuddled. And amazed at the young woman who,

only last week, it seemed, had been my baby sister. "No gun. But staying with me put you in danger. I don't care how sick the Nicholsons are, you're going back."

Nell narrowed her eyes at me. "Ain't no way, sister mine. I ain't going."

"Why not?" I demanded. "Give me one good reason."

My little sister showed teeth at me in fury. I realized I was going to have to pay for braces, but that thought shredded and vanished like a wisp of candle smoke on the wind. "Larry Aden is out on bail and he's back home on church property. That there is the real reason Sam brung me to you'un."

SEVENTEEN

"What were the bracelets?" Margot asked. Her dark-skinned face was slightly gray with shock.

The team was in the conference room, eating pizza provided by Soul, who just happened to drop by. Lucky that. Or not. Maybe something else, as if she had been notified. Or as if she knew things.

The Assistant Director of PsyLED was curled up like a cat, with her long skirts wrapped around her bare feet on the chair seat in the corner of the conference room, her shoes on the floor. She was all in silvers and grays today: platinum hair and dark eyes, silver earrings, and a shalwar chemise type dress, pants, and shawl in a gauzy fabric that looked cool and comfy. And not at all regulation. I sent a glance to JoJo, with her turban and shimmery skirts. Jo was more dance club than Indian, but there was a definite correlation.

Soul, like the rest of us, was working on her laptop and analyzing the video footage, trying to deal with the facts and the trauma of the attack, chatting with PsyLED DC and the National Guard and probably someone in the Department of Defense, tryign to get us backup. Her gaze kept shifting to Rick, evaluating, worried. She had said her reason for being here was to keep an eye on her only mostly para unit. She had explained that she was here solely as an observer, but she warned us that how we handled this situation would impact future para units.

No stress there. No. Not at all.

It was a few hours before dawn and things had settled down some after the paramedics and city cops left. The emergency team—who had entered wearing double pairs of gloves and white Tyvek biohazard unis in the presence of werecat blood—had bandaged Margot's arm and worked to stabilize Loriann before carting her to UTMC, running lights and sirens. Evidence had been collected by our team and by the FBI evidence collection team jointly, something FireWind worked out. No one had mentioned to any of them that Margot might go furry.

Soul had sent a request to the Dark Queen, Jane Yellowrock, requesting that one of her Mercy Blades come and try to keep the taint from taking. Rick claimed that Mercy Blades had the ability to keep a human from getting the were-taint. It hadn't worked on him, however. Jane hadn't responded. I had sent a similar request with identical results. Nothing. I wondered if Jane was suddenly out of range, in some arcane Cherokee ceremony, or on a ship at sea. No one knew and Alex wasn't answering his cell either. Sudden radio silence wasn't like Jane.

"The cuffs are similar to these," T. Laine said, tapping a key on her laptop. Overhead, a series of photos of bracelets appeared, looking like something a museum might put together. "I contacted the leader of the NOLA coven, Lachish Dutillet. She's in a null room prison for some reason, but her keepers let me talk to her. I had to tell her things that might be classified, and the witches were surely monitoring her calls, so feel free to write me up and bring charges." Soul and FireWind both shook their heads and T. Laine went on. "She suggested it was possible to charm an amulet with a spell calculated to control a demon, once it was captured. She said there were old tales of amulets created for that purpose."

I stuck a hand into my pocket and the evidence bags there. I hadn't turned them in or admitted to having them. I had Loriann's blood. I had shot Jason. I had a handful of tissues still damp with his blood. There had been enough for the crime scene techs, but I had collected my own too. For some reason I hadn't told my team I had any of it. What could I do to a blood witch when I had his blood?

Could I feed him to Soulwood long-distance? Death was a judgment and sentence that belonged to the witch council of the United States. They governed all witches accused of capital crimes. If I drained him for the land, it would be murder.

But . . . My land hungered. I could feel the desire like an ache in my belly, crushed down but painful and demanding.

"Loriann was still keeping secrets," Rick said. "But at last, finally, she knows her brother has taken up with evil." He had dressed and helped with the aftermath, but he couldn't look at Margot. Hadn't looked at her even once. Guilt was a nasty emotion. It changed relationships and made things that used to work no longer work.

My cell dinged with a text from Yummy, or someone using her cell, and I tapped it open. It said, *Our people's amulets have taken us to a bend of the Tennessee River. We know where Godfrey lairs.* I read the text aloud and though it was nothing to go on, the entire team turned to their laptops and tablets and started tapping away. The cell dinged again. *Our team will go in at half an hour before dusk to rescue our people. We will behead the daywalker who wishes to rule Ming's lands, and stake his scions. I'll text you the address ten minutes before we penetrate. Be ready with ambulances to come where we request.*

"Ming is giving us the minimum legally required headsup," JoJo said. "At least we can put EMS and the local LEOs on alert. You really gotta get that chick's real name."

"Last time I asked, Yummy told me no. I ain't magic."

"That was an order," JoJo said, her tone laughing.

"No. I kinda like 'Yummy,' " I joked, sending my vampire friend back a *K*.

Too softly, the words breathy and sere, FireWind said, "You tell your superiors no with regularity, don't you? That's insubordination and grounds for censure or dismissal." The team went silent and still. The words carried enough of an edge and threat to make me put down the cell and focus on the special agent in charge of the eastern seaboard. FireWind was an unknown. An unknown with power over us all, and power over our jobs. That made him scary. And . . . his inscrutable expression was no longer in place. It was . . . maybe cracked wasn't the right word, but it was different. The banter between JoJo and me was just that. Banter. FireWind had to know that, so something else was going on here.

I considered all that had happened in the last hours. FireWind had made the decision to let the blood witch inside his unit's headquarters. He had promised he'd fight off Jason and had failed. His team had then been attacked. The FBI liaison was possibly turned into a black wereleopard. His probie was the only team member to get off a defensive shot. The grindys had killed no one so far as we knew. Yet. But Rick might be in their sights. Ayatas and Rick had some sort of conflict going on so he probably felt guilty about maybe getting his SAC grindy-killed. Also, FireWind was going to take some heat for a failure in protocol and building security. Worse, his upline boss, Soul, was here, watching. He was visibly upset.

I looked to Soul but her chair was empty. I hadn't seen the boss-lady leave. But that was a problem for later.

The mamas had always said to start out like you intend to proceed. I needed to address this.

JoJo started, "I was just—"

I held up a hand to stop her and said, "Would you folks give me a minute with the boss man?" The cats reacted and I thought they were about to disagree, or worse, try to protect me. I shook my head at both of them and stood, pointing to the null room. FireWind followed me in. The door shut behind us. The cold that had nothing to do with temperature and everything to do with antimagic instantly started seeping into my bones. Into Ayatas too, if his face was anything to go by.

"You have my undivided attention," FireWind said, the words pointed and stiff, like a stick to the eye.

I sat on the edge of the table, laced my fingers in my lap so I'd present the most nonthreatening image possible. I looked up at him and turned on church-speak because it was disarming. And a disarmed enemy was the best kind. "See, Ayatas FireWind, it's like this. I like being a cop. I like solving crimes and helping people. I like my job. I like this team and they are dang good at what they do. I consider them friends." I leaned in to make sure he was listening to what I was saying. "You'un come in here and take over because you'un consider yourself the peacock with the biggest tail. The best of the best. And things didn't go like you'un planned and now you'un're scrambling in the aftermath of unexpected disaster. And you'un, right now, are trying to take it out on me because you need a release valve and I'm handy."

FireWind's eyebrows went up in surprise. "Please continue," he said, "and address why a probationary employee should not be released for insubordination."

"Last part first, then. This team's got no one who can read the land. *No one.*" I let a little more church into my voice. "'Acause whatever I am, I'm whatchu call a one-off. A one-of-a-kind."

"Your sister scents of *yinehi*," Ayatas said, eyes shrewd.

"My sister don't grow leaves. She can't read the land. She can't do what what I do." All true. Sorta. I mentally promised myself to keep my other siblings away from Ayatas' *yinehi* sniffer and continued on my attack. "In fact, PsyLED can't do its job thoroughly without me. PsyLED needs me more than I need it. Also"—I dropped a fraction of my church-speak and let my tone go hard—"I was the only special agent to get off a shot at Jason Ethier when *you* let him inside and he attacked HQ. So you don't scare me when you huff and puff and blow the walls down by threatening my job. I got a job offer outside of law enforcement anytime I want, so I wouldn't suffer financially if we parted ways. I ain't insubordinate. None of this unit is. Jo and me was making a joke."

"Job offer?" he asked.

The angst had begun to clear from his eyes as I talked. Start as you intend to go forward. Challenging him seemed to be effective. I said, "With Clan Yellowrock."

There was no way to miss the shock that jolted through him.

"Yeah. Your sister's . . . court, I guess you call it. As part of the Dark Queen's retinue. I know my value. I ain't got the big head, but I know who I am and what I got to offer. So don't threaten me. You can ask nicely or you can fire me. Until such firing, PsyLED has my total, undivided loyalty. We'uns clear?"

"Perfectly. As clear as when you kicked Rick LaFleur in the crotch."

"He had it coming," I said, unrepentant. That had been early in our acquaintance, before I joined PsyLED.

"Hmmm."

That *hmmm* was pretty good, but I'd been *hmmmed* by churchmen. FireWind was an amateur compared to that kind of censure. I leaned in even farther and smiled my sweetest churchwoman smile. "I done been threatened by burning at the stake since I was five years old. Being fired from a job ain't nothing." A small expression of surprise flashed across FireWind's face. He hadn't known that part of my history, which meant he hadn't spent much time looking over my personnel papers. That was interesting. I eased back, resettling my weight on the table. "Now. You got a plan of action or you gonna waste our time testing us to see what we're all made of, 'cause frankly I think you'd do better to wait till all this is settled."

With a bite to his words, FireWind said, "PSY CSI is delayed. Before you stop for the morning, I'd like you and Kent to go back to the stockyard and see what you can find out by daylight. Wear Tyvek uniforms."

"Good by me. I gotta drop my sister and her dog off at home first." I stood and walked to the door. Put my hand on the handle and stopped. "I ain't hard to work with. I'll support you and your decisions to my last breath, even when you get your butt kicked. But"—I looked over my shoulder at him—"you and me got off on the wrong foot. In fact, you and the rest of the unit got off on the wrong foot. I'm betting you're used to working with white male human teams. Unit Eighteen is composed predominantly of paras, not humans, a mixed male-female team, too. You can't treat this team the way you treat others and still have a fully functioning unit. This team has a lateral organizational structure, not an old-timey vertical one. Going forward, I'd like to be polite and respectful. I'd like the same from you." I started to open the door.

"Jane offered you a job?"

I stopped. Jane Yellowrock. "Yeah." I opened the door and left the icy room that tried to melt my own magic in my bones. But . . . I noticed that the hunger, the bloodlust, was completely gone. Breathing was easier.

In the conference room, I told T. Laine our orders. "We'll have to take your car because my truck is too small for the three of us and the dog."

As we were walking down the hallway, I heard FireWind say to Rick, "You were a willing sacrifice when you were tattooed. Loriann used you, then also made you a slave to protect her brother and to track him. Would you be insulted if I asked you to stay near your cage for the duration of this case?"

"I've already addressed that," Rick said. "And I've been bunking here."

"I see. I think that was a wise move."

I made a soft humph. Seemed FireWind could learn new tricks after all. I woke my sister and gathered her things and the dog, thinking about Rick and everything he had gone through. As we headed down the stairs, FireWind shouted to us, "Be back at four p.m. Full crew. We're going to breach and contain the house where Jason and Godfrey and the vampires are lairing before the local Mithrans even wake up for the night."

"Ten-four," T. Laine said.

We left Mud at Sam's house, outside, playing with her dog and trying to stay out of the way of the new baby and the mamas and away from the virus that had gripped the church. She was alone, but in line of sight of my brother, as safe as she could be with Larry Aden free from jail and a danger. It wasn't safe on church grounds, but it was safer than with me for now, despite the future possibility of her growing leaves and being burned at the stake. And that was a distinctly uncomfortable thought for me, who wanted to get custody and take her away from the church. Mud was in danger no matter where she lived.

T. Laine was driving and I was resting. I was way more tired than I admitted, and when I was tired, I went quiet. Exhaustion and sleep deprivation seemed to have the opposite effect on the unit's witch, and Lainie was running on thirty-six hours with little or no sleep. She finished off a thirty-three-ounce coffee on the way to the stockyard and talked my head off, asking questions about me and what I'd said to FireWind off the record, none of which I answered. That didn't stop her chatter.

She looked wide awake when she braked the car in front of the crime scene tape and got out to speak to the deputy guarding the site. I followed more slowly, my feet kicking up puffs of dust. I could hear the flies and, in the heat, the stench of rotting meat and blood was already strong. My bloodlust was awake and eager, but more like a curious puppy than a slavering starving hellhound. So far.

T. Laine chatted with the lone deputy as we both dressed out in Tyvek uniforms, the onesies worn by evidence collecting teams. The two were gossiping, agreeing that guard duty was boring and we really needed rain and it was hotter than the opening to hades. Lainie had thought to bring cold Cokes and some ice, and that made them best friends. I showed my ID, signed in to the official record, and moved into the heated, reeking stockyard, my paper uniform stifling.

It was still and silent in a locale that was probably usually loud with animals and machinery and the occasional worker. A hot breeze blew through, sweeping up dust devils. Flies buzzed like a chorus of buzz saws. Turkey buzzards were everywhere. A kettle of them soared overhead. I had no idea why a flock was called that, but all the names of buzzard groupings were bizarre. A committee, a venue, or a volt, they were perched on the rooftop, with the braver members of the scavenger pack sitting on the outer pen walls of the covered areas. A flock of feeding buzzards was called a wake, and three of the most brave, or the most dominant, were having a wake at the carcasses. It wouldn't be long before the stench drew multiple species of predators and scavengers from everywhere if the cleanup crew wasn't allowed onto the site.

Flies dive-bombed me as I approached the pens and walked into the shade under the metal roof. Buzzards perched on fencing. Dead animals were everywhere: three goats in the first pen, a miniature horse in the next, a sow and piglets. The animals had bled out from every orifice.

I dug out a small spiral notepad and walked down the wide aisles, beginning a listing of the animals with roman numerals. That was when I saw the man. Like the animals, he had died horribly—blood down his face, across his chest, dried and crinkled on his clothing. He was Caucasian, bearded; his blue eyes were clouded over, his light brown hair caked with dried blood. He was wearing jeans and a plaid shirt, and, like the animals, he had bled from every orifice. I backed a step away before I remembered that this was my job. I stopped, swallowed acidic bile that rose in my gullet. Quickly figured it out.

The man was lying on a sleeping bag, barefoot, half-covered by straw. A pack rested beside him, with a bag of canned goods, a twelve-pack of cheap beer, and a bag of trash. He was homeless. He had made the unfortunate decision to bed down yesterday in a pile of straw. And now he was dead.

"Nell," T. Laine called out.

"Here! We got a DB." Dead body. Not a homeless man, not a person with a past and a name and hopes for a better tomorrow. But a DB, to keep our souls distant from the awful part of the job of a cop.

T. Laine strode into the shadows and the buzzing of flies, saying, "Check for ID. Then back away. We're still waiting on PsyLED crime scene investigators."

The stench grew and the clouds of flies buzzed like a speeding engine as they laid eggs. We ascertained that there was only the one human body, hunted for ID, and anything arcane or black magic. There was nothing. and we left the stench of the pens for the witch circle, sweating like church-women.

Lainie had been reading arcane texts and had brought along a version of a *seeing* working. She wanted to see if she could re-create a vision of the spell at its inception, as it was drawn and cast, and then determine what the circle was doing now. I was more interested in the bodies we had left in place in the circles. Vampires were known to burst into flame in sunlight and we'd had a lot of sun already today.

"The vamp bodies are gone," T. Laine said, "and the circles are still intact. No one has been here but us. I don't even see a pile of ash."

Not that I intended to tell Lainie, but when I fed the earth, the ash was eaten by the land. There was nothing left at all. Jason had found a way to do that. If there had been vampire ash, it had soaked into the earth. Which meant that Jason might have used vampires in other circles and the remains were gone by the time we got there. That would explain the maggoty feeling. Ming had her scions locked down, but some might have gone missing in the months before we knew about Jason's circles. And . . . maybe the invading vamps had do-nated vamp prisoners for sacrifice.

"What do the vamps who are helping Jason get out of this?"

"Best guess? Jason's such a blood junkie. They think they can control him and use the demon's power vicariously, maybe even drinking the power down with Jason's blood. All the power, none of the side effects of being demon ridden."

"Oh. That makes sense."

"Stay back and take readings," she said.

I retreated to the shade and leaned against a tree, calibrating the psy-meter 2.0 and testing the readings against T. Laine. She read pure witch. But the circle didn't. It read witch and vampire and fluctuating levels of one and four.

I didn't have my blanket, but I touched a pinkie finger to the earth and yanked it away. *Nasty. Maggots. Death.* I wanted to gag and promised myself to never, ever do that again at a scene filled with dead animals and filth of demon.

At the circle, T. Laine walked sunwise around the circle, pausing every few steps, her eyes on the center. When she finished one complete revolution, she stopped and studied it, put an amulet on a silver chain around her neck, and removed a plastic zipped bag from a pocket. It contained blue powder. She opened the baggie and tossed a few grains of the blue stuff over the edge of the circle. They fell slowly and . . . stopped. They hung in midair.

T. Laine called to me, "Keep measuring and film this on your cell. If I explode, see that my family never learns I was stupid enough to do this."

"Do what?"

"Measure!" she demanded.

I set my cell on a tree limb and focused the video on the circle. I tapped the small button to film Lainie's activities. Then I extended the psy-meter's wand and hit record. "Go."

T. Laine took a fistful of the blue dust and tossed it high. It went up and out and was caught by the breeze; it swirled and settled across . . . the *hedge*. Nothing happened. She tossed another. Then another. She finished by upending the baggie and shaking out the last of the blue dust. It didn't spread out perfectly, but enough settled that I could make out the form of the *hedge of thorns*. It looked exactly as if someone had upended a massive, shallow, splotchy blue bowl.

T. Laine held out her arms and leaned down. Gingerly, she touched a patch of blue dust. I saw the magics as they were enacted. From the circle's point at the south, a line of blue raced around and back to the beginning as the circle was cut and chalked into the earth. The energies sparkled for a moment, then moved down the spoke closest, to the center. They sparkled again, growing in intensity, and shot out the spokes to meet the outer circle. The vision dimmed.

A red circle rose inside it, concentric, smaller than the blue one. It too dimmed. A small smearing of blue energies at the north point led to the center of the circles. Another smearing. And two more. They faded. And then the red circle sprang into place, followed by the blue one. They stayed in place, visible to human eyes in the daylight, stable and unwavering. I understood that it was an image of what had been, created by Lainie's working. It made no sense to me at all, but T. Laine was grinning like a cat with a bowl of cream.

She called to me, "The circles were two spells in one. The inner one called the vampires and a black cat, and imprisoned them in the center. The outer one—"

A black light burst from the ground. T. Laine jumped back. Something long and smoky and dark moved from the earth. Two more, then two more. They were . . . fingers and a thumb. An amorphous blue-ish hand reached out of the pit. It was wearing a ruby ring. It made a fist and withdrew into the land. The red circle winked out. The blue one blazed up high, sparkling in the sunlight.

T. Laine raced away from the edge of the outer circle. Dropped flat to the ground. As if—"Get down!" she screamed at me.

I dropped, clutching the psy-meter to me. The blue circle glared so bright I had to look away. I duck-walked behind the tree. The blue energies exploded. Brilliant. Silent. They evaporated. I peeked out from behind the tree to see a ring and spokes of bluish powder. There had been only light, nothing kinetic.

T. Laine rose from her crouch. She was breathing hard. Panicked. Sweat ran down her spine and dampened dark half circles beneath her arms. She backed away. Stumbled. Caught her balance and turned to me. Raced close. I looked down at the psy-meter 2.0. It was bouncing all over the place, all the levels, jumping up and down.

"Son of a witch on a switch," she cursed. "That wasn't supposed to happen. I'm pretty sure no one has ever seen that before and lived to tell it. Except Jason."

Uncertain, I said, "That was a demon's hand, wasn't it?"

"Holy hell and back again, yes." T. Laine opened a bottle of water and poured it over her head, splashing us both with the icy contents. She gasped and shivered once and opened a Coke, which she drank down, crushing the plastic bottle to force it down her throat fast. She burped. Burped again as the Coke's carbon dioxide bubbled in her stomach.

I saved the reading, turned the meter and the cell off. Carefully, I asked, "Did you free the demon?"

"No! I'm adventurous, not stupid. The blue powder is part of a . . . let's call it *review* working. It lets me see recently executed spells. Once. It's like a delayed reflection; it triggers nothing, the demon is still trapped. You get the video?"

"Whatever my cell managed to capture." I walked to the edge of the circle and bent to look at the blue talc. A few grains had spilled to the side and I gathered them up, without touching the circle itself. The powder felt oily and coarse and rough all at once. I carried it back to the tree and put it in a paper evidence bag.

T. Laine said, "This spell drained the blood from every farm animal on the property and a human and, if we guessed right, the vampires that were sacrificed in the circle." She caught her breath and stared out over the stockyard. "Demons suck dill pickles. Come on. PsyCSI is working up a paranormal scene in New York. They won't get here until tomorrow. Let's get out of here before we further contaminate the crime scene."

As she drove back to HQ, T. Laine talked as if her mouth had lost its brakes, the words pouring out nonstop. She needed to talk, the vocalization a result of what she had seen and the huge coffee she had downed on the way. And the Coke. I couldn't forget the Coke. I was exhausted, thinking about the earth and communing with it, using a pinch of bluish powder. On the way I got a text from Sam.

Larry Aden's first wife came to see my baby. She spotted

Mindy and was caterwauling about how Mindy was supposed to be hers. I feared it might attract the Jackson crowd so I took Mindy and the dog to your place.

My sister and her dog were alone at Soulwood. Alone.

I needed to get there, but we had to tell FireWind what we had discovered and write up our end-of-day reports. The new boss met us at the top of the stairs. I touched my cell open and handed it to him. A video was worth a thousand words.

I cleaned up in the locker room and followed the sound of their voices to the break room.

FireWind and T. Laine were studying a drawing on the table. Lainie said, "This is Tandy's rendition of Rick being spelled by Loriann when she tattooed the tat magic. Tandy was finally able to get him to talk about it some."

The drawing was pencil on lined paper, depicting a barn and a straw-covered floor. There was a black marble square in the middle of the open floor and an iron ring, and shackles. There was a crack and a small broken place in the stone. Something about the shape of the broken place drew my attention and it took a bit to figure out why. When I did, my brain began to put things together.

To the side of the huge black stone crouched a female figure, her hands busy. And upon the black square stone a naked man was stretched, arms and legs spread. Rick. The tattoos unfinished, dark smudges.

"Rick finally got around to describing the inking. It was . . . pretty horrible," Tandy said.

"Okay," I said, putting the page down. I didn't want to see the event of my boss's torture. *First* torture. He'd been attacked and tortured by a werewolf pack too. And by Paka. Rick LaFleur had been beaten by life so badly it was hard to comprehend how he got out of bed in the mornings. "Did you see the hand in the video? Did you see the ring it wore?"

FireWind started. Almost in unison he and T. Laine said, "Ring?"

I leaned in to my cell and tapped it on. Hit the play button. FireWind moved to face the computer system and the video appeared on the overhead screen, much larger, though pixelated and grainy. It wasn't easy to see, but the ring was there, a brownish gold (though gold wasn't supposed to tarnish) and in the center a brownish red stone was mounted. I didn't know much about stones. There were shapes incised into the stone, but they were impossible to make out, even with a little computer sleight of hand to enhance it.

FireWind said, "Soul is calling the Vatican. She's sending their lead investigator all we have on the demon. We hope someone there will know something."

T. Laine made a sound of breathy laughter. "And I called *my* experts, the U.S. Council of Witches. Between the two opposing sides, we should learn something. Hopefully not things in total conflict with each other."

I nodded, feeling like a bobble-head doll, and looked around. Occam wasn't here, either off for a few hours of rest or away doing things for the investigation. Rick and Margot Racer were in the sleep room, talking softly. I was tired and worried and I had too much to do before I could rest. There was a Shakespeare quote, something about exhaustion, but I was too tired to remember it. I downloaded the video to the main system and left.

My sister was setting up an agility course in the backyard using found objects. A length of rope, some pointed wooden stakes from the woodpile, a stack of cement bricks, a few two-by-ten boards, and two shovels. Mud and Cherry were racing to and fro in the heat, the silly little dog wearing herself out.

I waved to Mud and carried my pink blanket into the woods, back from the house, deep under the heavy foliage. There was a spring back here and a rill of water. It was dark and cool and silent. I hadn't been here recently, though I remembered walking here when I was coming back from being a tree.

The rocks were a tumbled mass in the near-vertical hillside and the pool was deeper than I remembered, the bottom clay, lined with a layer of leaves from last fall. The trees around the pool weren't old growth, though they looked like it. Until I first fed the land with the body and soul of the faceless man who had attacked me, right here, they had been only twenty-five years old. Now it would take several tall people to hold hands around the trunks. The boles were massive. This was home as no other place on the face of the earth would ever be home. This was the heart of Soulwood.

I dropped the blanket to the surface of a flat rock and sank down on it. I laid out the things I had stolen and secreted away. The bits of tissue, stained with Jason's blood. The gauze, brown with Loriann's blood. The grains of blue talc. There was also a bit of Rick's blood that had splattered in his office. No one had seen me take it, either.

I wasn't a witch. But my magic was, and always had been, blood magic.

By every definition I had ever learned, I was a black-magic practitioner. It was time to test out that theory.

EIGHTEEN

Anywhere else, and I would have been cautious reading the earth. I had learned the hard way not to dive into the land, but to touch it with a fingertip and ease into the ground. But this was Soulwood. This was home. I toed off my shoes and placed my bare feet on the ground. The soil against my soles was dark and rich, composed of organic compounds and minerals; this close to the rill of water and the broken stone of the hillside, it had rock chips throughout in dozens of browns and tans and blacks. I leaned against a boulder, cool and sturdy at my back, and let down my hair. It was sweaty and thick as a tangled ball of tree roots; it curled around my face and shoulders. I worked my fingertips into the soil, scratching with my nails until fingers and palms were below the surface of the earth.

Rootlets coiled up to my flesh as if inspecting me, but they didn't try to grow into my skin. A simple nudge sent them into place, touching, but not drinking, not damaging me. Oak and poplar and maple, even a Douglas fir, shoved against my flesh, the soil rippling, quivering, and rising as the roots reached for me, dislodging the sediment. When they ran out of room, they rose above the ground and arched over my feet and hands like loose socks and mittens. I sighed in contentment.

Time passed. I sank into the land. Knew it. Knew everything on it. The coyote family down the hill. The small herd of does and young nibbling grasses. The smaller but more rowdy bachelor herd. Squirrels sleeping in the heat of day. Birds pecking at the ground, several at a small pond of water, bathing, splashing. A feral cat, ready to pounce on them. A bobcat watching them all, curious about the smaller cat but not hungry enough to take its meal. An owl nest with juveniles and two adults. A dozen turkey buzzards perched near the road at the bottom of the hill, ripping at a carcass, a deer hit by a car sometime in the last week.

I reached for the vampire tree, which was enormous now. The biggest part of the tree was at the original site, where I had pulled on the tree to heal me after I was shot and lay dying. The bole of the trunk was massive there, bigger than some houses, more than twenty feet across. The branches twisted and draped, so heavy they had settled to the ground like huge sinuous snakes. The root system covered the entire church land, having sent rootlets out in every direction, poking up a small stem and a few leaves every few yards, as if tasting the air, testing the world in that spot. The tree had formed a twenty-foot-tall hedge behind the chain-link fence at the church's gates. It had even tested a few places on my own land, but it hadn't claimed the ground as it had the church lands. The vampire tree was interested in something taking place at God's Cloud, enough so that I could do what I wanted without attracting it to me.

I reached through the land to the bits of bloody tissue. Rick's blood was easy to recognize and access because I had claimed him for the land as I healed him. He was a part of Soulwood. Not sure what I was looking for, I studied the blood, the twists and turns and things that didn't feel human. I studied Loriann's. I turned my attention to the blood I had collected from Jason, not to claim him, but to find him. I studied the blood, felt the ways it was different from Loriann's, from Rick's, and even different from my own. I hadn't studied much biology beyond Paranormal Physiology 101 at Spook School, and I was curious. After inspecting all the blood samples through the power of Soulwood, and setting aside the ones that belonged to my land, and the one that had come from Loriann, I *searched*.

The blood guided me through Oliver Springs and Oak Ridge into Knoxville and toward the Tennessee River. And past the city into the countryside on the far side of the city. I didn't know where I was at first. And then the feeling of the earth, of the soil, hit me, slamming solidly into me like a big fist. The sensation rattled my teeth. *Magic. Blood. Death.* I had been there today. The stockyard.

Jason Ethier was less than a mile away from his witch circle, sleeping in the arms of a vampire. Sex and magic and darkness. Need and rage. Sickness eating away at his body. Secrets and pain eating away at his soul. Dark and bloody and twisted things in his mind. Things I didn't want to look at.

The sorcerer was protected by magical *hedges* so strong they raked along my consciousness like electric cacti, burning, stabbing, cutting. The *hedges* were tied to the vampires and the moon, the working powered by the blood of humans. I couldn't touch his blood through them, couldn't drain him into the earth. I tried. It was like trying to pick up sewer water in an open hand. Jason had tied himself to the *thing* beneath the stockyard and its foulness had coated Jason's soul. The smoky fist of filth.

It was lethargic in the daylight, and from the safety of Soulwood, I studied the ring on its colossal finger. Engraved into the red stone was a stretched-out, flattened-looking *X*. Below that were the initials *B, K,* a lowercase *u,* and an *L,* like gang signs, except they glowed with what looked like black flame. *B'KuL.*

I slipped away from the *thing* in the earth, away from the sickness of Jason Ethier, out of the house where he slept. It was at the end of a long drive less than a mile, as the buzzard flew, from the Knoxville Livestock Center and all that putrefying meat and drying blood. And the *wrong* thing in the earth.

I started to tug myself completely free, back to my body, but contact with Soulwood had jarred something loose in my brain. I paused and tried to bring it to my conscious mind. Some little something. Some tiny inconsistency. A single question unanswered. *What did Jason* really *want?* He could have killed Rick at a calling circle. In the office with the gun. And he hadn't.

I eased my hands free of the plant mittens and the leafy socks. We were missing something. Interpreting something incorrectly.

I stood and shook out my faded pink blanket. Yummy and Ming and the vamps didn't give us an address because they wanted the op all to themselves. They didn't want their hands tied when they killed everyone on the premises. They wanted medic primed to go into action just in case. But. If they killed

Jason Ethier, that might set the demon free. How did one stop an almost-free demon?

I put on my shoes and stood, carrying my blanket to the house, thinking as I walked, carrying with me the peace I always felt when I communed with my land. Before I reached the edge of the trees and the grassy acres where my home and garden were, I stopped and found my cell phone and accessed a map. Located the land and house where Jason slept. It was a house on Roseberry Road. Dialed T. Laine.

She didn't answer hello. She answered with a sleepy, grouchy, "This better be good, Ingram." Clearly I had waked her.

"Two things. One, the demon hand was wearing a ring."

"Already established, Ingram."

"I just figured out what it looked like. It was an *X*, squished, so the sides were longer than it was tall."

"Gebo, merkstave," she said, coming awake, "well, not merkstave. Gebo can't truly lie in merkstave, but it can lie in opposition. Gebo properly indicates balance in all matters like exchanges, contracts, personal relationships, and partnerships." She fell silent.

"What happens when Gebo is in opposition?"

"Greed, privation, obligation, dependence." She added, "Bribery, loneliness, oversacrifice unto death."

I described the other initials and said, "Bukul?"

T. Laine said, "Son of a witch on a switch. Don't ever say that out loud."

"Why?"

"That's its summoning name," she said. "We can use *B*, *K*, *L*—just the initials. And I can use the summoning name to . . . do something. Good. Yeah." She was fully awake, lit by excitement. "I've been reporting to the U.S. witch council, and they've been trying to adapt a *shoot to kill* working for this situation." Her mouth clicked closed on the words as she heard them. *Shoot to kill a kid with cancer.* T. Laine took a slow breath, her excitement dissipating. She cursed softly. "Attempting to summon a demon is a death sentence."

"Will they be here to help?" I asked.

"No. They can't fight demons. They told me to evacuate. They say me killing Jason is the best they can do."

"Why? I don't understand."

Lainie took a slow breath. "My species tends to run from demons. With good reason. A demon can run through a family blood line like lightning, using us all."

I hesitated, thinking about what I had sensed when I found Jason in the arms of a vampire. He had been broken as a child. He had taken that brokenness and built a house of hate and fury around it. He had shaped himself into a creature of utter darkness. The brokenness had not been a choice. What he did with that brokenness was. And Jason was legally an adult now. Giving Lainie the address assured Jason's death, and Lainie might have to carry out the death sentence herself. Alone. Not giving it meant a vampire war and Jason might get away in the battle and also free the demon. Or share his sister with it by accident. Like me, Lainie might have to learn to live as a killer. And then I remembered that one master vampire would be awake, the daywalker, Godfrey.

T. Laine could not take on a blood-witch and a master vampire alone.

I said, "The other reason I called? I know where Jason is. A house on Roseberry Road, under a *hedge* of protection, with a lot of vampires. Probably the rogue vampires and Godfrey. We know what he's calling. He has to be stopped—now. We can storm the place while most of the vampires are asleep. Call the witch council and get your permission."

Not that we needed it. If I could get close to Jason, inside his magical defenses, I could feed him to the earth. I had his blood.

"Later," T. Laine said, disconnecting.

I still didn't have an answer to my question *What did Jason really want?* Another possibility, half-seen from my communion with the land, crawled up from the dark and rooty recesses of my mind. I dialed Ayatas FireWind. He sounded alert and reserved, as always. "What can I do for you, Ingram?"

I told him what I had learned about Jason's location and magical protections, and asked, "Do you know a lot about demons?"

"Too much." The words sounded tired and beaten.

"In Spook School, I learned that when a witch calls a demon, they contact the demon, make a bargain, and slit the throat of the sacrifice. The blood frees the demon into the circle with the sacrifice and seals the bargain with the blood. When the demon drinks or absorbs the blood, the demon is then free. And that gives the witch rule over the demon and his powers for a specified time period. Yes?"

"More or less. Though the bargain Jason negotiated required a blood sacrifice to even contact the demon," Ayatas said, his tone pedantic, impassive. "That contact and bargain was what you saw in the *review* working cast by Kent."

"Who will be the sacrifice that gives the demon freedom?"

"Vampire prisoners dedicated to that purpose and Rick LaFleur."

"What happens if Jason dies now? Before he frees the demon?"

"It would be a half finished summoning. Anyone could take over and free him, and the agreed upon bargain would no longer be in play. It's what demons hope for in the first place—getting free, having access to the earth and the humans in it, unrestricted by bargains."

"And if Jason is dead and the demon is still trapped in the circle?" I asked.

He hesitated, a slight hitch in tone. "There may be those in our government and military who think they can control a demon, can rewrite the bargain if Jason is gone and the demon is still trapped in the circle."

"So we have to finish this fast, and tie up all the loose ends."

"I fear so."

"And if we take Jason out after the possession?" I asked.

"It will be difficult to kill Jason with the tools we have on hand once he's possessed by the demon. That's usually part of the bargain. Magical protection from attack for the duration of the contract."

Tools we have on hand. That was an interesting phrase. I took a slow breath and said, "I know where Jason is. And our timeline window is small. We have to take him out today before Ming gets to him at sunset. Do containment vessels have a size maximum?"

There was a short, sharp silence on the other end of the connection as FireWind processed my question. "You think it's a Major Power."

"Yes. When I read the land, I got a good look at the ring on the demon's hand. The red stone was embossed with a rune. T. Laine says it's Gebo in opposition."

The reserved, unemotional FireWind took a hissing breath.

"We have its calling name, based on the initials *B.K.L.* I think it's huge and powerful and tied to the magma working its way up through the earth's crust," I said.

"Hmmm. There are hot springs and other signs of geological activity in the Appalachians. In answer to your question, yes, containment vessels do have a maximum suppression and restraint assessment, but no one knows how to measure demonic energy, so PsyLED labs haven't tried the systems with anything larger than your garden-variety flesh-eating imp."

"So we can't contain it, and we can't kill it, and Jason is under the magical protection of a powerful *hedge of thorns* until he lets it drop to free the demon. And we have to act before sunset and the vamps rise."

"Yes. But until the bargain is completed, the demon's power is fundamentally and effectively limited." I could almost hear the frown in his voice when he added, "We thought Rick was being called for two reasons: revenge, and to power the working to call the demon. But something is off."

"Right," I said. "Why shoot Rick? Why try to turn himself into a werecat?"

"Best guess is blood spatter for the calling, and were-taint to heal his cancer. Jones found a diagnosis of leukemia in his history." He made a ruminative sound. "Tonight is the total dark of the moon. The new moon rose around dawn. It is up but invisible all day, and will set around seven p.m., before sunset in Knoxville in summer." He made the pensive sound again. "Since nothing magic happened when it rose, the curse must be timed for the interval between moonset and sunset. Thank you, Ingram. This is invaluable information. We have a great many logistics to work out, and our timeline to stop Jason may be a very narrow window."

"From the time Jason starts the spell and drops the *hedge*, to the moment he's killed enough sleeping vampires to free the demon, but before the demon is actually set free. And then we have to figure out a way to send the demon back," I clarified.

"I suppose that's correct. Anything else, Ingram?" FireWind asked.

"Has anyone thought about putting Rick on a plane for the Vatican?" I asked.

"Several times. It's still in discussion."

"Last question. What if the vampires with Jason don't know what we do about the demon and its summoning? Godfrey is an old vampire who probably knows a lot about magic, but this is a brand-new curse-working. What if Jason is using them for more than we think?"

I felt FireWind's attention narrow onto me. "I'm listening."

"What if the curse part of the spell isn't just for Rick, but also is directed at the other group that hurt him? What if the curse is directed at all the vampires in Knoxville? Or even all the vampires in the state? Or think bigger. What if the curse is directed at the life force, or un-life-force, of every vampire in the world all at once? Just causes them to bleed to death like the cattle did at the stockyard."

FireWind went quiet and the silence stretched out. "What you're suggesting is, or should be, impossible. But . . . a vampire kidnapped him and killed his grandmother in front of his eyes. Yet he's working with a vampire now."

"If Jason starts the curse after moonset and before sunset," I said, "in the last ninety minutes of day, before the vampires rise, he'll have sleeping vampires available to bleed into his curse, the way he bled the cattle at the livestock center. He wouldn't even have to cut them. That narrows our timeline even more."

FireWind muttered something that might have been cussing in another language. "He gets revenge on Rick, kills him, is healed by vampire blood or the were-taint, kills large numbers of vampires, and has a demon at his disposal for as long as their agreement lasts. The little sorcerer is brilliant." There was reluctant admiration in FireWind's voice.

"If we miss our window," I said, "Jason will have the demon to grant him power for as long as he lives, which might be a long time as a werecat or a vampire."

FireWind agreed thoughtfully. "Logistics will be a nightmare and we don't have much time to prepare."

"And that narrow window," I said.

"The unit is exhausted. New-moon set is less than an hour and a half before sunset. This will be tricky. Get a nap. Be at HQ by four p.m. And, Nell, see that Mud is elsewhere. This will not be the safest place on earth."

The connection ended. The safest place on earth. As far as I was concerned, that was Soulwood. I wondered if I could get the vampire tree to babysit. I needed sleep, but my family was more important. I needed . . . I needed to claim the church land. I needed a sacrifice.

I shook my entire body like a dog shakes its fur. *No.* I was not killing someone to claim the land. At my feet a tendril pushed through the soil, and a single thick, green leaf uncoiled, resting against my ankle.

In the yard, Mud screamed with laughter and rolled on the ground with Cherry. Overhead, a bird sang, long and sweet. I smelled wisteria and the grape Kool-Aid smell of kudzu in bloom. The vampire tree tendril coiled up my ankle and wrapped around it. Not trapping me. Just . . . making me aware. Reminding me, as if it had access to my mind. And maybe, on some level, it did.

Larry Aden had been wounded by the vampire tree. The tree had his blood. The tree could . . . sacrifice Larry, and I could claim church land through it.

And that would be murder. Not self-defense to protect myself. But premeditated, cold-blooded murder. An icy thrill rushed through me like a broken dam of glacial water. My body clenched. Goose bumps flew across my skin, pebbling my arms and legs and up my chest.

I looked out over Soulwood, over land that was almost holy. "I'll find another way," I whispered, staring at the sprig of the vampire tree on my ankle. It now had three leaves and was about six inches long. I bent down and plucked the sprig. I carried the vampire twig to the back porch and tucked it into an unused pot of soil.

Today was the total dark of the moon, and though the moon was up now, and would actually be above the horizon all day, it wouldn't be visible at all. The darkness of the night sky would be brightened only by stars. And whatever curse and demon-summoning Jason had planned.

Inside the house, I showered and crawled into bed. I fell fast asleep. I still didn't know what I'd do with Mud when I went back to work, but my brain needed sleep and I could problem-solve after some rest.

I dropped Mud off at Esther's, though I didn't get to see my older sister. Esther didn't come to the door when Mud and I knocked. Jed opened the door, a man at home in the daylight, when by church codes he should be working.

"Jed," I said.

Jed looked tired and angry and had a three-day beard. He didn't meet my eyes. "Nell."

I remembered Esther's fingers at her hairline, so much like mine when my leaves were trying to grow. If being plant-women ran in the family, as I believed, Esther was likely to grow leaves too. But she hadn't talked to me.

He pushed open the door, but I caught Mud's shoulder. "If Esther needs my help keeping things trimmed back, you let me know."

Mud laughed and skipped inside. Jed's eyes flashed fire and he closed the door in my face.

"Hospitality and peace to you too," I shouted through the door. I probably shouldn't have stirred that pot. But if my sister was growing leaves . . .

I got back in my truck and took off for HQ.

It was just past four, and T. Laine was talking as Tandy put the last pencil traces on the sketch of the smoky fist of the devil trapped in the earth. "The New Orleans coven and I agree. The spell Ethier is likely using to summon his demon is a shared power spell. It can be called *totality*. It's a bargain type of spell, one where a witch and a demon share witch and demonic strength and power at different times and for different purposes. For instance, the demon might use the witch's strength and youth to power itself to the surface, in which case, the demon steals years, the witch ages, the demon gets free. Then the bargain reverses as the demon extracts more power from the deeps along his pathway, which he then gifts to the witch. The witch ages, but he ends up with one *major* power/working/curse/whatever. That's the way it's supposed to work."

"Except that Jason isn't aging. Rick is," I said.

"Jason added levels in a working so complex I may never understand it. Jason sacrifices Rick—maybe from a distance, since Rick's blood is now mixed with his own—and maybe sacrifices all the vampires in the house with him too. With such a big sacrifice, he survives handling and channeling the evil of a Major Power through his body and his circle. The demon possesses Jason, enacts the curse, and—if Ingram is right—destroys all the vampires everywhere. After that, un-aged, healed from the leukemia, healed from vamp-blood-addiction, Jason will have whatever years are left to him, riding a demon—to use Ingram's term. Perfect spell. And scary as hell."

Tandy stepped back from his drawing, studying it.

T. Laine took a deep breath, her eyes on Rick. "The last DNA test results came back from the lab. One vial of liquid was your blood. I'm betting Jason has even more, which is how he's draining you. It's how he can reach you even inside the null room or a silver cage. Maybe the blood was drawn by Loriann during the inking. Maybe stolen from a hospital lab or something, prior to you being infected with were-taint. Security in hospitals is set up against humans, not witches. But how he got it doesn't matter. Now he has fresh blood *inside* of him. I'm hypothesizing that with the blood, Jason added an extra layer to the curse. He has Rick's human DNA. He's been using Rick's blood and life force to power the spells. Rick is aging fast. The demon, however, doesn't know what's happening. It's a bait and switch with Rick's life in the balance, made worse because Jason likely infected himself with Rick's were-taint. Jason kills Rick and curses the vampires who hurt him in one fell swoop. If he loses his bargain with the demon, then the were-taint might heal his cancer anyway."

Rick looked out the window at the western horizon. His silvered hair seemed awfully bright, the black strands fewer now, in spite of the were-taint, which was supposed to give

him a much longer life span. Now it made sense. Rick was
dying. The pencil drawing of Rick being tattooed was on the
table. I spun the paper, studying the depiction. There was
something—

T. Laine interrupted my thoughts. "Only after the curse is
done will the demon realize that Jason hasn't aged, isn't old,
and he's been cheated. Then they live in powerful disharmony
until Jason dies."

Rick murmured, "Jason must really hate me." He was rubbing his shoulder, the one with the mangled tattoos, tats that
he'd accepted, a spelling that he'd suffered, to save Jason, the
child. A good deed, horribly punished, proving the old adage
that no good deed goes unpunished.

I couldn't stand watching my boss's face. I leaned to Tandy
and pointed to his drawing. "The arms of the X were more
squished. And there was a little hook right there." I pointed.
"Claws. I forgot the claws. The demon's claws were hooked,
like a cat's." Rick and Occam looked up at that. "Retractile."
The hand and the ring were coming to life on the paper, drawn
by Tandy's pencil. It was scary.

Rick asked, "What happens if we miss our deadline and we
have to kill Jason after he's possessed?"

"The last time that happened was December sixteenth,
1811, in New Madrid, Missouri," T. Laine said. "It resulted in
the largest earthquake in the history of the United States. It
had an estimated magnitude of eight point six on the Richter
scale. The earthquake raised and lowered parts of the Mississippi Valley and changed the course of the Mississippi River.
A thirty-thousand-square-mile area was affected, and tremors
were felt on the eastern coastline of the United States. Additional earthquakes went on for months. If that happens here?
An earthquake that big? The entire river valley will likely
suffer a substantial upheaval," T. Laine said. "The U.S. witch
council estimated an eight point five or higher. Every power
plant and dam in the valley will be damaged. Some will suffer
catastrophic failure. There will be flooding like we've never
seen. Nell's house might be safe as long as the hilly ridges
don't fall over. The rest of us will drown."

"Power plant," Rick said softly. "The nuclear plant?"

"Is not secure to an eight-point-five earthquake," T. Laine said.

"So the spell of *totality* is tied to LaFleur's tattoos," FireWind said softly.

"Yes," T. Laine said, just as softly. "I think so."

"If I'm dead will the spell be broken?" Rick asked.

My head snapped up. Was Rick talking about *suicide* to save the city?

T. Laine made a sound that might have been laughter if laughter was mostly grief. "Gebo in opposition means a lot of things, boss. Greed, privation, obligation, dependence. In your case, because of who you are, because of your natural protective instincts, it also means oversacrifice unto death. You die and the demon will just take the vampires targeted by the summoning/curse spell. You can't stop it by dying. Jason prepared for that possibility."

Rick looked old, the lines in his face deeply engraved, his skin sallow and tired. He turned away, spinning in his chair, his back to us, staring out over the city.

T. Laine said, "We knew the local witches were scared. We knew there was a Circle of the Moon cursing, a blood sacrifice, the Angels and Demons tarot spread, and a summoning. We knew something bad was coming."

"But not a major prince of darkness," FireWind said, sounding wry. "Not a curse to bring all the vampires to true-death."

"What about the Vatican?" T. Laine asked. "Are they sending an emissary or a cardinal or whatever?"

FireWind was leaning against the doorjamb, arms crossed, watching us. He said, "I've been in touch with them, through a PsyLED emissary. They are assembling an entire team of exorcists, but they can't be here by nightfall. And they aren't willing to sacrifice a few local priests to assist us and keep the vampires alive." He shrugged. "Undead. Their plan is to deal with the demon if the rest of us are dead and the demon is free."

Rick shook his head. Rick was Catholic. I had no idea how he felt about FireWind's statement. "We should have called them sooner," he said.

"Yes. But we didn't know, didn't guess what Jason was really doing, until we saw the hand rise from the circle."

"We have clues, but we still don't *know* everything," T. Laine said. "We weren't clueless or too stupid to see the writing on the wall. It was just too big a curse to focus on. And no one expected a Major Power or Principality."

"I've had encounters with demons," Rick said.

"There is only the one in your records—" FireWind stopped. "Ahhh. The one at Spook School, when you were present for a demon who was taken into a containment vessel, and the one involving my—Jane Yellowrock." He had almost said "my sister."

Rick glanced at his supervisor. "The one Jane killed on national TV was summoned by the Asheville coven leader. It was called the Raven Mocker. And though I'm sure someone has left messages with her voice mail . . . ?" He glanced at JoJo, who nodded. ". . . We're still not clear how Jane contained it or destroyed it."

"I didn't know you were there," FireWind said.

JoJo, already pulling up footage of the demon's death, said, "You can't kill a demon."

"Close enough," Rick said.

The footage appeared on the screen overhead. We watched as a demon killed some humans. Then Jane, now the Dark Queen of the vampires, Ayatas' sister, killed the demon. And the redheaded woman who had summoned it.

"Yowzers," T. Laine said. "I had forgotten the sequence of events here."

"Jane's rough on her friends," Rick said. Unspoken were the words "and her boyfriends." "According to Jane, there was an angel present and only with that angel's help was she able to stop it." Rick looked as if he might say more but stopped.

"Was that demon a Major Principality?" T. Laine asked.

"No."

"Anyone have an angel on speed dial?" Occam asked in dark humor. "Anyone try prayer?"

"Yes," Rick said softly. "Jane's angel hasn't answered."

Replaying the YouTube footage, T. Laine said, "I agree that this demon isn't as powerful as the one Jason Ethier is calling. He's killed two vampires and a buttload of animals in sacrifice and the demon's still not free. If B.K.L. gets loose, we are screwed six ways to Sunday."

I said, "The death of one wereleopard won't be enough. How many vampires will he sacrifice tonight?"

"He's in the lair with Godfrey and all his humans and scions," Rick said.

"Jason would have seen the witch amulets on the prisoners they took from Ming's. He would have known what they were. My money says Jason arranged for the local vamps to find out the address, bringing more vampires to them like lambs to the slaughter," Occam said. Which was very twisty but made sense. "If so, then Jason plans to drain every one of Knoxville's fangheads as sacrifice, including at least three master vampires, Godefroi de Bouillon, Ming Zhane, and Lincoln Shaddock."

"Where's Loriann?" Rick asked. "She was being treated at the hospital after Jason's attack."

FireWind said, "You are tattooed to be protective of her and her brother, so I have to ask. Why do you want to know?"

"She might be the only one in the world who could stop Jason. Or at least slow him down until the team gets to him. She and Kent could set up protections for us. Maybe something that could slow down the ascension of the demon to this plane of existence. If Kent is willing to work with Loriann."

"I will not authorize Loriann Ethier to work with our people," FireWind said, "though I will allow her to be on-site in case we have need for hostage negotiation. The wound in her chest was bloody, but the round just nicked a small artery, in and out. She's patched up and is currently in the null room, repenting of her ways." He raised his brows slightly and asked T. Laine, "Do you have the restraints ready?"

"Yeah. The level-five null cuffs are painful enough to fall under the Eighth Amendment's 'cruel and unusual punishment' clause, but since the U.S. witch council approved of them, no one seems to give a rat's ass. They'll hurt like hell, but they'll keep her power docile."

"Level five?" I asked.

"Brand-new," T. Laine said, her face grim. "They work by sliding minuscule silver needles under the skin and directly into the nervous system. I happen to have two pairs. Lucky me."

FireWind's cell chimed and he lifted it to see the screen. A look of satisfaction crossed his face. "If they get here in time, we'll have additional reinforcements in the form of the National Guard and a big brass observer from the DOD."

Relief pulsed through the room, but FireWind doused it with the words, "*If.* Moonset and sunset are awfully close today, about ninety minutes apart. If we are right about the timing of the curse, Jason will have to drop his *hedge of thorns* just after seven, and he'll begin his blood sacrifices. We'll need to take him before he's finished. Gear up." He added softly, "Every weapon at your disposal even if they grate against your morality. We will be joined by SWAT led by Gonzales, Special Agent Margot Racer leading a small FBI team, a team from the Tennessee Highway Patrol, and TBI." TBI was the Tennessee Bureau of Investigation. "I assume Ming's and Shaddock's former-military humans will show up prior to sunset and her former-military Mithrans just after dark. I'd like this operation in the bag when they show. Jones, you will handle communications from here. Dyson, you will be with me throughout the op. LaFleur—" He stopped. "Where is Soul? With the null room so easy to break out of, Soul is the only one strong enough to contain LaFleur."

I said, "She disappeared when Jane Yellowrock never called us back about the Mercy Blade to try and cure Margot."

FireWind cursed and studied Rick before shifting his yellow eyes to me. "Ingram, are you willing to drive your truck?"

I nodded.

"Is the truck bed empty?"

"Yes," I said, confused.

"Any extra gear that won't fit in the unit's van will be transported in Ingram's vehicle, along with the silver cage."

I blinked. *The silver cage?* Rick's *cage?*

"Kent," he continued, "shackle Loriann Ethier. Since Soul is AWOL, she and Rick will ride with me."

"You're going to let Rick be there?" T. Laine said, frowning, her eyes narrowed in disagreement. "Close to Jason and the demon?"

"Loriann broke out of the null room. Do you really think it will hold a were-leopard?" FireWind asked."If he's with us and in a silver cage, Occam can shoot him in the leg with silver to stop a shape-change." FireWind looked at Occam. "Do not let him free of the cage. No matter what." Occam dropped his chin in agreement.

Feeling numb, I went to my cubicle and gathered my weapons. In my gobag I secreted extra magazines, some marked silver-lead, the others loaded with standard ammo. In a plastic zippered bag I placed the bits of bloody tissue. My secrets. In my truck was a shotgun and a plant in a clay pot—the sprig of the vampire tree.

Occam stopped at my cubicle. "Nell, sugar," he said softly, "okay if I ride with you?"

"Fine by me, but you need to know that I'll likely be doing some B and E this afternoon." B and E meant breaking and entering and that statement made Occam pause.

After an uncomfortable length of time, he said, "You can take care of yourself, I know that. But . . . I'm thinking you might need backup if you're breaking the law."

I met his eyes, glowing a soft golden brown with his cat. "Oh. Well. In that case, I'd like you to ride with me, very much."

We detoured to Rick's house and found the new, hidden key. I didn't have to resort to the threatened B and E and shatter a windowpane to get in. Unfortunately, I knew my actions were going straight to JoJo at HQ from Rick's security cameras. All I could hope was that my illegal entry and theft would be forgiven. Or maybe the footage would disappear.

Later than we wanted, we cruised in to a prearranged address on Roseberry Road, at a small sign that said, FOR SALE. BANK OWNED. I motored down the drive, winding in until my C10 was deep in the scrub, well hidden from the street. At the back, there was a house, overgrown, ramshackle, windows and doorway boarded over. I got out, into the stifling heat, to overhear FireWind say to T. Laine, "We have the bank's permission to use the property. Were you able to get *any* of the local witches to assist us with a working here?"

"No. They haven't responded to texts, e-mails, voice mails, police stopping by with requests for help, or notes tacked to their front doors. They've gone to ground. I'm the only witchy woman on-site unless Loriann becomes suddenly trustworthy. And that's not going to happen, so why don't you tell me why she's *really* here, and not some silly hostage-negotiation tale."

FireWind glanced at the van. The side sliding door was open and Loriann was sitting on the bench seat, her legs dangling in the sunlight. Loriann was wearing a green dress with bright blotches of purple and red on it. Her hands were bound in front of her with dozens of thin twisted strands of silver wire. Among the strands were traces blood.

"The reason," FireWind said crisply, "is that I was hoping to turn her over to the local coven until Jason is taken down. Loriann broke the lock on the null room. Jason destroyed the outer door. We can't secure her in HQ. Jones will be alone handling comms and I don't want her to have to step away from comms to shoot a prisoner during an interagency op."

T. Laine blew out a breath. "Yeah. There is that. And we can't leave Rick there for the same reason. Here you can shoot his legs full of silver if he starts to shift."

"Precisely."

I got out my gear. Per FireWind's orders, I was going on a short hike, close to the house where Jason Ethier and a group of invading vampires laired. In the back of the C10, Occam snapped a blue tarp over Rick's empty silvered cage. I made sure the shade covered my little vampire plant. It was cute, and if the tree didn't eat puppies and try to take over the world, I'd market it.

It was still daylight, hours before the local vampires would show up at the address to attack the invading vampires. More unmarked cars and a few Highway Patrol cars drove into the deep, abandoned lot. A big SWAT vehicle, the shape of a bread truck, but heavier, bounced up the rutted drive. The bigwigs were gathering for the operation.

All across Knoxville and neighboring counties, Homeland Security and FEMA were on alert. The governor's office was flying in an observer. The public had been notified that an unspecified threat had been detected and citizens were being asked to stay off the streets.

I thought about Mud. About my family. About leaving Mud with Esther. I'd had no other sensible choice. I'd just left my sisters there, together, protected by Jedidiah as best he could.

If there was a major earthquake, no place in Knoxville except the heart of Soulwood would be safer than a compound full of hillbillies, supplies, and weapons.

I tossed my faded pink blanket over my shoulder and tied the laces of my field boots. I was going to read the land and see what I could see. And my cat-man was going with me. "That's close enough, Nell, sugar."

I stopped, the weeds up to my knees, beggar-lice all over my jeans, along with a few ticks. Beggar-lice were traveling seeds, hitching a ride on any convenient cloth or pelt or fur. I flicked them and the bloodsuckers away. "They're vampires, cat-boy. With the exception of Godfrey, who would have to slather sunscreen all over himself to step outside, they're asleep."

"The witch might be awake. Demons never sleep."

"Sure they do," I said, before I thought.

"And you know that how?"

Oops. I didn't answer, suddenly concentrating on a particularly insolent little tick who seemed to like denim. "I love every creature on God's earth, except ticks and roaches," I said. "Why can't ticks drain roaches and roaches eat ticks? That would be perfect, don't you think?"

Occam's voice dropped, all silky and dangerous. "Did you read the land alone? Go looking for a demon? *Alone?*"

"I was on Soulwood. I was safe." But even I could hear the defiance in my voice.

"When I'm hunting on Soulwood, you're there to protect me," Occam said. "I'm not trying to protect the *little woman.* I'm watching my partner's back, not trying to keep you from doing your job. When an evil is in the land and you read the land, you need backup."

Stubbornness welled up in me, not wanting to give in so easily, but . . . but, Occam wasn't talking about being dominant over me. He was talking about being my equal, about *mutual* dependence. Feeling guilty, I said, "Yes. I did it alone." I scowled up at him. "I promise not to do it again." Occam raised his mismatched eyebrows in disbelief. I turned away and stomped off through the brush. It grew thick and green right up to the road, which I crossed to trees on the far side. The shade was deep here and the soil loamy enough for there to be a springhead nearby. I was on the same side of the road as the house where Jason was supposed to be, assuming he was still with the vampires. "Stupid man," I grumbled.

"Say again, Ingram?" he said to my back, a hint of laughter in his voice. *Ingram.* Not *Nell, sugar.* He had heard me perfectly with his cat hearing.

I positioned the pink blanket on the slightly damp soil and sat on it. Touched a single fingertip to the ground, glanced once at Occam, and dropped deep and fast, like plunging a knife blade into the dirt. I was mad at my partner but still trusted him to have my back.

I didn't look for the demon or the circle, but I knew they were both there. I could feel the filth in the earth at the livestock center, like used motor oil mixed with clotted blood and grains of rotted wood and rat feces. It was a nauseating sensation and I stayed away.

Closer to me, partially overwhelmed by the sensation of the demon, maybe three hundred feet ahead, I felt . . . maggots. Thousands and thousands of maggots. They were all over the property but mostly on the left side of the house, in the basement. Avoiding the *hedges*, using the smallest hint of power, I eased my attention up through the gravel and the concrete of the slab foundation, trying to see how many vampires there were. I couldn't get close enough, but I hesitated, feeling something familiar. I pressed up just a bit. And touched wood in the walls. Local wood. The house had been built with local wood and I could feel through it, into the house. And I felt maggots. True-dead vampires. Undead vampires. Vamps in cages. Blood. Lots of blood. Rotting flesh.

Gagging, I heaved my mind away from the house. Accidently dragged myself through a mound of freshly turned earth. More rotting flesh. Human. I yanked away from the fresh graves. Seven of them. I wrenched myself out of the land and wriggled my cell from my pocket with shaking fingers. Called JoJo.

She answered with, "Ingram. Where are you? You and Occam aren't with the others."

"Looking for Jason. How many humans lived at the lair?"

"Five family members and two full-time help. The estate is forty acres of horse pasture and timber. The Blounts are a quiet, unassuming millionaire family who made their fortune in railroads and coal."

"Were."

"Huh? Were what?"

I said, "I just found seven graves."

"Drink some water, Nell, sugar. You don't breathe enough when you're underground, and you might not know it, but you ain't exactly yourself for a while after you read the earth."

"What kinda 'not myself'?"

He put a bottle of water in my hand and bent over me as if to speak quietly. Instead I felt him clip the leaves in my hairline. No need to advertise I wasn't human to the local LEOs.

Chagrined, I said, "Oh. The leafy kind."

Occam chuckled quietly, as he worked to slice through a vine on my thumb. "And the grouchy kind. And the bossy kind."

"If I was a man, it would be called taking charge or alpha male or something else good."

Occam tossed my leaves to the ground and squatted down beside me, his throat exposed in what might look like submission, but I knew better. His eyes were laughing. "You trying to lecture me about women's rights and misogyny, sugar?"

"No. I'm trying to say being bossy or an alpha isn't a problem if I'm right. I needed to be on that side of the road to read the house properly."

"Why?"

"'Cause tar tastes bad." I drank down the water, crushing the bottle.

His eyebrows went up again, his burned one a little lower than the other. "Oh. I didn't know that. And maybe I should have."

"Yeah. Let's go find Rick and tell him."

"You're in charge."

"Now you'un jist messin' with me."

"Pretty much," he agreed.

Rick wasn't surprised when Occam and I showed up, all hot and sweaty and covered in beggar-lice. I told him about the vamps and the graves. The sheriff's department had shown up and launched an RVAC, a remote-viewing aircraft, one with advanced cameras and sensors, and had seen the turned earth. They had also skimmed around the house and acquired infrared images through all the windows, giving them a head count of the living humans—fifteen. He and FireWind put their heads together, muttering, and wandered away, toward a group in front of the abandoned house.

The brass were standing around a makeshift table covered with house plans (which were on file with the county) and the security system (which had been provided by the company once a warrant had been delivered). They included the sheriff, the chief of the Highway Patrol, a TBI investigatory agent wearing suit pants and a jacket, and six SWAT team members in camo and laden with gear, most of it lethal. All of them were sweating in the heat.

The SWAT captain—Gonzales—was former military and opened the discussion with the words, "Listen up, people." He held up four fingers. "Ends, ways, means, risk. Strategy is like a three-legged stool, with ends, ways, and means balancing a plane of varying degrees of risk. We create strategy based on known variables and face risk depending on how we use our resources and what the enemy does. We have weapons, we have tools, we have floor plans, we have personnel. What we will *not* have is military backup before sundown. This is on us. Gather around!"

I yawned and ate an apple. SWAT and local LEO brass discussed ingress and egress and potential barriers and the proper times and places to use flashbangs, which were the perfect weapon against vampires, affecting their light-sensitive eyes and their better-than-human hearing. A well-timed flashbang was enough to knock an ordinary vamp on his butt for several minutes.

They also covered strategic choices such as bait and bleed, which would have meant letting Ming's people attack and the vamps fight it out among themselves. This would have let the demon loose and maybe killed Rick. They decided to keep the local vamps out of the picture and go in before sunset, which was a good thing, as I'd have gotten myself fired warning Yummy. To no one's surprise they decided on a blitzkrieg offensive with SWAT as the sole offensive wave.

Despite the fact that this was a paranormal crime scene, SWAT determined that PsyLED wouldn't be going in until the scene was contained and the house was cleared, because the hallways were too narrow and the chance of getting in the way of people with lethal weapons was too great. I listened long enough before I shouted, "What about sleep spells?"

The SWAT captain looked my way and saw a skinny female in jeans and a T-shirt, with a pink blanket over her shoulder. He grinned, one of the patronizing expressions a big man sometimes gives a woman who he perceives as a lesser being.

I didn't like his grin at all, and maybe I was feeling a little too prickly, but I scowled at him and said, "Kent, how many combatants did you take down last week with one spoken *wyrd*?"

T. Laine said, "I think it was twelve." That got Gonzales' attention. The captain looked from me to T. Laine and back, his grin fading.

"Magic keeps our side from getting hurt," I said. "You walk into a magically protected site with mundane weapons and you may not come out again."

T. Laine moved through the crowd, saying, "I'm Kent, a PsyLED witch. My intel says the vamps lairing in the basement have at least one very powerful sorcerer with magical protections and one daywalking vamp with superior mesmeric capability. *Wyrd* workings like the *sleep* spell are not the only offensive or defensive weapons in my arsenal."

Gonzales asked, "How long for my men to develop proper techniques with your arsenal?"

"Tell me, Cap," T. Laine said, halting in front of the group. "You go to an operation and turn your weapons over to someone with less training and experience?" Gonzales scowled. "I didn't think so. I'm a witch. I'm not giving you my weapons."

I glanced at Rick and FireWind, their faces carefully blank, observing.

"Your whole, entire plan," she said, "is mundane weapons against paras. You want a dynamic entry, rush in, fire a few silver rounds, round up everybody, and toss Jason to us. You have no contingencies except Unit Eighteen to deal with paranormal defenses and combatants. What if there are magical workings protecting the entry to the basement? What if they're prepared to repel boarders with any and all magical means? Godfrey de Bullion is a daywalker capable of clouding human minds. What happens if he stops your men cold? You guys ready to be munched on? What if the demon gets free ahead of schedule?"

Every eye was on T. Laine. Her head was back, shoulders back, her nearly black hair catching the light. "FireWind? You got something to say? You just came from an interagency confab to discuss exactly these types of problems."

The SAC East moved smoothly to the front of the group. "SWAT-Knox are top-notch against humans. But our evaluation suggests there's a blind spot in your training. All your previous military experience was in the Middle East, where there are very few witches due to ethnic cleansing of anyone with the trait." FireWind stopped about ten feet out from the SWAT team, his business casual clothes contrasting with the single long braid down his back, and with the military-style uniforms on the SWAT team. "All your paramilitary training since has been directed toward human targets and human situations. Here you have a mixture of human and para and you need Kent and the rest of us to meet your objectives."

"So what's *your* strategy?" Gonzales asked.

"Limited incursion from front and back doors. Take it slow. Clear the humans in the upper part of the house before entering the basement. Let Kent detect any magical defenses. Take it slow. We have the time."

Gonzales asked, "Former military?"

"In another lifetime." That was code for classified.

Occam hummed under his breath, then said, "New boss man's got him some style."

"Listen to FireWind and Kent," Margot said, loud enough to be heard across the grassy clearing. "Special Agent Margot Racer, FBI," she said, still speaking loud. Margot sauntered to, and then past, Rick. Margot was wearing long sleeves in the heat, covering up her flesh wound, the one that might turn her into a wereleopard. She was trailed by four feebs, one of them my cousin.

Surprise slapped through me. I hadn't seen Chadworth Sanders Hamilton, my third cousin from the townie side of the family, since before I was a tree. He looked different, but I didn't have time to figure out how exactly because Gonzales was staring at Margot as she walked into the mix of the big boys. They stepped back. The . . . maybe I'd call it the "balance of power" shifted fast and hard. I had to wonder who Margot Racer really was in FBI lore.

Again drawing the attention of the group, T. Laine stepped up with Rick, Margot, and FireWind, the four making a neat row of authority. "Considering your plans and the flashbangs, I suggest we add three offensive weapons. A unidirectional null spell, to proactively knock out magical defenses and any *wyrd* spells he might throw, a *sleep* spell to put any humans to sleep, and, if we have to retreat for any reason, I have one omnidirectional spell in a grenade-shaped device that makes sentient beings dizzy in a radius of twenty feet from point of impact."

"Do they work?" Gonzales asked our witch.

T. Laine shook her head, not saying no, but saying with body language that he was stupid. She put her fists on her hips and looked up a good twelve inches into the man's face. "Your weapons ever jam, bubba? Equipment ever malfunction?"

Bubba, aka Gonzales, grinned, and his shoulders dropped, tension easing. "From time to time. It's a pain in the ass."

Occam snorted under his breath and repeated, "Bubba."

"My weapons are just as likely as yours to fail when I need them the most. That's why PsyLED Unit Eighteen has a wide variety of both mundane and magical weapons at our disposal. Against mixed paranormal and human enemy combatants, a combination of weapons and techniques is your best shot."

"What about the dizzy weapon?" Bubba asked. "Omnidirectional means it hits us too, right?"

"Yes, if you're stupid enough to detonate it while inside the twenty-foot radius. And it works on dolphins, whales, dogs, pigs, humans, witches, and vampires. And if you ask really nice, the local coven might make you a few. For a price."

"It always comes down to money with women," a voice called out. The group laughed.

T. Laine said, "No one's paying me one silver dime extra to back up your sorry asses, though, are they?" That shut them up for just long enough for FireWind to step forward and introduce himself. Once again the dynamics of the group changed, bringing the meeting down to bureaucratic, political mode and police protocols.

By the time sunset was ninety minutes away, and the new, dark moon was beginning to drop over the horizon, the plan of attack was all worked out, with T. Laine joining SWAT in the first wave. Occam, Racer, and the feds were in the second offensive wave. The RVAC had done another flyover, a sniper in the trees reported no movement, and we needed to hit the place before the vamps died to power the demon spell. I made a bathroom break in the trees and picked another tick off of me. Nasty little buggers.

I ate another apple and geared up, adjusted my comms unit, and signed onto the para freq, utilized in this multiagency operation. I also untied my field boots. For me and the job I had in the offensive, shoes would be in the way.

The first wave of the assault team moved out on foot, into position.

Roseberry Road had been barricaded against all traffic. The nearest neighbors had been evacuated.

Occam and I got into my truck and downed bottles of water. The air-conditioning was like a blessing from heaven, not that I expected much of those these days. When the leaders' vehicles moved out, we followed. Rick and Loriann were with FireWind, in the car ahead of us. A few clouds on the horizon were sunset golden.

Over the comms channel there was little chatter. I glanced at my gas gauge and wished I had filled up. Occam said into my earbud, "I have the vest cams live. Thanks, Jones."

He held his tablet to me, and I tried to see on the screen, which was divided into small squares, one for each camera. I made out a man's hand, part of an assault rifle, someone's back, and what had to be T. Laine's hand holding the null charm. It was a copper-colored ink pen, but the ink in the chamber was antimagic.

The words blasted in my ear. "Gogogogogogogo!"

I revved the truck and smashed the pedal to the floor. Along with the others who would be holding the perimeter, I raced down the road and into the Blounts' yard, adding my C10 to the row of vehicles surrounding the property. Gonzales and his team were already inside.

NINETEEN

I leaped from the truck, grabbing my blanket and the pot of Soulwood soil with the sprig of the vampire tree. Heard shouting over the para freq. Heard the null pen go off. Felt it through my feet. I dropped to the ground behind the truck, half on the blanket, and touched a single finger to the earth. My other fingers were in the clay pot. Rick walked toward me and leaped to the truck bed. He crawled inside his cage and slammed the door, clearly fearing the surge of magic. We were running about six minutes late and the moon was dropping below the horizon as dusk settled on the land. The curse/summoning was waking.

Through the ground, I still felt the tidal forces of the new moon, its glow turned away from the earth. I felt maggots wriggling. I felt the power of the smoky fist, of B.K.L., in the stockyard. And I felt Loriann step onto the lawn. Her magic shot out like an electric charge, a *wyrd* that broke her shackles, sending them to the ground, along with splatters of her blood.

Blood on the earth. She was mine. It would be so easy.

But she didn't rush for the house and her brother. She walked to us. I heard the soft sound of Occam drawing his weapon. He whispered, "Jones. You seeing this?"

"Copy," JoJo said into my earbud. "Ethier is moving. Help is on the way. Hold tight." In the cage, Rick began gasping with pain. He mewled like a small child or a lost kitten. I felt Occam's cat stir and reached for him. I sent as much of Soulwood as I could to them, but my land wanted blood and violence; calm wasn't abundant.

In the field behind the stockyard, the fist began to open, drawing power from the deeps of the earth, hot and glowing.

Magma. Soulwood turned its attention to the new energies, intrigued. From deep and deep in the earth, the somnolent power that resided, motionless and waiting, stirred. If it woke, there would be earthquakes. Flooding. Destruction. If the demon got free as Jason died, there would be earthquakes, flooding, and destruction. Those six minutes might have cost us everything.

Loriann stopped beside the bed of the truck. I could feel Occam as he moved to block her access to the back of the truck, to Rick's cage, and to me. Gunfire rattled from inside the house and through our comms. Blood splattered on the walls and concrete floor. I felt it. Soulwood snapped its attention to the blood. *Hungry.*

Bloodlust, that simmering need, woke. And grew. I was tied to the land. I began to retreat, but the smell/feel/sense of the blood in the house was growing. Bloodlust reached toward it.

Occam ordered, "Get back. Get on your knees."

"Keep her talking," JoJo said.

Loriann said to Occam, "You're not gonna shoot an unarmed woman, so *listen* to me." I felt the power in the word *listen.* She had used a *wyrd* on him, forcing his compliance. "They'll kill Jason. They won't care. He's just another blood junkie to them."

I pressed on my bloodlust, forcing it down, wrapping it tight. I drew away from the blood and the need and concentrated on Loriann's voice. "If *you* go in, if *Rick* goes in, they'll be careful. You can keep Jason alive. Put the gun away. We're just talking."

JoJo cursed. "Sending help, Ingram. Hang on, Occam."

"Not interested in going up against SWAT," Occam said, sounding marginally himself. There was a soft clatter on the tongue of the truck. "See that? That's Bubba killing a bloodservant. Just broke his neck. Snap." I figured Occam was holding the assault rifle, trained on Loriann, and had placed his tablet on the truck, but I didn't risk a look, my attention on the house and the fight, my bloodlust snared by the violence.

"I can unbind the spell on Rick," she bargained, her words soothing. "As soon as Jason is safe. But you have to let him save my brother first."

"And we should believe you? On anything?" Occam said,

still fighting her attraction. His words echoed in my earbud. JoJo was recording all this.

Her tone waffling between desperation and threats, Lori-ann said, "He's being forced through a shift right now, even in the cage. You know how that feels, don't you, the need to shift while trapped in silver. You have to help Rick and he has to save my brother. Rick has no choice."

I wanted to hit her. Or drain her.

My fist clenched in the pot of soil, my fingers closing on dirt and the sprig of vampire tree. Four fingertips of my other hand were touching the soil beneath me. The land had tasted her blood. I heaved back and back on the bloodlust. It turned to me. And then to Loriann, whose wrists were bleeding. Small splatters fell to the earth near me. Eyes closed, I knew blood. I could feel each drop, could hear them pass through the air and hit the soil, even over the cacophony of the comms. Could taste them through the ground. Blood inside the house. Blood near me. Soulwood reached for the blood, wanting.

Over comms came the sound of screaming. Someone was hurt. One of ours. More blood fell.

The feel of magic rose through the earth, a wave of dark power. Jason had set off a magical attack. Something prear-ranged. A *wyrd* spell. Others of our crew began to scream. T. Laine was shouting in Latin. It was her *sleep* spell.

"Rick's shifting. He's in pain," Loriann said, cajoling. "Let Rick loose and he'll finish the shift and the pain will go away."

"And then he'll trot off and save your worthless piece-of-crap brother," Occam growled, "thanks to your blood magic."

"Hurry," I whispered into my mic to JoJo, eyes tight against the growing bloodlust.

"Once Jason is free," Loriann said, "I'll *break* the spell in Rick's tattoo. I put in a backdoor. I can do it."

"Don't believe you," Occam snarled, sounding too much like his cat.

Through the earth, I felt someone coming closer, as subtle and graceful as a cat. *FireWind. Notified by JoJo.*

"Listen to me," Loriann growled, almost sounding cat her-self, furious, attacking. "It's not too late. I can help Rick get in and back out."

Over the earbuds, on the para freq, I heard Gonzales say,

"What the hell is that? Open fire!" His words were drowned out by weapons fire.

"Kill it!" someone else shouted.

T. Laine screamed to be heard over the firing, "No! It isn't real. It's just a magic construct! Stop firing! Stop! Cease fire! Cease fire!"

Someone else screamed. Female. Vampire. The ululation of true-death.

"Too bad. I gave you a choice," Loriann said.

Magic slammed into me. Ripped thorugh flesh and bone. Occam screamed, a cat cry of rage. Rick screamed. I grunted as my muscles gave way. I slid flat to the ground, biting my tongue, blood and spit spattering as my face landed on the dirt. I'd have been bruised if I had been standing. Occam growled. Loriann had somehow coerced him into a shape-shift. A hard, brutal, fast change. Rick screamed again. I couldn't get my body to move, much less stand and fight.

Metal clanged. Loriann had opened Rick's cage door. Leaves erupted from the ground in the spots of my blood. In the spots of Loriann's blood as the earth responded. Tendrils of fresh vines reached for my bare skin. My bloodlust reached for Loriann. I hauled back on it, struggling to not take her for the land. Because what if she really *could* unbind Rick? I forced open my eyes. Saw Loriann, her back to me.

Numb, clumsy, I pushed away from the earth. Stood. Grabbed Loriann, my fingers on her bloody wrist. Hunger flooded through me.

Rick, in black cat form, and Occam's spotted cat lunged past us, toward the house. Grindylows raced in from somewhere, following. Claws out. I was too late.

Pulling on Soulwood's strength, I wrenched Loriann's fingers back and straight-armed her to her knees. "I felt magic," I said. "That was a spell! You're manipulating the tat spells on Rick. Right now."

Loriann laughed.

"She's using the tat binding," I said into my mic. But it was covered in my blood and I didn't know how clearly JoJo would hear. "She sent Occam and Rick to save Jason. Two grindys are after them." I could feel the magic coursing through her, following Rick.

FireWind finally arrived, silent. He clubbed Loriann to the ground, a single, vicious fist to the head. It knocked her unconscious. He strapped the silver blood-cuffs back on Loriann's wrists. With hands that were far stronger than a human's, he untwisted the wire of a second, similar cuff and wrapped it around her head. Her *wyrd* magic stopped. Like a clean slice through the air. But Rick and Occam were already inside.

FireWind was cold and brutal, his expression blank ferocity. "Can you call them back?" he asked me.

"I can try." I dropped down and curled my legs onto the blanket. "But you might have to cut me free. Use steel." FireWind ordered someone to watch Loriann Ethier and he knelt beside me.

I dug in the gobag, fingers finding the broken piece of black stone from the time of Rick's original inking. Stolen from Rick's house in my B and E. I had no idea why he kept it. I didn't care. It was part of the spell that had bound him. I had stolen it to use in a last ditch effort that might help him. I dropped it in my lap. Put a fingertip on the earth. Shoved my hand into the pot of Soulwood.

I reached for my land. And for Rick. There was strange power in the ground. A swirling miasma so thick it was like heavy oil and clotted blood. Light and dark energies, swirling, struggling. The fist was uncoiling, its dark energies anathema to the life of the earth. The fist shoved up through the stockyard ground, reaching for freedom it could only gain as the dark of the moon fell below the horizon. Magma boiled behind the fist, full of power.

The massive sentient sleeping presence beneath the earth, the soul of the land, stirred. The earth trembled. Demon, Soulwood, and the spirit of the earth were about collide. This would be very bad.

Closer to me, magics clouded the air and beat against the surface of the ground, contained but powerful. There was blood everywhere. I called to Soulwood and through my land I called to Occam. My spotted cat answered with a growl, always human enough to know me. I called to Rick. And . . . there. There he was. I found him.

His magic was hot and cold and prickly and furred. Burning bright. He was different from the last time I touched his

power. He was more . . . more were-creature. He *was* magic.
He *was* power. Flaring, intense. He was an alpha, one who
carried magic in every cell of his body. Yet that magic was
constrained, packed down, restricted. Unfocused. Inward
turned. Trapped.

His magic was trapped.

As if in a net.

The tattoos were the trap I sensed, the magics holding him
back.

"Ethier!" FireWind coming to his feet. Shouting. Blood in
the house. Gunfire. The sound of a body falling and the drum-
ming of running feet. Loriann getting away.

I reached out. Soulwood reached out. Rootlets and leaves
burst from the wood in the walls of the house. I placed Soulwood over the net that constrained Rick's power. Soaked Soulwood into the fibers of the spell that controlled him. It burned.
The cold burning of witch magic, wrapped around and into the
hotter magic of the wereleopard. Geometry and mathematics
in every tiny, microscopic witch strand. Soulwood stretched
and sprouted, like rootlets seeking water. And grew into the
witch magic . . .

The strands were . . . the tiny punctures that once punched
ink and magic into his skin. The pigments of the tattoo. And
the vampire blood. *There.* That frozen, clotted bit of magic.
Soulwood found the blood and took it. Broke it down. Whisked
it away and into the earth. Ate it. And more foreign blood
there. Cat blood. Easy to use, a useful sacrifice for the land.
And . . . Jason's blood.

Rick screamed. Occam screamed. Silver. Silver was everywhere. Silver and blood and burning. My magic was ripped
away from the tattoos.

Occam's leopard took him over, an emotional reaction so
fast, so full of fear, Soulwood couldn't follow. It was *fear-flee-
death-flame-burn-run-death* . . .

I reached through Rick's eyes. Saw the cats had been
caught in a silver mesh trap, one with spines that shoved
through their pelts and into their flesh. Jason had set a magical
and physical trap to capture Rick. He had instead caught both
cats. And both grindys.

Black cat blood. Spotted cat blood. Both of them magic.

Two grindylows. Surely magic too. Their blood on the magical cuffs Jason wore.

The new moon below the horizon.

The spell in the earth.

The ground beneath me quivered. Shook.

Earthquake.

The fist in the circle, in the stockyard, beat against the power that had imprisoned it in the dark eons ago.

Light. Might. Purpose. Some unimaginable power holding it trapped.

The fist beat that cage. Cracks began to form at the point of impact. The witch circle fed power to the fist's battering. My mind was open and aware of everything the magic touched, everything and everyone.

Rick screamed. His cat in agony. The fist hardened. Solidified by the power in Rick's cat blood. Trapped in Jason's spell. The silver net stealing Rick's life. The fist hit the boundary of the power holding it in stasis.

It burst free. The earth at the circle erupted, rock and dirt flying into the air. The fist opened into the evening air. B'KuL's open hand, reaching for the curse, reaching for the blood that powered the spell.

Jason summoned B'KuL, the sound of the name vibrating through the land. I felt blood flow. The blood sorcerer had cut the throat of a waking vampire. *Calling.*

Dark power blasting, the open hand of B'KuL flew through the night. Into . . . into the house where T. Laine and SWAT were. Where Occam was. Where Rick was. Where Jason was.

The hand of power wrapped itself around Jason. Jason's spell reached for Rick.

I might kill my boss. My friend. But—

I concentrated on the broken black stone. And I shoved the entire might of Soulwood through the stone into Rick's tattoos. Shredding the magic in the ink. The magic that held him, bound him, used him. The magic that tied him to Jason and, through the blood witch, to the demon. And maybe tied all the magic to Rick's soul. The broken chunk of black marble shattered.

Rick's were-magics sizzled. Exploded. Magic like a flash-bang. But bigger. Hotter. The magical mesh constraining

Rick's tattoo magic erupted. I yanked Soulwood from him. Freeing Rick from the tattoo magic. And from Soulwood. Rick tore himself from the tatters of the old spell that had trapped and tortured him.

His power burst free, burning through the last strands of the tattoo magic. But he was still trapped in a silver net with a raging, panicked Occam-cat and grindys. He opened his mouth and I thought he said my name.

Soulwood and I shoved a single vine of our might against one tiny spot on the silver net.

I thought of life. Of the roots of trees that broke apart boulders. My land, my tree, forced a hole through the silver net that held the cats and grindys, and attacked it from within. Growing, wrenching, ripping the silver needles from the cats' flesh. Tearing into the spell set within it. Cleaving the spell. It fell into shavings and strips and strands of silver that tinkled to the concrete beneath the cats. I ripped Soulwood away.

The demon needed a sacrifice to push more of his power to the surface. B'KuL's hand curled around the blood witch, evaluating the life and years and time in the cells of his summoner. Jason made a gurgling sound. "Your sacrifice is there. Take his years," he pointed at Rick.

Rick and Occam were free, but disoriented. Weak. The cats were staggering away from the silver wire, crawling to the doorway behind them. The grindys rode the cats' backs, holding on, cat fur in their cute little hands. The cats pushed through the vines waving in the air and headed for an exit.

B'KuL dropped his host to the floor, into a springy mass of leaves. But instead of reaching for the cats, the demon shifted his attention from Jason to the explosion of power that was Soulwood. I yanked myself away. But the fist of demon power opened and reached for my land, running its metaphysical fingers through the energies of life, through the leaves filling the basement, as if entranced.

I rolled away. Or tried to. I opened my eyes. Saw that the roots along Roseberry Road had grown up and trapped my feet. "Cut me!" I shouted. "Cut me free!"

The steel blade slashed through the roots anchoring my feet to the land. But my arm was rooted to the pot of Soulwood soil. The vampire tree had grown a cage around me. Trapping me to itself.

"Stupid tree! Fine. I'll use you. Cut my feet free!"

"I'm trying," FireWind snarled. He hacked through the roots tying me to the ground. His single black braid whipped back and forth with his effort. The pressure fell away. My feet were unshackled.

I thrust upright, grabbed my gobag, and raced to the house. Fell against the wall, to the ground, cracking the pot and dumping the soil and the sprig of the vampire tree against the house. It had grown roots, a twisted mass of them. I landed on the gobag. From my pockets I yanked the baggie with the smear of Jason's blood and tore through it with my teeth. Dumped it onto the soil of Soulwood and onto the vampire tree.

"This one," I said to the tree. "Stop him. He's yours."

The roots sent me an image of the Green Knight. Leafy armor. Pale green horse. It tunneled through the ground. Growing faster than was possible except for the power that was Soulwood. I fed my land to the vampire tree. It was eager. It was hungry. So was my land. *Blood.* It wanted a sacrifice.

So did the demon. But the earth power of Soulwood slipped through his clawed fingers.

The boy who called the dark power cut a still-sleeping vampire. Jason whispered, "Not enough. Not enough. I need more." The vampire woke, screamed in terror, and bled. The dark fist wrapped around the vampire and sucked the undeath from him. The vamp disintegrated into ash.

SWAT retreated from the dark power and T. Laine threw up a *hedge of thorns* to protect them.

B'KuL's hand whipped back to Jason. Its forefinger sliced the skin of Jason's chest. Reached inside. Jason made a strange sound, strangled, shocked, full of terror. The demon was attacking him. Possessing him. The bargain Jason had planned to betray was instead folding back onto him, devouring him.

And I had given that same boy to the Green Knight. I followed the tree through the earth and up through the openings in the walls made by the local flora as it burst into leaf. Soulwood and the vampire tree unfurled; vines and thorns and reaching tendrils wrapped themselves around the blood witch. The tree extruded thorns and jammed them inside him. Blood splattered. Feeding the earth. I had a momentary fear that the demon would turn on the tree, but it seemed that the fist of B'KuL had no frame of reference for the vampire tree that was stealing its prey. The demon didn't even notice.

Jason writhed in agony. But the tree wanted more, cutting into the life and undeath of humans and vampires in cages, even as it claimed the blood witch. I hauled the tree back from the cages. Consumed with its own needs, its own bloodlust, it almost refused my call to save the prisoners.

The sun set. The power of the curse grew.

Through the vines and leaves and thorns I felt/saw/tasted/ *knew* the energies of the blood sorcerer. And Loriann, racing into the fight to save her brother.

Elsewhere, the blood and the power of the vampires were being spilled in the house. The ones in cages, the Green Knight and I ignored. The ones free and barricaded in the back of the room, those the tree and I went after. Roots and thorns grew into them. Living stakes. The vampires awoke and fought. But the tree, sentient and eager, would not be stopped. *Taking a sacrifice. Just like the demon did,* I thought.

From belowground, local vines pushed through cracks in the concrete slab foundation and into the walls, the wood once grown on nearby land. The wood in the walls, awakened by my blood, *bloomed*. Put out roots. Growing. They twined with the vampire tree. Roots and vines and thorns. Jason screamed in unearthly agony. Dying.

Using the vampire blood I *fed the earth.*

Loriann threw herself at the body of her brother, held in the demon's fist, trying to save him. The fist and the tree both accepted her as a willing sacrifice. She was dead before she could scream. Her ashes scattered across Jason. Ashes and dust clogged the air; bits of dissolving vampire clothing, shoes, hair, and desiccated flesh fell and were devoured by the roots that broke up the concrete slab foundation. The tree tore apart the house and the vampires and their humans. Soulwood took its due, and sucked the remains into the earth. Ashes to ashes, dust to dust.

Jason laughed, the sound all wrong. "I did it. It's all mine."

A different voice shivered through the ground and into the house. "I accept the bargain." The power of the demon began to unfurl within Jason. The vampires in the cages began to bleed and to scream as the bargain was sealed.

My roots found the most powerful of the vampires and slammed thorns into him like wooden blades. Wood like stakes. The vampire tree drank his blood. I had never met Godfrey. I had seen him twice, as he tore out the throat of a store clerk and later killed a young boy. But he wanted to rule this hunting territory, drink down its people, destroy the life in the land. No one ruled here but Soulwood. I gave Godfrey to the tree. The Green Knight and I reached to the vampires still alive in cages and twined around the bars. Ripped them apart. The freed vampires raced away. Terrified of the living wood. The vampire tree was gaining strength. I didn't care. Because Soulwood drank too, drank down the sacrifices that gave it power. Bloodlust was slowly diminishing.

I looked through the blood and the life and death all around me. Determined that Unit Eighteen and all our humans and cats were safe and free, standing in the perimeter of the yard, keeping Ming's vampires from approaching. Good.

I found the fist inside of Jason, the demon fighting for its power, its freedom, Jason bargaining for his life. I looked back along the track to the circle. The magic was active, open. Clouds of power bloomed into the night behind the stockyard. The demon was rising. The earth shuddered, bounced, roiled like boiling water.

Earthquake.

The circle was open and protected. Any attempt to close it or break it was doomed. But . . . no one had ever tried to close a circle from belowground, using the power of life, the power of the earth. If I could break it before Jason was fully possessed or died . . .

I directed the vampire tree to find the witch circle. The roots tunneled through the earth, seeking the power of the circle. Seeking the dead flesh at the stockyard, so much not yet carted away. The tree and Soulwood found the bodies of the Blounts, buried in the yard, and together, devoured them.

B'KuL shoved through, rising into the night. The stench of sewage and plague and rot filled the air. It rose, an arm, a leathery wing, a brutal, muscled shoulder. I wasn't going to be in time.

The tree roots and Soulwood found the circle in the same instant. They tore into the power structure belowground. The land vibrated. The demon saw the powers tearing into the mathematics of the circle. The fist opened, clawed at the power of Soulwood, but the magics were too dissimilar. The smoky fist caught nothing. It tore into the tree, but the roots were too thick, too many, and they began to siphon off the magics in the circle. And then the magics of the demon. The roots regrew, the Green Knight ripping the demon energies apart, sealing up the earth from below. Life cutting into the darkness and the filth of the demon's passage, disrupting the bargain with Jason.

B'KuL dropped the sorcerer. The fist of B'KuL ripped away and traced its own power signature back to the witch circle. Inside. Fighting the unfamiliar energies, poisoning the roots with death and disease. But Soulwood healed the tree, destroying the death magics of the demon.

B'KuL, threatened on all sides, reached back to Jason, but the sorcerer, drained by sickness and demon magic, his blood a sacrifice to the land, stopped breathing. Too soon for the bargain. Too soon for the demon. Jason's heart stuttered. Stopped.

The vampire tree tore apart the circle from below, from the center out. Trapping the demon in place. B'KuL screamed in fury. Inside the house, Jason's body fell apart. Ashes to ashes.

The somnolent presence deep and deep in the earth rolled over in its sleep, uneasy, as if prodded by a bad dream. The earth shuddered. Foundations across the river valley cracked. Water in rivers and reservoirs rippled deep, where they touched the land. The sleeping soul of the land jolted.

B'KuL thrashed and fought. Trying to pull himself free. Trying to retreat into the earth, to safety.

The new moon was too far below the horizon. The sun had set. The curse had been strongest between the setting of the new moon and the setting of the sun, that sliver of time when everything was open, the sky a bright, wide, sunset expanse. I felt the power of the curse diminish. And then it was gone.

The circle closed over the dark power.

The earth shook and trembled. A single sacrifice would free the half-trapped demon.

A small quake cracked foundations and popped windows. A few dishes shattered.

And even that went still. Silence reigned in the land. The spirit of the earth, that presence in the deep, fell back into its rest. And slept.

All across Knoxville, up into the hills and down into the river valley, the earth was nourished.

Soulwood was satisfied. So were the new, gigantic trees on the Blounts' property. So was every acre and square foot of land I had ever claimed. Trees that had been young now wore the girth of old growth. Where there was pasture, now was young forest; where the land had been spoiled by man, now there was the freshness of life.

More vampires had appeared on the land near the house. Yummy and Ming and Shaddock. Vampires left. Witches came, unknown witches, strangers, but Lainie liked them so I didn't drain them. The land and I rested.

Hours passed. The stars moved through the blackness of the night sky.

In the new forest a mile away, I felt Lainie and four other witches make a new circle in the land. It surrounded and covered the blood-magic circle in the pasture that had become a deep wood. With magic, they sealed off the demon's access. B'KuL would never get his sacrifice. His power remained locked away.

More time passed. The sun rose and circled the sky. The dark of the new moon set.

"There she is," a familiar voice said. "Son of a witch on a switch. She still looks human."

"Damn tree. Damn tree is everywhere." Occam. I smiled.

"Can't burn it. Can't poison it. All you can do is cut it and hope it doesn't kill you." Sam.

Why was Sam here?

"Can you get to her?" Lainie. Worried.

Something furry rubbed against my shoulder and chittered. A grindylow. How . . . odd.

I felt the vines and the roots give way. Felt the tree give me up. Felt my body lifted and held against Occam's chest. He was purring. I wrapped my arms around him and remembered to breathe.

"Got you, Nell, sugar. I got you."

EPILOGUE

I pushed off with my bare toes against the wood decking of my front porch. My silky skirt brushed my calves as I toed the swing slowly back and forth. What with the heat and being a tree and the ways my life had changed, it had been almost a year since I sat in my swing. I had missed it.

The night air blew through the covered porch, cooler since the weather front had come through, a comfortable seventy-something. The temps wouldn't last in summer in Knoxville. They never did. But for now it was pleasant in the aftermath of the slow-moving storm.

Mud and the new dog, Cherry, were staying with Esther and her husband tonight, as she would all three nights of future full moons. Jedidiah would drive her to school when the full moon fell on a weekday, and take her to church services when the full moon fell on weekends. I had refused when Jed first asked me to let Mud stay with them, but I'd changed my mind for several reasons.

The first was that Larry hadn't been seen since the night of the dark of the moon. He had disappeared on the way home from devotionals. There was no sign of foul play except a bloody patch of disturbed earth found near the original trunk of the vampire tree. I figured the tree had gotten hungry and good riddance.

The second reason I relented was that Esther was growing leaves, possibly due to the burst of Green Knight magic. Or possibly because she was pregnant and hormones had caused her to sprout. She needed help, and Esther was still afraid of me and my inhumanness—though that reticence was thawing now, thanks to her leaves. Jed, on the other hand, was having trouble with his wife being nonhuman. I hadn't expected that, but being a churchman ran deep in his blood. I didn't mind Mud helping Esther and keeping an eye on Jed a few days out of the month. I was enjoying the privacy and would enjoy not having to get up as early to drive my sister to school before I went in to work.

The boxes on my porch were blocky shadows, stacked out of the blowing rain, and they would be gone soon. Brother Thad had given me an estimate on the installation and construction that I couldn't say no to, and with the court date for Mud's custody hearing moved up, the porch would be cleared by the end of the coming week. My sister and I would have more than double the air-conditioning I was used to, more than triple my previous solar panels, a bathroom upstairs, remodeling in the old bath, and upgrades here and there, and at a cost I could afford. With a line of credit on my house and land. There was always that.

Brother Thad assured me he wasn't losing money on the deal, but I figured he wasn't making any either.

I was no longer living completely off the grid and my feelings were mixed about joining the twenty-first century.

I toed the swing harder, staring at the full moon dropping into the tops of the trees in a lacy veil of cloud. It was the last night of the full moon, some two weeks after the hellmouth—Tandy's name for the witch circle—had been ripped apart by Soulwood and sealed by the makeshift coven put together by a few of the local coven members and T. Laine. Despite the refusals of the coven leader, Rivera Cornwall, Theresa Anderson-Kentner, Suzanne Richardson-White, and Barbara Traywick Hasebe had responded to T. Laine's plea for help and were now being touted by the local law enforcement and national media as heroes. And they were. T. Laine had kept her name out of the papers and gave all the praise to the local coven.

No one had seen the Blood Tarot deck. If it had been in the house with Jason, it was ashes now. If not, then it would turn up. Black-magic items always turned up.

It had been a busy two weeks, and I had lain low, hiding in the office or at the house. Not that anyone except Unit Eighteen and Ming of Glass associated the sudden growth of trees with me. The rest of the world, from the governor to Gonzales of SWAT to the FBI and the CIA, had been assured that Jason Ethier, an insane blood-witch, had made all the changes. The public had begun to associate the use of magic with old growth forests, and since both Ethier siblings were dead, and the demon had been safely sealed in his prison, all was good.

Except it wasn't.

Unit Eighteen was quietly dealing with the fact that our enemies had been turned into ashes and dust. And that I had done it. Again. Or Soulwood had. Or the Green Knight had. Either way the result was the same. Just like when I destroyed the salamanders.

The debriefing had taken place between Rick, Soul, FireWind, and me. Behind closed doors. With no recording devices. I had told them a lot, but not everything. It wasn't like I had a choice. I had killed people. Or the land had. My superiors accepted that the land was responsible but there was no doubt that the land had only acted because of me. At my behest. That was the term FireWind had used. Behest.

The reports they wrote up were carefully neutral, but they knew more than they reported and they suspected much more than that. Internal Affairs was sniffing around and that had made things tense at the office. With the exception of my work life, I was satisfied.

Yummy had knocked on my door at two a.m. the third night I spent at home, which was a perfectly acceptable time of visitation in vamp terms. Not so much in human terms. But Yummy assured me that this was a ceremonial visit and that to refuse was a gross breach of etiquette. Yummy had brought a gift from the Master of the City of Knoxville. So I had let a vampire into my home while my sister slept upstairs. If the court system ever found out, I might be denied custody, but I was between a rock and a hard place. Yummy was flawlessly polite throughout the visit. So were the blood-servant guards that kept watch on my front porch.

She had stayed in my home for an hour, chatting and drinking tea. I was assured by Yummy that Ming now owed me two boons. The MOC had sent me some very nice, very expensive, loose-leaf oolong called Tieguanyin tea. I was told by Yummy that the tea sold on the market for three thousand dollars per kilo and was named in honor of Guan Yin. Guan Yin was the Buddhist goddess known as the goddess of mercy. The tea was accompanied by a small card inscribed in Ming's own hand, thanking me for the bodies and blood of her enemies. Yummy and the vampires somehow knew that I was responsible for the dead vampires.

Through Yummy, I learned vampire gossip. Lincoln Shaddock had retaken his clan home and hunting lands with a minimum of bloodshed. Or so he had reported to Ming. I interpreted the statement as meaning that he had drank down his enemies and thrown out the drained husks, but I might have been wrong.

Cai had survived as a human, though he was now both dreadfully scarred and particularly powerful.

Ming was upgrading her clan home's security systems, and had discovered cameras in the walls. Alex Younger's backdoor into the vampire's lair had been compromised. Yummy seemed to think I would know all about it, and I managed not to lie in any meaningful way, or in any way she could smell.

It had been strange to have a vampire in my home, especially considering that she and Occam had dated before I joined Unit Eighteen. *Dated* meaning sex and blood. But Yummy assured me that she had no claim on the wereleopard and she begged my forgiveness for trying to "poach your lover on your land," as she put it, when she was injured and bleeding to death. It was a very strange conversation. Even stranger that I liked her.

Occam had been healed in the burst of magic. Not totally, of course, but vastly improved, and while I never did learn why he had been so shy about his scars, he had a full head of hair growing in, his ear had grown back, his smile was no longer twisted, and his fingers were no longer fused. They didn't bend. He still had scars, but as he said, "I don't scare small children on the streets." He looked pretty good to me.

I was different too. I had scarlet hair. Flame bright. My eyes were the deep, vibrant green of emeralds. I had a full line of leaves around my hairline. My fingernails and toenails had turned to wood—polished, beautifully grained wood, and one woman who noticed them at the grocery store wanted to know how I achieved the look. I had to pluck my leaves every morning and sand back my nails at night. I could still pass for human if I worked at it, though I hoped the effects would pass with time and I'd look more human. I was just glad I hadn't grown thorns.

I laid my head back on the swing and scratched at my leaves as the day lightened around me. Waiting. The full moon would be setting soon. The wereleopards would shift to human form and come visiting as they had every morning of this first full moon—a spotted wereleopard and two black wereleopards in human form. I would offer them coffee, eggs and bacon, and we would chat. And I would share some of Soulwood's peace with them all, soothing their pain and their spirits.

Rick (and his cat) was more self-controlled than I had ever seen him, exuberant because his magic was stronger, yet pained because his blood had turned Margot. Margot was still grieving her loss of humanity. Occam just liked being soothed. He said it made his cat happy.

Over the last two weeks, Rick and Margot had spent a lot of time together and that shared time as cat and human had begun to develop into what looked like the beginnings of an office romance. From New York, FireWind had called and offered the former FBI agent a position at PsyLED and Margot had accepted. She would have to attend Spook School, and she had accepted that too, though starting out as a probationary officer had hurt. I, however, was no longer a probie, but a full-fledged PsyLED special agent. With the concomitant raise in pay, a bump in security level, and a move to day shift, which made child care nearly effortless.

The vampire tree had put roots down in the stockyard with a huge, massive tree in the center of what had once been a blood-witch circle. It hadn't talked to me since it took on the guise of the Green Knight and went to war. That suited me just fine. Talkative trees were just scary.

I pushed off on the swing. Time passed. The dawn sky brightened. I felt the energies of were-creatures shifting in the woods, faster than once before.

From the edge of the woods three forms emerged. Margot was nearly invisible, her dark skin blending into the gloom. One was still cat-like, lithe and healthy, his blondish hair visible, long and swinging, his blondish beard scruffy, the way I liked it. The last one was easily recognizable. Rick LaFleur's white hair and beard were a beacon. He had aged in the magic of the new moon curse, but we thought the aging had stabilized and, what with the were-taint in his veins, he'd still live a much-longer-than-human life span. As JoJo said, Rick was craggy and harsh, but still gorgeous, a chick magnet. At his feet two grindylows gamboled and then took off for the woods again.

The human cats reached the porch and I poured coffee into four mugs. Margot and Rick slid two chairs close together and sat. Occam walked up the steps and kissed my lips sweetly.

I had asked him to stay over today. In my bed. Not sleeping. I had been very clear about what I meant, so as to satisfy his promise to let me do all the asking. He had promised to show me all the tenderness and love in his heart—to the full moon and back. I was looking forward to it, my human heart beating fast as his lips met mine, my leaves shivering in delight.

My life wasn't safe, but as William Shakespeare had written, "Security is the chief enemy of mortals." At least I'd never be bored.

Read on for an excerpt from
the third Soulwood novel

FLAME IN THE DARK

Available now!

I walked the length of Turtle Point Lane near Jones Cove, my tactical flash illuminating the street and the ditch, trying to keep my eyes off the lawn and runnel of water and mature trees to the side. *I should be in the trees, not here in the street, wasting my gifts on asphalt.* I hated asphalt. To my touch, it was cold and dead and it stank of tar and gasoline.

But the K9 teams had dibs on the grass and were already in the backyard, the mundane tracker dog and the paranormal tracker dog, with their handlers, and lights so bright they hurt my eyes when I looked that way. As a paranormal investigator, I had to wait until the human and canine investigators were finished, so my scent didn't confuse the Para-K9s. Standard operating procedure and forensic protocol. But that didn't mean I had to like it.

Armed special weapons and tactics team—SWAT—officers, on loan from the city, patrolled the boundaries of the grounds, dressed in tactical gear and toting automatic rifles. Knoxville's rural/metro fire department patrolled inside the house along with uniformed cops, suited detectives, and federal and state agents in this multiagency emergency investigation.

The PsyLED SAC—special agent in charge of Unit Eighteen, and my boss—had put me to work on menial stuff to keep me off the grass and out of the way until the dogs were completely done. As a probationary agent, I did what I was told. Most of the time.

My steps were slow and deliberate, my eyes taking in everything. Crushed cigarette butts stained by yesterday's rain, soggy leaves, broken auto safety glass in tiny pellets, flattened aluminum cans in the brush and a depression: an energy drink and a lite beer. A gum box. Nothing new from the last twenty-four hours. I was surprised at the amount of detritus on a street with such upmarket houses. Maybe the county had no street sweeper machine, or maybe the worst of the filth ended up hidden in the weeds, hard to see, making the street appear cleaner than it really was. Life was like that too, with lots of secrets hidden from sight.

I had already searched the entire street with the psy-meter 2.0, and put the bulky device in the truck. There were no odd levels of paranormal energies anywhere. A small spike on level four at the edge of the drive, but it went away. An anomaly. The psy-meter 2.0 measured four different kinds of paranormal energies called psysitopes, and the patterns could indicate a were-creature, a witch, an *arcenciel*, and even Welsh *gwyllgi*—shape-shifting devil dogs. I had nothing yet, but I headed onto the lawn to do a proper reading. I'd get my wish. Eventually.

I searched the area around a Lexus. Then a short row of BMWs. I took photos of each vehicle plate and sent them to JoJo, Unit Eighteen's second in command and best IT person, to cross-check the plate numbers with the guest list. The air was frigid and I was frozen, even though I was wearing long underwear, flannel-lined slacks, layered T-shirts, a heavy jacket, wool socks, and field boots. But then, along with uniformed county officers, I'd been at the grounds search for two hours, since the midnight call yanked me out of my nice warm bed and onto the job at a PsyLED crime scene. Field examination was scut work, the bane of all probie special agents, and we had found nothing on the street or driveway that might relate to the crime at the überfancy house on a cove of the Tennessee River.

To make me more miserable, because I had drunk down a half gallon of strong coffee, I had to use the ladies', pretty desperately. I stared at the Holloways' house, trying to figure out what to do.

"I just went to the back door and knocked," a voice said.

I whirled. I'd been so intent that I hadn't heard her walk up.

A young female sheriff's deputy grinned at me. "Sorry. Didn't mean to startle you," she said.

"Oh. It's okay." But it wasn't. I was jumpy and ill at ease for reasons I didn't understand. There were woods with fairly mature trees all around, water in the cove nearby, and well-maintained lawns the length of the street, all full of life that should have made me feel at home. Instead I was jumpy. All that coffee maybe. "I'm Nell. Special Agent Ingram." I put out my hand and the woman shook it, businesslike.

"You don't remember me," she said, "but we met at the hospital during the outbreak of the slime molds back a few weeks. You gave me your keys and let my partner and me get unis out of your vehicle. I never got the chance to thank you. May Ree Holler, and my partner, Chris Skeeter." She pointed to a taller, skinny man up the road.

"Your mother escaped from God's Cloud of Glory Church, like I did," I said, referring to the polygamous church I grew up in. "I remember. Her name was Carla, right?"

May Ree grinned at me, seeming happy that I remembered. "That's my mama. Hard as nails and twice as strong." She indicated the dark all around. "Us females always get it the worst on these jobs. The male deputies can just go in the woods, but it isn't so easy for women. The caterer let me in to use the bathroom. Even gave me a pastry." May Ree was short and sturdy with a freckled face, brown hair, and wearing her uniform tight, showing off curves. She had a self-assuredness I would never achieve. Her hair was cropped short for safety in close-combat situations, but her lips were full and scarlet in the reflected glare from my flash, and she was fully made up with mascara and blush, even at the ungodly hour. "Go on. And if they offer you something to eat, bring me another one of those pink iced squares. I missed supper."

"I will. Thanks," I said. If I couldn't get her one I'd give her a snack from my truck when I came back out, presuming the bread wasn't frozen. Still moving my flash back and forth, covering my square yard with each pass, I walked from the street, up the drive, and to the back door, where I snapped off the light. I thought about knocking, but I had learned it was easier to apologize than to get permission. Not a lesson I had

learned at the church where I was raised, but one I had learned
since coming to work with PsyLED. I might get fussed at or
written up, but no one would punish me for an infraction, like
the churchmen did to the churchwomen.

Opening the door, I slid the flash into its sheath and stepped
inside. The warmth and the smell of coffee hit me like a fist. I
unbuttoned my jacket so my badge would show and blinked
into the warmth. My frozen face felt as if it might melt and
slide off onto the marble tile floor. I breathed for a few moments and tried to unclench my fingers. My skin ached. My
teeth hurt.

The arctic front had no regard for global warming. It had
hit, decided it liked the Tennessee Valley, and decided to stay.
This was the second week of frigid temps. Snow I liked. This,
not at all.

Once the worst of the personal melting was done, I looked
around. The kitchen was empty, a room constructed of stone
in various shades of gray on the floor and the cabinet tops and
the backsplash. The owners must have taken down a whole
mountain to get this much polished rock. The ceiling was
vaulted with whitish wooden rafters and joists. Cabinets with
the same kind of treated whitish wood rose ten feet high. A
ladder that slid on a bronze rail was in the corner. The stove
was gas with ten burners and a copper faucet over the
stovetops, which looked handy unless one had a grease fire
and thought to use water to put it out. There was a commercial-
sized coffeemaker with a huge pot half-full, two big, double-
glass-door refrigerators, and a separate massive two-door
freezer. I spotted the small powder room off the kitchen and
raced into it before anyone could come in and tell me to get
outside and use the trees.

I was one of maybe twenty-five law enforcement officers
and investigators from the various law enforcement branches
and agencies called in to the shooting at the Holloway home.
The FBI was here to rule out terrorism because a U.S. senator
had been at the private political fund-raiser when the shooting
started.

PsyLED—the Psychometry Law Enforcement Division of
Homeland Security—was here because a vampire had been
on-site too. The fire department was here because there had

been a small fire. The local sheriff's LEOs were here because it was their jurisdiction.

Crime scene investigators were here because there were three dead bodies on the premises, though not the senator—he was shaken up but fine. The grounds search was because the shooter had come and gone on foot. It was complicated. But dead and wounded VIPs meant a lot of police presence and a shooting to solve, especially since the shooter got away clean.

When I came back out, the kitchen was still empty and I decided a bit more of the "ask permission later" was called for. Most anything was better than going back outside to search the road and paved areas for clues into a crime I had not been informed about. Two automatic dishwashers were running softly. The pastries were taped under waxed paper, including little pink iced squares. May Ree would be disappointed. There were four ovens, and all but one was still warm to the touch. I inspected the planters under the windows. At first glance they appeared to be full of herbs—basil, rosemary, thyme, and lemongrass—but the leaves were silk. Which was weird in a kitchen that looked as if someone loved to cook.

Trying to look as if I belonged, I wandered through a butler's pantry, complete with coffee bar, wet bar with dozens of decanters and bottles, and wine in a floor-to-ceiling special refrigerator. Beyond the butler's pantry, stairs went up on one side and down on the other, proving that the house had multiple levels, not just the two obvious from the outside. Picking up on the smell of smoke and scorched furnishings was easy here.

I stayed on the main level and meandered into a formal dining room on one side of the entry. There was more stone here too, and wood in the vaulted ceilings. The twelve-foot-long dining table was set for a party, though I didn't recognize any of the food except the whole salmon and the tenderloin of beef. It seemed a shame to let the food go to waste when May Ree was hungry, but there was blood on the floor in the doorway, leading from the back of the house to here. Since there was blood, the food itself might be evidence, so I kept my hands to myself and stepped carefully.

I had seen EMS units racing away as I drove up, so I knew

there had been casualties, but seeing blood was unsettling. My
gift rose up inside me, as if it was curious. Not trying to drink
the blood down, not yet, because I wasn't outside, my hands
buried in the earth, but more like a mouser cat who sees movement and crouches, trying to decide if this is something worth
hunting.

A formal living room decorated with a Christmas tree and
presents and fake electric candles in the windows was on the
other side of the entry. It had real wood floors and a ten-foot
ceiling with one of those frame things set in the middle to give
it even more height. Maybe called a tray ceiling; I wasn't sure.
Life in the church hadn't prepared me with a good grasp of
architectural terminology. The entire room felt stiff and uncomfortable to me, maybe due to the fact that all the plants
were fake. Fancy tables, tassels on heavy drapes, carved
lamps, furniture that looked showroom-fresh. This wasn't a
place to kick up your feet.

The room was full of people in fancy dress, and oddly, I
knew two of them, Ming of Glass, the vampire Master of the
City, and her bodyguard, a vamp I knew only as Yummy.
Yummy flashed me a grin, one without fangs, which was nice,
but she mouthed, *Opossum*, at me, which was a tease I didn't
really need. I mouthed back, *Ha-ha. Not.* Yummy laughed.

All but three of the partygoers in the room looked
irritated—two vamps and a human. Vamps tended to expres-
sionless faces unless they were irritated or hungry, both of
which were a sign of danger. The human was sitting on an
ottoman, and he looked devastated, face pale, his tie undone,
a crystal glass in one hand, dangling between his knees. I
figured he was the husband of one of the dead. There was
blood spatter on his shirt and dark suit coat. A man who didn't
belong in the expensively dressed crowd stood beside him,
taking notes. A fed, I figured as I slipped away, before I got
caught, to wander some more.

I passed uniformed and suited LEOs here and there, two I
recognized as local and one unknown wearing a far better-
fitting suit. Probably another fed. The firefighters left through
the front door, big boots clomping, and gathered on the street.
Two crime scene techs raced into the room off to the side, carrying gear. No one paid any attention to me except to note that

I had a badge on a lanyard around my neck. I hooked my thumbs into my pockets and moseyed over, probably a failure at looking as if I belonged.

The action was in the game room and the stench of fire grew heavier. Inside was a pool table, comfy reclining sofas, and a TV screen so big it took up most of the wall over the fireplace. On the opposite wall were antique guns in frames behind glass. Cast metal that might have been machine parts was protected within smaller frames. What looked like an ordinary wrench was centered on the wall in a heavy carved frame as if it was the most important thing hanging there. People commemorated the strangest things.

There were also lots of old, black-and-white photographs of stiff-looking people wearing stiff-looking clothes. Their hats and the way the women's clothes fitted said they were rich and pampered. The men's mustaches and thick facial hair made them look imposing, at least to themselves; they had that self-satisfied look about them, the expression of a hunter when he was posing with a sixteen-point buck. However, their expressions also made them look like their teeth hurt. Dental care was probably not very common back whenever these were taken.

Standing in the doorway, I spotted Rick LaFleur, the special agent in charge of Unit Eighteen, talking to Soul, his up-line boss, the newly appointed assistant director, and another woman. If body language was a clue, the PsyLED agents were arguing with the African-American woman in the chic outfit. She wore the tailored clothes as if they were part of her, as much as the scowl and the aura of power. I figured she was the new VIP in charge of the Knoxville FBI. They were too busy to pay attention to me, so I strolled in. Saw things. Smelled things. Touched things with the back of my hand, here and there.

The gas logs had been on, but were now only warm to the touch. A game of pool had been interrupted and balls were all over the tabletop. The solids were mostly gone. One cue stick lay on the floor in two pieces. Drinks of the alcoholic variety were on every available surface.

The entire room smelled of fire, the sour scent of a house fire—painted wallboard and burned construction materials, lots of synthetics. The stench was tainted with what might have been the reek of scorched flesh. Icy night air blew in through the busted windows; blackened draperies billowed. Charred furniture and rugs spread into the room from the window. The fire seemed to have started there.

There were bullet holes on the wall opposite the windows. And there was a pool of blood on the floor. A body lay in the middle of it. She had taken a chest shot. Dead instantly if I was any kind of judge. There was no taped outline. No chalk outline. Just the blood and the body, still in place.

I stared at her. The victim was middle-aged with dyed blond hair and blue contacts drying and wrinkling, shrinking over her gray eyes. She was wearing a pale blue sweater top and black pants, three-inch black spike shoes. Diamonds. Lots of them. There was blood spatter on the wall in an odd outline, as if someone had been standing behind her. Blood on a chair and small table. Blood on a shattered glass on the mantel near her. That bloody pool beneath her was tracked through by the shoe prints of the people who had tried to save her. There was a lot of blood.

My gift of reading the land—and feeding the land with blood—was less reticent now, more focused. Hungering. But I had been working with it, trying to harness it, and I stroked the need like the hunting cat I compared it to, flattening its surface, pushing it into stillness. Proud of myself that I had the strength of will to not feed my hunger and the earth beneath the house, I turned from the body.

By now, the crime scene had been captured in photos and video and cell cameras and drawn out on paper by hand. Multiple redundancies. Crime scene techs were still working, but oddly, there were no numbered evidence markers in the room. I had to wonder why. Maybe they had been placed there, then already removed as CSI gathered up the physical evidence.

I approached the broken windows. Outside, a coroner's unit waited, lights not flashing, not in an upscale neighborhood. The EMTs and their vehicles had left with the wounded, three, I had heard, one critical. Farther beyond, a media van waited, a camera on a tripod and a reporter in front of it, filming for the morning news. In the dark of the driveway, where the cameras couldn't get a shot, two uniformed figures lifted a gurney with a body bag into the coroner's van. There was already one gurney inside. Three dead, three wounded at this scene.

The window glass was shattered, in pellets all over the floor. It reminded me of the automobile glass outside, but this was clear and the vehicle glass had been tinted and well ground into the asphalt.

The cloth blinds were burned and tattered, the drapery seared. The walls were scorched all around them, and up to the ceiling. A table by the window was mostly shattered charcoal and candles had melted across the surface. A blackened glass was on its side. It looked as if the shots had smashed the glass, spilling the alcohol and toppling the lit candle. I guessed that the fire had spread quickly, but I wasn't a fire and arson investigator. I knew to keep my opinions to myself unless asked. Opinions went into the evidentiary summary report in the "Opinion" box, where they were mostly ignored. They weren't facts.

I slipped out before someone asked me what I was doing. Next door was the master bedroom. Master *suite*. Yes, that sounded right. It was full of people. Instead of pushing my luck, I slowly went up the staircase onto the second level.

On the second floor were six bedrooms and four full baths. Counting the servants' powder room, the en suite in the master, and the two guest powder rooms on the ground floor, that was a lot of bathrooms. I had grown up in a house that technically had more square footage and more bedrooms than this one, but it was nowhere near as fancy. The Holloways' home was luxurious, what T. Laine probably called "new-money decadent." They probably paid their decorator more than the yearly income of most American families.

I traipsed back down, hearing T. Laine's and Tandy's voices from the master suite. T. Laine was Tammie Laine Kent, PsyLED Unit Eighteen's moon witch, one with strong earth element affinities and enough unfinished university degrees to satisfy the most OCD person on the planet. That was how she had introduced herself to me. Tandy was the unit's empath, who claimed his superpower was being struck by lightning.

I'd wandered around as much as I could without entering the master suite, but I was nosy, so I stood just outside that door, taking the excuse to see, hear, and learn what I could before being banished back into the cold by Rick. Who was now standing in said master suite. He was in front of the window, facing the door and me, being dressed down by a well-suited FBI-agent-type in an expensive suit and tie, regulation all the way. Rick's black hair was too long to be regulation, his black eyes were tired, and his olive skin looked sallow. Rick had aged in the last weeks, though he looked a bit better now that he had learned how to shift into his black wereleopard form and back to human. He frowned at me, but didn't interrupt his conversation.

"This isn't one of your magic wand and broomstick investigations," the fed said. It was said in the tone of an older kid to a young one, insult in each syllable, in a local, townie accent. "This was an attack on a house party and fund-raiser with some of the biggest movers and shakers in Tennessee. Super-wealthy business and political types, with their fingers in every financial pie in the nation."

Toneless, Rick said, "With all due respect, there were witches and vampires at the party. The strike could have been aimed at the Tennessee senator, Abrams Tolliver, as you *assume*, or at Ming, the closest thing Knoxville has to a vampire Master of the City, with whom he was speaking."

I knew of the Tollivers. Rich, powerful people who made their money when the Tennessee Valley Authority stole the land of all the state's farmers and changed the face of the South. The men of God's Cloud preached about the entire Tolliver family going to hell, and maybe taking up their own special circle right next to the devil himself.

"Or just the fully human victim, or one of the human homeowners, which is far more likely. This is not your case," the suit said. "This is a joint FBI, ATF, and Secret Service investigation, not some trivial magic case."

"You are incorrect," Soul said. I stepped quickly to the side, because the assistant director of PsyLED was standing behind me and I was blocking the door. My heart started beating too fast, and my bloodlust rose with my reaction. I pushed down on it, anxious about its agitation, but not worried enough to leave the house.

"You need to return to the living room with the other guests, lady," the suit said. He sounded frustrated. And unimpressed at the vision Soul presented, all gauzy fabrics, platinum hair, and curves.

"On the contrary. I am exactly where I belong, young man."

"Who the hell are you? If you're law enforcement, where is your badge and ID?" he replied.

The room fell silent. I covered my mouth and moved inside quickly, along the wall, to keep them all in view. Soul walked slowly closer to him, silvery gauze waving in a rising wind that wasn't really there. I didn't have the same kind of magic as Soul, but I felt her power on my skin like small sparks of electricity. *Arcenciel* magic was wild and hot, a shape-shifting ability that defied the laws of physics as scientists understood them. It wasn't common knowledge—in fact, half of Unit Eighteen didn't know—that Soul was a rainbow dragon, a creature made of light. But even without that knowledge, if the suit didn't know a stalking predator when he saw one, then he needed to spend more time in the wild, to hone his survival instincts.

"What. Did. You. Say?" Soul asked.

"Hamilton!" a woman barked. "What the bloody hell."

It was the woman from the game room, the African-American woman who wore the power of her office like a crown and robe. Her ID was clipped at her collar and her name was E. M. Schultz.

Soul didn't turn to her, keeping her eyes on the suit and saying, "I've been on conference call to PsyLED director Clarence Lester Woods, the secretary of Homeland Security, and the director of the FBI, as well as the head of Alcohol, Tobacco, and Firearms. This is a joint investigation between four, not three, branches of law enforcement. You may address me as Assistant Director, PsyLED. And your services are no longer needed at this crime scene." She turned her head as if looking for something.

In a tone that wasn't quite a question, not quite a demand, she said, "Special Agent Ingram?"

I jumped. Soul kept on talking. "Take Mr. Hamilton

outside. Give him your flashlight. Teach him how to do a perimeter grounds search. Then come back in here. I need your services."

I was staring at Hamilton, his name touching down in my mind, in the place designated for it. Chadworth Sanders Hamilton, his father's second son from his second wife, named for his mother's grandfathers. And my third cousin, by way of Maude Nicholson, my grandmother. My distant cousin from the townie side of the family. I'd heard he had graduated from the FBI academy at the top of his class and come back home to make his mark. This embarrassing dressing-down was likely not the mark he wanted to make.

I held up a hand to identify myself and silently led the way to the kitchen. There, I found foam cups, poured coffee from the coffeemaker, and put them on a tray with napkins, a bread knife, and a spoon. I could practically feel the embarrassment and fury emanating off Hamilton as I worked, my back to him. At least the anger would keep him warm for a while. And there was no way I was going to tell him that we were related when he was so furious. Maybe later. Maybe . . . Carefully, tray balanced, I left the warmth of the house, my cousin on my heels, not offering to help with the load. I didn't know if that made him a jerk or just oblivious, but so far, my cousin was not making a very good impression.

Outside, I flashed my light three times, handed it to Hamilton, and said, "Forty-eight hundred lumens. Battery will last another two hours before it has to be recharged. One yard squares, from the middle of the ditch to the middle of the lane. This'll be the third pass so it should be pretty clean."

"What's up, Ingram?" May Ree asked, joining us at a jog. The other deputies followed, and so did three SWAT officers, until we had a small crowd.

"Coffee," I said, unnecessarily, as they reached in for the cups. "Keys." I placed them in May Ree's hand. "There's a loaf of bread in the passenger seat of my truck and a jar of jam. Bring the knife and spoon back in when y'all are done. I'll get some fresh coffee out here as soon as I can." May Ree dashed down the road to my car. I continued to the others, "This is Hamilton. Probie. Looks like he came out without a coat, so he'll be cold."

"It's all right, kid," a deputy said. The county cop was six-six easy, and had a chest like a whiskey barrel. "We've all been stupid from time to time." Several officers laughed.

Hamilton flinched and burned hotter, probably thinking about the dressing-down he'd just received, not the coat he'd forgotten. Probably furious that he'd been called "kid" by a county cop, someone an FBI officer might look down on, in the hierarchy of law enforcement types. But he kept his mouth shut. He looked pale in all the flashlights and totally out of place, underdressed in his fancy suit.

The deputy continued, "I got an extra jacket in my unit. It'll hang to your knees, little fella like you, but it's clean. Hang on, I'll get it." He too jogged off.

I didn't laugh at my cousin's expression at the words *little fella like you.*

Hamilton accepted a cup of coffee. And the coat. And a slice of bread and jam. I waited until the cups were gone and Hamilton was wearing the borrowed coat and starting on the road. He was all but kicking the pavement like a kid. I hadn't told him who I was, that we were distant cousins. My grandma Maude had been disowned when she married into the church. I doubted that Hamilton knew I existed.

Back inside, I figured out how to work the coffee machine and got coffee gurgling, found a gallon-sized carafe, a table-cloth, more napkins, and foam cups. When the coffee was ready, I took the tray back outside, placed the tablecloth on the hood of a county car, the tray atop it, and went back inside, where I made another trip to the powder room and put on fresh lipstick. The assistant director of PsyLED wanted me for something. That made me nervous. I had learned that lipstick gave me false courage. False was better than no courage at all.

Ready to find
your next great read?

Let us help.

Visit prh.com/nextread

Penguin
Random
House